Luathara

Book Three of the
Otherworld Trilogy

Autumn –
Always keep your
dreams within reach.

FaerieCon West
2014

by

Jenna Elizabeth Johnson

For the Sisters of Mercy, who first introduced me to the mystical world of Ireland.

Contents

Wathara

One

Purpose

The creature was utterly disgusting, whatever it was. Faelah, yes, but I didn't have a name for this unfamiliar beast. Not yet, at least. So, what to call this one . . . I'd have to come up with something creative, some new word to describe the half-dead creature resembling a possum, coyote and rabbit all rolled into one. Perhaps I could combine the first two letters of the names for each of the animals: po-co-ra. Huh, *pocora*. It even sounded like an Otherworldly term.

The thing, the pocora, jerked its head up from whatever poor creature it feasted on, bony jaws dripping with gore. My stomach turned, and not just because of the brutal scene. The faelah was eating one of Mrs. Dollard's cats, the chubby one that obviously hadn't been able to outrun this particular enemy. I gritted my teeth. I wasn't attached to my neighbor's cats, despite the fact I once spent a summer caring for them, but the poor thing hadn't deserved to die at the mercy of an Otherworldly monster.

I took a deep breath, pulling an arrow free of the quiver slung across my back and deftly positioned it in my bow. I'd become quite good at this in the past several weeks; arming my longbow with an arrow quickly and without making a sound. I stretched the bowstring back and aimed the arrow's tip at the creature, steadying my arms while trying to concentrate. With a twang, I released the string and fixed my face with an expression of satisfaction as the arrow pierced the mummified hide of the pocora. The creature squealed like a pig and fell to the ground, kicking and clawing and attempting to remove the hawthorn arrow. If I had used any other wood, the faelah might've stood a chance, but even as I watched the small monstrosity struggling to regain its feet, smoke lifted from where the hawthorn shaft burned through nonliving flesh. I crinkled my nose at the acrid smell and turned away. Generally, I didn't like killing anything, but the faelah of Eilé were an entirely different matter. And they weren't technically alive, either.

The creature's screams ceased and it went still. I waited a few more moments before moving close enough to pull the arrow free. I always kept the arrows from my hunts. It wasn't like I could go down to the local sporting goods store and ask for arrows made with hawthorn wood. I wiped it on a nearby patch of grass out of habit. Whatever remained of the faelah would already be gone, however, burned off by magic. I glanced back over my shoulder as I left the small clearing behind, but the pocora had already disintegrated into ash, its glamour no longer keeping it alive and whole in the mortal world. I sighed and turned my eyes to what was left of Matilda Dollard's cat. I would pay her a visit later and tell her I'd found her pet's remains in the swamp. Another poor victim of a coyote attack.

Clear, a bright thought said in my mind, forcing my thoughts away from the gruesome scene.

I shaded my eyes and glanced up into the eucalyptus leaves only to catch the brilliant white flash of a small bird of prey darting through them. She had been scanning the forest for more faelah. I grinned.

Did you catch anything? I sent to my spirit guide.

Meridian chittered and sent back a joyous, *Tasty.*

That would be a yes.

Purpose

I heaved a deep breath and pulled my quiver back onto my shoulders. Mid-morning had become late afternoon and I knew Mom would be worried if I didn't get back soon. After having confessed to my family I was Faelorehn, an immortal being from Eilé, the Otherworld, and that a vindictive goddess was out to get me, she had been a little more protective of late. I guess I couldn't blame her.

Meridian finished up with whatever she had caught and then set her focus on accompanying me back to the house. The walk home took a good fifteen minutes, but I didn't mind taking my time this afternoon. I had a lot on my mind, after all. Actually, there had been a lot on my mind since my junior year in high school when all of this stuff concerning the Otherworld got dumped on me like a ton of bricks, but for the past month I had even more to worry about.

I made my way back to the main trail leading out of the swamp and thought about what had transpired just before graduation. It sometimes made me sick with anxiety, but I couldn't help that. The Morrigan had tricked me, once again to my chagrin, into thinking she meant to go after my family. A few years ago, she would have been happy just to kill me. Now that she knew I possessed more glamour than the average Faelorehn, she was intent on using me as her own personal supply of endless magic. She probably would have succeeded if Cade hadn't stepped in. *Cade . . .*

A pang of regret cut through me and when I reached the spot in the trail where a fallen tree blocked my way, I leaned heavily against the rough trunk and pulled a well-worn note out of my pocket. The message wasn't from Cade, but from his foster father, the Dagda. I unfolded the edges and began reading.

Meghan,

Cade is improving every day, yet he is still very weak. I know you wish to see him soon, but please give him a little more time and don't cross into the Otherworld. The Morrigan has been lying low; no one has seen her lately, but that doesn't mean she isn't lurking in the shadows, waiting to cast her net. For now, you are safer where you are. Cade will come and get you as soon as he is recovered.

    -Dagda

The note should have made me happy, and it did when I first received it a week and a half ago, but I longed to visit Cade so badly I ached. I needed to know he was safe and I needed to witness with my own eyes that he was healing.

I folded the worn paper into a perfect square and returned the note to my pocket, then climbed over the log and kept on walking. Last May I'd been all set to go to prom with the guy of my dreams, Cade MacRoich, the gorgeous Faelorehn boy from Eilé who appeared one day like some guardian angel to save me from the Morrigan's faelah and to tell me all about my strange heritage. Unfortunately, on the day of the prom we both got tricked into running headlong into the evil goddess's trap. Only, Cade wouldn't let her have me, and right before he took on almost a dozen of her monsters, he told me he loved me. And then he died.

I stopped for a moment, craned my head back and leaned on my longbow, soaking in the filtered sunlight trickling down between the leaves above. I shut my eyes and tried to tell the knot of worry in my stomach to go away. Cade had died, he died defending me and the trauma of such a terrible experience forced my power to surge forth, scaring the Morrigan away, at least for the time being. The sudden rush of my glamour had soon faded and the reality of what had happened slammed into me like a train. I was convinced my heart would tear itself asunder, for Cade had sacrificed too much.

Only after recovering from my hysterics did I remember Cade's foster father, the Dagda, an ancient Celtic god-king, happened to own a magical cauldron with a reputation for reviving the dead. A frantic horse ride against a driving storm later and I dropped like a fly at the Dagda's door, a lifeless Cade in my arms. I'd arrived just in time; Cade would recover. But he never got to hear me tell him I loved him, too.

I had returned to the mortal world, an emotional and physical wreck, only to finally confess the truth to my family: I was an immortal from the Otherworld, the daughter of a Celtic goddess and the high queen of Eilé, and one day I'd be going back to the world of my origins. Let's just say after such an ordeal, I needed something to keep me distracted, to give me purpose so I wouldn't lose my mind completely. Thus, I had taken up hunting for the faelah on my own. Heck, before the Morrigan's attack Cade constantly pestered me about practicing my archery and this way I could kill two, maybe three, birds with one stone. I was getting some much-needed practice in, I was clearing the swamp of dangerous faelah, *and* I was keeping my mind occupied. Yup, three birds.

I fingered the note in my pocket once more as I stepped onto the equestrian trail leading to my home. I hoped the Dagda was right; that Cade was recovering. I so desperately wanted to turn around and head for the dolmarehn in the heart of these woods, to travel back to the Dagda's home and see Cade, but like the Dagda said, I'd be an easy target in the Otherworld. And I agreed with the other thing he'd mentioned as well. I had no doubt the Morrigan would be looking for me.

Gritting my teeth, I turned my mind away from those dark thoughts and picked up my pace. By the time I reached the end of the path, I welcomed thoughts of a shower, a sit-down with a good book, and some hot chocolate. Summer was in full swing, yes, but the coastal fog was already creeping in and the early evening would turn chilly.

I planned on crossing our backyard and slipping in through my sliding glass door, but a barrage of young boys accosted me before I could even step foot on the lawn. Apparently my brothers had been waiting for my return.

"Meghan!" Logan whined as he rushed forward. "We wanted to go with you this time!"

He crossed his arms, and yes, actually stomped his foot.

I blinked at him and my other brothers as they gathered around me, a small army of Elams.

"Huh?" Despite my claims that my hunting ventures helped purge my mind of everything Otherworldly except the faelah themselves, my wandering thoughts still found ways to wrestle free of the bonds I'd placed on them. I didn't have a clue what he was talking about. I'd been too busy reminiscing.

"We want to help you hunt!" Bradley offered, thrusting out a fist which happened to be clutching a small bow.

Oh. *That.* I cleared my throat and took a breath. When would they realize no meant no? I was still getting used to the fact that my parents and brothers knew about my Faelorehn blood. After keeping my identity a secret for so long, I found it easy to forget I had told them (and shown them) what my Otherworldly power could do.

I squatted down so I would appear less imposing to them. Hah, me, *imposing . . .*

"I'm sorry guys," I said, feeling only slightly guilty. "But you can't go faelah hunting with me. It isn't safe for you."

"You go," Bradley put in.

I rolled my eyes. "I'm Faelorehn Bradley. I have magic, remember?"

Not that it would make any difference. Whatever power I managed to store up in Eilé during my last visit had most likely burned out after my battle with the Morrigan. I was running on empty and it would take another extended stay in the Otherworld to get me back up to a level where I could do some real damage. But they didn't need to know that.

"And I'm glad you didn't come with me," I continued. "I encountered something really creepy today."

Purpose

And just like that, their scowls were replaced with wide eyes. "What?" Jack and Joey, the twins, whispered together.

I grinned, despite the fact that the encounter had been more ghastly than usual.

"Well, I'm calling the faelah I killed a pocora, but I'm not sure what it's called in the Otherworld."

They remained silent, waiting for me to continue. "It looked like a cross between a rabbit, a possum and a coyote, and I think it might have been mummified."

I had explained early on, right after telling my family the truth, that anything concerning Eilé would have to be kept top secret. I made all my brothers double swear, spit and shake on it (tantamount to a blood oath, or in the Otherworldly sense, a geis). They were not to repeat a single thing they saw or heard to their friends or classmates. Having to keep this promise, and not being able to go on my hunting adventures with me, was practically killing them. So, whenever I came back from one of my faelah target practices, I distracted their disappointment with a detailed description of whatever I happened to kill. Worked every time.

"Did you shoot anything else?" Logan piped in, forgetting his previous irritation at being left behind while I got to have all the fun.

"No," I said.

Their shoulders slumped, so I thought the conversation was over. I started to stand back up and nearly fell over when Bradley blindsided me with a completely different question.

"So, when do we get to meet your boyfriend?"

After regaining my balance, I blinked down at him. "What?"

"Your *boyfriend*," he crooned, "the guy in the Otherworld you always talk about. When do we get to meet him? Or is he imaginary?"

I blushed and gritted my teeth. I did *not* always talk about Cade. Always thought about, yes, but I only ever talked about him with Mom, long after my brothers' bedtime. Little, eavesdropping cretins . . .

"He's not my boyfriend," I grumbled, glaring at Bradley.

Then I paused. Or was he? Before the Cúmorrig had overtaken him, Cade had told me he loved me, but the last several weeks had given me plenty of time to think about it. Did he really mean it, or had he only said so because he realized he wouldn't survive the fight? Did it mean he might have acted rashly? Of course, it didn't change the fact that *I* loved *him* . . .

"Sure he isn't," Bradley snickered.

"I bet you let *him* go hunting with you," Logan muttered.

I scowled at him again. I'd have to try and analyze my scattered thoughts later. "He's my friend, and he'll meet you guys when he's better. He's very sick right now."

That's right, because being brought back to life and recovering from what had killed you in the first place could be considered a sickness . . . sure.

To my immense relief, my younger brothers decided not to hound me about Cade anymore. We all headed back up towards the front of the house, but before we even got clear of the backyard, Meridian dropped from her perch in the eucalyptus trees above and came to rest on my shoulder.

The boys all started arguing and crowded in again, forcing me to stop so I wouldn't trip over them. They absolutely adored Meridian. She used to use her powerful glamour to keep herself hidden from them, but now she understood it was safe to be seen and she no longer bothered with the disappearing act. Besides, I think she was rather infatuated with my little brothers as well, and I often wondered if she thought of them as her own little merlin chicks.

Chase game! Meridian sent as she chittered excitedly, leaping off my shoulder and darting around the backyard as my crazy brothers ran after her. She loved playing this game with them. Even Aiden, all too often happy with simply watching from the sidelines, joined in. My heart warmed at seeing him play like a normal boy, but a painful lump rose in my throat again. This was all temporary. I couldn't stay with my mortal family forever.

Feeling rather morose, I reached into my pocket again and brushed my fingers against the thick paper of the Dagda's note.

Be safe Cade and come back to me soon, I thought.

I turned to sneak back into the house, but the sudden presence I detected near my leg made me pause and glance down. Aiden. Apparently he was done playing chase. Yes, I would be leaving the family who took me in and raised me so I could live in Eilé, where I belonged. In Aiden's own quiet way, he was telling me how we all felt about it: none of us wanted to let go. I wasn't human, though; I needed the safety the Otherworld and its magic would grant me, especially now that my power had shown itself. Moving to Eilé would be hard, and I think I would miss Aiden the most, but I had to be brave.

Fighting the well of pain in my chest, I removed Aiden's hand from my shirt and curled my own fingers around his. He looked up at me, his blue-green eyes trying to tell me something, but like always, his autism kept him from saying what he needed to say. Luckily, I'd become rather good at reading his face.

Taking a deep breath, I stood with him as my other brothers kept at their game with my spirit guide. I set my quiver down and leaned my bow against the house, then bent over and pulled Aiden into a rib-crushing hug.

"I know buddy, I know," I whispered as he wrapped himself around me. I managed to hold on a little longer before a tear escaped. "I'll miss you too."

~Two~
Recovered

The next morning I woke up feeling groggy and slightly dejected. I didn't know exactly when I'd be going back to the Otherworld, but I knew it was inevitable. I wanted to go, don't get me wrong, and not just because it meant more one-on-one time with Cade. There had been something about feeling the full extent of my very own Faelorehn glamour that urged me to return, almost like a drug I couldn't get enough of. Despite the terror and anguish I had felt when facing down the Morrigan, the whole experience had been exhilarating. It was almost as if the magic of Eilé itself was crying out to me; coaxing me to cross over into the Otherworld and soak it in like warm sunshine.

Yet, there was also that part of me that hated leaving my friends and family. Not that I would disappear and never come back, but to not wake up and see my brothers every day? To never find my dad reading his newspaper while the house erupted in chaos? To wake up without the smell of my mom's cooking filling the kitchen? The ache that swelled next to my heart threatened to overwhelm me, but I quickly got a hold of it and banished it away. All children left their parents' homes at some point in time, whether to go to college or start a life of their own. How was this any different? Okay, most young adults weren't going to live in a different dimension full of magic, monsters and goddesses bent on destroying them, but hey, most people my age were human.

Sighing to dispel some of my negative mood, I rolled out of bed and headed to my shower. I took my time this morning, letting the steaming hot water pour over me, imaging it was washing away all of my worries. After the shower I brushed my teeth, combed out my unruly hair and threw on a pair of old jeans, a t-shirt and a sweatshirt.

It was still foggy out and I planned to go down into the swamp to get some more practice in with my longbow. I wasn't about to slack off, despite the fact that I'd found only the one faelah creature the day before. I located the torque and mistletoe charm Cade had given me on my desk, placing them around my neck as if they were pieces of armor. Ever since the day I'd returned from Eilé in late spring, I'd been wearing them almost constantly. I had been questioned by Robyn almost immediately about the torque (let's face it, the piece of jewelry kind of stood out and Robyn knew her Celtic stuff), but I had merely brushed her off and told her that Cade had given it to me. She was still the only one of my friends who had actually met him. Of course, she thought he was human, a conviction I wasn't about to correct. Soon I'd have to tell them the truth, or at least some version of the truth, but for now I'd let them go on believing the lies as long as possible.

I sighed and placed my hands loosely on my hips, scanning the room for my spirit guide. Meridian, another gift from Cade, snoozed in the corner, making soft chirruping sounds as she slept. I grinned. I hated to wake her, but she was my bodyguard on mornings like these.

Meridian, I sent to her.

She snoozed on. I smiled and tried again.

Meridian!

She woke with a snort, well, her version of a mental snort. *Up!* she sent as she ruffled her feathers and tried to act as if she had been alert the whole time.

I laughed, threw my quiver over my shoulder, grabbed my bow with my left hand and held out my forearm to her.

Ready for practice? I asked

Yes. Hungry.

She landed on my sleeve, then crawled up my arm to settle herself on my shoulder, tucking her head back under her wing.

I turned towards my sliding glass door, expecting to see the fog-dimmed vista of our backyard and the eucalyptus trees that trailed down into the swamp. But something else was waiting for me and my heart nearly leapt out of my chest. There, standing on the concrete slab that served as a small patio stood a huge, white wolfhound.

My bow thlunked to my carpeted floor as I dropped it, my eyes wide and my jaw hanging open in shock. The dog panted and scratched at the door, his tail wagging. But all I could do was stand there, frozen. The memories of the month before flashed through my mind: the Morrigan, the faelah, Cade dying, Fergus nowhere to be found. He had fallen somewhere during the battle, dying when his master had, and we'd been forced to leave him. But if he was here now, alive and eager to get my attention . . .

"Cade!" I cried out, barely even a whisper.

My senses returned to me in a rush and I bent down to scoop up my bow, nearly tripping over its length in my rush to get to the door. Meridian dug in with her claws as she got jostled about on my shoulder. I dove for the handle of my door, flipped the latch, slid it open and tumbled out. Fergus took a few steps to avoid me, but he wasn't fast enough to escape the hug I threw around his great neck.

"I'm so glad to see you!" I proclaimed as he panted next to my ear.

I let go and he gave me a quick canine grin before trotting towards the horse trail. I didn't even hesitate to follow him, my heart lurching once again when he didn't stop at the oak tree to indicate Cade had left me a note. Could Cade really be here? I shook that thought from my mind before I tripped over myself in a jumble of nerves, but the idea wouldn't leave me alone. My heart sped up even more. The last time I'd seen Cade, he'd been lying in bed in one of the Dagda's rooms, barely alive. Would he be glad to see me? Would he regret what he had done? I bit my lip and tried to move faster to keep up with Fergus.

We came to the point in the trail where the path led over the small land bridge and between two thick rows of willow trees. On the other side was the small meadow where my normal, well, somewhat normal life had all started to go downhill. I passed it without giving the memories of my first meeting with the Cúmorrig a second thought. I walked a few steps further down the road, and then stopped dead in my tracks. Leaning against a tall eucalyptus tree stood a tall young man. *Cade.*

For a few breathless moments I merely stood there, my eyes taking him in, my heart galloping in my chest as my emotions tried to settle. He wore the clothing of the Otherworld; brown leather pants with knee-length boots and a loose, cream colored shirt beneath a beautifully worked leather vest. Instead of the old trench coat he had worn when we'd first met, he wore a long green cloak lined with fleece, the hood thrown over his head. But I could see his face well enough. He was pale, but not as pale as he had been after fighting the Morrigan's - his mother's - monsters. His green eyes met mine and he smiled, but it was guarded, as if he was unsure of how I would react to his presence. He looked worn down, weary, older almost, but I had never seen anything or anyone more beautiful in my entire life.

Finally he spoke, only one word, but it was enough to make my scattered emotions burst forth.

"Meghan," he said, his tone so quiet I barely heard it.

That was all it took. The sob that had been hovering in my throat broke free and I dropped my bow and quiver. Meridian took off in a flurry of white feathers and irritated chattering as I sprinted across the small space that separated us.

Cade straightened just in time to step into my aggressive embrace. I buried my face in his shoulder and threw my arms around him, forcing myself to be gentle when he rocked back against the tree. He was still recovering from death, after all, and squeezing the life out of him might not be the best thing for his health at the moment.

I cried into his cloak and held on. I could hear him murmuring words in the ancient language of Eilé as he stroked my hair. I was pretty sure I could stand like that all day, but at some point I pulled myself away, or maybe he somehow pried me off of him. Either way, I found myself gazing up into his face, wanting so badly to kiss him but not having the gall to make that move on my own.

He grinned, his eyes tired, and brushed a loose curl away from my forehead so he could kiss it. I shivered.

Somehow, I managed to find my voice. "How are you? Are you okay?"

He lowered his hand to take mine and squeezed it, grinning. It made his expression seem less grim, so I smiled back and relished the feeling of his hand in mine.

"I am," he said.

An awkward silence fell over us, as if we were two strangers or casual acquaintances meeting for the first time. Finally, Cade spoke again, his demeanor stiffening. He dropped my hand and leaned back against the tree once more.

"Meghan, the Dagda wanted me to come see you, he thinks-"

He paused and took a deep breath, running his hand through his hair and pushing back the hood at the same time. "He thinks you should come to Eilé as soon as possible."

My heart nearly stopped its erratic sprint. *Go to the Otherworld.* I knew it was coming, heck, I'd been planning on it. But so soon? I had just received the Dagda's letter less than two weeks ago.

I opened my mouth to speak, but all I did was croak, "Why, why so suddenly?"

Cade cringed and I could almost feel him withdrawing somewhere deep inside of himself. I didn't like that feeling.

"We think the Morrigan is planning something, and now that your geis is broken, we don't want to risk her getting to you here."

I blanched. It was my own fault my geis was broken. Two years ago, when I had first met Cade, the Morrigan had tricked me into entering the Otherworld. At the time I had just learned I was Faelorehn, from the Otherworld myself, but I didn't know that my mother had placed a geis on me. Apparently I was safe from all Otherworldly creatures, as long as I never entered their domain. Now I was as vulnerable as a popsicle on a hot day.

"Can I . . . can I at least say goodbye to my family?" I whispered harshly, retreating into my own emotional bubble.

Cade flinched, then reached out a hand to me. Reluctantly, I took it, slightly ashamed at how much comfort that one act brought me. He brushed his thumb over mine and my unease melted.

"We don't have to leave right away. I was hoping," now he paused again and looked away. He heaved a great sigh and forced himself to look me in the eye. "I was hoping I might stay with your family for a time, perhaps a week or so. Get to know them, let them get to know me, so they don't feel as if I'm just tearing you away from them."

Immense joy, then terror, shot through me at the thought. Cade? Stay with my family? So he could be glared at by my father, studied by my mother, and harassed by my brothers? Part of me tingled at the thought of having him staying under the same roof as me, but another part was petrified that my family might actually drive him away.

While I was slowly panicking, Cade turned away and reached behind the tree, pulling a large bag and his own longbow and quiver of arrows from where they had been sitting.

"I'm prepared to stay for quite some time," he said, somewhat uncertainly.

I cleared my throat. "Of course you can stay with us, it's just-" *My dad will probably interrogate you at gunpoint, my mom will most likely ask you embarrassing questions under the pretense of making small talk after she's coerced you into helping her in the kitchen, and my brothers will launch an all-out attack.*

I cringed at the image of Cade stirring a pot of gravy while Mom prattled away about starting a family and settling down properly while my dad stood looking on, his arms crossed and his expression grim. Then, when Cade went to move the pot of gravy off of the burner, my brothers would burst out from behind the kitchen island and attach themselves to his legs, causing him to spill the hot sauce all over my dad while my mom tsked at his poor domestic skills . . .

"Meghan?"

I snapped myself away from the horrifying image and felt my face turn pink. Oh, this was *such* a bad idea . . .

I smiled and said, "I think that would be wonderful. You staying with us for a while."

The look Cade gave me made me think he didn't quite believe me, but he smiled anyways. He set his bag and bow back down and crossed his arms, looking me over carefully. I squirmed, but inside I was glowing. The old Cade had returned and he no longer looked so uncertain. And, despite my fears about immersing him in my family, he was coming to stay. With me. I could have hopped up on the closest log and done a jig. If I knew how to jig. And if I didn't mind embarrassing myself to death.

"How's your archery coming along?" he asked, changing the subject.

I smiled, a genuine one this time, and said with utmost confidence, "I've practiced all summer, and I think I might just be able to beat you now."

He lifted an incredulous eyebrow, so I picked up my bow, strung it, and proceeded to prove my claim.

As we practiced together, I tried to forget about what my parents might say when I walked through the door later that morning with Cade in tow. I tried to block out the uncomfortable images of my brothers and my father and their own version of welcoming my guest. Most of all, I tried to block out the niggling feeling that something wasn't quite right. There was so much Cade and I needed to discuss: the Morrigan's attack, my outpouring of magic, the fact that he had told me he loved me . . .

I'd let my joy of seeing him alive and well overwhelm me, so I hadn't noticed that Cade greeted me like an old friend, not as someone he was in love with. Hadn't he said those words to me? Just before sacrificing himself so that I might have one last chance to escape the Morrigan? The memory was still so strong for me; his declaration of love, the way he had held me, his kiss . . . I nearly lost my balance as I remembered that kiss. Had it all been an act? Or worse, had he just said those things on a whim? Had he just kissed me to make me feel better because he knew we were going to die?

I bit my lip and focused on the target far ahead of me. After all, I had just boasted that I could beat him at archery, and the last thing I needed to do was fall apart and lose my concentration. I took a deep mental breath, centered my arrow on the bull's eye of an old target from our last practice, and released the bowstring. Funny how the glorious sound of my arrow hitting the central red dot was an eerie reminder of just how I felt at the moment.

After over an hour of target practice, I ran out of ways to stall the inevitable. I'd tried small talk and telling jokes, anything to avoid the one thing we both didn't want to talk about: the Morrigan's attack. We could have easily called it a day and headed back up to the house, but I was trying to avoid that as well. Unfortunately, small talk was called small for a reason, and honestly, I wasn't that good at telling jokes, so we gathered up our things and headed up the equestrian trail.

It wasn't long before Cade and I were standing outside the front door of my house. At first I was just going to walk in with him, but I had given it some thought on the way up from the swamp. My family knew the truth about me now; I had told them at the end of the school year, when I had gone missing for the weekend. As soon as I had returned home and after the police department had been called and informed that I was fine, I had burst into tears and told them everything I'd learned about my heritage.

Now, once again I stood on the threshold of another one of those situations where I was going to hit my parents and brothers with another whopper.

I licked my lips, took a deep breath and said, "Let me go in first, okay?"

My hand reached for the doorknob, but I paused before turning it. So Meghan, what to say to them . . . *Hi guys! Guess what, Cade's back! You know, the guy I told you about? The one who enlightened me about who I am? The one that was so sick? Yeah, he's better, and guess what! He wasn't really sick. Nope, he was murdered by his mother's Otherworldly monsters and I took him to the Dagda's Cauldron . . . what's that? Oh, long story, but it basically brings people back to life. So here's Cade, standing here before us now. And he's come to take me back to the Eilé with him!* Yes. That would go over very well.

I blinked up at Cade and found him giving me an odd look. Oh, oops. Must have let my mind wander again . . . what had I just said? I was going to go in first, right.

I shrugged. "I think it's best that I let my family know what's going on before we both come bursting in."

I looked him up and down, biting back a grin of admiration. Oh yes, he sketched a fine image indeed, but my family wasn't used to seeing anyone quite as, uh, *striking*, as Cade. His broad shoulders and unusual height, his perfect face framed by dark auburn hair, and those changeable green eyes . . . Combine all that with his Otherworldly clothes and he looked like some fairytale prince who'd just stepped off the pages of a book.

He relaxed a little and nodded, setting his bow and travel bag down next to the old rickety bench that guarded our front porch. He crossed his arms and sat down, the wood creaking in protest against his weight. I feared the bench might break, but I had more daunting things to worry about. Steeling myself, I tried the doorknob, grateful it was unlocked. I cast Cade a final, nervous smile before slipping inside.

The energetic melody of a video game soundtrack greeted my ears and the smell of Mom's pancakes infused the air as I stepped into the great living room. The quick snap of folding newsprint told me that Dad was sitting in his recliner, catching up on the local news.

"Logan! You just shot me!" Bradley complained as his digital self crashed down in flames.

"Meg, is that you?" Mom called from the relative area of the kitchen. "Want to come cut the tops off of the strawberries?"

I took a deep breath. *Keep cool Meg, this doesn't have to be so difficult.* Despite the fact that it was almost eleven, the Elam family was just getting started on breakfast. During the summer months, morning in our household generally began anywhere between nine and ten in the morning, sometimes later.

I walked into the kitchen, taking note of where everyone was located. Bradley and Logan were glued to the TV and Dad was absorbed in his paper. Aiden was watching the video game commence as if it were a cartoon, and Jack and Joey were busy constructing something out of blocks, presumably a city for their toy T-Rex to destroy. I could see the green dinosaur waiting in the wings, a mouth full of white, plastic teeth ready to do some damage. I shivered and told myself that it didn't remind me of some of the faelah I'd seen.

The strawberries were in the fridge, still tucked in the green plastic crates they always came in. I pulled them out, dumped them in a colander, and wandered over to the sink where I rinsed them off. Cade had been sitting outside for a good two or three minutes. Maybe five. I had better get this over with before he took it upon himself to knock on the door and proceed with introductions on his own. I picked up a knife and started to carve the green stems off of the red berries.

"So, Mom," I started off weakly.

"Yeah hon?"

Her back was to me and she was busy pouring batter on the griddle. I clenched my teeth. *Just tell them already!*

"Remember the boy from the Otherworld, Cade? And how he had been very sick?"

I waited for her response, and it seemed like it was taking her a long time. We had talked about Cade a few times before. They hadn't been long conversations, but I had fed her enough information that she should remember him. I glanced over my shoulder to find my mom looking at me carefully. Uh-oh. I knew that look. I had her full attention now; no going back.

"Well, he's much better and, well, he's . . ." I fished around for the right way to tell her he was currently sitting outside the front door, expecting to stay with us for a week. Before I could come up with the right words, however, the sound of Bradley's voice cut through the room.

"There's an elf on the porch!"

I almost choked. Oh *crap!*

Several things happened at once. First, Mom's attention got diverted from me. Okay, good. Then, all of my other brothers promptly stopped what they were doing to run to the window and peek through the blinds like Bradley. Third, my father stood up and set the newspaper down on the coffee table with a slap. And finally, Mom said, "What on earth are you talking about?"

By this time everyone had migrated to the window. I could only bury my face in my hands, my cheeks turning bright red in mortification.

Eventually, I said, "That isn't an elf, that's Cade. And he's come to stay with us for a while. If that's okay."

Good. I'd said it. But now everyone was staring at me as if I'd sprouted feathers. Ugh. This was not how I wanted this to go . . .

"You're boyfriend's an elf?" Logan asked.

"Logan! He's not my boyfriend! And he's not an elf."

My frustration was ringing clear, because everyone became silent, quietly watching me.

"Look," I continued, "can I invite him in? It's kind of rude to just stare at him through the window, don't you think? He met up with me down in the swamp and I asked him to wait outside while I broke the news to you."

"What news?"

So far, Dad had remained relatively quiet, taking everything in with a grain of amusement. Now he looked serious again.

Oh Dad, I thought miserably, *you know what I'm going to say, don't you?*

I let my shoulders slump and said, "I'll be going to the Otherworld soon. Cade said I'll be safer there and that we should be leaving in a week or two."

"Meghan, I don't think you should just run off with this young man. How can you even know if you can trust him?"

Mom would worry, and I couldn't blame her. I decided to go with the truth without telling her everything.

"Trust me, Mom. Cade and I have been through a lot together. I can't tell you everything because it would make you worry even more. But believe me, he has my best interests at heart."

I could tell my parents didn't like the situation at all, but they knew, as well as I, that I was eighteen, legally an adult, and that I could leave the house whenever I wanted to without their permission.

"So, are we letting the elf in now?"

"Bradley!" my mother hissed, then looked at me.

I nodded and moved towards the front door, burning in embarrassment and hoping Cade hadn't heard anything that had been said. I opened the door and stepped outside quickly, before my family could get a better look at him. He sat on the bench where I had left him, the hood of his cloak pushed back and his longbow resting in his lap. Despite the uncomfortable scene I had just left behind, I couldn't help but smile. No wonder Bradley thought he was an elf; he looked like a character out of one of his video games.

"Um," I said, my hands behind my back, one still grasping the doorknob, "my family is ready to meet you."

Cade merely nodded, then stood, placing his bow beside his travel bag. My heart began to speed up again. Was he nervous? Would he scare my family? And more likely, would they scare him?

I thought it prudent to warn him before we went inside. "My family," I began, then took a deep breath. "They can be overwhelming. They are going to be curious about you, just so you know, and my brothers, and Dad and Mom, might ask you some awkward or inappropriate questions."

I gritted my teeth and studied my toes, feeling embarrassed again. The light touch to my shoulder brought my gaze back up. Cade was looking at me, his mouth turned into a crooked grin, a mischievous glint in his eye.

"They can't be any worse than my family, can they?"

I stared blankly at him for a moment or two, wondering if he was referring to his mother, the Morrigan, his father, the Celtic hero Cuchulainn, his foster father, the Dagda, or his sister, Enorah, the wild woman of the Weald. It didn't matter. His statement made me laugh and my anxiety instantly melted away.

"No, I guess they couldn't. Though my brothers can be fierce in their own way."

Cade smiled for real this time, his eyes crinkling at the corners. "Good. I've always wanted brothers."

Before I could even fathom exactly what he meant by that statement, he gently nudged me aside and opened the door.

Three

Welcome

To my utter surprise, my family's reaction to Cade went quite well. After introducing himself to everyone as Caedehn MacRoich with an annoyingly impeccable display of manners, my brothers moved to ambush him, as I had anticipated. But just before pouncing, they stopped short and gazed up in awe at the Faelorehn man who now seemed to take up the entire room with his presence. I had to bite my lip to hide a grin as Logan and Bradley, and even the twins, all burst out with ridiculous questions. They wanted to know if he had magic like their sister, if he owned a sword, if he lived in the forest, why he was so tall . . . The only one remaining silent was Aiden, but that was normal. Instead, my autistic brother just watched the whole thing unfold from a distance, his eyes wary but curious.

Mom was the one to pull me away from the scene. "You boys be nice to our guest. Logan and Bradley, why don't you show him to the spare room and help carry his things in."

My brothers groaned but obeyed, chattering like chipmunks as they grabbed Cade by the arms, leading him away like a prisoner. He didn't seem to be bothered by it at all. As soon as they disappeared around the corner, Mom grabbed my upper arm and wheeled me into the kitchen. "Oh Meg! What a nice young man, and so handsome!"

I went crimson and nervously pushed a loose strand of hair behind my ear. "Careful Mom," I murmured, trying to lighten the mood, "Dad will get jealous."

She snorted and waved my remark off as she promptly got me working on the strawberries again. Dad stood off in the living room, eyeing me carefully and making me feel even more awkward than I already did. When I felt a pair of arms wrap around my waist, I knew Aiden hadn't joined Cade and his flock of admirers. I glanced down at my brother only to find his eyes swimming and his lip quivering. I stopped what I was doing and took a steadying breath. I placed a hand on his head and whispered, "Not yet Aiden. I'm not leaving yet."

Cade emerged from the hall ten minutes later with a water gun in his hand. I arched a brow and paused in my current task of setting the table. He had a huge grin on his face and his eyes glinted.

"Bradley and Logan have challenged me to a battle," he proclaimed.

I heaved a great sigh and placed my hands on my hips. "You know you don't have to cater to their childish demands, right?" I told him.

The look he gave me was one of pure disbelief.

"What? Forfeit and lose my honor?" he asked, placing a hand over his heart.

I couldn't help it, I laughed, and then my two younger brothers emerged from the hallway with their own weapons.

"Don't get too dirty! Brunch is in half an hour!" Mom called after them as they disappeared outside, the squealing twins right on their heels. Even Aiden left my side to go watch.

Twenty minutes later, Cade stepped in through the door, followed by my brothers. They looked like a litter of puppies trailing after the alpha dog, eagerly leaping up and vying for his attention.

"You have to teach us how to sneak around without making any noise!" Logan demanded.

"And how did you duck away from me like that?!"

Bradley's face was glowing with admiration.

I turned away and bit my bottom lip again as I carried a pitcher of orange juice to the table. This introduction could not have gone any better.

"Boys," Mom said as she carried over a plate full of pancakes, "leave our guest alone and come to the table. Breakfast is ready."

We all took our customary seats, with Cade and Dad sitting at opposite ends of the table and the rest of us filling in on either side. I chose to sit closest to Cade and tried to hide a small blush when my mom gave a knowing look.

The food was passed around and I noticed that Cade politely took a little of everything. For a few minutes, we merely ate in silence, and I couldn't help but feel the knots growing in the pit of my stomach. This was where serious conversations took place, at the dinner table, and I was nervously waiting for one of my parents to break the ice.

"Tell me, Caedehn is it?" Dad asked.

My fork almost skittered off the plate as I missed the strawberry I was aiming for. *Oh no. Here it comes . . .*

Cade carefully finished chewing his food before looking my dad in the eye and answering, "Yes, but please, call me Cade."

"Alright, Cade, do you mind telling me what your intentions are towards my daughter?"

Oh good lord . . . The happy sound of silverware scraping and cutting came to an abrupt stop. The room went dead silent and I could feel my face going white. Cade reached under the table and took my hand, squeezing it as he straightened his shoulders in what I imagined was meant to be a confident posture.

Welcome

"I intend to bring her back to Eilé, the Otherworld, so that she may learn how to use and control her power. I wish to be her friend and to provide what help I can."

That seemed to satisfy my dad for the rest of meal. Thank goodness. I was relieved, sure, but I was also disappointed. A friend? Was I just a friend to Cade? I cast him a sidelong glance, but he had returned to his pancakes. Sighing, I decided I should follow his example and not draw any more attention to myself.

The rest of the day was spent sharing stories. Cade answered all of the questions my brothers threw at him and thankfully, Dad's prodding followed a more typical male theme that didn't fall under the 'Let's Embarrass Meghan' category. Mom asked him about his own mother, and Cade had to pause before answering. I was the only one to see the dark expression cross his face, though. He never mentioned the Morrigan, but told my family about his sister and how she had helped raise him until the Dagda took him in. I laughed along with everyone else as he recalled some of his more rambunctious exploits as a boy. By nine that evening, everyone was ready to call it a night.

"Oh, Meghan, I forgot to tell you," Mom said as she got up with Dad to head to their room. "Robyn called while you were out this morning and wanted to know if you were going camping with them this weekend."

I winced. I hadn't planned on it.

"I think you should consider it, dear," she gave Cade a quick look. "Your friends will be heading off to college soon and you'll be going . . . well, you might not be seeing each other again for quite some time."

Yes, I would be going to live a new life in the Otherworld. She didn't need to say it, and she was right. I should go camping with them. But if the faelah found me . . .

"Cade could go with you," Mom continued, smiling over at him. "Then your friends could meet him. It's this weekend, so it gives you two plenty of time before you have to leave."

Cade cleared his throat and said, "It sounds like a great idea."

Mom smiled. "Good, it's settled then. Goodnight you two, don't stay up too late."

Despite a strong temptation to take advantage of some alone time, I bid Cade goodnight as well. I was tired and emotionally overwhelmed by the day's events and I could use some time alone to think about . . . things.

After Cade assured me he had everything he needed for the night, I gave him one last smile and headed downstairs with a slightly heavy heart. He'd been the perfect gentleman and it was clear that my brothers loved him and my parents, at the worst, tolerated him. Mom liked him, it seemed, but it was harder to tell with Dad. Sighing, I burrowed under my comforter and tried to focus on sleep. Only problem was, there were still so many questions I wanted to ask, but I had no idea when I'd get the chance (or gather the courage) to ask them.

For the next few days, Cade settled in with my family like a long lost friend. He played with my brothers, showing a patience I had seen only practiced by my parents. He helped my mom with preparing our meals and he took part in insightful discussions with my dad. After that first morning at the dinner table, when Dad had established his authority as my father, the tension surrounding all of us seemed to ease. I grinned, realizing that Cade had passed the rigorous Elam litmus test.

The few times Cade wasn't being held captive by my family, he accompanied me into the swamp and helped me eradicate any wayward faelah we stumbled upon. When I showed him how much my archery had improved by shooting one of the demented, Otherworldly squirrels that were common in the neighborhood, he smiled broadly and gave me a look that was enough to melt my heart. He even showed me some basic sword and fighting techniques, promising I'd be learning a lot more once we left for Eilé.

I enjoyed the training. Not only was it exciting and exhilarating, but it gave me one more excuse to be close to Cade. My favorite move, by far, was one which required him to wrap his arms around me in order to show me how to escape. I was really tempted to just succumb to the attack, but a girl shouldn't be too obvious.

One afternoon, after we were done with our practice for the day, but before we returned to the house, Cade invited me to sit next to him on one of the old, fallen eucalyptus trees that were so common in the swamp. I silently obeyed, wondering what he wanted to discuss. He had that look on his face, the serious one that meant something weighed heavily on his mind. My heart sped up, half fearful, half hopeful.

"There is something else I'd like to teach you Meghan," he said, his tone almost grim.

Uh-oh. Why did he sound so reluctant?

"Okay," I answered, my fingers absent-mindedly pulling at the bark of the tree.

"We, the Faelorehn, have another gift, one you have already started using to some capacity," he went on.

Okay, I said once more in my mind, subconsciously urging him to spit it out. What could it possibly be?

"You see," he dropped his head and joined me in peeling away old bark. "We have the gift of mind-speaking."

Huh? What was that exactly?

My arched brow and silence must have expressed my confusion because he smiled at me and seemed to relax a little.

"How do you communicate with Meridian?"

I blinked, not expecting the question. "Uh, she tells me things, in my head and I answer her back the same way."

"How do you do it?"

I shrugged. I couldn't tell him. True, he had told me that when she was old enough, Meridian and I would be able to speak telepathically, but I couldn't tell him *how* we did it. It just sort of happened.

"It came naturally, correct?"

I nodded.

"The Faelorehn can also speak, mind to mind, to one another. I'd like to teach you how."

He went quiet again and that gave me a few moments to gather my thoughts. So, did that mean I could speak with him the way I spoke with Meridian? I shivered inwardly, delight suffusing me. To be able to communicate telepathically with Cade? It seemed so . . . intimate.

I turned back to him and smiled. "I think that would be a useful skill."

He released a great sigh and returned my smile. Why was he so nervous about this?

"I was afraid to tell you Meghan. I was afraid you might think I've been reading your mind all this time."

Ah, that explained his nervousness. And made me reconsider my earlier thoughts. I froze. *Had* he been reading my mind? And if so, what had he seen? Oh no, had he seen all those times I'd daydreamed about him? Could he hear what I was thinking right now?

He must have noticed my panic, because he lifted a hand and moved over an inch. "Meghan, I swear to you, I've never once read your thoughts."

"Then how is it you know what I'm thinking right now?!" Oh crap, oh crap, *oh crap* . . . How mortifying! I could feel myself blushing to the roots of my hair and I stood up, ready to bolt.

"Meghan, I don't need to read your thoughts, they are written plainly all over your face."

Welcome

There was laughter in Cade's voice and darn him, he reached out and gently took my hand. It had the opposite effect of lightning, soothing me instead of jolting me.

"Sit, and let me explain." He patted the spot next to him on the fallen tree.

Sighing and willing my burning cheeks to return to their normal, paler color, I sat down, grumbling under my breath.

"Mind-speaking, or *shíl-sciar*, is different than communicating with your spirit guide. First, the conversation takes place in a completely different part of your mind. When you share thoughts with Meridian, they appear on the surface, within the shallowest part of your conscious. Shíl-sciar with another Faelorehn, however,"

He paused and seemed to be reluctant to go on.

"Mind-speaking, uh, *shíl-sciar*, with another Faelorehn . . . ?" I prompted.

Cade took a breath. "It requires something more. Trust, of the deepest kind, and complete honesty. One cannot lie when conversing using shíl-sciar."

How . . . interesting, and daunting. I wondered how that worked, considering I'd lied often enough to myself. And people lied all the time in regular conversation, why couldn't they do the same with mind-speaking? Maybe it was a Faelorehn thing and not a human one.

The sound of Cade's voice again prompted me to leave my thoughts for later.

"When we use shíl-sciar our thoughts, our internal words, come from the same place where our emotions reside, so mind-spoken words are the purest form of conversation, even more pure than words spoken aloud in the most sincere way. The words often show up as writing, appearing and disappearing across the darkness of the mind."

"Like typing on a keyboard?" I asked.

Cade nodded. "It's slightly different with each individual. The words are also accompanied by a feeling of who the person is and tinged with the color of the emotion they are conveying."

I crinkled my eyebrows.

Cade's mouth quirked in a smile. "It's an indescribable sense. The only two people I mind-speak with, at the moment, are the Dagda and my sister. I can tell them apart by the feeling that I get when I receive their words in my mind."

I nodded. I guess that made sense. After all, I got a different feeling each time I interacted with my brothers and parents. They were all feelings of love, but they were all different in their own way.

"Anything else I should know?" I asked.

"Yes. The words are also accompanied by colors. Each color represents the emotion the speaker is feeling. Reds often depict forms of distress, blues represent calm, yellow caution and so on. You'll come to learn them as you get better at mind-speaking."

"So, how does it work?"

"First, I need you to find the place in your mind that is most perceptive to magic."

I gave him a look. How was I supposed to do that?

Cade smiled and said, "Close your eyes and seek out your Faelorehn power. Remember how I showed you how to find it when we were in Eilé?"

Oh, I remembered. It was the first time he had kissed me. Well, the first time he had kissed me when I had been fully aware of it. I shivered and then my skin grew hot as my mind conjured up the memory.

I gulped. "Uh huh," I whispered.

Cade moved closer to me. "It's almost the same thing, only instead of trying to feel it, you are going to try and see it. Close your eyes."

Okay . . . Shrugging I did as I was told.

"Concentrate on the feel of your magic. It won't be very strong since you've been in the mortal world for so long, but it will be there."

I focused, trying to block out everything but the darkness of my mind. Slowly, a small pinprick of light came into view. It grew brighter until I was seeing a blue flame glowing in the darkness. It warmed my heart and made me smile. My magic.

"Have you found it?" Cade asked.

"Yes," I said with a smile, still keeping my eyes closed.

"Good. Now I need you to look away from your magic, into the darkness just beside it."

I did as he asked, feeling a bit reluctant to leave my beautiful fae power behind.

"Okay," I said, "all I see is darkness now."

The words, *Very good Meghan*, scrawled across the dark space, pale blue in color, accompanied by the whispering echo of Cade's voice.

I gasped and my eyes flew open. I stared at him, my face surely white with shock. Yes, I had heard his voice, but not with my ears. What the hell . . . ?

Cade held up a hand, his own face looking uncertain. *Don't be alarmed. This is mind-speaking. I want you to try to project your own words towards me. You have to think about what you want to say, find the dark spot next to your magic, and then say them, in your mind.*

Once my initial shock wore off, I took a deep breath and closed my eyes again. I found the dark cavity next to my magic and thought of something to tell Cade. *How is this possible?* I sent.

Cade's words and essence blossomed, a warm yellow in my mind. *It is because of our Faelorehn glamour.*

This is so weird, I sent back, wondering what color my words were in his head.

ḷaᵀḫara

It is strange at first, but you'll get used to it. Shíl-sciar can be a very useful skill, especially once we reach the Otherworld.

I gulped, trying not to think about the Otherworld.

Until then, Cade continued, *we will practice.*

Okay, what shall we talk about? I asked, starting to like this way of talking. It was odd, no doubt about it, but it was nice as well.

I can tell you a little more about your glamour and how to use it. The essence of our magic, like I told you once before, stems from the earth but is cultivated in our blood. We borrow from the earth, and being in Eilé makes our glamour more powerful, yet it is in the blood where our magic is most potent. That is why some of the tribes of ancient Ireland made blood sacrifices; they thought they could harness the power of Faelorehn magic through the blood of animals. Unfortunately most earth born creatures don't contain nearly as much magic as those from the Otherworld. It is often said that a wounded Faelorehn is far more dangerous than one that is not. An open wound has the potential to release an incredible amount of magic since the skin is not there to keep it in check. Think of it as an electrical wire that is encased in rubber. You won't get shocked unless you touch the bare wire. Your blood is the conductor and your skin helps keep it in check.

I listened to Cade's lesson, letting his words flow into my mind. I had never thought of magic as electrical, but I guess it made sense.

When you call upon your magic, and if you are very still and concentrate hard enough, you can sometimes feel it coursing through your veins, along with your blood.

Another thing you need to know is that using your glamour can be dangerous for you. Magic is something that must be carefully administered and controlled. If you use too much at once, it can damage you, even kill you.

Worry tainted the pale red words Cade scrawled across my mind, and I realized he was telling me this not only because it was something I should know, but because I had been careless with my magic before. Not that I could have known any better. I thought about how I had overcome the Morrigan's faelah army after Cade's defeat, careful to keep those thoughts away from the place in my mind that would project them towards Cade. Could I have killed myself that day?

I swallowed. *How do you know if you are using too much?*

Cade moved closer to me and I could feel the heat pouring off of him. I resisted the urge to close the distance between us and simply sat there, willing my heartbeat to slow down. He placed a hand over the spot where my magic resided, next to my heart. My mouth went dry and my heart sped up.

Whenever you need to use a large amount of magic, always remember to bring it into your inner sight so that you can monitor it. Meghan,

Cade's words stopped flowing into my mind and he placed his hands on both my shoulders, turning me so that I faced him. He looked into my eyes, his own a deep, golden green. I wondered what color mine were at the moment.

Meghan, never, ever, let your magic burn out. If the flame that represents your glamour ever becomes faint and starts to flicker like a candle about to extinguish itself, you stop whatever it is you are doing and pull your magic back into yourself. To let your magic burn out is to die.

The grip on my shoulders tightened and I actually cried out.

"I understand," I croaked as I tried to pull away from him.

Cade released me, taking several steps back. He ran his hand through his hair and took a deep, shuddering breath.

"Meghan, I'm sorry," he said aloud. "I didn't mean to hurt you, it's just-"

He sighed again as I stood back and rubbed my shoulder. He had gripped me pretty hard.

"It's just?" I prompted.

He glanced up at me, his eyes even darker than before, his mouth cut in a grim line. "It's so easy to over-extend your power, especially if you have not had proper training in how to utilize it. If anything ever happened to you because you didn't know how to rein in your glamour, I'd . . ."

"You'd what?" I asked immediately, the slight pain in my shoulders forgotten as my heart raced to catch up with my thoughts.

Cade lifted his head once again and gazed at me, the look in his eyes so beguiling that I almost started drooling.

He opened his mouth to speak again, but at that very moment Bradley decided to scream at the top of his lungs from somewhere up the equestrian trail.

"MEGHAN!!! Mom says dinner's ready!"

Cade straightened immediately, losing his intense composure.

No, no, no! What were you going to say?! I wanted to scream at him.

Instead I gritted my teeth and we started up the trail. I was dying to know what he had been about to say, but I guess it could wait for later. Perhaps we could find a private moment this weekend while at the lake. Then again, did I want to risk Robyn, Tully and the boys overhearing? But if it involved another declaration of love followed by a passionate kiss, I don't think I'd care very much who was there to see it.

Four

Truth

opez Lake was crowded with the usual family vacationers, looking for a weekend away from lying around the house. The buzz of motorboats and the muffled sounds of radios playing across the campsites drifted through the window of Cade's Trans Am as we rumbled slowly through the camping area. Robyn, Tully, Thomas and Will were meeting us there, and as we drew closer and closer to our destination, the knots in my stomach became even tighter. The night before, Cade joined me in my room after everyone went to bed so we could discuss the camping trip and the meeting of my friends.

"I want to tell them everything," I'd said nervously. "Well, not everything. I want them to know the truth about what I am. They have been my closest friends all through high school and they deserve to know why they won't be seeing me so much anymore."

I had kept my head down, talking to my hands as they worried away at the tattered cuffs of my sweatshirt's sleeves. Cade had gently taken one of them, distracting me from my nervous fretting, and squeezed my fingers.

"Then you should tell them, and I'll help you."

He kept my hand in his for a long time before dropping it, and once again I'd wondered about the big question that was my constant shadow. Would we just go on forever pretending like nothing had happened between us? I tried to forget it as I'd tossed and turned in my bed after Cade left, wondering if he was doing the same thing in the guest room upstairs. Eventually, I managed to force the thoughts from my mind, *again*, and fell into a fitful sleep.

"This looks like the place," Cade said, jerking me out of my reflection.

He turned his car down a paved lane that ended in a cul-de-sac of sorts mere yards from one of the lake's small inlets. I noted the numbers of the campsites until I spotted the one that matched the name scrawled on the paper I held: Toro, site eight. If the sign hadn't been an indication, the image of Will and Thomas struggling with a partially raised tent while Robyn and Tully looked on in mild disapproval would have cinched it.

Cade rolled up next to Thomas's van (on loan for the weekend) and killed the engine. I'd been too busy finding amusement at my friends' expense that I had completely forgotten that I was about to spend a night alone with Cade with only my friends to chaperone us. Friends who knew nothing about him, nor how I had met him . . . My heart shuddered to a stop as the last rumble of the Trans Am's engine came to an end. Not even Robyn knew how I'd met Cade. For some reason, she had been so dazzled by his Otherworldly beauty that she'd kept her boundless curiosity alive only on the tidbits I was willing to feed her.

Okay, she had asked me once where I had found him, but I had flippantly responded that he had found me. Sooner or later my friends were going to want to know more about my good-looking, mysterious pseudo-boyfriend, and I would have to either invent something or bite the bullet and do what I'd planned to do all along: tell them the truth. For some reason, informing my friends that I was an immortal, Otherworldly being who'd met Cade while being attacked by monsters seemed far less daunting than admitting I wasn't all that clear on what our relationship status was. Yeah, and just what did that say about my sanity?

I took a deep breath and climbed out of the car, putting on my best smile as my high school buddies came to greet us. In all honesty, I still wasn't ready to tell them about my unusual ancestry, but I had a weird feeling that Cade and I weren't going to leave this camping trip without something happening that would give us no choice.

To my immense relief, no one charged at me spouting questions regarding Cade and his sudden appearance. They all had been aware of his existence for a little while (or, according to everyone but Robyn, his *feigned* existence), so his appearance wasn't too shocking. Last spring, Cade was supposed to go with me to prom and he would have met everyone then, but that was before his mother sprung her neat little trap and kind of ruined my whole weekend. Now, as the two of us slowly walked up the short drive to the campsite, I would finally get the chance to show them I hadn't invented him after all.

"Meghan! Cade! So glad you guys could make it!"

Robyn dropped the tent stakes she'd been holding and came sauntering over. Though not as short as my best friend Tully, I still had quite a few inches on her and I had to bend down to give her a hug. Robyn let go of me and I looked up at everyone else, expecting the same casual, Aw-shucks-how's-your-summer-been? expressions on their faces. What I saw instead made me want to laugh out loud. Tully, Will and Thomas stood ramrod still, their eyes wide and their mouths open in different stages of shock. Their gazes were fixed on Cade, like a Pointer spotting a duck. I covered my mouth to hide my amusement. Yes, even in his civilian clothes Cade had that effect.

Robyn hadn't given Cade a hug, but she did give him a once over. I noticed admiration on her face, but it wasn't the dumbstruck look she had plastered on him the first few times they'd met.

I cleared my throat. "Cade, you know Robyn of course, and this is Will, Thomas and Tully."

I gestured towards my mute friends as I named them. Cade smiled politely and nodded at each of them in turn.

"Pleased to meet you all," Cade said. "Is there anything I can do to help?"

He indicated the tent and, as if some hypnotist somewhere snapped his fingers, Tully and the boys became alive with purpose, instructing Cade on how he could be of assistance. I glanced at Robyn, but she only gave me one of her sly looks.

"I'll get our stuff out of the car," I blurted, and turned on my heel before she could start interrogating me.

Half an hour later the tent was up, our food organized in the cooler, and our camping gear stored securely inside our canvas abode. The tent itself was big enough to hold eight people and had two smaller rooms off to the sides, their fabric doors rolled back to let it air out before nightfall.

"I moved yours and Cade's stuff to one of the side rooms, you know, in case you two want some privacy."

Robyn winked at me and I gritted my teeth. It didn't help stop the blush, however. I pushed past her and went to join Will and Thomas, who had taken out their fold up chairs and were each enjoying a soda. I plopped down next to them and released a great sigh.

"In case you're wondering," Will said after taking a loud sip of his drink and pushing his glasses back up the bridge of his nose, "your boyfriend decided to take a walk."

I had been leaning back in my chair, my eyes closed against the warm sun above. Upon hearing Will's comment, I did a full body cringe and leaned forward, my hair falling into my face, as I glared at him.

"He isn't my boyfriend. He's just a friend."

Yes, I wanted him to be my boyfriend, but I couldn't tell my friends that without talking to Cade first. The last thing I needed to do was ruin our friendship by going around and telling people something that might not be the truth.

"Well, if that's the case, can I have him?" Thomas asked.

My annoyance disappeared in a flash and I cast him a quick look. He gave me his crooked grin, brown eyes dancing with mirth. I snorted out a laugh and in the next moment the tense mood had vanished.

"What are you guys talking about?" Tully asked as she and Robyn came walking up the road.

"How hot Cade is," Thomas answered wistfully as he dug around for another drink in the cooler.

Will groaned and rubbed his face, but I only smiled. I kind of felt sorry for him, getting stuck with all us girls and Thomas and the gorgeous son of a goddess and the Celtic version of Hercules. It was definitely going to be a long camping trip for him.

Tully took a seat next to me and looked like she was about to ask me something when Cade appeared out of nowhere from the oak trees behind our tent. He startled all of us into a fit of laughter and when it died off, Will clapped his hands together and proclaimed it was time to start the fire so we could barbecue the chicken.

Cade offered to help and Will begrudgingly accepted. Thomas, without an ounce of shame, offered to watch, which only resulted in Will casting him an annoyed glare. Not surprisingly, I had to stifle another laugh. Cade, to my relief, didn't seem to notice his newest admirer and proceeded to make a teepee out of the wood they'd gathered earlier.

I helped Robyn and Tully get the meat and vegetables ready, and since Cade was in the immediate vicinity, we kept our conversation to books, movies and the like, though I could almost feel the waves of curiosity rolling off of them, Tully especially. She had been my best friend since childhood, but ever since I stumbled into the swamp in the middle of the night and met Cade for the first time, we had been drifting apart. Not that it was anything she or I meant to do, it's just how everything had turned out. I regretted keeping things from her, but I had done it for her own safety.

The sun was dipping low on the horizon, but the chicken was over the fire, the potato salad waited on the table with the chips and drinks, and we had all retreated into silence. Of course, the sounds of other campers nearby intruded on our thoughts, but I think for the most part we blocked it all out.

After eating and packing away the extra food, we gathered around the fire pit and cracked open the graham crackers, marshmallows, and chocolate. Thomas and Will sat across from me in their fold out chairs, Tully and Robyn on either side of them, and Cade and I took up one side of the bench. We had dragged it closer to the fire so we could make our own s'mores.

I flicked a glance at Cade. He gazed into the flames, his expression free of any emotion and his eyes dark. He had remained relatively quiet the entire time, taking part in polite conversation but only speaking when he needed to. Perhaps he was taking this time to study my friends; to get a sense of what they were like. Mostly, though, I imagined he was deep in thought about what awaited us in Eilé. I bit my lip and turned my eyes back towards the fire. I didn't want to think about what might be occupying his mind at the moment.

I returned my attention to the marshmallows turning golden brown over the fire. Mine was done, so I got to work making a s'more. Cade watched me with curiosity, and then began mimicking my actions. I was simply glad that look of deep contemplation was gone from his eyes. It always worried me when Cade adopted that expression.

With nimble dexterity, Robyn plucked the crispy marshmallow off the end of her own fork and wedged it between two graham crackers with a piece of chocolate. "So, now that we are all here with no pesky parents to eavesdrop, why don't you tell us how the two of you met?"

I inhaled a cracker crumb and proceeded to cough uncontrollably. Cade gently patted my back as the blood rushed to my face and my eyes watered. When I regained my composure, I looked up at him while blinking the tears from my eyes. He didn't look at all phased by what Robyn had said.

How couldn't he be? She had just insinuated that we were an item. And it only bothered me because he had never indicated one way or another that we were (or were not) an item. Somehow, between the day he arrived in the swamp at the beginning of the week and this very moment, Cade and I had never found any free time to discuss it. Okay, if I was being completely honest with myself, I'd admit it was because I was scared to death to broach the subject, but it was easier to blame it on time constraints. Yes, a week simply wasn't enough time to ask the boy who claimed he loved you if he wanted to be your boyfriend.

I opened my mouth to give an answer, what answer I wasn't sure. Cade, however, beat me to it.

"My little sister goes to school with Meghan's brother, Aiden."

The unformed answer died in my throat. I turned my surprised face towards his, but he was looking at Robyn.

"I had to pick her up one day after school and Meghan happened to be there as well."

Robyn grinned and took a bite out of her s'more, chewing with relish and losing that gleam of mischief in her eyes. I quietly exhaled my relief and Cade turned to study me, a soft look in his expression and a gentle curve at the corner of his mouth. Wait, what just happened? One minute Robyn was swooping down, talons open, to tackle the mystery of Cade once and for all, and he just stepped right in and thwarted her with a simple little lie.

I turned my attention back to the fire. Robyn was never that easily diverted. She had been surreptitiously fishing for information; trying to get one of us to claim Cade and I were a couple, and he had stopped her dead in her tracks. Normally such a question would be followed up by another more intrusive one, especially given his answer, but no. Robyn was content with Cade's response, one that neither claimed nor denied what our relationship status was. Had he used glamour to suppress her curiosity? I blinked and looked at Cade again. He was still gazing at me, his features calm, calculating. I swallowed. Could he be waiting for *me* to acknowledge our relationship? But how could I do that when I didn't even know what our relationship was? Ugh!

"Well, I'm bushed," Tully said, yawning as she pushed herself out of her chair.

Eventually, the fire died down and my three other friends claimed exhaustion and climbed into the tent. Robyn, of course, was the last one to rise.

"Goodnight you two, don't stay up too late."

In the dim light of the dying fire, the suggestive waggle of her eyebrows made her appear downright demonic. I glared at her and she chuckled, the harsh grating sound of the tent zipper sealing her inside and cutting her amusement off.

Truth

Cade and I sat in silence, side by side on the wooden plank of the bench, gazing into the orange glow of coals. I took a slow breath and swallowed back my rising fear very carefully. All week I'd managed to put off saying anything about what had happened between us on the battlefield with the Morrigan. At home my family acted as a nice distraction, but now I only had the gentle lap of the lake a few dozen yards away, the quiet rippling hiss of the fire, the general racket of fellow campers joking and enjoying the night, and my own heartbeat to chase my errant thoughts away.

Stop being such a coward Meghan! He said he loved you, didn't he? And are you going to try and convince yourself that that kiss meant nothing?

I gritted my teeth, squeezed my eyes shut, and told my conscience to take a hike. I turned to Cade with every intention of bringing up the subject we were both avoiding, but the words died in my throat. First mistake: I should not have glanced at his face. Second mistake: I should have diverted my eyes right away.

"Uh . . . um." I raked my hair behind my ears and glanced down. I couldn't do it. I couldn't find the words. Cade sat there, patiently, expectantly, and I knew, somehow I just knew he was waiting for me to say something, anything. What could I say?

I licked my lips and tried again. "I-I think I'm going to go to bed. Do you mind putting out the fire?"

And because I was such a wuss, I stood up quickly and headed into the tent without so much as wishing him a goodnight.

Way to go Meghan. I think you just blew it. I didn't even bother opening the tent quietly and I'm sure the muffled grunt was Thomas's way of letting me know he didn't appreciate being tripped over.

I pushed past the nylon divider that cut off the small room on my side of the tent and plopped down on my sleeping mat. I never liked sleeping zipped up in a sleeping bag; made me feel claustrophobic, so I was the dork who always brought a sleeping mat to lie on so that I could use my sleeping bag as a comforter. I yanked the sleeping bag over my head and did my best not to burst out of my own skin. I took several deep breaths and tried to calm my heart and settle my mind. It didn't help.

Something tickled my cheek and I reached up, expecting to find a mosquito or some other unpleasant insect taking advantage of me, but when I pressed my fingers to my skin all I felt was moisture. I turned over on my side and burst into tears, great, big muffled sobs that I hoped no one else heard.

A few months ago I had had my heart wrenched from my body because I believed Cade was dead. And now he was here, right in front of me, and I didn't even have the courage to tell him I loved him. No, apparently I only had the nerve to do that when he had no way of responding or understanding my declaration.

I can't say how long it took me to fall asleep, but eventually my body stopped shaking and I dozed off, wondering if I had ruined my only chance to really tell Cade how I felt.

Sometime later that night I woke up with a start. I was lying on my side, staring at the outside wall of the tent, the bright moonlight shining down through the mesh roof above me. I strained my ears, thinking that maybe some noise had woken me, but I heard nothing except the soft snoring of my friends and the occasional cough from a neighboring campsite. I sighed and focused on getting back to sleep before I could remember why I felt so empty inside.

Meghan?

Truth

The sight of my name popping up in my head, blue script against a black abyss, made me jerk. And when I did, my shoulder came into contact with something, no, *someone*, just behind me. Cade?

Meghan, are you awake?

Blue again, but not as harsh. I could detect Cade's essence in the words and I relaxed.

Yes? I sent back.

I was hoping we could talk, like this.

Oh. He wanted to have a conversation using shíl-sciar, a conversation that no one else could hear. Why now, in the middle of the night? And then the memory of what had taken place around the campfire came rushing to my mind like an unexpected wave on the shore. My skin flushed with anxiety.

Alright, I answered tentatively as I tried to swallow.

I'm sorry I've been distant these last several days, but I wanted to give you space and give myself time to think. I've been trying to figure out the right words to use . . .

He sighed out loud, but then the silent words returned to that dark place in my mind.

What happened on that plain, with my mother and her Cúmorrig, I didn't want you to have to ever see me like that.

Ah, so here it was: the conversation I had been yearning for and avoiding at the same time. So far it sounded as if Cade was just as afraid as I was, and I guess I could understand that. He had been rather frightening when the battle fury took over. Both his appearance and what he had done to those mutated hounds was enough to give the Grim Reaper nightmares. Not that I blamed him, nor was I in the least bit ungrateful for what he had done. Maybe this was why he had been so quiet on the matter since coming back to the mortal world; perhaps he had been worried about my reaction all along.

And-

Cade's word hung in the darkness for a long time, fading towards yellow in my mind.

And? I prompted, my heartbeat quickening.

He released another sigh, but this one wasn't physical. It was a feeling that appeared in my head as a wash of blue and green.

And I didn't want you to think you were obligated in any way. I didn't want you to feel like you owed me a debt for what I did.

This night, and the entire week if I was being honest, had been an emotional roller coaster for me, so my ability to process simple thoughts was a bit off. I rolled over to face Cade, hoping I might be able to discern something from his expression. I could see him clearly enough, his features limned in the silver light of the moon. His eyes looked darker than usual and his hair was slightly mussed from sleep. Only when he lifted a hand and placed his fingers gently against my cheek did I realize that he had crawled under my open sleeping bag with me. I tensed slightly as my heartbeat kicked up its pace once again, but the soft stroking of his thumb against my temple soothed me.

I meant what I said the last time I saw you in Eilé, before I fought the Morrigan's hounds.

All uncertainty was gone from his eyes. The entire week he'd kept his distance, being careful not to touch me too often or let his gaze linger too long. Now he looked as if he saw nothing else in the world but me; as if he had given himself a pep talk after my rude departure earlier that night and was ready for the challenge ahead of him. This was the Cade who had held me close before taking on the Morrigan's monsters; he was holding nothing back. My toes and fingertips started to tingle, and I bit my lip, not allowing myself to breathe.

I am in love with you, Meghan Elam, and you mean more to me than you can possibly know.

The proclamation was so soft, so sincere, his words in my head so pale blue they were almost white. Tears began to form in my eyes and a cloud of butterflies took flight in my stomach.

I love you, he sent again, his thumb continuing its soothing caress, *but I don't want you to think that you owe me anything for what I did for you. I don't want you to feel that you need to love me ba-*

I cut off his thought process by leaning forward and pressing a kiss against his mouth. I don't know what possessed me to be so bold. It was as if my mind had stopped working and my heart had taken control.

Cade didn't miss a beat. He deepened the kiss, bringing both of his hands forward, lacing his fingers in my hair and molding his body to mine.

Reluctantly, I pulled away so I could catch my breath and suddenly I was ready to talk.

You didn't hear me after you . . . after you died that day. You couldn't hear me, I sent to him, my own words rich with emotion.

Cade's fingers loosened their hold in my hair, but he didn't let go completely. Taking a deep breath and trying to make my head stop spinning, I managed to continue. *But I'll repeat what I said when you were gone and as Speirling carried us across Eilé: I love you too, Caedehn MacRoich, and I want to be with you more than anything else.*

He smiled, his eyes shining in the moonlight.

And since my fear was now obliterated and since we were being so openly honest, I continued, *I was afraid you had changed your mind. That you regretted what you had said to me.*

Cade's hold tightened for a split second and his face grew stern.

Never, his pale words whispered across my mind.

He drew me forward for another long kiss that sent me reeling, and then he wrapped his arms around me. I snuggled against him, resting my head on his chest, my heart glowing contentedly. Cade did love me after all, and now I had no fears about going to the Otherworld, for he would be with me. I fell asleep listening to his heartbeat and the occasional terms of endearment he sent into my mind as he drifted off. For once in what felt like a very long time, I was indescribably happy.

Five

Evidence

think it was the horrendous screech scraping at my eardrums that woke me up again. I jerked and flung out an arm, wondering why I felt disappointed when it only tangled in my sleeping bag. Then I remembered. Cade had told me he loved me, again, after curling up next to me last night. And this time he heard me tell him I loved him back. I recalled falling asleep in his arms, but he was obviously no longer lying next to me. A black shadow formed above me and I nearly screamed, but it was only Cade, crouching low in the dark.

"Meghan," he hissed, "there are some faelah in the campground. I need to go take care of them."

I sat up, the color draining from my face. I knew this was going to happen! This was exactly why I hadn't wanted to go camping in the first place.

Cade moved to stand up, but I grabbed his hand.

"Wait, I can help," I insisted.

Sure, the thought of confronting faelah in the middle of the night wasn't my idea of a fun camping trip, but I didn't want to be *that* girl: the one who sat quivering in fear as her boyfriend took on the role of knight in shining armor. I grinned despite my fear and annoyance. Cade really was my boyfriend now, wasn't he?

"No, you'll stay here."

It wasn't really a demand, but I crossed my arms and narrowed my eyes. "I've been practicing with my bow, which is in the back of your car, and this is a much more public place than the swamp. What if the faelah decide to start searching tents? The people two campsites down from us have a baby."

Cade hesitated, then drew his mouth into a hard line.

"Alright," he finally conceded, drawing me up so he could give me a quick kiss.

My stomach fluttered again and I was disappointed when he pulled away.

"Put on some shoes and a sweatshirt and follow me."

I quickly obeyed and soon we were picking our way over the lumps of my sleeping friends.

"Wha . . ?" Robyn mumbled as she sat up from her sleeping bag.

"Shhh, lie back down Robyn," I told her.

"What's going on?" Will grumbled.

Robyn slumped back down and turned over in her sleeping bag. "Meghan and Cade are sneaking out for a lovers' tryst," she huffed. "Go back to sleep, it's probably three in the morning."

I didn't correct her assumption, nor did I grow annoyed at her claim. As much as I would have liked to be fulfilling Robyn's hypothesis, I had more important things to worry about at the moment.

The sound of the tent zipper as Cade opened it was much louder than I thought it should have been. We stepped out into the night, still bright with moonlight but obscured by the dark shadows cast by trees, trailers and tents. Cade took my hand again and we went straight for his car. He unlocked the door and drew out my bow and quiver, leaving his own behind. I gave him an odd look, barely discernible in the pale moonlight, but before he could answer my questioning gaze, he had somehow flipped the seat bottoms up in the back of his car to reveal an impressive collection of weapons. My eyes grew wide when he chose a sword. Not just any sword. This thing was a good three feet long, plus another foot for the hilt. Cade's grin told me my jaw had dropped open.

"I need you to pick off the little ones Meghan," he said. "Can you do that?"

I nodded numbly, wondering just what we were going up against. I had a sneaking suspicion it wasn't going to be those demented gnomes or even one of the bigger things I'd managed to take down over the summer. I got an arrow ready and started following Cade quietly, my heart beating a fierce tattoo against my ribs. I wanted to go back to the tent and hide under my sleeping bag. Then I gave myself a mental kick. *Stop being so pathetic Meg! You wanted to go with Cade, and besides, you'll be facing this stuff every day very soon. You won't last a week in Eilé if you can't handle a few stray faelah.*

Breathing deeply to calm my nerves, I crept silently along, always following Cade and keeping my ears open for stray sounds. I felt a little ridiculous sneaking around the campground in the middle of the night, dressed in my pajamas and tennis shoes, holding a bow like some sleepwalking nerd who had taken her hobby of live action role playing a little too seriously.

Eventually we came to a low spot in the campground, only a few dozen yards from the closest tent, the one with my snoring friends in it. I caught a clear glimpse of the lake in the distance, the moon pooling in the silver dimples over its black surface. A dumpster and several trash cans formed a dark obstruction of the view, and the dozens of oak trees clinging to the hilly campground offered many good places for faelah to hide.

A sudden crash sounded to our left as one of the trashcans fell over. Cade whipped around, keeping his sword low but pointed away from him. I fought the urge to press myself against his back. Instead, I lifted my bow and got ready for battle.

A heartbeat later, two small creatures came rolling out of the trash bin, snarling and fighting over a chicken bone. At first glance they looked like raccoons, but as I watched them I could see they were definitely Otherworldly. Bushy tails and patchy fur covered their hides, but it was the legs and heads that made me blanch. The faelahs' arms looked mummified; shrunken skin stretched over bone, and their heads were completely devoid of flesh. Cade tapped his sword tip on the asphalt and the horrid creatures stopped their argument to look at us. I felt my stomach turn. Bloody eyes peered out from gore-stained skulls.

"Now Meghan," Cade hissed under his breath.

Pushing aside my fear and disgust, I drew my bowstring back, took aim, and let an arrow fly. It pierced the side of the first creature, causing it to scream in agony. The other one scrambled to get away, but I had already found a new arrow. As it tried to scurry up the hill into the shadows, I took aim and released my bowstring. This time the arrow lodged into the back of its neck.

I grinned, very proud of myself, and it was only when Cade leaned in to give me a one-armed hug and plant a kiss on the top of my head did I realize how badly I was shaking. I had always managed to stay relatively calm in the swamp, but then again, that was always during the day and practically in my backyard. Here, it was dark and there were other people who could be immediately hurt.

"You did great Meghan," Cade whispered against my hair.

I didn't have much time to enjoy the moment because the dark campground was shaken by the roar of some Otherworldly monster. Cade's grip tightened right before he released me and stepped away. He made ready his sword again, this time positioning it so that its length protected his torso.

Evidence

"What was that?" I breathed, feeling cold sweat break out on my forehead.

"Cúthra," Cade growled, his jaw tight. "They don't normally visit the mortal world, unless-"

He paused, so I prompted him, "Unless?"

"Unless they are sent by someone with great power," he finished, turning his head to give me a grim look.

Sent by someone with great power . . . The Morrigan. I gulped, tempted once again to run and hide, but I never got the chance. In the very next moment the huge beast stepped out of the shadows of the trees. I think the smell hit me first, that clinging scent of death and rot and evil. The monster was about the size of a Clydesdale horse and walked on all fours. Instead of hooves it had long-fingered hands and feet with wicked claws at their tips. A bedraggled mane ran down the back of its neck all the way to its small tail. Like most of the Morrigan's evil faelah, it appeared to have been dead for a week. Its face, so disturbingly similar to the two faelah I had killed, was broad and ridged with bony spikes. Saber-like teeth lined its mouth and its small eyes glowed with a malevolent orange.

As if the Cúthra's size and muscle mass weren't terrifying enough, it stopped and stood up on its hind legs. Oh, it could walk like that too? Now it could use its long, powerful forearms like spiked wrecking balls. Wonderful.

"Meghan, I want you to go back to the tent, wake your friends, and get out of here."

Huh? My mind was still numb from processing what it was seeing.

"What?" I rasped.

Cade whipped his head around, his eyes fierce. "I want you to get out of here!"

"No!" I said without even thinking. "I'm not leaving you!"

Cade gritted his teeth. "You don't understand. I have to use my ríastrad against the Cúthra, so I want you as far away as possible."

Ríastrad. Cade's battle fury. The same battle fury he had inherited from his father, Cuchulainn. I had seen it once before, when he had died protecting me from the Morrigan's mutated hounds.

I placed a hand on his arm and forced him to turn and look at me. "I have seen you use it before Cade. I'm not afraid of you."

His mouth was set in a grim line, the sword in front of him gleaming in the moonlight. "I don't want to hurt you Meghan," he murmured.

I tightened my grip on his arm. "You won't. But I'll keep my distance just in case."

Terrified as I was, I couldn't leave him to fight this battle alone.

His shoulders drooped insignificantly and then he nodded once. Reluctantly, I stepped back several paces before turning and looking for a good place to watch the battle. There, behind two boulders marking the boundary of the campground. My heart was in my throat and I was tempted to crouch behind the stones, but Cade might need my help. I positioned myself so that I faced the monster, then drew an arrow from my quiver.

The creature moved forward, close to fifteen feet tall now that it stood on its hind legs, and swiped at the air in front of Cade with a massive paw, its razor sharp, bear-like claws almost making contact. It opened its mouth and let out a great roar, its nose, eyes and throat glowing with red coals like the Cúmorrigs' had. My knees went weak again and what little sense I had left spent its energy wondering how this thing wasn't waking up the other campers. Perhaps its glamour disguised the sounds it was making, or maybe they thought it was a bear and they were hiding in the false safety of their tents.

Evidence

I didn't have much longer to think about whether or not the Cúthra could actually be heard, because in the next second Cade lunged at it. I almost screamed as I ducked my head. What was he thinking? That monster's reach was far greater than his and it was obviously much stronger. When the Cúthra bellowed again, I risked a peek. Cade was back to where he had started, his chest heaving, his sword, dripping in near-black blood, held to the side. He had managed to cut the faelah, but now it looked angrier than ever.

Cade hesitated, and as I squinted in the pale moonlight, it looked like his eyes were closed and he was trying very hard to concentrate. The Cúthra moved forward slowly, back on all fours, twitching its tail like a lion about to pounce. I wanted to shout out a warning, but then I realized what was happening. Cade began to grow larger, his hair gathering in spikes. His arms seemed to dislocate and his eyes grew wild. The ríastrad. When he was done with his transformation, he was a full two feet taller than usual and more closely resembled the Cúthra than the young man I loved.

The sword he carried looked like a dagger in his hand, but as his battle fury took full control of him, Cade made quick work of the Cúthra. It wasn't an easy fight, not in the least, but I could tell by Cade's quick movements and the monster's flagging strength that soon the problem would be gone and we could return to the tent.

As I watched the fight from afar, I spotted a few more of those little faelah I'd shot before the Cúthra arrived. A pack of them, like rats smelling blood, waited on the outskirts of the ensuing struggle. Feeling a rush of adrenaline, I aimed my arrow and shot. The first creature squealed and fell to the ground, twitching. I readied another arrow and took aim at another one. Twelve arrows later, they were all dead. I wondered at their intelligence, since none of them fled after witnessing their comrades fall. Perhaps they were too focused on the smell of blood to care.

"Well done Meghan."

I jumped. I had been so fixated on killing the faelah I hadn't noticed that Cade had finally killed the Cúthra and morphed back into his more human-looking self. I grinned sheepishly and glanced up at him. He looked tired and bedraggled in the torn remnants of his clothes, but not nearly as exhausted as he had the day he fought the mutated Cúmorrig.

He must have seen something cross my face because he asked, "What's wrong?"

"Oh," I flapped a hand, "nothing. I just thought you would look more, uh, worn out after your ríastrad."

He grinned, that grin that made my bones melt.

"Normally it takes a lot more out of me. But a Cúthra, in the mortal world, isn't that tough to defeat."

I blinked up at him. He thought that had been easy? Of course, I shouldn't be that surprised. After all, he had managed to take on ten of the Morrigan's giant hounds at once.

We headed back to our tent, staying alert in case any more faelah showed up. It was when we were returning our weapons to Cade's car that the glare of a flashlight fell on us.

"Meghan, what the hell?!"

I froze. Robyn. Of course.

"Is that, is that a sword?! Crap, I thought you guys were just going out for a make out session or something."

She gasped. "Is that blood?! What happened to Cade's clothes? What have you two been doing?"

I sighed and started to turn around. Maybe I could make up some excuse . . . But when I noticed Tully, Will and Thomas standing behind her, all three of them with looks of horror on their faces, I knew there was going to be no easy way out of this.

"What's that smell?" Tully asked, crinkling her nose.

Oh no.

Evidence

"Hey, what's that over by the dumpster?"

Will adjusted his glasses and picked up a lantern, Thomas close behind. Robyn cursed and started after them.

"Wait up!" she grumbled.

Oh no, oh no, *oh no!*

I twisted around and shot Cade a panicked look. Would they be able to see the dead Cúthra? His face was grim.

In the next breath, Cade's words entered my mind: *Meghan, it hasn't been dead long enough to turn to ash and it no longer has control over its glamour. They are going to see it for what it truly is.*

Crap! What do we do?! I sent back.

Cade sighed, then gave me a long steady look, his eyes appearing black in the pale moonlight. *We tell them the truth.*

Could we? Tell them the truth? I mean, I'd wanted to tell them something about my true identity, but could I really do it? After hiding it all these months, and would they believe me? Was I really ready to tell them?

A panicked curse coming from Will and a blood-curdling scream that could only belong to Robyn was my answer. I let my shoulders slump as Tully bolted towards our other friends. Ready or not, my friends were about to learn what I'd been keeping secret for the past few years. That I was from an entirely different world than they were, one that grew monsters like old bread sprouted fungus. And I thought the worst part of the night was over . . .

Half an hour later, we were sitting around the inside of the tent. Cade had changed into a new set of clothes and I had pushed back the screen that separated our small alcove from everyone else. And at the moment we were being very closely scrutinized by my friends, the light of the two lanterns we'd switched on illuminating four unreadable expressions.

"So," Robyn said, her voice sounding uncharacteristically subdued.

"So," I repeated.

I had just finished telling them, in a rush, everything I had been withholding from them for the past two years. I told them how I had always heard voices, how I had stumbled upon Cade in the middle of the swamp, how he had told me about Eilé and how I'd been jumping back and forth between the two worlds for some time now. I didn't, however, tell them about the Morrigan, only that the creature they found by the dumpster had come from the Otherworld and that it was Cade's job to take care of them. Cade had held my hand the entire time and I was certain he was only being a gentleman by not complaining about my death grip.

Now we sat silently, Cade and I, facing my friends and waiting for the judgment, the questions, and the horror to come pouring out of them.

Next to Will I could hear Thomas muttering something about God and the devil in Spanish. I couldn't blame him. The Cúthra had looked like something straight out of hell.

"I must admit," Robyn said, "that this all seems a bit far-fetched, and I would in no way shape or form believe you if it weren't for that, that,"

She gave me a hard look.

I closed my eyes and released a deep breath.

"Cúthra," Cade offered, his voice a bit clipped and defensive.

Robyn cast him a quick, wary glance. "Yeah, that, thing lying next to the trash bins in plain sight. But, I mean, how is it even possible? This is the stuff I've been telling you about for years Meghan! It's mostly mythology. It isn't real!"

I blinked in surprise. It was the first time I had ever seen or heard Robyn doubt her Wiccan beliefs.

"But Robyn, I thought you believed in this stuff," Will said, voicing my question aloud.

"Well, yeah, some of it!" Robyn answered. "There are spirits and ceremonies and the like that need to be observed, but nothing like this!"

She gestured towards Cade, and I sucked in a breath, suddenly feeling resentful. Cade must have felt it too because I could have sworn he growled under his breath.

"What more proof do you need!?" I hissed, pulling my hand away from Cade's so that I could throw my arms up in annoyance.

Robyn snorted and crossed her arms, turning her head to stare at the wall of our tent.

I gritted my teeth, trying not to grow angry. This is exactly why I didn't want to tell them.

Then Will surprised me by saying, "How the hell could you be keeping this from us Meghan? I thought we were your friends."

I opened my mouth to respond, but the emotion that had been building up got caught in my throat.

But Tully, who had remained calm and quiet this whole time, only nodded somberly. "No Robyn, Will, you're both wrong. How could Meghan have told us something this big? Think about it. Would you have told anyone?"

And that was Tully. Always level-headed, always coming up with the right answer to smooth out all of our problems. She was probably life's greatest gift to me simply because she knew that not every predicament could be solved by talking about it.

Tears burned my eyes. I had lied to her all these years and she should be upset like Robyn and Will and Thomas. But she wasn't. No, she understood. Somehow, with all the hurt and anger and fear that was permeating the space around us, she understood. I was going to miss her more than anything when I left for Eilé.

"Oh Tully," I cried, swiping at a wayward tear, "I've been such a horrible friend."

She only smiled sadly and crawled over to give me a hug. "No you haven't Meghan. I knew something must be bothering you all this time, but I knew you would tell us when you were ready. Of course," she added with a soft laugh and a smile, "I never imagined it could be anything like this."

I sniffled and returned her hug.

Robyn, Will and Thomas had quieted down and were now donning looks of guilt.

"I'm sorry Meg," Robyn finally said, the tone of her voice telling me she had let go of her anger, "I didn't mean to yell at you, it's just, well, this is a big shock is all."

I nodded grimly. I didn't think I deserved such kindness. Deep down, I thought what Robyn and Will had said was true. They were my closest friends and I should have told them the truth.

"Well, now what?" Will asked, crossing his arms after adjusting his glasses.

"There's no way we'll ever get back to sleep," Thomas offered quietly as he eyed Cade suspiciously for what seemed like the hundredth time that night.

Or was he just checking him out again?

I bit back my amusement, glad to be distracted with silly thoughts instead of angry, hurtful ones.

"I don't know about you guys," Robyn said with her usual brusque confidence, "but I would kill to hear more about the Otherworld."

I grinned again. So, Robyn was finally going to admit this was real, huh? And just like that, Cade started in with details and stories from Eilé and my friends hung on his every word. I relaxed and moved so that I was settled between his legs, my back leaning into his chest. I sighed when he draped an arm around me as if it were the most natural thing in the world. I added a few tidbits here and there as he retold some of our experiences in the Otherworld, but left most of the talking to him.

We stayed like that until dawn, exchanging stories like kids spending their first night with their cabin buddies at summer camp. At some time during Cade's regaling, it dawned upon me that I may have told my friends where I was from, but I hadn't told them I was going back.

"Well," Robyn said, yawning as Cade finished off another story, "anything else we should know?"

Cade looked at me and whispered in my mind, *Well?*

I think I should tell them that I'm leaving.

I studied my fingers, folded together over the hand Cade had placed against my stomach.

Now would be a good time.

His thoughts were gentle, soothing.

Gathering my courage, I took a deep breath and let my eyes trail over Thomas, Will, Robyn and finally Tully.

"Yes, there is one more thing you should know." I took a deep breath and dropped my gaze. "I'll be leaving soon, with Cade. I am going to go live in Eilé."

"What?" Tully asked, her voice quiet and slightly strained.

And that's when the lump, which had snuck up on me in the last few seconds, lodged itself in my throat.

"I don't belong here Tully," I whispered.

I drew my legs up to my chest and wrapped my arms around my knees. Cade tightened the arm he had draped around me. I felt somewhat comforted but not entirely.

"But, your family, your friends!" she said, a little louder but not shouting. Tully never shouted.

The guilt was nearly overwhelming. She had been so calm earlier, so ready to accept the fact that I was much more different than she had always thought. Now it was Tully's turn to let me know how upset she was.

"They know, and now you know," I murmured. "I'll be living in Eilé Tully, but it doesn't mean I'll never come back and visit you again."

Tully made to say something else, but then closed her mouth and gave a short nod.

"Can we come visit you?" Robyn asked eagerly.

I grinned despite my sadness. Yes, now that Robyn was willing to believe my crazy story, she would be the first one to hitch a ride through the dolmarehn. If only she could . . .

I sighed. "You can't come visit me. Humans can't cross into the Otherworld."

Her face fell and I could almost feel her disappointment weighing heavily in the air.

"But Meghan, what about that demon you guys killed," Thomas said. "There must be more of them in the Otherworld."

I regarded him and gave a small smile. He was worried about me. It was a nice change from the distrustful anger. I took a deep breath to answer him, but Cade beat me to it.

"I won't let anything hurt her."

His voice sounded determined, fierce even. My smile broadened. "Besides," he continued, "Meghan is extremely strong. She has more glamour than most Faelorehn and as soon as we get to Eilé, her magic will grow even stronger."

That caused everyone to pause and look at me with great awe.

"Magic?" Will practically breathed. "Oh Meghan, can you show us?"

Cade shook his head. "She's been in the mortal world too long. She needs to spend some time in the Otherworld in order for her magic to work properly."

"Oh, darn." Will sounded so disappointed, but then Cade released a soft chuckle.

"She can't," he said, moving to stand up, "but I can."

Evidence

What followed was a modest, yet impressive, display of Faelorehn magic. Cade simply gathered his glamour in the palm of one hand and proceeded to make a dark green flame flicker and dance and take on the shape of various images: a bird, a leaping fish and a raindrop splashing into a puddle to name a few. I merely sat back and enjoyed the show alongside my friends. I had seen Cade do so much more, but I appreciated this little offering. It helped to ease the tense mood and took my mind off of what had passed earlier in the night.

By mid-morning we had packed up our sleeping bags and taken down the tent. Before leaving for home, I wandered down to the lakeshore and just stood there, staring out over the water as the breeze tugged at the loose strands of my hair. I closed my eyes and breathed in deeply through my nose, my thoughts wandering off into the Otherworld.

"You know, I always thought there was something special about you Meghan Elam."

I jumped, then turned to look at Tully. She was smiling, but her eyes were sad.

"Oh Tully," I said quietly, lowering my head and returning my gaze to the lake. "I can't believe you still want to be my friend after the way I've treated you these last few years."

Tully didn't say a word. She merely stepped forward, bent down to pick up a flat rock, and threw it out across the lake. We watched it skip four times before it dove below the surface. Eventually she shrugged.

"Sometimes the measure of a good friend is knowing when to simply be there in case you're needed."

"Tully," I said, my voice harsh, "I practically ignored you for the last year and a half! What kind of a friend does that?"

She reached out and pulled me into a hug. I couldn't return it because my arms were crossed, but I let my chin rest on her head.

"You didn't ignore me Meghan," Tully murmured. "You just didn't know how to tell me what was wrong, and I knew that."

She released me and stepped back. "I'll miss you," she said, sniffling a little, "but I'll just pretend you've gone away for college. Promise you'll come back and visit?"

I took a deep breath and placed my hands on Tully's shoulders. "I promise."

We both turned back to watch the small waves ripple across the lake once more.

"So," Tully said, all traces of sadness gone from her tone. "Cade. Was he your reason for being such an emotional wreck last year?"

And just like that, we were teenage girls once again, talking nonsense and giggling with reckless abandon. Soon I would be facing down the worst Eilé had to offer, but at that moment I just wanted to be young and carefree one last time.

Six

luaThara

Cade and I left for Eilé the next morning. I tried to hold it together as I packed what I could carry into the Otherworld with me. Most of my stuff would be left behind, and Mom had told me it was because I would need somewhere to stay when I came to visit. Every weekend. I had smiled at that. I would try to come back as often as possible, but I was sure that getting settled in to my new life would take a while. After all, I had to learn how to use my magic, somehow make peace with my birth mother, and avoid the Morrigan all at the same time.

I sighed, gave my room one more remorseful glance, and headed upstairs. Cade was in the living room, standing at attention with my family gathered around. I gulped. It felt like I was going to my execution.

"I guess this is it," my mom said with a trembling lip.

No Meghan, you will not cry . . .

And then Aiden ran up and gave me a fierce hug, followed by the rest of my brothers. It took me a long time to compose myself enough to speak.

"It's just like if I was going off to college," I assured them as I sniffed. "As soon as I've got my life in order in Eilé, I'll come back for a visit. I promise."

"Cade, a word if you don't mind," Dad said, opening the door and gesturing for Cade to follow.

My mouth went dry and my stomach plummeted. *Oh no.*

Cade gave me a calm look and used shíl-sciar to speak to me. *It will be alright Meghan.*

I took a deep breath. I had to believe him. He was the son of a goddess and could turn into a faelah-killing superhero on a whim, but I feared for his safety when he was alone with my dad.

They were gone for twenty minutes, twenty agonizing minutes. While we waited, I helped Mom and the boys make some cookies, one last family activity before I left. When Dad and Cade finally returned, we all stopped our laughter and chatter. Dad's eyes had a misty quality to them and Cade looked the same way he had before he left. I bit my lip to keep the tears from coming.

Before Cade and I started down the horse path, my brothers handed me a picture album my family had put together for me. The photos depicted scenes from my life. My mortal life. I hugged everyone for a long time, crying silently as I hung on to them one last time. I would miss them, but I would come back to visit. They were still my family.

Cade whistled for Fergus, who had been keeping a low profile in the bushes, and I called out to Meridian. She swooped down from the treetops to settle on my shoulder, nibbling me affectionately to try and cheer me up.

Sorrow? she sent.

Yes, I answered, *but it will get better.*

I smiled. Mind-speaking with Meridian seemed less colorful, less complicated than the shíl-sciar method with Cade, but her words were comforting nonetheless.

We reached the dolmarehn fifteen minutes later. I took a deep breath and tried to will my tears to stop falling. Cade looked at me and I was tempted to ask him what my dad had said to him. Tempted but currently too afraid. *Maybe someday I'll get the nerve to ask him*, I thought to myself.

"Are you ready, my love?" he asked gently, stepping up once again to take my face in his hands, my heart singing at his term of endearment. He wiped away the tears with his thumbs, a gesture that I was quickly becoming addicted to.

I nodded and he leaned in to give me a gentle kiss. He dropped his hands and reached one out to me. I took it and he carefully led me into the small cave. Fergus had run ahead of us and I could feel Meridian's talons digging into my shoulder as she hunkered down.

We moved slowly through the dark and my mind kept itself busy by thinking about where my life was headed. I had left my family behind and I was going home, to the world where I belonged. I was terrified and depressed, but I was also filled with excitement and wonder. I'd learn how to use my glamour properly, now that it was fully awake, and I would have Cade by my side. I allowed myself to smile through the tears, but before I could contemplate another thought, that familiar tug of Otherworldly magic latched onto me and we were pulled into the deep darkness of Eilé.

The Otherworld was the same breathtaking sweep of green rolling hills and ancient forest I had grown used to, welcoming me in that cool rush of ancient magic that could never be found on Earth. We quickly made our way towards Cade's castle, and once there I gaped at the difference. The ruined fortress was alive with activity. Men worked at replacing old crumbled stones and broken windows. Women and children were interspersed throughout the fields, tending to what looked like a combination of potatoes, carrots, onions and several grains. As we took our time walking up the dirt road, I got a full view of the side of the castle facing us. The stone wall that surrounded it was being patched up, but a narrow gap that still needed attention gave me a glimpse of a small kitchen garden that I hadn't noticed the last time we'd visited the castle.

I looked up at Cade and he merely smiled down at me.

"I wanted to make Luathara ready for you, so you'd have a place to stay in case you didn't want to live at the castle in Erintara," he said.

I shivered at the idea of staying with my mother, under her suppressive rules. I didn't think she'd allow Cade to visit me even if I asked nicely. No, I wasn't ready to jumpstart a working relationship with my birth mother, the high queen of Eilé. Best get my bearings in my new world first.

I sighed and let my eyes sweep the castle once more, then I remembered what Cade had said. I blinked up at him. "You did this all for me?"

Cade nodded.

I regarded the old castle, the one that had somehow worked its way into my dreams those many months ago. *Luathara* Cade had called it. I liked that name.

"The construction isn't quite complete, so after tonight we'll be staying with the Dagda for a while."

My face split in a huge smile. I loved Cade's foster father and I couldn't wait to see him again. The Dagda was an overwhelming presence, but he had shown me nothing but cheer and acceptance since the moment I'd met him.

"Unless, of course, you'd rather go to Erintara," Cade added with a smirk.

I punched his arm. "No, I wouldn't. I mean, yes, I eventually want to go see my mother again, try to make peace with her, but I'd much rather stay with the Dagda for now."

As we passed through the castle gates and stepped into the noisy courtyard, we were welcomed by a man Cade introduced as Briant, his steward. He was a kind looking man, tall, middle-aged with brown hair and intelligent eyes. Like all Faelorehn, he had a handsome quality to his looks.

"So this is the young Miss Elam. Welcome, my lady."

I blushed, as usual, but took his hand and allowed him to escort me deeper into the courtyard. All around, people in work clothes were bustling about. Men and women both hauled stones in wheelbarrows while those who were younger carried baskets full of berries and fruits to be prepared and stored for later. My head swiveled on my shoulders as I tried to take it all in and Briant laughed, a hearty, strong chuckle that reminded me of the Dagda. Cade strolled leisurely by my side, and when I glanced up at him I realized he was watching me with a soft smile on his face. I recognized that look. It was a look of pure bliss. I returned the smile, unable to help myself.

At the large door leading into the castle's main hall, a tall woman with strawberry blond hair, snapping blue eyes and perfect posture greeted us. She came off as stern at first, and when Briant caught her glance he dropped my arm and handed me off to Cade.

"Melvina!" he exclaimed. "Cade has come back with the Lady Meghan!"

The woman lost a little of her sternness and her rigid face melted into a brilliant smile. The result was enchanting.

My distraction at the change in the woman standing before us was short lived when the steward spoke next.

"High Queen Danua's daughter. The princess."

I flinched so hard Cade felt it. He glanced at me, one eyebrow arched and a look of amusement painted across his face. I glowered at him.

Melvina's bright eyes widened and she descended into a graceful curtsy that would do my birth mother proud.

I gritted my teeth. When I managed to find my voice I said, "Please, I'm the furthest thing from a princess."

Cade detected my distress and stepped in closer to me, the cloak he had thrown on that morning sweeping his sides and partially blocking me from those who had been close enough to hear Briant's loud announcement.

He pulled my head close, pressing his lips to my hair, and whispered, "Technically, you are a princess."

I reached out and grabbed the loose fabric of Cade's shirt with my hands and drew him closer.

"A princess is someone who grows up in a palace, wears expensive clothes, has nannies to raise her and servants at her beck and call. You saw where I grew up," I hissed.

You are the daughter of Eilé's high queen, Meghan. I know you don't like it, and I understand why the title grates at you, but it doesn't matter where you grew up. Danua's blood runs in your veins and you are her daughter.

The silent words were soothing, and I understood Cade's point. Didn't mean I had to like it. I released a deep breath and pulled away, glancing up at him.

Fine, I returned, *but please, could you ask them not to call me 'princess'? Just because I'm the daughter of a queen doesn't mean I want to be treated differently than anyone else.*

Cade grinned and kissed the top of my head again.

"Briant, Melvina," he turned to both of them. "Meghan would be eternally grateful if you would forget who her mother is while she's at Luathara."

They both widened their eyes in horror, but Cade stiffened his jaw and gave them both a stern look.

"What will we call her then?" Melvina asked, her voice warm and welcoming. The very tone made me relax.

"Meghan, just call me Meghan, please," I said, stepping away and holding my hand out to the woman at the top of the stairs.

She took my hand as if she had no idea what to do with it. I shook, and she quickly caught on.

"It's nice to meet you," I said.

"And I you, Meghan."

She smiled again.

"As Briant said, my name is Melvina and I am the head cook here at Luathara. If you have any complaints with the food, please let me know and I'll do all I can to improve it."

Briant huffed and said, his voice full of pride, "No one can make a better meal than my wife."

Melvina pulled a dish towel from the belt she wore around her waist and smacked him with it.

"Hush you!" she hissed, her cheeks turning slightly pink.

I turned and looked at Cade. First a steward, now a cook? Where had all these people come from? They hadn't been here the last few times I'd visited the castle. I asked him using shíl-sciar.

They all have homes in Kellston, but I invited them to live in the castle and aid me when I started the construction. Melvina and Briant have an older daughter who is married and she now lives in their old house. We can't live in a castle without the proper staff.

I swallowed. *We.* Living together . . . in a castle. Sure, he had said it was up to me whether I lived with Danua or stayed with him, but it really hadn't hit me until just now. Was this really happening? Had he discussed this with my dad? Was I really going to live in the Otherworld with Cade in a castle? I snorted inwardly. And to think, I had just told him I wasn't a princess.

Once we were properly ushered inside, and my wayward thoughts were left for another time, I discovered more wonderful changes. Colorful rugs decorated the floor and detailed tapestries hung on the tall, stone walls. All the windows were repaired and clean, making the place feel bright and airy. Melvina excused herself, claiming she had to prepare the evening meal, something that would be grander than usual since I had arrived. I tried to tell her not to worry on my account, but she only brushed me off and disappeared down one of the many hallways branching away from the entrance hall.

"Well, I shall leave you two alone then," Briant said, clapping his hands together. "But there are some missives in your study you might want to look at, my lord."

He bowed to Cade and then turned to leave.

I arched a brow and gave Cade a questioning look. He only smiled.

"My lord?"

He shrugged, unbothered by the comment.

"When you own a castle in Eilé, you officially become the lord of the castle and the land belonging to it."

"How much land?"

Another shrug. "Several thousand acres."

I dropped my arms and gaped. Several *thousand*?!

"Cade! Why did you never tell me any of this?"

He backed away slightly, stepping out of the ray of light streaming in from one of the tall windows. Some of that smugness he'd been exuding a few moments ago vanished and he looked uncertain. He ran his fingers through his hair and took a breath.

"For the same reason I never told you about the ríastrad and my own heritage. I was afraid you would realize I wasn't good enough for you."

Tears sprung into my eyes, not because I was hurt he hadn't trusted me enough to tell me these things, but because he had been afraid to do so.

"Oh Cade."

I stepped forward and pulled him close, wrapping my arms around him beneath his cloak. Cade returned the embrace and rested his cheek against my hair, one hand placed behind my head.

"How could you ever think you weren't good enough for me?"

"You are the daughter of our high queen, and I am the son of her worst enemy," he whispered.

I cringed, remembering the conversation he had overheard the last time I'd talked to, no, *argued* with, Danua.

I pulled away just enough to look him in the eye. I lifted my hands and held his face, the way he often held mine. "Nothing will ever convince me to stop loving you Caedehn MacRoich, nothing."

He sighed and I reached up to kiss him, a gentle brush of our lips that left me wanting more. I dropped back down to lean into him again, resting my head against his chest so I could hear his heartbeat. We stood like that for goodness knows how long, the bright mid-day light streaming down into the massive entrance hall, bringing the brilliant earthy reds, greens and golds of the rugs and tapestries to life. The sounds of men shouting, children laughing and stones being fitted into place rung throughout the castle, but I didn't mind. This was my new home and I wanted to soak in every last detail of it.

Eventually, Cade planted a kiss on my forehead and took a step back.

"I have to check on those missives Briant was talking about. Why don't you go rest or find one of Melvina's undercooks to make you some tea."

I regarded him with an arched eyebrow but only said, "I'd like to explore the rest of the castle, if that's okay."

Cade grinned, seeming pleased. "I'll be in my study if you need me." He indicated a carved oak door down one of the side passages, opposite to the one Melvina had disappeared down earlier. I nodded.

"Your bags were taken up to your room if you need anything. Your bow and quiver as well."

Cade's eyes glittered and I wondered if maybe he had set up an archery range somewhere on Luathara's several thousand acres. I shivered in anticipation. I had grown very fond of my bow and arrows. Perhaps we could practice later.

A sharp bark and the familiar screech of a merlin broke through the general ruckus outside, and Fergus and Meridian came flying through the open door. Well, technically Meridian was the only one flying, but Fergus was moving at top speed.

I smiled again. Somewhere between the dolmarehn and Luathara's courtyard, I'd lost track of them.

Meridian came to rest on my shoulder and started cuddling against me with excitement.

Home! Magic! Happy! she sent.

I laughed. *Yes, pretty Meridian. Home.*

Cade gave my hand one more squeeze, then dropped it and headed down the hall. I took a deep breath and spun around, Meridian clinging to my shoulder with her sharp claws. It was a little daunting, exploring Luathara while everyone around me seemed busy with work. Perhaps I could find someone who could use my help. Despite having visited the castle a few times before, I'd only ever seen this entrance hall, my room upstairs, and the great patio out in back that led to the cavern full of dolmarehn in the hillside.

"Want to explore with me?" I asked my spirit guide.

She chittered happily and fluffed her feathers. Fergus panted and wagged his tail at my side. Looks like I'd have company after all.

Smirking like an imp ready to make mischief, I decided to start with the first floor.

Luathara was filled with many rooms, some small, some larger. Most of them looked like spare bedrooms, but a few spaces resembled studies as well and I even found a set of doors that led down further into the belly of the fortress. I imagined a wine cellar or even an old dungeon awaited at the bottom. Shivering at the thought, I didn't venture any further than where my imagination took me.

At one point I popped into the kitchen, the vast room bright, spacious and warm from the fires in the ovens, to see if

Melvina needed any help. She promptly shooed me away, claiming that she wanted the meal to be a surprise and that she didn't want Fergus getting into anything. I had just enough time to catch a glimpse of the dried garlands of herbs and vegetables hanging from the rafters and to detect the scent of something delicious bubbling in a cauldron over one of the fires before my curiosity was cut off with the click of the door closing in my face.

Of all the rooms I discovered, however, the library was the most impressive by far. Located towards the back of the first floor, it was the largest room next to the entrance hall and just a tiny bit bigger than the dining room I'd stumbled into just a few moments before.

Several comfortable looking chairs and a few couches were scattered about, and a giant, diamond-paned window stretched from ceiling to floor, taking up most of one wall. The rest of the walls were dominated by bookshelves housing tomes that looked as old as the Book of Kells. I desperately wanted to take my time exploring this one room, but there was so much more to see. I shut the door with a soft click and made a mental note to come back one day when I could take my time looking around.

Once I was finished with the inside of the castle, I made my way out the front door, Meridian still gripping my shoulder and Fergus trailing us like a puppy. The courtyard was noisy and dusty, what with all the construction going on, so I looked around for a way out. If I wanted to get away from all the ruckus, I could simply slip through the portcullis and cross the bridge. Perhaps I might even find Speirling, Cade's black stallion, grazing in the fields. But I already knew what lay that way. I wanted to see more of the castle grounds. A sharp whistle pulled my attention to a small stone archway. Fergus released a bark, then took off to chase a young boy through a small gate. Aha, that would be a good place to start . . .

I quickly followed after him, passing through the arch and stepping into the small gardens I had seen earlier. Up close, the space appeared to be much larger, the far end backing into the same hillside where the waterfall and dolmarehn could be found. Luckily, the water cascading down the hill fell on the other side of the castle, so no mist bothered us here, although a narrow creek snaked along the garden's edge to disappear under the great stone wall I recognized as the base to the patio on the second floor. I suspected it flowed past the garden to join up with the larger stream that formed a makeshift moat around the castle.

Fergus barked somewhere in the maze of herbs and plants up ahead, so I followed the crushed gravel track around flower beds overflowing with lavender, rosemary, thyme, yarrow and a variety of other herbs whose names I didn't know. I trailed the wolfhound's excited barks and after bypassing a bed of mint, a happy scene greeted me. In the center of the garden stood a small fountain and around the fountain ran the boy who'd whistled at Fergus. Two little girls, their looks so similar they might have been twins, chased after the dog and the boy, squealing in delight, their light red hair trailing in braids behind them.

"Niall!" a young woman kneeling in a muddy flowerbed shouted. "Stop playing with that dog and get back over here and help me with these weeds!"

"He's not a dog! He's a spirit guide, Lord Cade's spirit guide!" the boy responded, out of breath as Fergus yipped at his heels.

Play! Meridian sent before leaping from my shoulder.

Before I could say anything, she dropped from the sky and made an arc in front of the boy. I knew she was just joining in the game, but her sudden appearance startled him and he jerked to a halt, letting go a small screech. Fergus didn't have time to stop, so within the time span of two seconds, the boy, the spirit guide and the two little girls were in a jumbled heap, legs and arms, both Faelorehn and wolfhound, scrambling to get up.

"Niall! Oriana, Wynne!" the girl weeding the flowerbed cried, jumping to her feet and lifting up her mud-stained skirts to run towards the others.

"Oh no!" I shouted, bolting from where I stood to join her. "I'm sorry, it's my fault. My spirit guide, Meridian . . . she likes to play."

I felt guilty, even though I know Meridian meant no harm. Eventually, the girl was able to pull the boy and two other girls free of Fergus, and to my relief they only had a few scratches. The two little girls were crying, but only sniffling at the shock of being rolled around on the gravel with a giant wolfhound. Fergus had trotted off to the side, tail between his legs and looking somewhat shamefaced.

I knelt down to help. "Is everyone okay?"

The young woman looked up for the first time and I saw Melvina's double, only younger, gazing back at me. The expression of concern on her face was briskly replaced with surprise.

"Who are you?" she asked.

"Uh, sorry, I'm Meghan. Meghan Elam." I held out my hand and grinned, but the girl's eyes only widened.

She stood up and backed away, giving a quick curtsy, then glanced at her skirts and grimaced.

"Forgive me, Princess, I'm not looking my best."

"Princess!" the boy shouted.

He quickly scuttled behind the older girl, clutching at her skirts and trying to hide.

"Niall!" the girl hissed, kicking him lightly with her foot and nodding towards me.

The boy, Niall, reluctantly let go of the girl's skirts and stepped forward, sketching a bow that might have been featured at court.

I hadn't realized I'd been standing there gaping like an idiot until the older girl cleared her throat.

"I'm sorry Princess Meghan, my name is Birgit, and this is my brother Niall and our sisters Oriana and Wynne. Our father is Briant, the steward of Luathara, and our mother is Melvina the cook."

The two girls scuttled from where they stood to go press against their sister's other side.

Finally, my voice learned how to work again. "No, don't, I'm not-" I babbled.

The four of them gave me an odd look, and somehow I managed to find my composure.

"It's very nice to meet you all, but please, just call me Meghan, or Meg."

I tried out a smile, but they looked even more frightened.

"But mum says we have to always give respect to our elders. What if I called you Lady MacRoich instead?"

Birgit hissed at her brother again, and I couldn't tell what shocked me more, the fact that he considered me an 'elder' or that he thought I should be called Lady MacRoich. I'm sure I paled, and then flushed scarlet right after.

I cleared my throat. How had this strange encounter grown so awkward? "Um, no, I'm giving you permission. I'm not Lady MacRoich so you can just call me Meghan. I'm not that much older than you."

"Why can't I call you Lady MacRoich? Aren't you the one Lord Cade brought back from the mortal world?"

"Niall! Do I need to glue your mouth shut?" Birgit growled, giving him a look that would scare the audacity right out of me.

Before I could let his question sink in, Birgit plastered her face with a smile and said, "Don't mind my brother, he has this horrible habit of speaking without thinking, *all* the time. Is there someone you were looking for Prin-, uh, Meghan?"

I could tell Birgit wasn't very comfortable using my name, but I was determined to show the people of Luathara that I was one of them.

"No, I was just exploring the castle and Fergus took off through the fence. I think I've seen everything, though. Would you like some help with the garden?"

Birgit's eyes grew wide again. "Oh no, you can't be pulling weeds!"

I arched a brow. "Why not? I used to do it all the time at home with my brothers."

The sudden thought of home and my brothers brought a pang to my heart, but I shrugged it off.

Birgit looked like she was going to protest again, but I walked past her before she could speak and knelt down in the partially weeded flowerbed.

"Um, you might want to show me which ones are weeds. These don't look anything like the plants in the mortal world."

I peered over my shoulder to find Birgit, frozen in place with Wynne and Oriana still clinging to her skirts. All three of the girls resembled Melvina, but Birgit had her mother's graceful posture, despite the mud and dirt. Niall, on the other hand, was a spitting image of his father.

"I'll show you!" he cried, instantly getting over his fear as he sprinted up to me.

I studied him as he slid into place beside me. His hair was dark with a bit of curl to it, and his dark brown eyes were flashing to gold as he pointed out the weeds and explained that they had to be grabbed at the base if you wanted to get them all the way out of the dirt.

We had created a nice little pile of discarded plants before Birgit joined us. She remained silent, and I wondered why she was so quiet until I remembered that I was a princess to these people. I sighed, but kept at my work. Cade must have told them about me, but how much had he told them? Obviously they knew I was Danua's daughter, but wouldn't he have told them that the high queen and I were estranged? Yet maybe he felt that it was my place to share that bit of information. Then Niall's words from earlier hit me full force: *Why can't I call you Lady MacRoich? Aren't you the one Lord Cade brought back from the mortal world?*

What had he meant by that? I shook my head, reminding myself that my goal at the moment wasn't to analyze the ramblings of young boys, but to try and make friends with the residents of Luathara.

I cleared my throat. "So, uh, Birgit, how long have you and your family lived in the castle?"

She was quiet for a moment, methodically pulling weeds from the flower bed.

"A few months now. Lord Cade asked my parents if they would like a position at Luathara Castle, and they happily agreed."

She paused and pressed her hands to her thighs and looked at me with a small smile. "We all love this place and it has been empty and sad for so long. It's good to know that it will be occupied once again."

I yanked at a weed and felt the satisfying tear of roots leaving the soil.

"Do you always call him Lord Cade?"

She shrugged and got back to work. "Mother and father insist upon it, though he would rather we just call him by his first name. He says it makes him feel strange, but Mother and Father would be angry if they knew. It took them long enough to stop calling him Lord MacRoich."

I nodded. I knew exactly how Cade felt. He and I had a somewhat similar past, growing up with foster parents and not really ever belonging. Just as being called 'Princess' felt so very wrong to me, I'm sure Cade shied away from the title of 'Lord'.

We spent ten more minutes pulling weeds, Birgit telling me about life in Kellston and Niall piping up every now and again to add his own details while their two younger sisters, who I learned weren't twins but only a year apart in age, played in the flower bed a few yards away. I thought about my own family back in the mortal world and I had to suppress the pain. I wondered when I'd get a chance to visit them again, if only to make sure Aiden was okay. He'd taken my departure the worst.

A sharp bark and the sound of heavy footfalls on the gravel drew my attention away from the weeding.

"Over here, my lord."

I glanced up to find a young man following Fergus. And behind him was Cade.

Cade stopped in his tracks and eyed me from head to toe. I glanced down at my jeans and shirt and suppressed a grimace. I was filthy.

I met his eyes and gave him a sheepish grin, blushing a little, then shrugged my shoulders. "I wanted to help."

Cade simply crossed his arms casually and shook his head, a humorous look on his face, his green eyes flashing to pale gray and back again.

Birgit and Niall had leapt to their feet the moment they saw Cade and now had their heads slightly bowed. I was still kneeling in the mud, so I had to crane my neck to look up at them. Ugh, I was so not used to this kind of behavior. I would expect it at Erintara in my mother's court, but not here.

"Thank you, Arlen." Cade nodded to the young man.

Arlen bowed his head once, then he glanced up and gave Birgit a quick smirk before turning and leaving the garden. I craned my neck again and noticed the slight blush and smile on

Birgit's face. I felt the corners of my own mouth curve upward. Looks like I'd have something to ask Birgit about the next time we met.

Cade strode forward, so I made some effort to get up. My legs were stiff from kneeling on the ground for so long and Niall was quick to come to my aid. I thanked him when I was on my feet and his eyes widened with pride. I laughed. He'd be a charmer when he was older.

I turned my head and found Cade standing right in front of me, arms still crossed and one eyebrow arched in question.

"Look, I made some friends," I said, turning to indicate my weeding partners. "Birgit, Niall and their little sisters. They told me that Briant and Melvina are their parents."

Birgit and Niall curtsied and bowed at the mention of their names, but Oriana and Wynne were too busy making mud pies to notice us.

"I see you've done a good job getting the anchor root out of the chamomile patch." Cade waved a hand to indicate our handy work.

"Anchor root?" I asked.

"Oh! That's what we've been pulling out!" Niall jumped in. "It's called anchor root because the roots are really hard to yank out of the ground."

I felt Birgit more than saw her stiffen behind me. Niall noticed too because he suddenly became silent and his brown eyes grew wider as his face paled.

"I'm sorry, my lord," Birgit said in a pained voice, "Niall has a problem with manners."

Ahhh, that's right, the whole 'lord' and 'lady' thing I was wholly uncomfortable with.

I glanced at Cade, hoping to gauge his reaction. To my great delight, he was smiling warmly and stood just as relaxed as ever.

"Birgit, we've had this discussion many times, you Niall and I. You don't have to call me 'lord' and you don't have to worry about offending me simply by sharing your thoughts. Please, I am the furthest thing from nobility and the last thing I want is for those who work and live here at Luathara to think that they are in any way beneath me."

"But, you're the grandson of-"

Cade raised his hand to stop Niall from continuing, and to my surprise, the boy stopped mid-sentence.

I arched a brow at Birgit, but she only turned her face away, scowling down at her talkative little brother. I gave Cade a sidelong glance, but he wasn't looking at me. He had never mentioned grandparents before, but with Niall's outburst I was curious. Very curious. Unfortunately, now wasn't the time to probe. I made a mental note to ask about it later.

"That doesn't matter," Cade said, answering the boy. "I know your parents wish for you to act a certain way, and I won't argue against that, but Meghan and I both would like you to feel comfortable around us. Show us the same courtesy you would your fellow neighbors in Kellston."

A strained silence fell over us all until Cade held his hand out to me and said, "Melvina has informed me that dinner will be ready in an hour, so if any of us needs to clean up, we best go about doing so."

He eyed me again, that glint of mirth in his expression, and I had to bite back a small smile. I took Cade's hand, wiping as much dirt off as I could before I laced my fingers in his. He didn't seem to mind. I turned and waved at Birgit and Niall and told them I'd see them later, then Cade and I made our way back to the castle.

"Did you have a good day?" he asked as we stepped through the archway into the courtyard.

Everyone seemed to be packing up for the night. The men and women who were rebuilding the crumbling wall climbed down from the scaffolding, and those already on the ground stacked loose stones up in neat piles.

I sighed, somehow gladdened by the scene. "I had a wonderful day. What time is it?"

"Five thirty," Cade answered as we ascended the few stairs that fanned out in front of the castle keep's main hall.

I almost tripped over the top step. "Five thirty?! Have I been in the garden that long?"

"Birgit and her brother and sisters must have made an impression."

Cade tugged me forward and we stepped into the hall, now suffused with the wonderful smell of home cooking. My stomach rumbled at the scent.

"Well," I said, "I might have spent a lot of time exploring the rooms of the first floor before actually heading out into the garden."

Cade smiled again and led me upstairs.

"I'm afraid there isn't a shower or tub in your room, but I have both in mine."

The thought of a shower after spending hours digging around in the dirt sounded blissful. We reached the top of the stairs and Cade led me down the hall, past the door to the room I had stayed in before, and on to his own. A large, four poster bed occupied the center of the room and a huge glass door stood open on the opposite end. A stone patio, complete with a balustrade, waited invitingly just through those doors.

"Oh, Cade!"

I couldn't help myself. I pulled free of his hand and made my way across the room. The view from this terrace was amazing. I could see the stone courtyard off to the right and the rolling, wooded hills and ponds scattered in the distance. To my left, a set of stairs led down to another small patio, then climbed back up once more onto the great terrace behind the castle. Directly below the low point of the staircase was the garden, its herbs and plants organized in a beautiful maze resembling a Celtic knot.

Cade stepped up behind me, so quietly he almost startled me. He wrapped his arms around my waist and rested his chin on my head.

"Do you like it?" he whispered.

I bit my bottom lip and turned around so that I faced him.

"I love it."

He bent down and kissed me. I wrapped my arms around his neck and returned his kiss, but he pulled away before I was ready.

"Dinner soon," he whispered. "I need to show you how the shower works."

I nodded, disappointed but also eager to get clean.

In Eilé, they didn't have modern plumbing like we did in the mortal world, but they had something close. The shower looked familiar, like something I'd find in a nice house in my hometown. The entire interior was composed of stone and sunken deep into the room so that a shower door or curtain wasn't necessary.

"The water is drawn up from a well and kept above the showerhead. All you need to do is release it with this knob," Cade indicated a lever, "and warm the water with your magic."

I turned and blinked at him. "How do I do that?"

He grinned. "It's really simple. Fortunately, it doesn't take much glamour to heat water. All you do is press your hands to these stones and let some of your power loose. The more you release, the warmer the water becomes."

He showed me and then I tried. It was simple and I almost got us both wet when I turned the nozzle to check to see if it was working.

Before leaving, Cade informed me that I could find my bags in my room, then he pointed out the robe and towel neatly folded on the countertop. The distinct click of a closing door informed me that Cade was gone, so I moved forward and began searching the bathroom shelves for soap. After opening and closing two cupboards, I finally discovered what I was looking for. Five minutes later I was standing under the steaming stream of water, thinking about what I'd learned during my exploration earlier. Luathara was a beautiful castle, there was no doubt about it, and Cade seemed to want me here as well. Yet I was still bothered by what Niall had said about calling me 'Lady MacRoich'. Did he think Cade and I were married? That sent shivers down my spine, despite the hot water. I sighed and worked some liquid soap I'd found in a jar into my hair. The strong scent of lavender suffused the air, helping relax my nerves a little. Cade and I had admitted our feelings for one another, but was he ready to take our relationship to that level? Was I?

The water momentarily became cold and I had to turn and press my hands against the stone again, tainting it with my magic. My bags had been sent to my own room, so I could safely assume that he wanted to take this slowly. I breathed a sigh of relief, despite the tiny pinch of disappointment. I wanted more than anything to be close to Cade, but I also didn't want to mess things up by moving too fast.

I finished rinsing away all the stray soap and turned the knob. I dried off using the towel on the edge of the stone basin Cade had said was the tub, and wrapped myself in the robe. I pushed the bedroom door open and checked the hallway, darting to my own room when I realized no one was wandering about on the third floor. I changed into a clean pair of jeans and one of the nicer shirts I'd packed. Dinner might be formal, and the last thing I wanted to do was make a bad first impression.

~Seven~

Interruption

The hall was busier by the time I made it downstairs. Many of the people I had seen working earlier stood around looking less dusty than before. Cade spotted me from the middle of the crowd and walked over to meet me at the bottom of the stairs. He too had cleaned up a little, though he wore the same clothes he had worn that day. The hall grew quiet when the crowd noticed me. I felt odd again, like the time I first met my mother in Erintara.

"Everyone, this is Meghan Elam. Meghan, these are the people from Kellston who are helping to rebuild Luathara."

I smiled, despite my awkwardness, and everyone nodded and murmured something about being honored to meet the daughter of the high queen. To my immense relief, nobody said anything about my being a princess.

"They'll be joining us for dinner," Cade continued, smiling happily as he took my hand and led me down the hall towards the dining room.

A great rectangular table, loaded down with dishes brimming with a variety of food, greeted us as we entered. I liked the dining room. It was situated on the side of the castle closest to the waterfall and had windows that ran from ceiling to floor all along the outer side. A narrow patio sat just beyond the windows and I was able to get a clear view of the fall in the near distance.

Cade led me to the far end of the table where two chairs waited. We sat down and I felt a little ridiculous, images of a nobleman and his wife dining before their subjects coming to mind. I winced. Maybe that was a bad analogy, considering what I'd heard in the garden and what had occupied my mind only a half hour ago.

The image vanished from my mind as everyone started pulling out chairs and taking their seats, casually talking to one another. I soon learned that even though Luathara was a castle, and although Birgit and her family insisted on addressing Cade and I with the proper titles, it was nothing like the formal court at Erintara. Thank goodness. People started passing around bowls and plates, chatting and laughing and sharing gossip. I blinked up at Cade only to find him watching me closely. I smiled and he returned it, but I could tell he was wondering how I was taking all this. I reached down and grabbed his hand under the table, squeezing it to let him know I was doing fine. After that, his composure was much more relaxed.

I glanced up and spotted Birgit and invited her to come sit in the chair next to me. Never in the mortal world would I be bold enough to actively seek out new friends, but that was the old Meghan. Besides, I really liked Birgit and I was in desperate need of some friends now that I was starting a new life.

Birgit's eyes widened as she made her way gracefully to my side. Before she sat down, I noticed her glancing towards the opposite end of the long dining table. The boy from earlier, Arlen, was watching her carefully. I had to hide a grin as she turned to give me a shy smile.

Borrowing some courage from thin air, I took a sip of mead and said, "So, tell me about Arlen."

Interruption

Birgit choked on her own drink and I cheerfully patted her back as she regained her composure. When she glanced back up at me, her blue eyes were wide with surprise and her face had grown redder than her hair. I only beamed at her. So that's how I looked all those times Robyn prodded me about Cade.

"You don't have to sit next to me, you know. You can go sit with him if you want."

Birgit took a deep breath and shook her head. "That's alright. My father doesn't really approve of my spending time with him."

All of a sudden, all the fun of talking with her about her crush left the room. I frowned. "Why?"

She shrugged. "He thinks Arlen isn't interested in more than what he sees."

Birgit blushed again and I nodded. I wondered if that was the truth or if Briant was just being a typical father. I wished to find out more, but I didn't want to spend the evening talking about a sore subject between father and daughter, so instead I asked Birgit about growing up in Eilé. Any thoughts regarding Arlen soon left our minds as my new friend answered all of my questions. The meal lasted long into the night, and as the dinner plates were exchanged for dessert, I turned to Birgit once more.

"Do you see many faelah around here?"

Birgit finished a bite of pie before turning to me to answer. Unfortunately, I never got a chance to hear what she had to say because the distinct sound of breaking glass cut through the dining room like a gunshot.

I jerked back only to catch sight of something pushing its way through the window twenty feet up. People started shouting and screaming and moving out of the way as another window shattered.

I stood, almost knocking my chair over, but before I could so much as duck under the table, strong arms grabbed my shoulders and a large body folded over me. Cade. The sound of shattering glass continued to permeate the room, so I pulled my head free of Cade's arm and glanced upwards. Dark creatures were struggling to crawl through the broken windows, their shapes almost impossible to trace because they matched the black sky outside.

"Briant!" Cade shouted over my ear, "Gather those with fighting experience and go get some weapons from the arms room, then spread out. It looks like they've got us surrounded!"

Briant's strong voice cut over the panicked ones and I caught a glimpse of several people trailing him out of the dining room to follow Cade's orders. Birgit had left my side to join her father and I wondered whether she was seeking to find a safe place to hide or if she was going to help fight off the creatures.

Cade pulled away from me just enough to grab my hand.

"My sword is in my room," he said as he half-dragged, half-led me into the main hall. "And your bow and arrows are in yours."

I stopped my stumbling and gained my feet but didn't let go of his hand. My heart pounded and I could feel my magic stirring. At first I thought it was fear, but to my surprise and delight, I realized what I was feeling was excitement. I was getting another chance to test out my archery skills on some of the Morrigan's monstrosities and I was looking forward to it. I didn't know if I should be proud of myself or shocked.

Cade let go of my hand at the top of the stairs and I sprinted to my door as he headed for his. I flew into my room, not bothering to pause, and walked into chaos. My window had been broken and Meridian, who I had let in before dinner, was flying around in the dark, screeching.

Meridian! I sent.

Angry! she returned, *Kill creature!*

Interruption

A quick, blinding flash and a sharp screech informed me that Meridian had zapped whatever faelah had managed to invade. I shuffled over to the corner where my bow had been earlier, relying on touch since the room was so dark. The acrid smell of scorched death greeted my nose and I had to fight back the urge to be sick.

Meridian, shoulder, I demanded, and in the next moment I felt my spirit guide's talons digging into my skin. Her overly tight hold told me she wasn't happy about the rude awakening.

I came back out into the hallway in time to meet Cade, brandishing his sword before him. Something black covered half the blade and I had a feeling his room had been broken into as well.

"Are you alright Meghan? I shouldn't have let you go into your room without checking it first."

"I'm fine," I breathed, "Meridian zapped whatever managed to get in."

Together, we ran down the stairs, Cade holding his sword in front of him while I slung the quiver on my back and readied an arrow in my bow.

The main hall was deserted, only a few torches and lamps burning to lend us light.

"Where is everyone?" I asked, my voice panicked. Could the faelah have hurt them?

"Most likely outside," Cade answered.

Something flashed in the corner of my eye and I breathed a sigh of relief when I realized it was only Fergus. He crept up close to us, a silent ghost with his hackles raised. Cade paused for a moment and then the wolfhound shot off ahead of us and through the open doors of the hall. I assumed he'd given his spirit guide instructions to wreak havoc on the Morrigan's creations.

Meridian, I sent, *do you think you can help Fergus?*

Yes, she replied eagerly, *attack!*

Meridian took off from my shoulder the moment we stepped through the door and into the courtyard. What greeted us was nothing short of pandemonium. The people of Luathara had spread out, all brandishing swords, spears, bows and clubs. Several torches had been lit and placed in iron sconces hanging along the walls, and someone had started a fire in a stone pit in the center of the courtyard. I almost wished they hadn't, for the flames cast a plume of bright light over the army of faelah. Odd, winged atrocities that resembled mummified possums crawled along the castle walls. Dark, rotten dog-like creatures snapped and snarled at someone with a battle axe, and some of the demon bats I remembered from the football game last fall swooped down at us, screaming and trying to whip people with their barbed tails.

"Meghan," Cade growled, "see if you can't take out some of the faelah crawling up the wall. I'll help with the others."

I nodded, my mouth going dry. My blood felt chilled and my heart pounded in fear, but this was my life now. I had a feeling that I'd never get away from the Morrigan's minions, so I would have to fight them instead.

Cade moved to leave, but before he leapt off the stairs, he grabbed me and pulled me close. The air whooshed out of my lungs and I hardly had time to take a breath before his mouth pressed hard against mine. The cold blood in my veins caught fire and I almost forgot about the monsters and the sounds of battle around us. Before I could really enjoy it, however, the kiss was over and Cade released me.

"Be careful," he whispered harshly before stepping away.

It took a few moments for my knees to grow solid again, but once they did I took a deep breath and jogged down into the courtyard and joined a group of people with bows. I allowed myself a split second of delight when I found Birgit among them, her serene face cut in anger and concentration as she let loose an arrow, piercing one of the creatures crawling up the castle's side. It shrieked and fell from the wall, slamming against the stone below with a sickening crunch.

I came to a stop several feet away from her and breathed, "Nice shot!" before readying an arrow and letting it go. To my relief, I caught one of the faelah in the wing, not killing it but bringing it down so that someone else could finish it off. It would have been mortifying to miss on my first attempt.

The battle cries of the Faelorehn combining in the air with the angry baying and howling of the faelah brought back memories I'd rather not revisit, but I tried my best to block the noise out. The small group of archers I'd joined managed to pick off most of the creatures climbing the walls, so they turned their attention, and their arrows, towards the faelah that were still airborne. When I noticed no more black shadows crawling towards the upper windows, I paused to see if I might be able to help those on the ground. What little glamour I'd soaked up since arriving in Eilé this morning burned in my chest, recognizing its homeland and clawing to be set free. I ignored it for the time being, remembering what Cade had said about using too much. I was still untrained, and the last thing I wanted to do was kill myself by letting my magic lose control. Besides, I might hurt the people who were on my side. It was frustrating, not being able to use my magic, especially knowing what it was capable of, but I simply clenched my teeth and focused on the battle.

I can't say how long we fought the faelah, but it couldn't have been very long. Cade and Briant and everyone else wielding swords and spears seemed to be driving the remaining creatures out of the courtyard, and only a few demon bats were diving at us now. I jogged to reach Cade's side just as he thrust his sword into one of the half-dead dogs I'd seen before. Not a Cúmorrig, to my utter relief.

I kept my bow in my hand, an arrow ready just in case. We drew closer to the open drawbridge, pushing the monsters out so that we could close the gates, but then something bizarre happened. The handful of faelah who were still fighting us simultaneously froze. A heartbeat or two later they turned and darted under the newly built portcullis, over the drawbridge, and then disappeared into the night. I stopped and let my arm drop. What the hell? It was as if someone had broadcasted a silent command, telling them all to flee in unison. Luathara's defenders, covered in sweat and some sporting bloody cuts, lowered their weapons to their sides and grew still. I glanced around Cade's large form and caught sight of what had silenced the monsters.

Just outside the gate several torches flickered, casting just enough light to reveal something horrifying, something familiar. I gasped and dropped my bow, covering my mouth with both hands.

The creature opened its mouth, revealing sharp, rotting teeth and spoke in a voice that conjured up images of deep, dark chasms and skeletons rattling in the wind.

"Hellooo Meghaaan, spaaawn of Danuaaa," it hissed, drawing out its words.

Despite the bravado I'd displayed that night, I reached out to Cade and pulled myself against his body. The horrible thing chilled me to the bone and its fetid stench burned my nostrils.

"Puca!" someone growled nearby. It sounded more like a curse than a statement.

So that's what this particular faelah was called . . . The last time I'd seen this creature I had been running for my life down my street, trying to reach home before it caught up to me. Luckily, that was before I'd broken the geis my mother had placed on me. I'd been terrified then and I was terrified now, especially since it had taken up the gift of speech. The faelah, the puca, resembled a twisted molding of a human and a goat. It had the torso and arms of a man, but the head of a demented goat, complete with burning eyes and long curved horns. The puca made me think of a satyr who'd visited Hades but had managed to somehow escape by swimming across the river Styx.

The creature lifted one cloven foot and slammed its hoof down while letting out a terrible wail. I gritted my teeth when its call was answered by similar screams from the hills and trees surrounding Luathara.

"My Queeen wishes to seee you, Meghaaan," it continued, its eyes burning with dark magic.

"No!" Cade growled, squaring his shoulders and moving so that he stood more solidly in front of me. "I'll give you one chance to turn and walk away. You know what I'm capable of puca, and you know I will not hesitate to kill you and any other faelah that come within ten yards of Meghan."

For several moments, all I could hear was the whispering of torch flames and the slight noises of the shifting feet of the people around me. The faelah, wherever they had disappeared to, remained eerily quiet. Then the puca started to laugh. It began as a light chuckle and soon grew into an echo that played across the expanse of Luathara. I had never felt so cold in my life.

"So, you dooo live, after aaalll Caeeedehn MacRoich. There waaasss taaalk you had risennn from the deaaad. My Queeen will waaant to know of thisss. For nooow, Caeeedehn, I shall not haaarm the little Faeloraaah. But youuur mother is ooowed a debt, and sheee'll be wantiiing payment sooon. There isss nowheeere to hiiide."

The puca opened its mouth, the lower jaw dropping further than what would normally be considered possible. A deep, horrifying rumble rose from its throat and a black, swirling cloud poured from its mouth. In one moment the puca was there, gaping as if it meant to swallow us whole, and in the next second the swirling black cloud engulfed it and the nightmare was gone. The magical backlash hit me like a sudden headache, but the pain soon passed. I hadn't realized how tense I'd been until I collapsed against Cade.

"Meghan!" he hissed, turning to support me as several others rushed forward to help.

"It's okay lass," a gruff male voice said, "evil magic like that can knock you off your feet if you're not expecting it."

I turned to see a huge bear of a man, black hair and silver eyes regarding me. Despite their fierceness, there was kindness in those eyes. I remembered spotting him working on hot iron when I'd explored the grounds earlier. The local blacksmith maybe? His appearance certainly fit the stereotype.

"Thank you, Torec," Cade murmured as I gained my balance.

"What do you want us to do for the remainder of the night?" the giant called Torec asked.

Cade's face grew grim and I wondered what he thought, but the look vanished as he said aloud, "I thank all of you for your help, and I can't express how sorry I am that you had to fight my mother's abominations tonight when you should have been heading home to your families."

A woman, tall and with the build of a warrior, held up a gloved hand and shook her head. "Lord MacRoich, you have given us a castle and a home to defend once again. We are happy to help you."

"I agree with Liadan," Briant spoke up from further back, "let us set up a guard and keep watch in shifts, just in case the Morrigan's minions decide to return."

There was a general murmur of agreement and Cade relaxed a little. I leaned into him and put an arm around his back, hoping to add my own form of comfort. He returned the gesture and nodded.

Interruption

The guard was posted in pairs, one couple for each wall of the castle, and four people to stand guard on the tower of the drawbridge, which was now shut tight. The rest of us filtered into the great hall where Melvina used her glamour to get a roaring fire going in the massive fireplace. It shouldn't have been cold out, since it was still summer, but the faelah had left a nasty chill we couldn't seem to get out of our bones.

Once inside, Cade pulled Briant and me into his study. The room was dark, but after lighting some candles, I took note of more bookshelves, an oak desk and thankfully, a window that hadn't been smashed.

"We can start cleaning up in the morning, and I'll send a message to the glazier to start making replacements for the glass that got broken."

Cade stepped up behind his desk, placed both hands on its smooth top, and released a deep sigh. I quietly took a seat in one of the stuffed armchairs by the fireplace, waiting to see what Cade had to say.

He glanced up at me, his eyes sad and his face grim. My heart quickened. I did not like seeing Cade like that, and if it wasn't for Briant's presence, I would have walked over to him and done my best to erase that look from his face.

"We'll be leaving as soon as possible," he said quietly, so quietly I almost didn't hear his words.

Cade glanced at his steward, and the man merely blinked at him.

"Meghan and I. We'll have to forego our stay at the Dagda's and go directly to the Weald, but I'll need to contact my foster father and the other Tuatha De to find out how much they know."

Cade looked at me again. "I didn't see the damage Meghan caused that night the Morrigan cornered us, but from what my foster father told me, it was something to behold. We should have had more time than this-"

He cut himself short, his eyes glimmering with worry as his gaze lingered on me.

"For the Morrigan to be able to bounce back from such an attack so soon . . . it makes me think she is receiving help."

Briant gasped. "From who?"

Cade gritted his teeth and shook his head. "I have my suspicions, but that is all they are, suspicions. Until I know for sure, I need to get Meghan somewhere safe. The rest of you should return home. The Morrigan isn't after any of you and I couldn't bear it if any of you were hurt while her monsters tore the castle apart looking for us."

Goose bumps broke out along my skin as Cade's words registered. The Morrigan, getting help from someone else? She was terrifying and volatile enough on her own.

"Is it safe for you to go now?" Briant murmured.

Cade stood up and ran both hands through his hair, then dropped them to rest on his hips.

"The dolmarehn that leads to the Weald is in the caves, and I doubt there will be any faelah waiting for us on the other side. As soon as we're done here, we'll pack what we need and go."

Briant nodded and I remained quiet, my mind reeling. Just this morning, I had been making cookies with my mom and brothers, looking forward to the Otherworld and seeing the Dagda's friendly face again. Now Cade and I would be taking off in the middle of the night to go to the Weald, the huge forest that covered much of the western edge of Eilé, a place dripping with wild magic. But I knew why Cade had chosen the magic wood, and it wasn't just because his sister lived there with the wildren, the unwanted children of this world, but because the Weald was the one place in Eilé the Morrigan could not reach us. And since I still needed to recharge my magic, it would be the best place for me to be at the moment, especially if the bane of my existence had found someone to nurse her wounds and assist in quickly refurbishing her army of monsters.

Cade gave his steward a few more directions on how to proceed with Luathara's construction and what to do with any more faelah that might show up before turning towards me. His eyes were cheerless, but a fierce determination shone through. Briant glanced between Cade and me, then excused himself to give us some privacy.

The moment the door snapped shut, Cade let loose a deep sigh. "I cannot even begin to apologize Meghan. I hoped to show you the progress here at Luathara before heading to the Dagda's, but instead you've been met with violence and fear."

He dropped his gaze and took another rattling breath. Quietly, so much so that I almost didn't catch it, he added, "I had hoped we would be able to avoid this for a little while longer."

I cleared my throat and decided to speak for the first time since entering the room. "I knew the Otherworld would be more dangerous than the mortal one, so you don't need to make apologies, Cade." I leveled my eyes with his. "I made the choice to come here with you, and despite what happened tonight, I won't change my mind."

I smiled, despite my rattled nerves. The encounter with the puca and the other faelah had been terrifying, but I couldn't help but admit, the pulse of my magic mixing with adrenaline as I helped defend the castle had been intoxicating. It felt good to finally have the means to fight back.

"Are you up to traveling to the Weald tonight?"

I shrugged. "Sure. Besides, if we stick around here that puca might come back."

The very thought froze my blood, and although wandering into the caves and then through the dark trees of the Weald was just as daunting, it was better than listening to that demented goat-man speak to me about the Morrigan's hatred again.

Cade nodded, his eyes softening a little.

"Very well, let's go pack and be on our way before my mother's servants have a chance to tell her where you are."

I was out of the chair and through the door before Cade even finished speaking. Apparently, it didn't take much to motivate me when I though the Morrigan might be arriving at any moment.

Eight

Departure

The caves were dark, darker even than the night sky we had just left behind, so I had to rely on Cade's guidance to lead me to the dolmarehn. It had only taken me fifteen minutes to pack since most of my stuff was still in the suitcases I'd brought along. The short time it took us to cross the space between the third floor doorway and the cavern's mouth seemed minutes longer than usual. I kept waiting for the faelah to return and overwhelm us. Meridian clung to my shoulder, as usual, and Fergus remained a silent guardian at our sides. Didn't matter. I was still jumpy after what had happened earlier that night.

Cade led me by the hand through the caves and I had to trust that he knew his way in the darkness. Eventually, he stopped and pulled me closer.

"Ready?" His voice was a rasp against the rough, damp cavern walls.

I swallowed hard and nodded, then remembered he couldn't see me.

"Yes," I whispered back.

I felt a small tug as the dolmarehn pulled me into its depths. When the magic spit us out on the other side, the black, towering beast that was the Weald loomed before us. The air was cool and held the sharp smells of a summer night. Thankfully, there were no corpse hounds with glowing eyes or other zombies waiting to ambush us. We didn't linger long, quickly making our way to the edge of the Weald and finding the trail that would take us to the village where the wildren lived. Cade had borrowed a torch from Luathara and sacrificed a few minutes to light it, so at least we weren't tripping around in the dark.

Fergus led us, always moving at an easy lope and staying well ahead. Meridian clutched my shoulder, grumbling in her avian mind about traveling at night. I spotted many eyes, flashing in the shadows as we passed. My bow was in my hand, an arrow ready just in case, but I drew closer to Cade when the eyes started following us. He had told me before that the Weald was safe from the Morrigan's henchmen, but it was clear my nerves were suffering hearing loss.

When I crashed into Cade for the fifth or sixth time in the same number of minutes, he held up the torch so I could see who the eyes belonged to. I smiled with relief when I recognized the twig people through the flickering light, the twigrins, trying to spy on us from the trees. Their tiny arms and legs were covered in lush, green leaves. I looked back at Cade, who was just a step ahead of me. His mouth curved in a small smile, his eyes lighting up and making the night seem less dark.

At Spring Solstice, I'll bring you back and you can see them when they're in bloom.

My smile chased away any lingering, dismal thoughts. He knew what I was thinking without even asking me.

Our nocturnal trek eventually brought us to the edge of a small community, and we were greeted by some of the older wildren standing guard. Cade quickly explained to the young man and woman that he needed to see his sister immediately. The woman left to wake Enorah, and Cade and I joined the other guard around a small campfire. By the time Enorah came marching up in all her determined glory, several of the cabins closest to us had started showing signs of life. Despite the early hour, it looked like word had spread about our arrival.

Enorah, taller than me by a few inches, her softly curling brown hair pulled back in a neat braid, stopped a few feet in front of us and drew herself into a domineering pose. She wore an outfit similar to the one she'd been wearing the last time I saw her: leather pants and vest, an old worn cotton shirt, and knee-length boots. The string of her longbow cut diagonally across her torso and I suspected that that was the hilt of a sword peeking over her shoulder. If I hadn't met her before, I'd be shaking and cowering behind Cade. I had half a mind to do so anyway. Enorah pursed her lips, her sharp eyes running over the two of us like a wolf assessing a possible threat.

"So, you've come to visit again have you? And at such a horrendous hour."

Her voice sounded casual, but I could tell she was suppressing her joy at seeing her brother.

Cade smiled and strode over, scooping her up in a bear hug. Enorah actually squeaked and spluttered, surprised at her brother's show of affection.

Eventually, Cade put her down and she punched him. "What is wrong with you?!"

Cade only smiled as he rubbed his arm. "Glad to see you too, sis."

At that moment, she glanced at me, her look of irritation disappearing. "Meghan! Have you no sense girl? What are you still doing hanging around my oaf of a brother?"

She strode over and gave me a hug, though not as powerful as Cade's. I returned it, truly glad to see her despite our relatively new friendship. A moment slipped by and she held me at arm's length. I almost gasped at the look on her face. Her grey-green eyes were swimming with unshed tears.

"Thank you," she whispered harshly, "for bringing Caedehn back to the Cauldron."

Ah. I had been so swiftly swept back to the mortal world after taking Cade to the Dagda that I had forgotten there were people who cared about him in the Otherworld. And with everything that had happened in the last twenty four hours, I was sure it wouldn't be the only thing that slipped my mind.

I smiled tentatively and grasped her elbow with one hand. "You don't need to thank me," I glanced over at Cade. He had his arms crossed and was watching us closely in the bright light of the campfire. "I would do it again in a heartbeat." I took a breath and carefully added, "Your brother means a great deal to me."

Enorah blinked, her tears fading away as her eyes grew wide with joy. "Did the idiot finally admit that he's crazy about you?"

I bit my lip, trying not to smile, and nodded once.

Enorah snorted and threw an arm around my shoulders. "It's about time! Oh, we shall be like sisters now!"

Out of the corner of my eye, I saw Cade stiffen. Uh, this could be disastrous if not handled properly.

"Well," I said, clearing my throat and pulling away from Enorah. I methodically hooked my hair behind my ears as I fished for something to say. "We've just-"

Just what Meghan? my conscience asked me. *Started dating?* Did the Faelorehn date? *Okay, he had just started courting me.* Eww, no, that sounded lame. *Uh . . .*

"Oh, calm down you two! I'm just teasing. Now, do tell me, what on Eilé possessed you to come stumbling into our village before dawn?"

I released a great breath, feeling intensely better. I braved a glance at Cade and was pleased to see he had relaxed again as well. Despite my relief, something must have been bothering me about the whole exchange because I could feel a little prickle of pain in my heart. What could I be upset about? It was the truth. Cade and I may have admitted we loved one another, but it wasn't like we were a serious couple. It wasn't like we were . . . engaged.

The very word sent prickles of fear and joy through my nerves. *Whoa Meghan, you're only eighteen. Way too young to think about marriage.* But why did it make me feel so giddy to imagine myself engaged to Cade?

I glanced up at him once more and noticed the shadows in his eyes.

"The Morrigan has decided she doesn't want to wait," he said in a glum tone. "A contingency of faelah attacked Luathara several hours ago and a puca gifted with the power of speech threatened Meghan."

The joy that had lit up Enorah's face vanished and her smile disappeared.

"Oh no," she murmured. "But how, Cade?"

She darted her eyes in my direction before returning her gaze to her brother. "I thought Meghan's release of power put a nice dent in the Morrigan's armor."

Cade nodded, his own face grim. "I think she has recruited help."

Enorah flinched, her crossed arms tightening about her. "Who? The Fir Bolg? Fomorians?"

I blinked between the two of them. I hadn't heard of the first thing she mentioned, but I had heard of the Fomorians. Heck, my father was of Fomorian descent. But why would they help the Morrigan? All Tuatha De despised the Fomore. Unless she, or they, were desperate. I swallowed hard. Oh, if my glamour had done the damage everyone seemed to think it had done, then the Morrigan might very well be desperate enough to recruit the help of a sworn enemy.

Cade released a ragged breath. "I don't know, but I intend to find out."

Before the conversation could continue in its current direction, we were attacked by a flock of small children, all yelling and laughing and trying to get a better look at their visitors.

Enorah laughed and scooped up a small red-head, the same girl who she'd kept a close eye on the last time we visited.

"What are all of you doing up?! Honestly, if there were chores to be done you'd all still be hiding in bed."

She turned to face Cade and me. "Come on the both of you. Enough serious talk, let's go get a good fire going and make something to eat! Apparently everyone is ready for breakfast."

I readily stepped forward to join her, but Cade caught her arm and said, "I'm afraid I can't stay."

Enorah furrowed her brow at him, then set the girl down and drew herself up to her full, authoritative height.

"What do you mean you aren't staying?"

I was just as surprised as Enorah, but Cade's sister beat me to the question on both our minds.

"Meghan is staying, but I have to go inform the others that she is here and that we need to start thinking about how to deal with the Morrigan, because you know she won't rest until she gets what she wants or until someone stops her."

Enorah looked like she was about to argue, but Cade cut her off. "Someone has to tell them, and you know Meghan can't come with me. Her power isn't strong enough yet and this is the best place for her until it is. If she comes with me then the Morrigan will surely hunt both of us. With just me she is less likely to care."

"Meghan, what have you got to say about all of this?"

Enorah turned to me, her face impassive. Honestly, I didn't like it one bit, and if I had been at all lucid during his meeting with Briant before we left, I would have paid closer attention to what was said. Cade had mentioned getting in touch with the Dagda and the rest of the Tuatha De. It just hadn't occurred to me that he meant to go visit them himself.

I hated the idea of him going out into the outside world alone. Yes, he had more experience in the Otherworld and definitely had more experience dealing with the Morrigan, but that didn't make me feel any better. Especially since I knew she was capable of murdering her own son. But Cade was right. It made more sense for me to stay in the Weald. As much as I despised the idea of him being vulnerable, I knew if I were with him then the two of us would be a bigger target. And unlike the last time we encountered the Morrigan, I didn't have a nice store of magic just waiting to wreak havoc.

I took a deep breath through my nose and released it before answering Enorah. "I don't like it, but I'm going along with it because Cade is right. I'm safer here than anywhere, and I'd just draw the Morrigan's attention if I went with him."

Enorah thought about that for a while, then nodded sharply. "Very well. And of course Meghan can stay here with us."

Cade released his breath, clearly relieved, then addressed his sister, "While she's here, I was hoping you could teach her how to control and use her power properly. I had hoped to teach her myself, but now that the Morrigan seems to be preparing for war, Meghan will need all the knowledge she can get, as soon as she can get it. Perhaps you can even take her to the Tree of Life."

I blinked in surprise. The Tree of Life? Where was that? *What* was that?

Enorah nodded. "I'll take her once she's had a chance to sleep. From what you've told me I can safely presume you've been up the whole night."

Cade nodded then opened his mouth and called, "Fergus!"

The spirit guide trotted up to us, as silent and ethereal as ever.

"Go wait for me down the trail."

Without so much as a wag of his tail, the wolfhound took off towards the edge of the settlement, disappearing down the path.

Cade turned to follow him, but paused and gave me a long look. *Accompany me to the edge of the village?* His shíl-sciar voice felt smooth in my mind.

I sighed, then closed my eyes. I didn't want to do this, not this soon. I had hoped for at least a good week or two in Eilé before I had to worry about the Morrigan. Now Cade was leaving me in the care of his sister and I wasn't even sure if I'd ever see him again. *No tears Meghan!* my conscience told me as my eyes threatened to well up.

I took a deep, shuddering breath and whispered back to him using the same, private method of communication. *Of course.*

Cade stepped away from Enorah, but she caught his hand before he could move any further. "Be careful brother. Now you have two women who would be heart-broken if you never came back."

He gave her a curt nod, then looked at me again before walking away.

"I'll be just a minute," I told Enorah. My voice shook a little, but I hoped she didn't notice.

"Take your time Meghan, there is no need to rush and it's still plenty dark out."

Despite the somber mood, she managed to lighten it by winking at me. Ugh, I could appreciate her attempt to make me feel better, but I didn't appreciate the flush creeping up my neck . . .

Shaking off Enorah's suggestive remark, I wrapped my arms around myself and followed after Cade. We walked like that, in silence, until the village was out of sight and we were blocked by a bend in the trail. The sky was still very dark, but I could see the beginnings of pale grey coloring the eastern sky. My skin prickled with goose bumps, but I knew it wasn't just because of the cold. I was worried beyond belief. True, Cade knew what he was doing. He was a faelah bounty hunter for goodness' sake and the son of a goddess. But I had seen what the Morrigan could do and I didn't ever want that to happen again. I'd be worried about him the entire time he was gone.

When Cade finally stopped walking, he stepped to the side and leaned against a great beech tree covered in moss and shoved his hands into his pockets, his cloak falling all around him like an extension of the green forest. I just studied him like that for several moments, grateful for the encroaching light of dawn. I sighed in appreciation. He looked like some long forgotten god of the old forest, beautiful, strong and intense. He was just standing there, still as the trees, but the power he exuded was almost too much to take in. I felt my heart swell again, reminding me how much I loved him.

I'll come back Meghan, I promise, his mind whispered against mine.

I know, I answered, my own thoughts shaky and raw as I transferred my gaze to the leaf-plastered ground. *When will you be back?*

He took a long time to answer, but finally he said, *No longer than a month. Maybe five weeks.*

A month! Five weeks! That was an eternity! *Cool it Meghan*, I told myself. *You've waited longer for him, remember?* Okay, so maybe it wasn't that bad, but it would seem like forever. I would just have to spend every waking moment focusing on fine-tuning my magic so that I could defend myself when it was time to leave the Weald.

The soft sound of rustling clothing was the first clue that Cade had moved from his resting spot against the tree. I glanced up, only to catch his gaze as he stepped towards me. My heart caught in my throat and I froze on the spot. When he was mere inches away, he reached up and took my face in his hands.

Without thinking about it, I lifted my own hands and placed them on his forearms. I knew my eyes were filling up with tears, and I knew it made me look pathetic, but I was too overwhelmed with emotion to care. I had just left my family behind, perhaps never to see them again, only to learn that Cade was leaving me for a month to traipse across the wilds of Eilé in clear sight of his bloodthirsty mother.

"Shhh," Cade murmured, resting his forehead against mine. "Hush, love. When this is all over, we'll go back to Luathara and start over again properly."

I tried to swallow, but there was an annoying lump in my throat. So, did that mean Cade wanted to marry me after all? If so, why had he nearly panicked when his sister joked about it? And, despite the fact that I loved him beyond all reason, was I even ready for such a huge life step, especially when I had the potential to live forever?

Shut up Meghan and just enjoy the moment while it lasts, my oh-so considerate conscience told me. Okay, good advice.

I licked my lips and turned my face up to Cade's. He smiled and leaned in closer, kissing me softly at first, but then deepening the kiss so that my nerves sparked all the way from the tips of my toes to the very ends of my hair.

I wrapped my arms around him and added my own fervor. Hey, why not play along if he was willing? Cade responded by wrapping his cloak around me and moving his hands from my face to my lower back. We were both lost in sensation for who knows how long, but at some point a screech from above forced us to break the kiss and we were left standing there, staring at each other as we caught our breath. Cade's eyes were flickering from green to brown to grey and I'm sure mine were doing the same. The screech sounded again and I saw a flash of white tear by. Meridian. I bit my lip to hide a grin as my cheeks turned pink.

Cade smiled back at me and leaned in to give me another kiss, this one not nearly as disarming as the last. I tried not to feel disappointed. After all, he did have to get going.

I grabbed the edges of his cloak and pulled myself up on my tiptoes to give him one last peck on the lips, then I forced myself to step away.

I quickly turned and walked back towards the village, glancing every now and again over my shoulder. Cade stood there, in the middle of the trail, looking like some cloaked avenger, watching me. I smiled and turned back around, telling myself the sooner he left, the sooner he'd return.

Just as I was entering the village again, I felt Cade's words sift into my mind.

A few weeks, my love. One short month.

I know, I returned. *Be careful and come back to me whole and alive or I shall make your life miserable after I take you to the Dagda.*

Cade's soft chuckle was the reply I got, but that heartwarming sound soon drifted out of my conscious like smoke in the wind.

Five weeks max, Meghan, I told myself as I met up with Enorah and the sleepy children in the center of the village. *Only a month.*

Nine

Guardian

When I woke up later that day, I nearly panicked. The bed I was lying in wasn't my own, the air held the distinct scent of wood smoke and damp earth, and there were several pairs of eyes (not belonging to my brothers) gazing at me with intense curiosity. Fortunately, I didn't scream, but I came darn close. Then it all came flooding back to me in one painful rush: leaving my family and home for the Otherworld, fighting off the attack on Luathara, the horrible puca delivering the Morrigan's threat, traveling to the Weald, Cade leaving to take care of business without me . . . A wave of emotion overtook me and a sob escaped my throat. I clasped a hand over my mouth before I lost it completely. That action alone scared the kids off, but they were soon replaced by Enorah.

"What's wrong Meghan?"

"I'm fine," I managed as I wiped away the stray tears.

I would not break down in front of Cade's sister. What was wrong with me? I had been fine earlier that morning after Cade left and I'd had something to eat. Perhaps the shock was just now wearing off.

Enorah sank down onto the thin mattress next to me and swung an arm over my shoulder, pulling me close and leaning the side of her head against mine.

"If you need to cry, go right ahead. You have every right to be upset right now. No one will judge you harshly for it."

I shook my head. No, I could control myself. I was just taken by surprise is all. I kept my tears at bay and refused to lose it. *Time to be strong, Meghan,* my conscience told me. And for once, I agreed. Instead of crying, I simply took several deep breaths, willing myself to remain calm.

Ten minutes later Enorah was leading me out into the middle of their small town. From the angle of the light pouring through the canopy above, I judged the time of day to be around noon. Huh, guess I hadn't slept that long after all. Would explain why I still felt groggy.

"Sorry, our accommodations are a little primitive, but we do have a shower," she said, grinning as she pointed out what looked like a shed with steaming cauldrons of water simmering beside it.

I smiled. Despite the rustic set up, a hot shower would help soothe my nerves.

When I was done cleaning up and had donned a fresh set of clothes from my backpack, I sought out Enorah again. She sat with a few other adults her age around the central mid-day fire. Several children, ranging in age from two to fifteen darted around, either helping their older comrades with chores or playing games of chase. There seemed to be a lot more kids than what I remembered from my last visit and quite a few extra adults as well.

I asked Enorah about this and her usually bright face turned gloomy. She nodded once and said, "The Morrigan's creatures have been more active of late. I think Cade is right; she is up to something and everyone in Eilé can feel it. Those who think they might have wronged her, and those who live too far away from established settlements to protect themselves have sought shelter with us and others who will take them in."

She turned and looked at me, her grey-green gaze hard. "A war is brewing Meghan, I can feel it in my bones. The trees can feel it," she glanced up at the boughs high above us, "the animals and the very earth can feel it."

A stone seemed to have formed in my throat, only to slide down to the pit of my stomach.

"Oh no," I whispered harshly, "this is my fault. Cade had warned me about this, when we first met, before I'd even come to Eilé." I looked up at her and I knew my eyes were flickering with my magic once again. "He told me that my mixed blood would bring turmoil to the people of the Otherworld."

Enorah only shook her head, then placed a hand on my shoulder. "No Meghan, don't look at it that way. Yes, your presence has brought about this change, but it has been a long time coming. The Morrigan has been working for years to inflict her reign upon our world. Only now does she think she stands a chance, but it is a risky bargain."

I furrowed my brow. "How so?"

"She wants you Meghan, she wants your glamour. If she succeeds, the power she steals from you will make her all but invincible. But if she fails, then she may be rendered powerless for centuries."

I shivered at that. I knew the gods and goddesses couldn't be killed, but *I* could, immortal or not. That gave me an even greater reason not to fight the Morrigan. And despite what Enorah said, and what the Dagda had once told me, I couldn't help but feel guilty about all of this. Only one thing to do about it though . . . I sucked in a deep breath and let it out just as forcefully.

"Okay, maybe I should start learning how to use this immense power of mine then."

I grinned, despite my unease, and Enorah laughed. "That's the spirit. Let's have some lunch and then I'll take you to the Tree of Life."

As we headed towards the village square, I said, "Cade mentioned something about that this morning. What is the Tree of Life exactly?"

Enorah's eyes took on that mischievous glint once again and all she said was, "You'll see."

Great, I thought, *more surprises . . .*

Meridian volunteered to be our lookout as we made our way deeper into the heart of the Weald. I had no idea where exactly this Tree of Life was supposed to be and Enorah wouldn't tell me. What she did do, however, was point out all of the wondrous creatures that lived deep within this magical place as we hiked. I saw several more twigrins, following quietly after us for a few minutes before disappearing into the branches again, and even some of the pixies that had greeted me in the swamp those many months ago. A few times we passed by a small clearing bedecked with what looked like a cluster of small, dome-shaped houses. I probably wouldn't have noticed them except several had streams of smoke rising from their roofs. I lifted an eyebrow at Enorah and she said with a smile, "A cranobh village."

"Huh?"

"They are distantly related to brownies but prefer to live in the forest. Cranobhs are generally shy and keep to themselves, but are incredibly strong and ferocious if you anger them."

My eyes must have been huge because Enorah let loose a string of laughter, pausing long enough to slap a hand against her thigh.

"Don't worry Meghan! The only way to offend a cranobh is by cutting down a tree in its presence. They are very protective of the forest."

We started walking once again, moving deeper and deeper into the ancient forest. On more than one occasion, I stepped on a moss-covered rock only to squeal when it jerked itself out from under my foot, scuttling off into the brush while emitting clicking sounds. The first time this happened I gave Enorah a look of horror, but she only smiled and said, "Litterbug."

Oh, right. I'd encountered one of those before, only it had looked different than the living rock version.

"Um, do they all blend in so well with their surroundings?"

If Enorah said yes, I didn't think I was going to make it through this day with my nerves still intact. And just like that, my wonderful imagination conjured up an image of me grabbing onto a branch for support only to find that it was some creepy crawly thing that didn't appreciate being touched.

Enorah chuckled and nodded her head to answer my question, looking like a woodland elf ready for mischief. Great.

Eventually, we came upon a wide, flooded meadow and the natural magic of the Weald, which had been brushing against my skin for the past several hours, intensified into something far more substantial. I glanced down at my arm, expecting to see goose bumps. Instead, an almost imperceptible pale blue glimmer shimmered just above the surface of my skin, making my blood sing and my own growing glamour flare ever so slightly.

Shaking my head, I tore my attention away from the sudden influx of magic and returned my eyes to the glorious scene before us. The water flooding the meadow was shallow, maybe two to three feet deep at most, and there were several large stepping stones creating a path across the natural moat. As beautiful as the shallow pool was, however, the enormous tree perched dead center on the largest piece of dry land brought me to a sudden stop. I felt my mouth drop open as I gazed upon one of the most beautiful things I'd ever seen. Most of the tree's boughs curved downward and several of its roots reached up towards the sky, intertwining with the twigs and branches above them. All around the entire tree, the roots and branches joined together like this, forming a great sphere of woven natural beauty. The leaves were gone from the tree, and I couldn't tell if it was always supposed to look that way or if this particular species lost its leaves in the summer. This was the Otherworld after all, and anything was possible.

"Meghan," Enorah said softly, all of her earlier mirth gone from both her voice and her face.

Cade's sister now donned a quiet demeanor of respect, one I was quick to mimic. I glanced down at her arm. She was indicating the pathway of stones that crossed the shallow pool. "All Faelorehn are welcome to enter within the joining of roots and branches of the great Tree of Life."

I stared at her in surprise, still under the spell of the tree and the magic that thrummed throughout this meadow like the resounding hum of a plucked guitar string. Releasing a great sigh, I looked more closely at the collection of stepping stones stretching out in front of me, my gaze tracing where they led. On the other side of the pool I noted a narrow gap in the tree's branches; an entrance large enough for someone to pass through.

Then Enorah's words hit me. "Wait, you want me to go in *there?*"

It didn't seem right. Sure, I was technically Faelorehn and the daughter of their queen, but I hadn't grown up here and it wasn't as if Danua was welcoming me into her castle with open arms. I knew next to nothing of their ways and although I had come a long way since my internet searches, I still had plenty to learn about my heritage. And Enorah wanted me to walk up to this tree, which looked to be as old as the earth itself and probably contained more magic than all the Celtic gods combined, and . . . do what exactly?

I almost leapt out of my skin when Enorah placed her hands on my shoulders. "The Tree of Life is here to help guide us, to give us wisdom and show us our true selves. And to soothe us when we are distressed. Can you not feel it beckoning you?"

I swallowed, but nodded. Yes, I could feel it beckoning me, almost like the feeling I got before being pulled through a dolmarehn. Only this sensation tugged on my heart, or maybe it was my magic. I couldn't quite tell, but it was there. Still feeling a bit reluctant, I took the first step towards the tree. After all, I could definitely use some guidance and soothing, even if it came from a giant, magical plant. Slowly but surely, I crossed the shallow moat, barely even noticing the enchanted aura of the meadow anymore.

When I was only a few feet away from the tree, I reached out a hand and carefully touched a knot on one of its roots. Instantly my nerves sizzled, as if icy lightning had struck my hand. I hissed in a breath, but didn't move my fingers away. Instead, I squared my shoulders and stepped through the gap. Suddenly, the world went quiet and all I could hear and feel were the whispers of hundreds of voices, all trying to speak to me at once in that Otherworldly language that seemed more ancient than time. My small well of magic flared, stronger than ever, and for a moment I thought my heart might burst.

The murmuring voices all came together and suddenly, I could understand them: *You have goodness in you Meghan Elam, but you are not meant for mere goodness. You are destined for greatness . . .*

The words swirled around in my mind, and although I could see them the way I saw Cade's thoughts when he used shíl-sciar, I could hear these words as well. What did they mean,

I was destined for greatness? Me? The nerdy teen from Arroyo Grande? But then again, that wasn't quite who I was. I was also Meghan of Eilé, daughter of Danua the high queen.

I gritted my teeth and let the meaning of the words sink in. Could I really be destined for greatness? I snorted. Sure, why not? I had gone from being the most unpopular girl at my high school to being an immortal Faelorehn princess with a powerful arch enemy and a hot, faelah bounty hunter as a boyfriend. My world of possibilities had gone from 'Not a chance in hell' to 'Anything could, and would, happen' in just a few months. And that's when it hit me, like the first icy drop of a winter storm, insignificant but shocking at the same time. I wasn't Meghan Elam of California, nor was I the daughter of a Celtic goddess queen. I was just me, but unfortunately I hadn't quite figured out who that person was yet. I mean, I had a pretty good idea, but I was still in the process of becoming who I was supposed to be. Maybe that is what the voices, the Tree of Life, meant. I was destined for greatness because I still hadn't discovered my true calling yet.

And just like that, my magic, which had been swirling around inside of me like a freight train tearing down a mountain side, died back down to the candle flame I always saw it as.

You are well on your way, Child of Eilé . . .

The voices whispered in unison one last time, dissipating as my heart rate slowed back into a normal pace.

Feeling suddenly drained, I plopped down on the bed of soft moss surrounding the base of the tree and rested my back against its gnarled trunk. I just needed a few moments to regain my composure, then I'd return to Enorah. I think I was at my limit when it came to powerful Otherworldly things for the day and I needed to clear my head to sort out the 'words of wisdom' the Tree had shared with me.

Taking deep breaths, I glanced around, sighing at the beautiful knot work weave of the interlinking branches and roots once again. Nothing in the mortal world ever grew like that, unless diligently trained by a gardener, and even then it didn't come close. I was so distracted with tracing the pattern with my fingers that I didn't notice the pale blue light slowly growing and overtaking the marshy glen. Eventually it caught my attention and I whipped my head around, expecting to see Enorah performing some tricks with her glamour in order to pass the time while I recovered.

What I saw instead took my breath away. A great stag, closer in size to an elk than a deer, stood stoically on the other side of the shallow pool. The numbing silence that had surrounded me melted away and the enchanting music of the forest played softly across the glen. As I tried to blink the incredible image of the stag from my vision, he took several soundless steps, moving gracefully through the water as if he were composed only of spirit. I stayed absolutely still, afraid that I might scare him away. Where had he come from? And where was Enorah?

And then something even stranger happened. That pale magic dancing around the Tree gathered behind the stag and he started melting into something different, something more familiar. By the time he reached the opening in the Tree, he had taken on the shape of a man with only his great antlers remaining. And all I could do was stare up at his impressive figure like an idiot.

He smiled, then tossed a lock of earth-brown hair out of eyes the same color and extended a hand out to me. I swallowed and continued my staring contest, trying for the life of me to figure out who he was. He wore leather hunting pants and simple moccasins, and his bare chest revealed toned muscles hidden only slightly by a deerskin vest. Around his throat was a torque, similar to Cade's and mine, only this one portrayed the heads of deer instead of hounds. Not too surprising, considering he had been one only a few moments ago.

"Don't be afraid Meghan," he said gently, his voice so in tune with the sounds of the forest.

"Wh-Who are you?" I croaked, still staying put on the ground.

He smiled again, his face lighting up and his gentle brown eyes flashing gold.

"A friend," he answered.

Feeling that I was trapped in this spherical nest of branches and roots, I took my chances and let him pull me up and out onto the stepping stones.

"Thanks," I mumbled, brushing off mud and leaf litter while at the same time casting quick glances in his direction.

He now stood with his arms crossed, studying me openly. He didn't feel threatening, but that didn't mean anything. He was tall and those antlers made him appear even taller. What was with that anyways? Obviously he was some sort of shape-shifter, but why wouldn't he get rid of the antlers after taking on his human form?

I tried to get a better sense of who he might be, but before I could ask any more questions, he sighed and said, "I've come to be of some help to you, Meghan."

"How do you know my name?" I whispered.

The strange man smiled. "The spirits of the forest told me."

Uh, *okay* . . .

"I know about your troubles with the Morrigan as well."

Ah, wonderful. First I had the spirits of the forest and a sacred tree telling strangers my name and informing me I was 'destined for greatness', and now I had some antlered shape-shifter I'd never met before telling me he knew about my biggest problem. Did everyone know everyone's business in Eilé? Or was it just because I was the clueless newbie? Or worse, was he here to escort me back to the mortal world? *Sorry Meg, we can't have you stirring up trouble in the Otherworld so you'll have to leave . . .*

"I also know who your mother is and that you are capable of producing great magic."

For some reason, that sparked enough anger in me to burn away my trepidation. "Oh? And did she send you? To try and talk sense into me?"

The last time I'd seen Danua, my mother, she had insisted I give up my friendship with Cade and move into the castle at Erintara with her to take on my proper role as her daughter. I had refused and she hadn't been too happy about it. Oh well. I hadn't cared at the time and I didn't care now. If she wanted me in her life, then she needed to make an effort to get to know me and not try to mold me into something I wasn't.

The strange deer man must have felt my irritation, but all he did was smile. It was a bit disarming because, after all, he had the same beauty about him that all the Faelorehn had.

"No, she didn't. I came on my own," he finally said. "As soon as you entered my realm I could sense your glamour. You have great potential to become very strong, but not strong enough to defeat your enemies. I am here to offer you a gift, a gift no other Faelorehn has ever been granted."

I opened my mouth to share a few more terse words with him, but choked on whatever it was I was about to say. Instead I offered a garbled, "Huh?"

"I am the Guardian of the Weald, Meghan, and all the wild things of Eilé. I know of the threat that looms over our world, and I know that you are a central player. The fight to overcome the Morrigan will not be an easy one, and since you are her main target, I thought you might benefit from a little extra magic."

I stared at him again and this time it wasn't because I found his antlers a bit disconcerting. How did he know all of this?

"Are you serious?" I finally managed, placing a hand behind me as I groped for something to keep me steady. A rough root or branch finally gave me some support.

"Would you like to have as much magic as one of the Celtic gods?"

I shook my head to clear it of my disbelief. If what he was telling me was true, then perhaps I stood a chance against the Morrigan after all. But a prickle of doubt pierced through me and I hesitated. What if this was a trick? I didn't know who this person was. Sure, he had emerged from the woods in the shape of a giant deer, the magic of Eilé clinging to him like a cloak woven from starlight, but I was in the Otherworld now. I really had no idea who was on my side.

Taking a deep breath, I opened my mouth to tell him I wasn't interested, but then an old memory played across my mind. It was an image of Cade, standing in the middle of a bloody battlefield, looking at me one last time before collapsing to the ground. The reminder of what the Morrigan was capable of made my chest hurt, and I had to grit my teeth and squeeze my eyes shut until the nightmare passed. Suddenly, I wasn't so certain of turning the shape-shifter's offer down any longer, and something, intuition or some deep instinct, made me think that this chance might not come my way again. I steeled myself, then looked the antlered man in the eye.

"Yes," I said, hoping I was making the right choice. It was so hard to think straight with so much magic saturating the air. "I would appreciate your help."

The stranger stepped forward and showed me his palm. "I'll have to touch you to make it work," he explained. "One hand I must place over the spot where your magic sleeps, the other I will place on your forehead. Is that alright?"

I bit my cheek, but nodded.

"Now, this might feel strange and it may even make you unaware of your surroundings for a while, but it will have no lasting effects, other than creating another pocket of magic next to your own. However, I must warn you," he paused, giving me a look that didn't reflect his general kindness, "this gift comes with a price."

I felt my stomach sink and a raw bitterness gnawed at my heart. Of course. I knew it must be too good to be true.

I swallowed my disappointment and whispered, "And what price is that?"

"A geis," he murmured.

I cringed and pulled away from him. In my experience, nothing good ever came from being pinned down with a geis. Would I be willing to pay the price? To have a taboo hovering over me in order to gain the power of a god? I thought about what I intended to do with that power once I got it: defeat the Morrigan so that she could no longer hurt me, my friends or my family. Yes, that was worth the price of a geis. But I still wanted to know what it was going to cost me.

I clenched my fingers into fists. "Very well," I said rather boldly, "what would the terms of this geis be?"

The antlered man studied me for a long while, then gently nodded his head before saying, "The power I lend you can be used only once, so you must use it wisely. It is also a secret and may not be shared with any other Faelorehn man or woman until after you've used it."

I blanched and gave him a look of horror. What!? I had to keep this a secret?

"Why can't I tell anyone about it?"

A flash of gold crackled in his brown eyes, and for a split second he lost his smile. Pressing his fingertips together he gave a slight nod, "It is just one of the conditions of your geis."

I gritted my teeth in frustration. What kind of an answer was that? Huffing a breath of annoyance, I asked, "So, what happens if I violate this geis?"

Hey, I needed to know all the details, right? Would be foolish to swear an oath without knowing all the consequences.

The man's humor vanished once again and his brown eyes darkened, taking on a somber aura. "If you share any details of this gift before you've made proper use of it, then you will lose all of your magic, never to gain it back again. You will become mortal; unable to live in Eilé."

I'm pretty sure my knees buckled, because one minute I was standing there, trying to look tough in front of this weird guy with antlers, and in the next moment I was sitting down in the shallow pool. The shape-shifter tried to help me up, but I really didn't care if I got soaked or not. I could lose my magic. All of it. Not that it was something I was terribly attached to. Heck, I hadn't known it existed most of my life. But if I had no magic, I wouldn't be able to protect myself from the Morrigan. Sure, she wouldn't want to make me her own personal, glamour cash cow any more, but after the fight I'd given her the last time we met, she would most definitely kill me simply out of spite.

Eventually, I allowed myself to be helped up. I had a decision to make. A life-changing, possibly life-ending, decision. The deer man must have known this because he stood patiently as if allowing me to think. Okay, he was offering to give me a lot more magic to be used only once, the kind of magic the Morrigan and my mother could wield. Enough to possibly defeat the Morrigan, someone who threatened everyone I loved. I had no reason to trust the validity of what he said, but something about the power that emanated from him and something maybe more instinctual, told me he wasn't lying. His offer was very generous, and tempting, but that was one heck of a gamble to take on a future I had no way of predicting. And even then, would it be enough? Could it stop the Morrigan for good?

Then I thought of Enorah and the wildren, and Danua and the Dagda. I thought of my family back in the mortal world. And finally, I thought of Cade. I loved them all, in one way or another, and the Morrigan was a threat to all of them. Yes, the Dagda and my mother were immensely powerful, and even Cade and I had our fair share of glamour. But what if the Morrigan had even more? Especially now that she had an ally. And who knows what other unknown advantages she had hidden up her sleeves. If I knew the Morrigan, she was no fool. She would have planned for everything and she would never take on her Tuatha De brethren if she didn't think she could win.

I took a long, deep breath and closed my eyes, trying to ease the ache in my chest. When I opened my eyes again, I found the strange man exactly where I had left him, standing only a few feet in front of me. His mouth cut a grim line across his face, his eyes studying me closely once again.

"I will accept your offer," I heard myself say over the fierce pounding of my heart.

I reached out my hand and he took it carefully, shaking to seal the deal. A jolt of magic coursed up my arm and joined the flame of my own glamour, sizzling and sparking for a brief moment before becoming that docile little flicker once again.

"Wait," I said suddenly, jerking my hand back. "Why me? Why offer this gift to me?"

The antlered man grinned and his eyes glinted. He may have been a deer, but that look was all predator.

"The Morrigan presumes too much; she takes things too far and thinks we'll sit back and allow her to do so. She is wrong. Besides, you're the one she wants the most. You need this magic more than anyone else."

I gritted my teeth. Yes, I was the little Faelorah with the gall to stand up to her without dying, so it was no surprise I was on the top of her 'People Who Must Die' list. I just wish everyone would stop reminding me of that fact.

"Are you ready?" the shape-shifter asked.

I nodded, bracing myself.

He took a step forward and lifted both hands, placing one on my chest just to the right of my heart, and the other on my head, as if I were a child he was blessing. Immediately, I felt my magic shimmer and quiver with life.

"This may feel strange," he whispered, "and when it is all over, I will be gone. My gift of magic will be its own separate entity, but it will reside next to your own glamour. Just remember what you promised, and follow your heart. It will tell you when it is time to use this gift."

Before I could so much as nod or voice one of the five hundred other questions that sat on the tip of my tongue, a great flash of light pierced the landscape and seared my retinas. I cried out in shock and felt myself falling once again. The candle wick that had once embodied my magic shuddered as a new flame, a much paler shade of blue than mine, flashed and burst forth like a super nova. Just as quickly, the great whirlwind of sensations overwhelming me vanished. The bright light that had accompanied the stag faded and I was left in a world caught between twilight and evening. Eventually I heard Enorah calling out my name and felt someone shaking my shoulders.

I wanted to keep my eyes shut; keep the world locked out until I figured out what had just happened, if that was even possible, but Enorah's frantic voice forced me to look in her direction.

"Meghan! What happened!?"

"The stag," I managed, "I mean, the man. I-I don't know."

A wave of painful dizziness swept over me and I felt my head loll to the side. Enorah grabbed me and shook me gently, forcing me to sit up and open my eyes.

"You stepped through the gap in the branches and sat down for no more than a minute Meghan, then you keeled over into the pool. I dragged you over here and tried to get you to wake up, but you weren't responding. You were out for a good ten minutes or more."

Enorah propped me up against a moss covered stone and looked me in the eye, her own eyes now pale grey and bright with worry. "What happened in there? Why did you black out? What did you see?"

My mind felt fuzzy and incoherent, as if I was chasing words around in my mind, trying to catch them and string them together to form lucid thoughts. I pressed a hand to my head and tried to think. That only made my head hurt worse, but I was able to recall a fragment of what had happened. Eventually, everything cleared and I licked my lips to answer Enorah's question.

"Didn't you see him? The giant stag?" I blurted, "He was standing right where I left you, then he came over to me and turned into a man, only he had antlers."

Had that been real? It seemed so real, but now that I was conscious again it seemed more like a dream than reality. Could I have imagined it all?

"What?" Enorah breathed in response to my babbling. Her grip on my shoulders tightening.

I bit my lip as the rest of my conversation with the stranger came flooding back. *Tell no one of my gift, it is a secret . . .* Oh no. I had sworn an oath and accepted a geis, promising the shape-shifter I wouldn't tell anyone about my new extra dose of glamour. Had I already broken my geis? I started to panic, but then a soothing voice, nothing more than a breath of wind, crooned, *I never said you couldn't speak about me . . . just don't tell her about your secret . . .*

I pressed a palm to my forehead and tried to think again, but Enorah pulled my hand away and cupped my face in her hands.

"Meghan! Do you realize who you saw?"

Guardian

I shook my head and frowned, then felt the blood drain from my face. *Oh no. Oh Meghan . . .* Had my first instincts been right after all? Had I just accepted a geis from one of the Morrigan's allies? Did I just sign my own death warrant? A sob worked its way up my throat and I nearly choked on it.

"Meghan? What's wrong? No, don't be upset!"

Enorah gently shook my shoulders, but the tears wouldn't stop.

"Meghan! You had a vision is all, a vision of Cernunnos! Don't be upset, please."

She pushed back my tangled hair and gave me a hug, trying to shush me and get me to stop crying.

"Cernunnos is the Guardian of the Wild, Meghan. He hardly ever comes this close to our village. Many people say that he lives in the farthest reaches of the Weald, where no one dares tread. It is said that his magic is so vast he is the wilderness itself."

She let go of me and held me at arm's length, smiling brightly. I sniffled, finally forcing myself into a calm state.

"He's not a friend of the Morrigan?" I murmured, my relief making my bones feel weak.

Enorah released a great sigh and then chuckled. "Oh no! Is that why you are so upset? Did you think the Morrigan was sending her minions to terrorize you when you were unconscious? Poor Meghan! I can't say I blame you, after what happened at Luathara the other night."

No. I was thinking I had just made a deal with one of her henchmen and I would soon lose all of my magic.

I wiped my sleeve across my nose, not caring that it was totally unladylike, and nodded. Hey, I had a secret to keep. It wouldn't hurt to let Enorah keep believing it was only my fear of the Morrigan that had forced me into hysterics. And the memory of the attack on Cade's castle helped me keep up the whole 'emotionally disturbed Meg' act.

"So, are you okay now?"

Enorah was sitting on her knees, her hands pressed against her thighs.

Finally, I took a deep breath and let it out slowly. "I'm fine, really. I'm just a bit tired of being clueless when it comes to the Faelorehn nobility. If another god or goddess pops up and doesn't bother to tell me who they are, I might just punch them."

I could have sworn there was another person laughing along with Enorah, someone with the smooth, rich voice of the forest, but I brushed it aside as she helped me up.

"Come on, let's get back to the village," she said.

"Good idea. I think I need to go to bed and not wake up until morning."

We made our way back through the forest and while we walked in silence I couldn't help but reach inside of myself to examine my new source of magic. Its wild flare had died down, but I could no longer picture it as a candle flame. Instead, I envisioned a pale sapphire rose, closed up tight as if it was sleeping. Brilliant, electric cerulean tendrils of light glowed between the tight petals, and somehow I knew that this is how I'd always see Cernunnos's gift. And then another thought struck me like a well-placed arrow. What if Cade noticed this new change in me when he returned? After all, he had been able to sense my Faelorehn glamour long before I even knew about it. Would he be able to sense this power too?

"Meghan, you okay?"

The weight of Enorah's hand on my shoulder made me jump.

She pulled her hand back immediately and donned a worried look.

"Sorry. I'm okay, really. Just thinking about what happened back at the Tree."

I gave a half-hearted grin, hoping she bought my lie.

Enorah nodded, then smiled and gave my shoulder a friendly nudge with her fist.

"Let's get a move on then. If we stick to this pace then we'll get stranded in the forest after dark."

I sighed, but started walking again. I really wanted to think about more pleasant things as we made our way back to the village, but what had happened with Cernunnos insisted on taking center stage in my mind. It would be hard keeping this knowledge to myself, I knew that for certain, but I also knew that the lives of those I loved (and my own life as well) depended on it. And then, when the time arrived, I would let that bud of power blossom and release its potent, brilliant blue magic and stop the Morrigan in her tracks. I just needed to figure out when that would be.

As the lingering, magical essence of the enchanted meadow wore off, I pictured the Tree of Life in my mind once more. Despite the stressful interaction I'd had with Cernunnos, the whole experience hadn't been all that bad. In fact, I had the itchy feeling that the Tree was pleased with my choice. How I knew this, I couldn't say. I only hoped that I'd made the right decision.

Ten
Training

*D*usk had begun encroaching upon the village by the time we got back, so Enorah fetched me a quick dinner then left me in one of the small cabins to sleep off my ordeal. Of course, I never told her it had been an ordeal, I simply explained that I was still tired from the night before. Either way, I was left to simmer in the near silence, listening to the children playing outside as I tried to gather my thoughts. So the wild deer man, Cernunnos, had given me an overdose of magic, enough to rank me among the Tuatha De; the gods and goddesses of the Otherworld. And I had to keep it a secret from everyone I knew and I could only use it once. *Alright Meghan*, I told myself, *don't screw this up. You made the right choice in accepting his help, now you have to figure out how you are going to keep something this big a secret.*

I turned over on the lumpy mattress and huffed a breath of frustration. I didn't think I would have any trouble keeping quiet with Enorah, the Dagda, my mother and any of the other Faelorehn I came into contact with, but how on earth was I going to keep this information from Cade? Especially now that I knew how to talk to him using only my thoughts. *Don't forget Meghan, just because you can communicate mind to mind doesn't mean you have to tell him everything.* Right. I simply wouldn't speak about it, out loud or internally. But would the guilt eat away at me? We were in a relationship now and the last thing I wanted to do was ruin it because I couldn't be honest with him.

Once again, the image of the Morrigan using Cade as a chew toy for her horrible hounds flashed across my mind. I ground my teeth. I would hang onto that image like a leech, despite the pain it caused me. If ever I was tempted to spill my discovery to Cade, the memory of his fight with the Cúmorrig would keep me in line.

Trouble?

The sudden thought from Meridian made me jolt upright. I sighed and leaned back into the pillow when I realized it was her. She had been scarce all day, so I wondered where she was now. Probably perched in the tree behind my cabin.

Yes and no, I responded, then paused for a moment. I could tell my spirit guide about my magic, couldn't I? She didn't speak with anyone else and spirit guides were the very form of loyalty. And she wasn't a Faelorehn man or woman.

I drew in a slow breath, deciding it best not to risk anything. *Just feel a little odd in this new place*, I sent. There, that should be safe.

Yes, new great magic inside, she said, *Bright Flower.*

My eyes widened in surprise, though there was no one to see me.

You know?

Of course, she responded, and I could just see her fluffing her feathers smugly. *Wild Lord told me.*

Huh. Well, if Cernunnos took the initiative to inform my spirit guide of my secret power, then I guess it was okay to speak with her about it.

We can't tell anyone, I whispered into her mind, *not even Cade or Fergus.*

No one. Secret.

I grinned. *Yes,* I sent as I finally allowed myself to relax, my eyelids fluttering shut as I lay back down. *Very secret.*

It wasn't long before sleep crept up on me, but before I lost complete awareness of my surroundings, a cool, inviting voice as old as the earth itself whispered against my mind, so gentle I wondered if I imagined it: *Rest now Meghan, for you will meet many trials before you can truly rest again . . .*

I woke to the sound of metal clanging and a male voice shouting, "Breakfast!"

Groaning, I sat up and placed a hand to my forehead. Had I slept straight through the night? Feeling somewhat sheepish, I crawled out of my cot and slipped on my shoes, then pushed the door open onto a scene of rambunctious chaos. Children, young and old, were scattering everywhere. Some squealed in delight, abandoning their morning chores, while others grumbled as they dragged themselves from their cabins, still in their pajamas. I followed the stream of children to the town center where a great fire heated the bottom of a pot-bellied cauldron. It wasn't as big or ornate as the Dagda's, but the vessel reminded me of Cade's foster father anyways. I smiled, a bit ruefully, wishing that the attack on Luathara had never happened. I could be at the Dagda's house right now, enjoying his company and warm hospitality.

I stood behind the others, not sure what to do, until a small girl thrust a wooden bowl and spoon into my hand and took off running, giggling as she continued passing out her wares. Small hands, belonging to a gaggle of boys no older than five, gently shoved me forward and I realized that I had somehow joined a line. Eventually I found myself face to face with a boy about my age. He lifted up a large ladle, dipped it into the cauldron, and pulled up a heaping portion of oatmeal. The smell of cinnamon and sweet spices hit my nose, making my stomach growl and my mouth water simultaneously. I blushed a little as I smiled. The boy emptied the thick oatmeal into my bowl and jerked his head to the side. I turned to find a group of young girls offering up baskets of steaming biscuits. I grabbed one from the smallest girl, holding her basket up with all her might as if the fate of the world depended on it.

"Meghan!" a familiar voice called.

I turned my head. Enorah was sitting on the great log of a fallen beech tree, surrounded by a few others I'd seen the day before. I side-stepped a few more of the wildren and made my way towards them.

"Feeling better?" Enorah asked.

"Much," I responded as I dipped my spoon into my breakfast. I took a bite and my eyes grew wide as the sweet, crisp flavors of late summer filled my mouth.

I quickly dug in, hardly noticing Enorah's dancing eyes as she watched me.

"Were you not feeling well last night?" one of the boys asked me.

I glanced up, my mouth closed over the spoon, and thought of an answer. He was tall, but looked a little younger than me. He had the natural beauty and grace I had come to expect from the people of this world, something that would have caused me to gawk a year ago. Being around Cade had raised my standards, apparently.

Enorah swallowed a mouthful of oatmeal, then waved her spoon around like the drunken conductor of a band.

"She isn't sick. She simply had a run in with Cernunnos when we visited the Tree of Life."

The comment had been nonchalant, but by the way everyone's eyes widened, I could tell my so-called run in wasn't something that happened every day.

I glanced up at Enorah. She merely grinned and winked. At the time of the incident, she had been rather floored herself. Obviously she'd had time to let the surprise wear off.

Eventually everyone got back to their breakfast, and by the time I was scraping the last bits out of the bottom of my bowl, it had grown brighter.

A flurry of small children scurried through the scattered diners, collecting dirty bowls. They were quick, too. One minute my bowl was in my hand, the next it was gone. I blinked as a young girl disappeared into the darkness like a twilight sprite.

"So, are you ready to start using that magic of yours?" Enorah asked, planting her hands on the trunk of the beech as she shoved herself back down to earth.

I froze, and for a split second I thought she was talking about the new magic Cernunnos had gifted me. Fortunately, my brain jumpstarted itself and I remembered Cade had left his sister with the responsibility of training me.

"Yes," I said, relaxing a bit, "I'm so ready to learn about my glamour."

"Excellent," Enorah piped. "Why don't you go back to your cabin and change and meet me back here."

I nodded, pushing away from the giant log and headed back towards the small cottage that had become my new, temporary home. I quickly pulled on a pair of pants, a clean shirt and a different sweatshirt than the one I'd been wearing the day before. I considered the small pile of dirty clothes before me and wondered if there was a way to get them clean.

I hope so, I thought, because I only had a few more spare sets with me.

Grabbing my longbow and quiver, just in case we met up with anything creepy, I pushed open the door and stepped out into the early morning light. Meridian, who'd made herself scarce the past several hours, dropped from the treetops somewhere and landed on my shoulder.

Hunt? she sent.

Not planning on it. Magic practice, I returned.

Training

Meridian grumbled her contentment and tucked her head under her wing for a snooze. Sometimes I thought I must have the laziest spirit guide in Eilé.

"Now I hope Caedehn has at least taught you how to find your magic," Enorah cast over her shoulder as she came to a stop at the top of a hill.

We'd left the wildren's village about a half hour ago, taking one of the many paths trailing off into the forest. The day was sunny and pleasantly warm, just as any mid-summer day should be. Enorah led the way, her stride strong and confident, reminding me so much of her brother. I bit my lip as a pang of longing hit me, but just as quickly I shook the thought from my head. *Honestly Meghan, he's been gone two days . . .*

Readjusting the quiver of arrows on my back, I tried not to think about it anymore. If I dwelled too long on what could be happening with Cade, then I was certain to drive myself crazy. Instead, I tried to remember what Enorah had just asked me. Oh yeah, if Cade had taught me how to find my magic. Taking a breath, I answered her, "Yes, he has."

I felt slightly winded from climbing the hill, but then the land leveled out. Enorah nodded towards a small clearing and started setting her own gear next to a large stone. She gestured for me to join her in the meadow, and once we were standing opposite each other, she crossed her arms and studied me for a moment.

"We'll start with just getting used to the feel of your magic and how it works," she said. "I want you to locate the source of your glamour, then let it expand to its furthest limits. Don't go too fast; you want it to suffuse your blood slowly."

I nodded and closed my eyes, picturing the small flame burning next to my heart. I almost gasped when the image of a pale blue rose jumped into my mind with it, but then I remembered that the extra magic had taken up residence next to mine.

The magical rose petals started to peel back and the glittering, pale blue power of Cernunnos's gift began to spill forth, hungry to be released. *No, not yet. You have to stay closed inside the flower until you're needed!* I bit my lip and thought about how I was going to do this without letting it all escape and without giving away its presence. I gritted my teeth and willed the petals to close just a little. Reluctantly, the new power obeyed and the bright blue magic dimmed. I took a deep breath and winced at my pounding head. Ignoring the ache in my temples, I shifted my internal view just enough to catch a glimpse of my own magic. The flame greeted me like an old friend, and to make sure I had the right magic, I made it dance and flicker ever so slightly.

"Got it," I hissed past the pain.

"Good, now let it grow. Fan the flame until it can't get any bigger."

Taking a deep breath, I carefully willed the flame to grow. Slowly, the fire next to my heart grew brighter, bigger. As my own magic flared, the blue rose of Cernunnos began unfurling again. This time it was harder to coax it into submission.

When it seemed like the rose wouldn't obey me any further, I quickly capped my own magic, not allowing it to grow any larger. The rose stopped blooming, and with sheer willpower alone, I forced it to close back up. Sweat beaded on my forehead and my jaw hurt from clenching my teeth so tight. The power in the rose tickled my senses, but I refused to let it go. I could feel more than tell the amount of magic that still wished to be released. Like the heavy weight of a massive lake pressing against an unstable dam. Well, I just had to figure out how to reinforce that dam.

Training

"Okay," I said, my mouth feeling parched, "I'm at my limit."

Technically, I felt like I could release loads more of my magic, but I was afraid it I did, the rose would burst into full bloom and join it. I'd just have to make do with what I had control over at the moment.

"Good," Enorah answered. "Now, all I want you to do for today is practice expanding and drawing in your magic so you get used to the sensation. Hopefully by the end of the week, if you practice every day, you'll be able to do it without consciously thinking about it."

I nodded, then drew my magic back down into a tiny flame and opened my eyes. A sharp pain cut across my vision as the rose tried to crack open once again, but the glamour obeyed me more quickly this time when I forced it down. A slight thrill of triumph shot through me. I was certain I could learn to balance both my sources of power with enough practice.

I made a mental note to wander off on my own whenever I could to practice that particular drill in full force. I wanted to be prepared when the Morrigan struck, but I had no idea what letting my magic flare to its full strength might do. Best to do it where no one could see.

For the rest of the morning, Enorah simply taught me some basic spells I could cast using my magic. As I practiced fluctuating my own glamour, she helped me memorize the words and actions that went along with these simple charms. For instance, by speaking the ancient word for 'sleep' and whispering it into someone's ear, or pointing my finger to my own while gathering a small bit of my magic, I could put someone or myself into a deep sleep.

When I arched my eyebrow at her, she merely shrugged. "It might come in handy some day. I've used it many times on myself when I didn't want the children disturbing me after a long night standing guard."

Once I felt like I had a good grasp on the expanding and contrasting exercises for my magic, she showed me how to gather up a small bead of glamour to use in the spells she'd taught me.

For another hour, I worked on drawing away small beads of my magic. It was simple, really, once Enorah explained the concept to me. First, I had to let my magic grow to a large flame, then I would simply pull away a tiny fragment of it, like gathering cotton candy on a paper cone, only instead of making a beehive of spun sugar, I was concentrating the glamour into a tiny pebble of magic. It took me a few tries to get it just right, but after several minutes I was whipping out beads of magic like I'd done it all my life. By the time we headed back for the village, I was glowing with confidence. Enorah couldn't stop telling me how well I'd done and that she was certain by the end of the month, I'd be a force to reckon with.

We made it back home just in time for lunch, and after I finished eating with the others, I sought out a quiet spot just beyond the edge of the village to think. I wanted time to let my thoughts wander, without any distractions.

Despite my determination, and so far, success, at hiding my new wealth of magic, I was still terrified that somehow I'd let it slip that an antlered being of power had placed a god's share of glamour into my hands. Yes, it was only my first day of practice and so far Cernunnos's gift had obeyed me when it tried to flare, but I had also only been able to expand my own magic to half its potential before I couldn't control that other source of power any longer.

Picking up a stick and pushing away a few of the leaves plastered to the ground, I opened up a small space on the damp earth and started drawing random images. After a few moments I paused, glancing around the open meadow I had settled in. I wondered if this would be far enough away to practice taming Cernunnos's magic. Regardless of my fear and trepidation, I was pretty certain that I could whip it into shape if I just worked with it; practiced that simple exercise Enorah had taught me over and over again until I could open my magic up entirely without affecting the pale blue rose that sat next to it.

You'll have your chance, I promised it.

As if the foreign well of power heard me, the rose pulsed once, a brilliant, electric blue, then settled back into being a young, dormant bud.

Breathing a mental sigh of relief, I continued doodling and another worry invaded my mind. I had no idea how I was going to keep this secret once Cade returned. Surely he'd notice I was hiding something and despite what he'd told me about the practice of shíl-sciar, I couldn't risk the truth slipping out that way.

"Something troubling you?"

I yelped at the sound of Enorah's voice, snapping the stick I'd been using to draw. She smiled and dropped down from behind the giant beech tree I'd been using as a backrest.

"So, spill. You can talk to me, I'm the only friend you've got right now in this strange and wonderful world of ours."

Enorah arched her eyebrows in anticipation and I allowed myself a little smile. I couldn't tell her what was really bothering me, so I went with what she probably already assumed.

"I'm worried about Cade, well, and all of us. I can't hide here forever and it's only a matter of time before the Morrigan figures out how to get beyond the magic that protects the Weald."

Enorah crossed her arms and leaned back against the tree. She nodded and sighed.

"True, but Cade is very capable. He's been dealing with her his whole life you know. If anyone can evade the Morrigan it's my brother."

"I know, but I still worry."

We remained silent for a while, listening to the fires from the village crackle, the scent of their smoke spicing the pleasant summer air. Animals, some familiar to me, some not, scurried in the branches above and the underbrush below, evading predators or searching out food. The brilliant colors of the forest seemed more vibrant here than they ever were at home, and I wondered if it was a result of the living magic that thrived all around us. I so wanted to forget about all my worries and drink it all in, but then a new thought occurred to me. Enorah had taught me a few handy spells this morning, could there be a charm that might help me hide the secret of my new magic?

Clearing my throat, I glanced over at Cade's sister. With her arms still crossed, she had her face tilted towards the sky. I imagined she was doing what I wished to do: taking in the beauty of the forest in all its glory.

"Enorah," I said tentatively.

She made a sound of acknowledgement.

I took a deep breath. Okay, here goes . . .

"Is it possible to use my glamour to, um, hide information I don't want anyone else to know?"

She lowered her head and trained her sharp eyes on me. I pursed my lips and reached for a new stick, hoping to seem only slightly interested in an answer.

"Why do you ask?" she said after some time.

I shrugged. "Just in case. There are some things I want to keep to myself for now and I'm afraid I'll accidentally let them slip before I'm ready to share them."

"No one can force you to share your secrets Meghan. Well, perhaps the Morrigan could if she got a hold of you and used her dark magic."

Ignoring her use of the word secret and instead latching onto the Morrigan's name, I nodded vigorously. I had only really been thinking about keeping the knowledge of my new magic from Cade, but if his mother found out . . . ? I shuddered. That would be beyond disastrous.

"Yes, that's exactly it. I'm safe for now, but as soon as I leave the Weald there's a good chance the Morrigan could corner me. I'd like to be prepared."

"There's a way," Enorah said slowly, quietly. "It isn't known to many, and I learned it a long time ago, when I lived a different life."

I arched a brow, but she held up a hand.

"Please, don't ask." She smiled a sad smile. "In fact, it's this very trick I'm going to teach you that keeps those memories away from prying minds."

My curiosity ached to know what her dark secret was, but I could tell from the sudden change in her demeanor that her past was a book best left unopened. Besides, Enorah was my friend and a good friend didn't pry.

"Oh," I said instead, "I'd never press you Enorah if you didn't want to tell me-"

Again, she held up a hand and shook her head, cutting me off. "I know Meghan, don't fret. Now," she inhaled and pushed away from the moss-encrusted tree trunk, "the convenient thing about this spell is that you only have to use it once for every secret you want to keep, and then it takes care of everything else for you."

I gave her an incredulous look.

Enorah merely smirked and said, "Imagine a spider, with a hundred legs instead of eight."

I wrinkled my nose at her. I had nothing against spiders, but they weren't my favorite things in the world. And to imagine one with a hundred legs? Eww. But if that's what I had to do, then so be it.

"Now, this spider lives in your subconscious, sort of like your magic, and it spins a web in the corner of your mind. Once it's established, you give it the knowledge you want to keep hidden from all prying minds and it will wrap it up like an insect and place it in the center of the web. Any words or other thoughts that come to you about the secret you keep will be snatched up by the spider's legs and added to the web. Only you can look at them, no one else can, no matter how powerful they are."

Wow. I simply gaped at Enorah. That was a convenient trick.

"Where on earth did you learn how to do that?" I breathed.

She shook her head. "Can't tell you that, and you mustn't let anyone know I taught you. Very few Faelorehn know how to cast this particular spell and it's not something I should be teaching others."

"Oh Enorah, I'm sorry," I reached out to her, feeling guilty that I'd put her in such a position. But I wasn't sorry I'd be learning this rare bit of magic. I needed it.

Enorah grabbed my hand, her eyes shining. "You are my friend, Meghan. And you are dear to my brother. Of course I don't regret teaching you. Now," she cleared her throat and smiled, "are you sure you're up to this? You did spend half the day practicing with your magic. Do you want to wait a day or two?"

"No," I said automatically.

At her slight look of surprise I smiled sheepishly. "I feel perfectly fine, honest."

"Okay then. Here's how you create your very own spider . . ."

I stood up straighter, all my attention on my tutor.

"First, you have to separate out a small granule of your magic, about the size of a marble, just like we practiced today. With me so far?"

I nodded and closed my eyes. Since it was so fresh in my mind, creating the marble-sized sphere of glowing blue was a cinch. And even better, Cernunnos's rose remained tightly furled.

"Next, repeat these words after me: *Caerah nost, foreth setten aevoreh feain.*"

I opened my eyes, almost losing control over my tiny ball of magic. "Huh?" I said. "What does that mean?"

"It basically means: *Hold fast the secret I wish to keep.* Simple enough words, but since they are spoken in the language of the ancients, they hold more power than others."

"Is that the same language I hear you and Cade and the Dagda speak sometimes?"

Enorah shook her head, her eyes somber. "No, that's a different language."

I opened my mouth to ask more, but Enorah interrupted me.

"Do you need me to repeat them?"

"Please," I answered.

She said the phrase several more times and when I was sure I had it, I closed my eyes again and found that little sphere of magic waiting for my instructions.

"Caerah nost, foreth setten aevoreh feain."

My accent wasn't as smooth as Enorah's, and I'm pretty sure I mispronounced a few of the words, but the blue sphere of my magic burst forth like a supernova. I squeaked and fell to the ground, my rear end making contact with a damp pile of leaves. I blinked away the shock and when I focused inwardly, I saw a tiny blue spider, busy making a web in the corner of my mind. She was pale turquoise, just like my magic, but had a lovely red and black pattern on her back. She was actually kind of cute.

"It worked!" I breathed.

"Good," Enorah said, standing somewhere above me. "Now, take whatever information you want to remain hidden, and hand it over to the spider. Just picture it and say it in your mind. When the spider grabs it and takes it to the web, you're all done."

I nodded, closing my eyes again and forgetting about the soggy earth soaking into my pants. I found the spider again, busy with her web, and told her about the secret magic Cernunnos had given to me and how I needed her to hide it and any other thoughts I had about it. The spider reached out with her multiple legs, long, delicate strands of pure, raw magic, and grabbed up all the thoughts about my extra source of power. She gathered them together, like those little word magnets used to write poetry on a refrigerator, and spun her beautiful silk around them, securing them in her web. I smiled again and sighed.

"All finished?" Enorah asked as she gave me a hand up.

"Yes," I said with relief.

"One more thing to know. You can destroy the spell any time you wish. Just simply find the spider and its web in your mind and speak the word *duantis*. It means 'done'. Also, if you let your glamour run down, like if you visit the mortal world and stay there for a long time, your spell with die off on its own."

I nodded, committing the word to memory with the others I'd learned.

Feeling a hundred times better now that I'd found a way to keep my secret safe, I headed back to the village with Enorah. We planned on going out tomorrow once again to practice with my glamour, but I had the whole afternoon free.

"So, is there anything else you'd like to know about our daily life here?"

Enorah's bright tone of voice was a pleasant change from her earlier, somber mood, so I took advantage of the situation and said, "Actually, I'd like to know how you clean your laundry."

Training

Laughing, Enorah swung an arm around my shoulder and led me towards the creek.

"Unfortunately, we have to do it the old fashioned way. However," she added, a glint in her eye, "I can show you another trick with your glamour that might help get the job done faster.

Eleven

Arrival

I kept a tally of the days Cade was gone. Yes, it was silly and pathetic and practically drove me crazy, but I couldn't help it. Besides, it helped me keep track of my progress with my magic as well. Every morning, Enorah and I would hike to that hilltop meadow, far enough away from the village that if my magic got a little out of control, it wouldn't damage anyone or anything. We would spend hours there, going over what I'd learned the day before and then Enorah would teach me something new. I always warmed up with the same expand and contrast drill from that first day, and as the days progressed, I became better and better at pushing my magic further without Cernunnos's glamour butting in. A few times it tried to join my own glamour, but I always managed to force it into submission. And anytime I thought about it, that little magical spider living in the corner of my mind would work furiously to keep it secret.

On the tenth day of my stay in the Weald, Enorah taught me how to create a shield of magic. By releasing small amounts of glamour, and sending it out in wide, flexible sheets instead of rolling it up into pebbles, I was able to construct a force field over myself.

Arrival

"Think of it as one of those fountains that looks like a sphere of water," Enorah said.

I wrinkled my nose and pictured water flowing in a continuous stream, a thin film of liquid pouring around a central geyser. Like everything new I tried with my magic, creating the shield was tricky at first, but gradually I became better at it. By the end of our lesson I had the hang of it, and when Enorah threw a stick at me, it bounced off of my invisible shield and clattered into the shrubs growing under the great beech trees surrounding us.

"Good!" she barked. "Now for invisibility . . ."

Invisibility was easily my favorite. Enorah coached me through the process of coating myself in magic. I closed my eyes and took deep breaths through my nose.

"It's just like the fountain, but this time the water pressure isn't nearly as great. You want it to feel like a steady stream of water flowing over every contour of a stone statue."

At first, my magic burst forth and I merely created another shield. My heart skipped a beat when this happened, because the rose tried to burst open once again.

No you don't, I growled inwardly, *you stay just as you are until I need you.*

An image of Cade, standing against the Cúmorrig with the beast's long claws stabbing into his abdomen came to mind. The sharp lick of pain that sliced my heart managed to force the wild magic back where it belonged and only the hairline cracks along the petals' edges showed pale blue. I hated drawing on those memories, but sometimes they were necessary to get Cernunnos's magic to obey. Every time it fought to be released, I got the impression that it was used to being free and didn't like its confinement.

"Okay, steady, let's start over again," Enorah's calm voice crooned.

I nodded and dashed away my fears and anxiety. *Focus Meghan, focus . . .*

An hour later I'd mastered it, and by the end of the second week I could create a shield, become invisible and even fling small bursts of my magic in long tendrils from my fingers or throw it like fireballs in one of my brothers' video games. It was exhilarating and terrifying at the same time, but I always managed to accomplish what challenge Enorah set for me without letting Cernunnos's power slip from my control.

The first few days of the third week progressed almost exactly as the previous days had. I would get up early and eat breakfast with the other wildren and then spend a few hours practicing (I only practiced now since Enorah was satisfied with my progress and thought it best if I just strengthen what I'd learned). After practice, we would return to the village and either play games with the younger kids or participate in archery with the older ones. Enorah even taught me some self-defense maneuvers that we tested out on the bigger boys.

After the evening meal, I would sometimes help out with the chores or read stories to the younger children as they got ready for bed. More often than not, they'd want to hear about the mortal world, so I'd tell them about my mom and dad and brothers, or share tales from my adventures with Tully, Robyn, Will and Thomas. I tried to tell them that my high school woes with my friends weren't real adventures, but they didn't care. They begged for them every night and I always gave in, grateful to somehow reconnect, even on this basic level, with the ones I'd left behind in my other life.

It was no surprise, then, that I soon lost track of the time Cade had been gone. I had grown so used to my new routine and had settled in so well with the wildren that I no longer had time to worry.

Arrival

Of course, when Enorah caught me gazing off longingly into the east one afternoon, she murmured only for my ears to hear, "Three more days Meghan."

I started, not realizing I'd let my mind wander, and then smiled back at her, returning my focus on the arrow I'd placed in my longbow. Gazing at the target in the distance, I took a steadying breath and drew the string to my cheek. *Three more days.* In three more days the four weeks would be up, and Cade would be coming back. My stomach fluttered with anticipation, and as my arrow found the ring just on the outside of the middle of the target, I only hoped that nothing would impede Cade from keeping his promise to return.

That night, I watched the wildren place the wood around the base of the cauldron, their movements well-practiced and fluid, and savored the smell of fresh smoke as the flames licked the side of the great black pot. The muted light of early twilight spread over us and I found my mind wandering off with thoughts of Cade once again.

Now that my magic was well under control, and with Enorah's reminder earlier this afternoon, my mind had the energy to conjure up an image of Cade standing on the edge of the village, telling me he'd be back soon. My heart sped up and I began to fidget with anticipation. I couldn't wait to see him, though I was also afraid of what news he might bring back. I'd been so fixated on getting my magic (and Cernunnos's) under control that I'd forgotten about why Cade had left in the first place. Had he been able to tell the other Tuatha De about the Morrigan's attack? Had he told my mother? And if so, were they going to help us do something about it?

"Thinking about my brother?"

Enorah's voice just a few feet away caused me to fall off the log I was sitting on.

I grumbled and brushed the dead leaves off of my pants as I made room for her. She sat down next to the spot I'd made and dismissed the older children who had managed to get the fire under the cauldron going.

"So," she said as they scattered to get in some good playing time before dinner was ready, "was I right? Were you thinking about Caedehn?"

It was hard to avoid her eyes, even when that was the only thing in the world I wanted to do at the moment, but I sighed and glanced up. There was humor there, like always, but warmth and sorrow as well. There was no doubt in my mind that Enorah loved her brother, but why did she look so sad? Didn't she know I loved him too?

The best way to go about this situation was to answer honestly and then go from there. "Yes, I was thinking about Cade." And just in case she any doubts, I added, "I love him, Enorah."

Enorah bent over, her elbows resting on her knees, and ran her fingers through her curly hair.

"I know you do," she answered softly, "I just need more time to get used to it is all."

I gave her a troubled glance. All this time she'd been helping me with my magic, treating me like a close friend, and she had doubts about my devotion to Cade?

Enorah shook her head and smiled.

"Oh no, not like that." She snorted, then ran her fingers through her hair again. "We've been so busy practicing your magic that we never had time to have this conversation."

I watched as the flames of the fire flickered in her eyes. Suddenly nervous, I swallowed and gave her my full attention. What conversation would that be?

Enorah took a deep breath and said, "I am so happy that my brother found you Meghan. You have no idea how grateful I am. It's just that long before he met you he would bring girls here to introduce to me. I could tell they made him happy, but there was always something off about them. Like deer in the meadow during summer. No inclination to look elsewhere until the good food ran out. They were simply waiting until something better came along. Cade couldn't see it because, well, because he thought he'd finally found someone to love him for who he was."

I listened to Enorah, remaining calm and silent. Strangely, I didn't feel any jealousy towards these previous girlfriends, though a few months ago I may have. Perhaps it was a sign that I understood that there was no need to resent the people who had been too blind or selfish to see the young man I'd grown to love; so shallow that they couldn't look beyond his unfortunate ties to the Morrigan and the battle fury that sometimes overtook him.

"Cade and I, we have been alive a long time Meghan, you must understand we've been looking a long time for that perfect companion." She smiled, but it was the furthest thing from joyful. "Some of us are still looking."

I glanced up and gave her a concerned look.

She shook her head. "Oh no, don't you dare feel sorry for me. I have chosen my life here, among the unwanted children of Eilé. I have enough love here to last several hundred immortal lifetimes."

She laughed, but I was not convinced. My heart gave a small twinge of remorse for Enorah's sake, but I didn't press the issue. Sometimes it was best not to talk about regrets.

"I just wanted you to know that it means a lot to me, that you care for my brother. For once, I feel like I can trust someone else with his heart."

Her statement was so honest, such a reflection of what I could see in her eyes and sense in her presence that I almost started crying. Here was a sister who genuinely loved her brother and although she was grateful for me, I was grateful towards her as well.

I sniffled and placed my hands no her shoulders. "And it means a lot to me too, knowing that Cade has a sister who loves him so much."

Enorah beamed at me, then wiped at her eyes.

"Don't you dare make me cry, Meghan Elam. I can't risk tarnishing my image."

We both laughed then and I gave her a hug.

"Come on, help me stir this soup until the second dinner shift gets here."

We stood, pulling each other up, then took one of the several, giant wooden spoons sticking out of the great cauldron. As we mixed the soup, we laughed and joked together. Enorah told me tales about Cade when they were younger and I told her stories about growing up with my brothers.

By the time the other kids showed up to keep the soup from scalding, both Enorah and I had tears running down our cheeks from laughing so hard.

That night, Enorah and some of the other adults brought out a few bottles of mead to celebrate Lughnasadh. The harvest festival was still a handful of days away, but as Enorah put it, "The denizens of the Weald begin celebrating early and stretch the party out for as long as possible. Besides," she added with an impish grin, filling mugs as she walked around after dinner, "we must acknowledge Meghan's progress with her magic lessons."

A few of the children knew how to play musical instruments, so in no time we had a full-out, forest festival underway in the village square. Enorah even pulled several people up to dance and as a group, we laughed and jigged around the fire, making utter fools of ourselves and having a great time.

By the time I made it to bed in my small cabin, I was dizzy from the mead and general cheer of the evening. As I fell asleep, I thought of the conversation I'd had with Enorah.

Arrival

Smiling, I welcomed dreams of friendship, love and loyalty, and for once I felt like I truly belonged in Eilé.

I woke slowly the next morning, my head still slightly fuzzy from the mead last night, only to find Meridian perched on my headboard. I had been letting her in before bed since the nights had been growing cooler, but she usually slept in the corner where I'd constructed her a small perch.

Meridian hopped down onto my pillow, then fluffed her feathers and nibbled at my ear. Ugh! What a way to wake up in the morning. Grumbling, I rolled over and grabbed the spare pillow, clamping it over my head. Meridian screeched in avian outrage at my attempt to ignore her.

Up! she blared into my head.

Meridian! Go back to sleep. I don't even know if the sun's up yet!

Outside! she insisted.

Groaning, I threw back the sheets in frustration, immediately hissing as the cold air hit me. I grabbed the warm cloak Enorah had lent me and slipped on my shoes, yawning and cursing my spirit guide at the same time. Honestly, the way she disdained the cold you'd think she'd want to stay in as long as possible.

I stepped outside into a fog bank, the light of dawn barely cutting away at the dark morning. No one else was stirring. Uh huh, just as I'd thought. I envied them their lack of pestering spirit guides. I wrapped the cloak more tightly around myself and turned to go back inside. I could probably get one more hour of sleep in before Enorah woke me up for breakfast, and I was more than ready to get back under the warm covers. Unfortunately, Meridian darted out the door and almost slammed into me.

"Hey!" I shouted, falling back so her wings wouldn't smack me in the face.

Glowering as she disappeared into the thick mist, I made to turn back towards the door when something caught my eye. I squinted into the distance, trying to figure out what was moving behind the thick wall of mist. A heartbeat passed and the shape grew more solid, mimicking a figure wearing a long, hooded cloak. I froze in place, my heart pounding against my ribcage. Who could be coming into the village this early and why hadn't the people standing guard warned us?

Just as I was about to dart into my cabin and bolt the door, the person stopped and pulled back his hood. I sucked in a breath and clasped my hands to my mouth. Cade. Forgetting my warm bed and that coveted extra hour of sleep, I bolted from where I stood and sprinted across the village square.

Cade watched my progress, his calm face slowly changing, as if a light within had been lit and was slowly growing. When I was five feet away from him I threw myself into his open arms. I couldn't help myself. I had missed him so much and his smile was enough to charm the common sense right out of me.

For a long minute I simply stayed where I was, pressed up against Cade's solid strength and blocking out all other senses. From the way he pulled me close, his arms like a vice, I could tell he shared the sentiment. I could feel the tears forming in my eyes, but I ignored them.

"You're early," I said.

Then I wanted to kick myself. *You haven't seen him for nearly four weeks, worrying almost the entire time that he might be getting torn to shreds by a pack of faelah, and that's what you come up with to say to him?*

"I would have been even earlier if I could have managed it. I missed you so much," he murmured into my ear.

Pure joy unfurled in my stomach and I sighed, leaning into him even further.

"Well!" someone said rather loudly.

Arrival

Cade reluctantly let me go, setting me gently on the ground. Oh, I guess I'd had him in another one of my tourniquet hugs . . . I bit my lip and turned my head, my hands still resting on Cade's arms.

Enorah stood there with her hands placed casually on her hips. Of course she was up. She was always up this early. And behind her stood a group of sleepy-eyed children. Yay! An audience for my lovely display of overactive hormones.

"If I knew keeping Meghan captive here would result in more frequent visits, brother, then I would have dragged her to the Weald long ago."

There was humor in Enorah's voice and after our conversation the night before, I knew there was sisterly affection there too.

Cade grinned and I relaxed even further.

"Hello, sister mine. I'm glad to be back."

"Breakfast is in half an hour." Then she added with a glint to her eye, "That should give you plenty of time to get reacquainted."

Enorah turned and walked away, barking out orders to the children who'd stood behind her. Groaning, they scattered to start getting the breakfast ready.

Suddenly, the village was silent once again, the approaching dawn softening the blanket of fog that surrounded us.

Meridian chittered in the tree above and a soft whine from behind Cade let me know she was talking with Fergus.

Go play, I sent to her.

She responded with a joyful screech and Fergus's spirited bark let me know that Cade had told him the same thing.

I turned my head and glanced up only to find Cade's green eyes regarding me so intensely that it became hard to breathe.

"Meghan," he said, right before pulling me close into another embrace.

I returned the hug and pressed myself as close to him as possible; to ensure myself that he was truly here and that he was real. Silently, Cade led me away from the center of the village and headed towards a small meadow, conveniently screened by a thicket of brush and large stones.

We were blessedly alone and there were a million things I wanted to ask him: did he find out about the Morrigan's plans? Was she organizing her army of faelah? Did she really have someone helping her? Could the Dagda aid us? Did we need to stay in the Weald longer? But none of those questions came up. Instead, I stood up on my toes and leaned into him, eager to simply absorb his essence.

Feeling suddenly mischievous, I whispered into his ear, "Would you like to see what I can do?"

I didn't wait for an answer. Drawing on my several days worth of practice, I merely allowed some of my magic to flood over me. Only the tightening of Cade's hold on my arms let me know I had disappeared from sight. I wiggled out of his grip and slipped away from him before he could realize what I was doing. He turned in place, reaching out as he scanned the surroundings looking for me.

"Not so fun when the joke is on you, is it?" I crooned from his right.

I had no idea what had come over me. I had missed him terribly all these weeks, and now that he was back I was trying to hide from him? But the idea of Caedehn MacRoich, faelah bounty hunter extraordinaire, fumbling around in a foggy clearing searching for me, sent a thrill of exhilaration through my blood.

Cade darted and I just barely missed getting caught. My heart was pounding and a flood of adrenaline helped me get out of the way. I'd have to be careful; he was incredibly fast and I needed to concentrate if I wanted the magic to keep working.

Cade repositioned himself and bowed his head, his eyes closed, as he took long, deep breaths from his nose.

What on earth was he doing?

Nervous, I took a small step back and a leaf crunched under my foot. I could barely hear it, but it was enough for Cade to locate me and pounce. I squeaked when his arms wrapped around me, secure but not painful. I squirmed, but there was no way I was going to escape that grip.

My back was to his chest and he lowered his mouth, pressing it against my ear, then murmured, "Looks like you're trapped. Whatever will you do now Meghan?"

His voice was low and seductive, and I couldn't stop the tremor that ran down my spine. Answering him was also out of the question. He kissed me lightly below my ear and I willingly turned in his arms. The cool sensation of my invisible shield of magic melted away and when his lips finally met mine, I no longer cared about escaping. I no longer *wanted* to escape. Cade's grip loosened and he dropped his hands to my hips. I mimicked him, but instead of staying at his waist, my hands began pulling at his shirt. Following my lead, Cade pushed his fingers under my t-shirt and ran his palms up my bare back, bringing me closer. I was utterly lost in sensation and all I wanted was to be as close to Cade as possible. The timid Meghan had disappeared, along with all my other inhibitions as well, apparently.

Someone cleared their throat and Cade stopped, dragging his mouth away from mine. One of his hands remained pressed against the bare skin of my back, while the other rested halfway up my stomach. My own fingers were gripping the hem of his shirt and we were both breathing heavily. From the look on Cade's face, his mind had to be just as scrambled as my own.

"I hate to interrupt your reunion," Enorah said, her voice dripping with amusement, "but there are young children present just around that rock outcropping and if I don't stop you now, I'm afraid you'll both forget you're in the great wide open. Besides," she added with a wide smile, "breakfast is almost ready and I'm sure you're both very hungry."

Enorah winked as she turned to leave, and I silently cursed her for the blush her comment caused. Cade hadn't seemed to notice, however. He pulled me closer, his arms wrapped around me again, and took a long, deep breath.

"I missed you," he murmured against my hair.

Forgetting my embarrassment, I returned the gesture. "Me too."

We walked back to the center of the village, hand in hand. Fergus and Meridian returned just as the first rays of morning light pierced through the fog. As we ate, Cade entertained the youngest of the wildren with tales of his battles against the faelah. Me, well, I just sat back and enjoyed the fact that Cade had come back to me in one piece.

Once breakfast was over, Cade and I helped everyone clean up, despite their protests. Afterwards, I led Cade away to the meadow where Enorah and I had practiced. We spent the entire morning there, with me showing Cade all I had learned and him demonstrating a few more tricks. By the time we returned to the village we had missed the noontime meal, so by nightfall we were starving.

Dinner that night was a casual event. Some of the older teens had gone hunting earlier, so we ended up roasting hunks of meat and vegetables over the bonfire. I did my best not to hoard Cade all to myself. After all, Enorah deserved some time with him as well.

As the fire died down, the younger kids headed off for bed. Eventually only Cade, Enorah and I were left. The logs crackled and popped, the hot flames whispering along with the sounds of the forest creatures at night. Silence descended upon us, but then Enorah let out a big yawn, dumped the dregs from her mug into the fire and stood up, stretching.

"I'm going to call it a night, but I'll see you in the morning, okay?"

She glanced at me, then her brother, and although it was hard to see in the dark, a glint of regret crossed her eyes. I frowned, but Cade nodded before I could ask what was wrong. With one last smile, Enorah turned and headed towards her cabin, leaving Cade and me to soak up the warmth of the fire.

Cade reached over and pulled me close, kissing my forehead and wrapping his cloak around me.

We have to leave in the morning, his shíl-sciar words brushed against my mind.

I sighed. So that explained Enorah's morose mood. I figured as much.

You seem disappointed. I thought you were eager to get to the Dagda's, he continued.

I am. I've just grown fond of the Weald, I guess.

Cade took a deep breath, letting it out slowly. *I would rather you stayed here, where you're safe.*

I can't hide forever Cade, and that's not the reason I'm reluctant to leave.

I lifted my chin up so I could see his face. *I like it here and I'll miss Enorah and all the kids.*

Cade chuckled and murmured, breaking the silence, "Oh, you're definitely a keeper if you have the patience to like Enorah."

I smacked him. "Is that the only reason you can think of for keeping me?"

I meant it as a joke, but his green eyes darkened and his voice grew deeper as he answered, "Oh no, far from it. You're so beautiful Meghan. Your eyes," he bent down and kissed each of my eyelids, then gently ran his fingers through my hair.

Kathara

"Your hair, your nose with its freckles." He smiled and nipped my nose with his lips. "And your unrelenting spirit."

He lifted a hand and pressed it against my skin, right above the space between my heart and my magic. And of course, my glamour let out a burst of energy, the blue rose next to it cracking open to see what was going on.

I felt as if I was melting under the warmth of Cade's endearments, but I had just enough sense to get control of Cernunnos's gift. *Stay shut, you*, I growled at it.

"You're perfect Meghan. How could I ever let you go?"

He bent down and kissed me for real that time, drawing it out so that I thought it would never end. The fire grew suddenly hot and I had to pull away to catch my breath.

I cuddled next to him so that my hand was placed over his heart. "I don't plan on ever letting you go either," I murmured drowsily, then yawned and felt my eyes drift shut. I could so fall asleep just as I was, with Cade as my mattress and blanket all in one.

Before I could register what was happening, Cade had lifted me up into his arms and was carrying me across the dark village square.

"What are you doing?" I murmured, my eyes still working to remain open.

"I'm going to get you settled in your cabin. You can hardly keep your eyes open."

"Not true," I said as I fought another yawn.

Cade snorted as he managed to push open my cabin door. In one second I was safe in his arms, and the next I was being tucked under my quilt. It wasn't nearly as warm and didn't smell quite as good as Cade.

Go to sleep Meghan, he whispered into my mind. *I need to check the perimeter of the village one last time, then I'll join you.*

A shiver coursed through me at his promise and I was determined to stay awake until he got back. Unfortunately, that

- 164 -

Arrival

resolve waned and I was asleep within five minutes of curling up in bed. I never even heard Cade come in after his inspection, and it wasn't until morning that I realized the warm sense of safety I felt was really his arms wrapped tightly around me.

Twelve

Lasair

The sky was still dark when Cade and I left the small village behind. Enorah was up to see us off of course, but none of the other wildren were awake.

Cade's sister met us outside of our cabin, her arms crossed with her elbows resting in her hands. She was like a silent wraith of the forest; serious and grim. Her current mood, so unlike the general cheerful one from the past several weeks, made my stomach churn into knots. She was worried about her brother; about the both of us. Suddenly, the idea of leaving seemed extremely unappealing. Why couldn't we just hide in the Weald with all the other castoff children? Why not just wait out the Morrigan's fury?

Because she will not rest until she has had her revenge, Meghan, or your power . . .

The words seemed to whisper in the wind, though the eerily still forest was blanketed in a thick, static fog. I shivered. The words weren't from Cade or Meridian, perched far above us. Nor were they from my own conscience. Yet I knew who they had come from, and he was right. Cernunnos didn't give me that magic so I could sit in the middle of the Weald and hide. He had given it to me so that I could go out and fight against the evil that threatened all that I loved.

Suddenly I was angry and that anger helped burn away the fear. How dare the Morrigan threaten me, threaten all of us? Who cares if she was an all-powerful goddess. What right did she have to take what she wanted and hurt those who couldn't defend themselves? For some bizarre reason, an image of Michaela West and Adam Peders and their gang of friends popped into my head. I hadn't thought about my high school tormentors in months, yet, in a way, they were very similar to the Morrigan. They too took what they wanted and treated people like dirt. Well, I had fought back against them and I'd fight back against the Morrigan as well.

"Meghan?"

Cade's voice snapped me out of my internal tirade.

I blinked up at him.

"Are you okay? You seem tense."

Quickly, I smiled and hoped my face didn't reflect the way I felt.

I leaned into him and said, "Yes, just a little sad about leaving."

Cade relaxed, then helped me settle my now full backpack and quiver on my shoulders.

"Before you go," Enorah said, lifting up her hands. Resting on her forearms were two daggers, one slightly larger than the other, enclosed in identical sheaths. "For both of you, to keep you safe."

"Enorah," Cade whispered, his voice gruff as he lifted the larger knife, "where in Eilé did you get these?"

He drew the dagger from its cover, the bright silver blade clean and sharp. It was about the length of his forearm and the head of a hound decorated the pommel.

Not knowing what else to do, I mimicked him and examined the other dagger. Mine was shorter and instead of a hound's head, the profile of a merlin adorned the top of the hilt.

Luathara

"This is so beautiful Enorah," I murmured, tears returning to my eyes.

"Keep them on you at all times, it will give me peace of mind."

Cade reached out and grabbed his sister into a tight hug. Enorah left one arm free, so she used it to pull me into the embrace as well, the three of us fighting our brimming emotions. Eventually, Cade loosened his grip and we both paid Enorah our final farewells, waving as we turned down the trail that would take us out of the Weald.

"Let me know what the final plan is," she called after us. "Those of us who are able would be honored to help in the battle against the Morrigan."

Cade only nodded, waving one last time as Enorah's figure disappeared behind the shroud of mist.

By the time we made it out of the cave behind Luathara, the sky was bright with morning light. The castle itself stood quiet, so different from how it had been when Cade and I had fled four weeks ago.

We entered the back of the castle, through the great oak door that now stood in the repaired wall. Inside, the castle was dark and cold and I could barely make out some of the colors in the tapestries decorating the walls.

"Where is everyone?" I whispered.

Despite my attempt to speak quietly, my voice carried through the vast hall.

"At their homes in Kellston. My mother could still target the castle just to spite me."

"Oh Cade," I murmured as I moved closer to him, "I'm sorry."

He stopped his forward movement and stepped up to me, taking my face in his hands.

"It's not your fault, Meghan. We'll continue with the construction when we've defeated the Morrigan."

I nodded, my thoughts grim nonetheless. *And how are we to defeat a powerful Celtic goddess?*

By pooling our resources.

I frowned at him.

He smiled and traced one of my eyebrows with his thumb. "I managed to visit most of the Tuatha De while you were stuck in the Weald with my sister, busy training your glamour to answer to your beck and call. Remember? They have agreed to meet with Danua and discuss our options with regards to the Morrigan."

Just because they'd agreed to meet, didn't mean they would help. I wondered if Cade had learned anything else about the person who was helping his mother regain her power so quickly, but that was a question for another time.

Taking a deep breath, I nodded, my head moving between Cade's hands.

"In a week we'll meet up with them at Erintara."

I tried not to wince, but Cade noticed and arched a brow. I sighed and glanced away, attempting to find something to focus on in the dark hallway.

"I haven't spoken to my mother since that day I told her I'd have nothing to do with her."

Cade chuckled and pulled me closer, resting his chin on the top of my head. "She is your mother, Meghan. No matter how often you might disagree, she will always care about you."

I took a breath and said softly, "You're mother doesn't care about you."

Cade stiffened and I immediately regretted my words. I pulled away and looked him in the eye, "I'm sorry. I shouldn't have said that."

He only shook his head and took my hand, drawing me towards the stairs. "No Meghan, it's the truth, and that's why I have no qualms about challenging her. She wishes to overthrow Danua and to be the new high queen of Eilé. Imagine what life would be like for all of us if she succeeds. That is why the entire contingency of the Tuatha De have agreed to this meeting. We must take action before it is too late. We can no longer turn a blind eye as the Morrigan grows in power."

As we wound our way downstairs, I thought about why Cernunnos had given me the extra power that day I visited the Tree of Life. Could he, for some reason I couldn't fathom, really be trying to help me? Or did he have some other ulterior motive? Naturally, that thought didn't comfort me as we stepped through the castle's main doors.

Speirling greeted us in the courtyard, whinnying and tossing his great black head. I smiled, forgetting my dismal thoughts. I'd missed the huge horse. Once we were both secure on the stallion's back, Cade led him out into the fields and up the hill towards the dolmarehn that would take us to the Dagda's. Meridian followed us from the sky and Fergus trotted ahead, keeping an eye out for faelah. Being at Luathara again had made me nervous, but between the castle and the large dolmarehn, we saw no sign of the Morrigan's underlings.

Once through the great stone gateway, Cade nudged Speirling in the ribs and the black stallion veered to the left, stepping gingerly around the stones and lumps of grass that decorated the otherwise barren landscape.

"Where are we going? The Dagda's is east of here, not north."

Cade turned and threw me a mischievous smile. "We have a stop to make along the way."

"What stop?"

I leaned forward and tried to see further ahead of us. A crop of tall, rugged hills loomed far in the distance, their jagged tips standing stark against the sun's early light.

You'll see, Cade whispered in my mind, his words a beautiful pale pink.

I grumbled to myself but simply leaned in closer to him and rested my cheek against his broad back. I inhaled deeply, and his scent helped calm my spirit. Speirling's easy breathing and rhythmic plodding must have lulled me to sleep because I jerked awake some time later.

How long have I been out? I sent to my spirit guide.

Meridian swooped from the sky and came to rest on my shoulder.

An hour, she answered.

That surprised me. Who would have ever thought I could sleep for an hour atop a horse?

I glanced around at our surroundings, not bothering to question Cade any further about our destination. I would find out eventually. We had reached the rugged hills I had seen earlier, but a broad, smooth river snaked along their base, cutting us off from the thick woods on the other side. There were plenty of trees on our side as well, but those across the river seemed to have a more powerful aura to them, as if they were guarding something.

"It's beautiful," I whispered.

Cade turned his head to glance down at me. He looked weary, but a smile graced his perfect face nonetheless.

"I have a surprise for you."

I returned his smile. "You always seem to have a surprise for me."

He laughed and nudged Speirling on.

We followed the river's edge for another half hour and I occupied my time listening and looking for the birds I could hear chirping in the trees. Eventually the land sloped downward and drew level with the river. A small stream flowed from the hills to meet up with the larger tributary and a wide beach on either side suggested that it was shallow enough to cross.

Cade pulled Speirling to a stop and slid off his back, helping me down once he was steady on his feet.

Fergus, who had been jogging between us and the unseen Otherworldly creatures he chased, broke free of the brush and joined us on the small stretch of bare land.

"Let's see if our friends are nearby," Cade murmured.

He lifted his fingers to his mouth and let loose a harsh whistle.

A moment went by, then another. In the distance a horse whinnied and Speirling answered it.

I glanced up at Cade, the question plain on my face.

He lifted a hand and grinned. "Just wait," he said.

I turned back towards the river, my eyes on the opposite shore. Soon the air filled with the voices of several horses, calling out to one another. A faint rumble followed shortly after, and then the rumbling overtook the sound of the wide, rushing river. A film of dense mist still hugged the low parts of the land, but the sun had managed to burn through a few patches of it, the bright rays painting pools of yellow on the ground.

The pounding grew louder and in the next moment a herd of horses broke free of the trees. Like a flock of birds, they moved as one and followed the stream down to the river bank. I gasped so loud that I stumbled in place, Cade catching hold of me.

Led by the most beautiful cream colored mare I had ever seen, the herd tore through the shallow river, sending up great plumes of water. I had half a mind to bolt; to find a tall bolder to take refuge on so I wouldn't get trampled, but the magnificence of the herd kept me glued in place. Well, that and Cade's firm grip on my arms.

The herd's leader didn't pause until she was a few feet in front of us. Her ears were pinned back against her head and she was breathing heavily.

"Steady now, you know me," Cade said firmly but calmly.

The pale horse drew back on her hind quarters and let out a loud whinny, but as she descended back to the ground, her form faded and morphed into something else entirely.

My mouth dropped open and my eyes grew wide. No longer was I staring at a horse, but a tall woman with great tangles of pale blond hair falling over her shoulders and reaching the backs of her knees. I had seen the Faelorehn transform before, particularly the Morrigan and then Cernunnos, but for some reason this change took me by surprise.

I made a sound that could have been a squeak and pressed myself against Cade. He only smiled softly, squeezing one of my hands in his own, and all I could do was chastise myself for being lame. Honestly, I had within me magic powerful enough to rival the gods, and I was afraid of a tall woman?

The woman who had been the horse just seconds ago turned to her herd and raised a hand. The agitated horses stilled immediately and perked their ears forward, their large eyes now gleaming with intelligence and curiosity. The woman turned back around and eyed me suspiciously, her sharp, clear grey eyes flashing to hazel then gold. She drew in a deep breath through her nose and I distracted myself by counting her freckles. I had a feeling I could be at it all day and I'd never reach the final number.

"Caedehn," she finally said, her voice clear and crisp and her eyes now trained on him. "What brings you to my realm? Is this the lost Faelorehn girl everyone has been speaking of?"

I instantly snapped out of my daze. Okay, two things. One, I wasn't lost and two, everyone was talking about me? Alright, maybe that was a pointless thought. After my mother had announced to her entire court that I was her illegitimate daughter, I couldn't be too surprised that I had become the latest source of gossip in Eilé. But I resented being considered *lost*.

Forgetting my earlier apprehension, I cleared my throat and stepped away from Cade. The horse woman snapped her eyes back to me and I ignored the unease that formed in the pit of my stomach.

"I am Meghan Elam, daughter of Danua, and you are?"

Cade stiffened next to me and for a dreadful moment I was afraid I might have said something to anger the woman. I didn't know her, after all, and the fact that she could take on the guise of a horse meant she was very powerful. Probably one of the Tuatha De; a goddess of the Celts.

I bit my lip and fought the urge to back down. Way to go Meghan . . .

The woman merely arched a pale eyebrow at me and, without smiling or adding any emotion to her voice, she said, "I am Epona, but some call me Rhiannon. I reside over the horses of Eilé."

For about five seconds I simply stared at her, at a loss. Then I remembered reading about her in some of the stories in my Irish mythology book.

"Oh, I'm sorry," I fumbled with my words. "I'm just tired of being talked about like I'm some sort of novelty. I didn't mean to offend you."

I stuck out a hand, hoping to make peace, but Epona merely stared at it for a split second, her own eyes wide. Eventually, her lips quirked up into what could only be considered a smile. She reached out her own hand and took mine, shaking it firmly. A jolt of power shot up my arm and I hissed, fighting the urge to let my own glamour break free. I struggled against the rush of power and gradually my magic quailed. Unfortunately, it took a little more effort to get Cernunnos's gift back in line. A half a minute (and a slight headache) later, it finally settled. Thank goodness I'd had all that time to practice controlling it . . .

Epona released my hand and took a breath, casting her glance on Cade. "So, she has spirit, your Meghan. I guess I shouldn't be surprised, considering she's Danua's daughter."

The horse woman crossed her arms and smirked at me.

Speirling, who had remained strangely quiet this entire time, decided to make his presence known and let out a small whicker, his ears pricked forward and his eyes bright with joy.

Epona forgot us for a moment and glanced over at the black horse. Her face broke into a genuine smile and she stepped forward, her hand reaching out to Cade's stallion.

"Speirling! My dearest, how is Caedehn treating you?"

Speirling tossed his head once and dug at the earth with his hoof.

Epona patted his face and murmured something in the language of Eilé.

Without looking back at us, she sighed and said, "I take it you've come for a horse for Meghan."

"Yes, if you have anyone to spare," Cade responded.

Huh? A horse for me? I blinked up at Cade and though his smile was small, his eyes were bright with humor.

"Very well, I shall ask them."

Epona stepped away from Speirling and faced her herd of horses. She crossed her arms and simply stared at them. As we waited, I took this time to study all of them. They all resembled Speirling: strong, sturdy animals with that aura of Otherworldly power and intelligence about them. Some were as dark as Cade's horse, while others were pure white or grey or brown. Many were all the shades in between and several more were multi-colored.

Finally, a red stallion trotted forward, tossing his head and whinnying. He was the most brilliant shade of chestnut I'd ever seen on a horse, and he was a bit smaller than Speirling.

The goddess eyed him and said, "Are you certain Lasair? You will be the horse of the high queen's daughter. That's a big responsibility you know."

The red horse merely dug at the ground and rumbled. I could only assume it meant he was sure about taking on the task of carrying me around the countryside.

"Very well," Epona replied, dropping her arms to her sides. "Come, meet your new mistress."

She reached out a hand and gestured for the horse to step up to me. I stiffened for a moment, nervous once again, but the Otherworld didn't have any cars and it would be nice to have my own horse.

"Meghan, this is Lasair, and Lasair, this is Meghan. You will need to rely on one another and trust each other's instincts if you are to work together. My horses do not belong to anyone, Meghan, they serve you willingly and may return to me whenever they please. If you wish Lasair to serve you, then you must be prepared to work as a team. Do you think you can do this?"

I nodded, trying not to flinch as she took my arm and placed my hand against the horse's forehead. As soon as my skin made contact, I could feel his thoughts and concerns. It wasn't exactly the same as speaking to Meridian or using shíl-sciar with Cade, but somehow I knew what he was thinking, what he was feeling.

"He'll obey you now, but you must never abuse his loyalty or his trust."

I pressed my lips together and nodded.

"Thank you, Epona," Cade said, giving her a slight bow.

She nodded sharply, and stepped away from us.

"We will see you in Erintara at the end of the week, I believe."

"Yes," she answered, her voice growing grim and her eyes burning with anger. "I am ready for the battle to come. I will lose no more of my horses to the Morrigan."

She glanced over at Lasair, who had pinned his ears back against his head. I could feel his anger pouring over me, and I took a step back.

"Fear not Meghan. He lost his sister to the Morrigan several years ago, and he has not forgotten it. I believe this is what encouraged him to become your companion. He is ready to defeat her great evil as well."

I nodded and reached out a hand to my new horse. I stroked his neck and slowly his anger melted away. I smiled, sending thoughts of encouragement his way.

We took the extra saddlebags from Speirling and draped them over Lasair's shoulders. He didn't seem to mind, holding still until we had everything secure, including my longbow. I decided to keep the quiver on my back. It seemed more secure there and I didn't want to lose any arrows, especially if there was a chance of being ambushed by faelah at any given time.

Cade gathered up Speirling's reins and climbed onto his back. He then reached out a hand and helped me up behind him before leading the black stallion over to the red one. I was reluctant to get onto Lasair's back without a saddle or bridle, but the horse was calm and I could sense his encouragement. Once settled securely behind his neck, we turned to look at Epona.

"Until I see you in Erintara then. Be sure to stay clear of the faelah and anything else the Morrigan throws your way."

With that, the goddess transformed back into the cream-colored mare, tossing her head and whinnying as she led her herd back across the river.

Lasair watched her and the other horses as they disappeared behind the trees on the opposite riverbank. He whickered softly and I leaned forward to pat his neck. I ran my fingers through his mane and smiled. I could feel his sadness, but his pride was stronger. Casting aside my own doubts and fears, I leaned forward and wrapped my arms around his neck. Lasair nickered with affection and before I knew it, we were on our way toward the Dagda's once again.

We followed the river for an hour before turning south again. The trees eventually gave way to the rocky ground I had grown so familiar with when traveling to the Dagda's. The horses moved at an easy pace, not too fast and not too slow. Just after mid-day I caught a glimpse of a familiar group of hills rising up from the level earth.

"Not much further now," Cade called over his shoulder. "Fergus, go on ahead and let them know we're on the way."

Fergus barked once and took off, Meridian chattering as she hurried after him.

Yes Meridian, I sent after her, *go right ahead.*

I smiled when she sent me an apology. She had grown rather fond of Fergus and ever since nearly losing him in spring to the Morrigan's wrath, she had been even more intent on watching over him.

Settling back into the rhythm of Lasair's smooth gate, I relaxed and prepared myself for an easy end to our journey. Unfortunately, that's not what Fate had in mind. The first wave of faelah exploded from the earth a split second before Meridian's warning screech tore into my mind. The dark creatures rose from the uneven ground as if the soil had been as heavy as tissue paper on their backs. Of course, by the way they were built it didn't surprise me that bursting from the earth was no difficult task. Compact and close to the ground but with powerful legs, the creatures didn't even bother to stop and shake the mud from their hides. They simply emerged and charged, their broad, crocodile-like mouths hanging open, their long spiked tails trailing behind them. Let's just say shock didn't even come close to describing my first reaction.

"Meghan, your bow, quickly!" Cade snarled from Speirling's back.

I snapped out of my stupor and reached down, trying my best to untie the knot holding my bow in place while simultaneously staying atop Lasair. We were still moving forward at a steady pace and the faelah were charging towards us, covering the distance at an alarming rate.

My fingers shook and I could feel sweat breaking out on my forehead. I gritted my teeth as my adrenaline surged, awakening my glamour. I would have loved to just fry our approaching enemy, but unfortunately I had to use my own power to suppress the magic Cernunnos had given me. The blue rose was fighting harder than ever to burst open and spill its magic into the world. Too bad my gut instinct was telling me this wasn't the right time to use it.

I cursed as the first monster slammed into Lasair. He gave a fierce whinny, but kicked out with his front legs, catching the faelah before it could do any damage. I slipped and almost fell, but managed to catch a handful of the horse's mane.

Lasair didn't shy away from the Morrigan's minions like Speirling did. Instead, he rushed towards the downed faelah, lashing out with his hooves and trampling the creature into the ground. For a mere moment I sat stunned, almost forgetting to shift with his movements so I wouldn't tumble to the ground. This wasn't just a horse, this was a warrior.

"Meghan!" Cade called out again.

I looked up to find him clear of Speirling's back. He stood still with his arms spread slightly.

"Don't let their tails lash you and try not to get bitten."

Cade let his head fall back and he closed his eyes, taking long, steady breaths. The reptilian faelah kept emerging from the earth and in the distance I heard the baying of the Morrigan's hellhounds; her Cúmorrig. We were under full attack. She had known we would eventually travel to the Dagda's. All she had to do was wait.

Lasair's furious scream reminded me that we had stopped moving. I glanced at Cade once more as the power of his ríastrad took hold, but a horrible noise demanded my attention elsewhere. I sucked in a breath. More of the scaled faelah had moved in. I gave up on trying to untie my bow and instead reached down and drew the dagger Enorah had given me from its sheath. Thank goodness I had taken her advice and kept it on me.

"Try to stay steady Lasair," I whispered as I crouched low against his back, my heart in my throat. I had practiced defending myself during my stay in the Weald, but none of it had covered fighting from horseback. Still, my instincts told me I stood a better chance if I could just stay on Lasair.

The red stallion whickered softly, his sides heaving from the effort he'd used to kill the first monster. Having Lasair on our side gave me a sense of security, but that slight moment of peace vanished as something dark appeared over the rise in land to the north. I squinted, losing my concentration for a moment as I tried to see what that darkness was. Then it dawned upon me and my heart dropped to my stomach. The hellhounds I'd heard earlier. Dozens of them, and several other faelah as well. Their numbers far outshone the ones we faced that afternoon the Morrigan had lured me into her trap. We were doomed.

Meridian, go get the Dagda. Tell him we need his help! I sent in desperation.

Yes, swift! Meridian sent back.

Lasair pinned his ears flat against his head and snorted in fury, baring his teeth and stomping his feet. I let the three faelah that had surrounded us see my dagger, but whatever Otherworldly magic it might contain, it did nothing to intimidate them.

The creature in front of us hissed and leapt, aiming for Lasair's throat. The horse moved quickly, rising up on his hind legs and striking out with his hooves. He caught the faelah in the head and it went down. Unfortunately that gave the others an opening. They both jumped at the same time and one landed on Lasair's rump. The other aimed for me but I reacted quickly and lashed out with the dagger, stabbing the creature in the chest. It screamed in agony, but the forward momentum threw me off of Lasair. I landed with a thud on the ground, the faelah landing on top of me. I gasped for breath and thrashed at the creature, nearly throwing up as its stench filled my nose. Finally I struggled free, then quickly scrambled to my feet, my dagger ready for another attack.

Fortunately, the creature was dead, a giant welt growing and spewing smoke and gore where I had stabbed it. I pressed the back of my hand to my mouth, fighting the sickness that threatened to rise up. The magic within me still struggled to break free, but I gritted my teeth and fought it along with the nausea. If that army of Cúmorrig fell upon us I might use it, but right now I was willing to fight with what I had.

A harsh whinny tore my attention back onto the battle scene and worry laced my blood as Lasair fought to remove the faelah. He bucked once, getting the one on his rump off, then reached around and bit into another, tearing it free and kicking it. I watched in awe and admiration as the horse pummeled the beasts with his hooves.

He tossed his head and screamed, jogging over to me and turning so that he stood between me and the approaching sea of evil. In the distance I could hear the rumbling of feet pounding the ground and Cade's harsh howl of anger as his battle fury aided him in taking out the first line of monsters.

This couldn't be happening. We were only yards away from the Dagda's home. We had to make it. I wasn't ready to risk using the magic Cernunnos had given me; I wasn't ready to risk losing my only secret weapon . . .

Suddenly furious, I shoved the dagger back into its case and then went to finish untying my bow from Lasair's saddle bag. More of those ground-dwelling faelah closed in, snarling and growling, but they didn't scare me. I calmly drew an arrow from my quiver, placed it in my bow, and took aim. The closest monster was only ten feet away, trying to get around Lasair. It lashed its long tail out like a whip and caught my horse on the shoulder. Lasair screamed in pain and I gritted my teeth, allowing just enough of my magic to flow free in order to ease the tension building inside of me. I released the arrow, letting it take some of my glamour with it. The arrow caught the creature in the throat and brought it down instantly. I sacrificed a few seconds to test my magic again. Straining against the strength of the other source of power, I drew just enough of my glamour out to establish a weak shield. Hey, something was better than nothing, and Enorah would be terribly disappointed in me if I couldn't create a simple defense after all my practice.

Once both my sources of magic were stabilized, I sought out another arrow and readied it, taking aim at one faelah, then the next as they charged towards me. I used just enough of my glamour to keep my shield up and to add extra killing power to my arrows. That other well of magic still burned and clawed to be set free, but I held it in place as sweat poured down my face. I took out three more faelah and listened for Cade among the clatter and cries of battle. His angry shouts assured me he was still fighting, so I kept up the combat on my end. Lasair, too, had proven himself a fierce fighter and he continued to kick and bite and trample as I aimed and shot my arrows.

A screech from above and the thundering of hooves tore me from my concentration. Meridian swooped down out of the sky, diving at the faelah who had managed to sneak up behind me. A shockwave of power hit me and I fell to the ground, my weak defense bursting like a bubble. Oh well, wasn't much of a shield anyway. The five monsters behind me collapsed and turned to ash, helpless against a spirit guide's power.

Dagda follows! Meridian sent as she moved on to another group of faelah.

A bark and a snarl announced Fergus's arrival as well. He must have gone with Meridian.

I stood up, wincing at the pain in my arm as I pushed against the ground. I glanced down at it and sucked in a breath. A long gash ran from my elbow and halfway down my arm to my wrist. The sleeve of my sweatshirt was soaked in blood. How had I missed such a huge injury? Had I been that focused on the battle?

A shout of fury rose above all the rest of the noise and I glanced up to see a small army of horses carrying men in chainmail charging towards us. Leading them was a huge man on an equally giant Palomino charger. Pale red hair streamed from beneath his helmet and he had a great sword raised above his head. The Dagda.

My knees buckled and I collapsed with relief. The Dagda and his guard thundered past me and behind them were dozens of other men armed with crude weapons and simple leather armor. I tried to stand back up so I could continue helping with the fight, but my legs wouldn't hold me. I mentally kicked myself for being weak, but there was nothing else I could do.

Lasair came up to me, his sides wet with bloody cuts where the tails of the faelah had lashed him. He knelt down beside me and at first I thought he was just as exhausted as I was, but when he turned his head to regard me with brown, intelligent eyes, I realized he wanted me to climb on his back.

Nodding grimly, I complied, trying to ignore the injured arm that had gone from aching to burning. I scooped up my bow before he rose and despite my pain, I continued to shoot the faelah from Lasair's back. The battle lasted a half an hour longer and although the Dagda and his men managed to kill several more of the Morrigan's faelah, most of them fled to return to their master.

"Meghan!" a familiar, yet muffled voice yelled.

I blinked and turned around, smiling in great relief.

"Dagda!" I nearly sobbed.

He still sat astride his large blond horse, but he'd removed his helmet, his red hair sticking out in every direction. His face was grim and his eyes burned with the fury of battle. He climbed down from his horse, the armor he wore clanging with every step. Without stopping, he reached me and pulled me up into a great hug. I yelped in slight surprise, but returned his embrace without a second thought. He smelled of leather and oil and sweat and the earth itself. I sighed and let the tension in my body melt away.

"Dear girl! Are you well?"

He put me down then held me at arm's length, checking me for missing limbs and any other injuries.

"Your arm," he murmured, taking my hand and gently stretching my arm out.

I winced, but held still. His mouth cut a grim line across his face.

"It looks bad, but I'm sure it will be fine once it's cleaned."

Throughout the Dagda's fussing, the last vestiges of the fight came to an end. The dead faelah were all but ashes thrown to the wind and the Dagda's men were wandering the great field, checking to make sure all the monsters that remained were truly dead. Well, dead in the sense that they wouldn't be rising up again.

The sound of approaching footsteps made me turn around. Cade stood there, looking tired but not nearly as tired as he had looked in the past after going through his battle fury.

He nodded at the Dagda, silently thanking him for his aid, then stepped up to me, pulling me from his foster father's protective shadow and into his arms before I could so much as squeak in protest.

"Are you well?" he said against my hair.

I only nodded, taking a shuddering breath, though that action alone was difficult with Cade's death grip on me.

A sharp whinny reminded me that Lasair was still hurt and bleeding.

"You're lucky," Cade said as he reluctantly stepped away from me. His eyes were bright and fierce. I attributed it to the remnants of his ríastrad, but it could have been something else entirely. I swallowed hard as my nerves started acting up again.

After looking at me like that for a good fifteen seconds, he cleared his throat and said, "You picked a good horse."

I laughed, despite our surroundings and my fresh anxiety. "I was lucky *he* picked *me*, remember?"

Cade grinned and took my hand, the sharp, primitive look in his eyes fading a little.

"Now, that's enough fraternizing for now. Let us return to my abode where there awaits a hot bath for the both of you and then a meal afterwards. We have a Lughnasadh celebration planned for this evening, and with today's success on the battlefield, my men will be eager to begin the festivities as soon as possible."

The Dagda patted Cade on the shoulder, though it was more of a wallop, then climbed back into the saddle of his own horse.

Cade squeezed my hand once, casting me another quick glance, then left to retrieve Speirling. I turned to find Lasair gazing at me with great brown eyes. I walked up to him, placed my hand on his forehead and sighed.

"Lasair, you did such a wonderful job," I said, trying not to think too much about the crushing power of his hooves.

At the sound of his name, his ears pricked forward and he pushed out his head, nudging me with his nose. I laughed and hugged him, happy to hear his contented whicker.

With the help of a nearby soldier, I was back atop the red stallion, and within ten minutes we were all headed towards the Dagda's home. It wasn't until we passed between the first two hills, however, that I noticed the large black raven glaring at me from the edge of a copse full of dead trees.

I sucked in a breath and Lasair slowed to a stop, his ears swiveling as he tried to detect what had alarmed me.

Danger? Meridian sent as she snoozed on my shoulder. The tightening of her claws let me know she felt my unease as well.

Yes, I sent swallowing back a lump of fear, *but it will remain at a safe distance.*

For some reason I knew the Morrigan would not act today. Mustering up as much courage as I could, I sat tall on Lasair's back and faced the raven straight on. A hundred yards separated us, but if I didn't know any better, I would have sworn I saw the horrid bird twitch.

That's right, I thought as the Morrigan released a low grumbling caw, *I have friends now to help me, and I'm not nearly as weak as you think I am.*

Tempted as I was to let some of my glamour flare, the last thing in Eilé I needed to do was hint in any way at the magnitude of my power. The Morrigan was far too observant and powerful. Magical spider or not, showing off in broad daylight would definitely give my secret away. Besides, it would be in my best interest to play the victim.

Yes Meghan, show her you are defiant, but under no circumstances let her know what power you now possess. Your life and the lives of others may depend upon it.

With one last lift of my chin, I turned back towards the Dagda and his soldiers. My arm ached and Cade waited for me up ahead. If that wasn't incentive enough, then the opportunity to get clean, have something to eat and then take a nap before the party cinched it. I sighed and urged Lasair onward. The Morrigan and I would find another opportunity to meet and work out our differences, I was certain of it.

Thirteen

Lughnasadh

The Dagda's underground home met us with the same overwhelming sense of hospitality and cheer I had grown used to. The grand hall was teeming with people preparing the mid-day meal (a bit late because of our little conflict), and the Dagda's female friends scooped me up the moment we entered the house and started leading me towards the ground floor bathroom.

I cast an exasperated glance over my shoulder, but the Dagda only slapped his knee and let out a roar of laughter. "Don't mind them my girl! They love to fuss over every young person who enters my home."

I gave him a wry smirk and shrugged. I already knew this, of course, but I could have done with a little less fuss at the moment.

Before they ushered me down the hall, however, my eyes fell upon Cade's face. Instantly, my smile vanished. He was watching me like a hawk, his jaw working as if he was grinding his teeth together. He stood utterly still next to his foster father, but if I didn't know any better I'd say he was having a very hard time keeping his battle fury in check. Which was odd, since he'd just exhausted quite a bit of it.

Cade's gaze flashed up to mine and he jerked back ever so slightly. His eyes lost their aggressive edge and he blinked several times, his shoulders lowering as he grew more relaxed. I lifted an eyebrow in question, but in the next moment I was swept around the corner and lost all sight of him. This strange emotion I'd seen in him worried me. He hadn't been like that before the battle and I'd never really seen him so worked up before after coming down from his ríastrad.

Sighing, I let my worries go for now. Later, when we had a chance to be alone, I could ask him about it. At the moment I was very much looking forward to a long, hot bath, and when the women leading me away pulled me into a huge, airy room, I almost melted in delight.

A great copper tub, modeled after the Dagda's precious cauldron I suspected, awaited me with steaming hot water. The women who had escorted me showed me where the towels and soaps could be found. When I was left alone, I gathered up one of the larger towels and a handful of lavender scented soaps. I quickly stripped out of my bloody, sweaty clothes and sighed in bliss as I immersed myself in the near-scalding water. I soaked for a while, then scrubbed myself down, cleaning all the grime and stench of the faelah from my skin, taking extra care with the cut on my arm. Once cleaned, the pain all but disappeared from the wound and it actually looked like it was healing before my eyes. Perhaps the magic of the Otherworld helped faelah wounds heal more quickly than they would have in the mortal world.

I can't say how long I stayed in the bath, but when I finally emerged into the great hall, my hair still wet and wearing the spare clothes the Dagda's women had left for me, I felt like an entirely new person.

I found Cade and his foster father sitting in the kitchen enjoying a cup of tea. As I approached, both men turned to regard me. To my great delight, the weird tension remained free of Cade's face and I had to stop myself from running and flinging myself at him. He, too, had cleaned up and was wearing the simple pants and tunic of the common folk of Eilé. True, I enjoyed seeing him in finer court clothes, but there was something about Cade in this very moment, his dark red hair still damp and curling above his collar, the way his mouth curved gently in an almost smile and his eyes . . . Right then, the way he looked at me made me feel like I was the only other person in the entire world. The dark anger that had dominated his eyes was gone and all that was left was the young man I just couldn't get enough of. I bit my lip to keep it from trembling and fought the sudden urge to cry. I never imagined that I could love someone as much as I loved Caedehn MacRoich.

I took a deep breath and continued into the kitchen, accepting a clean mug from a dark haired woman and smiling my thanks.

"The Dagda and I were talking about the battle, Meghan. I saw some of it, though I was pretty preoccupied myself," Cade said, reaching out a hand to take mine. "How did you manage to throw off that first faelah?"

Did his eyes just flash with that unfamiliar, aggressive emotion again? No, it must have just been a play of the light. I took a breath and said, "I used the dagger Enorah gave me, the one like yours. Well, and Lasair was a huge help."

My mouth curved in a goofy grin and I looked up at Cade. "That horse is a faelah killer Cade."

He smiled and squeezed my hand, a tremor running down his arm as he did so. Alarmed, I shot my eyes back up to his, but he had returned his attention to his mug.

The conversation stopped for a few minutes while we all got back to our own thoughts and sipped our tea. The savory scents of beef stew and fresh baked bread floated all around us and the warmth of the kitchen fire fought off the chill of the autumn air that seeped in through the windowpanes. I had to admit, sitting there in silence was eating away at me. I wanted to ask Cade if he had seen the raven after the battle, but I was afraid that savage look in his eyes would return if I did. Besides, the Dagda's soldiers had made sure all the faelah were gone. No point in bringing it up and making everyone worry.

A young boy and two servants entered the kitchen and walked over to the small cauldron hanging over the fire. The first woman, old enough to be the boy's grandmother, lifted a ladle and sipped the broth. After a moment's hesitation, she proclaimed it to be ready and started scooping the thick soup into wooden bowls. The boy and who I now assumed was his sister, placed a bowl in front of each of us, then set a basket of hot bread in the center of the great table before leaving to pass out more stew.

Before he even glanced at his stew, Cade cleared his throat, breaking the silence, and said, "I was wondering if your offer still stands, Dagda, for us to stay here as long as we need to. As you may well know, plans have changed. The Morrigan's attack on Luathara a month ago has made the castle too dangerous for Meghan to stay there."

He took a heavy breath and continued, his eyes now shifting to the bowl in front of him. "Meghan may decide she'd rather stay in Erintara with her mother, but I cannot ask the queen to extend her hospitality towards me. And now that this fight, this war with my mother, seems to be approaching at a much faster pace than I had previously anticipated, I cannot give you an exact time as to when I'll be able to return to Luathara."

Cade squeezed my hand. "But the bottom line is, the Morrigan is after Meghan and my priority is to make sure she is safe."

The Dagda arched a brow, though his face was serious. "Only Meghan is the target, you think? I would say you're a pretty big mark as well, my boy. Especially after defying her so openly. And now that you've been saved by my Cauldron, she'll be even more determined to bring an end to you."

Cade drew a long, ragged breath and said, almost too faintly for me to hear, "Meghan's life is the one most at risk."

I shivered, but hoped Cade didn't notice. His words frightened me, not because I knew I was in danger, but more so because they finally drove home what I had known all along but could never really fathom: my life may very well be over soon. Between the Morrigan's obsession to kill me and Cernunnos's unpredictable glamour, I was a walking time bomb or a match in a drafty room. Any day, any minute, I could go off or be snuffed out.

Before, the notion of dying was just this daunting idea hovering over me like a storm cloud, but now, for some reason, Cade's words took that storm cloud and expanded it until it engulfed me completely. The Morrigan wanted my magic, and she would stop at nothing to get it. She would kill me, and my life would be over. It was as simple as that. Or I could use the magic Cernunnos had given me. That option came with a heavy price as well. If I acted too early, I might end up breaking my geis and become mortal. I'd lived most of my life thinking I was mortal, I'm sure I could manage it again. But if I lost my immortality, I would lose Cade as well. The very thought made my heart clench with anguish.

I glanced up at Cade, brooding over his stew, and a sudden, desperate realization swept over me. I had been cautious my entire life, carefully living from one day to the next, expecting the future to be a constant stretched out far ahead of me. That was no longer a guarantee, and if I really thought about it, I hadn't been living at all. I'd just been existing, always worrying about what others thought or what the consequences of my actions might be. How those insignificant things would affect my future. Well, turns out I might not have much of a future after all.

My own glamour and its fussy neighbor started a slow burn in my chest, responding to my new, sudden determination.

It was time I started taking part in my life instead of just watching it drift by. Yes, I may not have much time left, but darn it, I would make it worth something.

The Dagda's great sigh broke me out of my internal, self-inflicted lecture. I clamped my teeth shut and wrapped my fingers around the warm bowl of stew, willing my nerves to settle.

"But of course you are welcome to stay with me as long as you wish, and Meghan as well," the Dagda continued. "Whether the battle comes to us tomorrow or next year," he added, throwing me a quick look, "you both are always welcome here."

I didn't want to think about my impending doom any longer, so I turned back to my stew, my stomach growling in appreciation.

We finished our meal in relative silence, the only sounds to disturb us being the general clatter and conversation coming from the great hall just beyond the kitchen door. When our bowls were empty, the Dagda personally escorted us to our rooms, located on the very top of the hill.

"Since you plan on an extended stay, you can have the two guest suites. They're adjoining you know. Just a single wall and door between them."

The Dagda winked and for once my face didn't turn bright red. Maybe my subconscious decided that being embarrassed was a waste of time. Yes, that had to be it. The new, fierce, I'm-ready-to-take-life-by-the-horns Meghan was afraid of nothing.

Cade moved aside, waiting for me to follow his foster father up a rather large staircase. We climbed the stairs to the very top and came out onto a circular landing. Three, evenly spaced doors greeted us.

"That one will take you out onto the wrap-around ledge." The Dagda pointed to the largest door, the one closest to the stairwell. "Back in the time when Eilé was overrun with Fomorians, that ledge served as a marvelous lookout. Now I'm afraid it only encourages me to play tricks on my guests. Tis a wonderful place to launch projectiles from."

I turned around and arched an eyebrow at our host. His smile was wide and his blue eyes sparkled silver with mischief.

The Dagda cleared his throat and turned towards the first door. "This will be your room Meghan, and Cade, yours is the door opposite."

He opened each door as he spoke and I took a moment to glance inside. The rooms were almost identical and richly furnished. I stepped inside the room he'd designated as mine. One, curved wall seemed to be covered in circular windows, their diamond-shaped panes glittering in the afternoon light. I cast my eyes around the comfortable space, noting the fireplace, the desk and massive shelves filled with books. The small room to the side I assumed was a bathroom. The thick rug on the floor looked soft and the large, four poster bed even softer.

Suddenly, I was incredibly tired. I had been through a lot that day and I really needed a nap, especially if there was to be a party later. The Dagda's home always exuded welcome and warmth, and I felt so very safe here. The faelah were gone, Lasair and Speirling were settled in the Dagda's famous stables, their wounds being tended to while Meridian and Fergus kept them company. My own arm felt a hundred times better and I was the cleanest I'd been in weeks. Enorah's makeshift shower was functional and lived up to its purpose, but there was just something about taking a hot bath with a variety of scented soaps to choose from that made a girl feel really refreshed.

I leaned back from the doorframe and attacked the Dagda with a fierce hug. He let out a small noise of surprise before returning my gesture.

"Thank you," I murmured, my eyelids drooping sleepily as his beard scratched the side of my face.

Gently, he peeled me off and held me in front of him. "You're always welcome here, darling girl."

I smiled and then glanced over at Cade. He was watching me carefully, an expression of sheer admiration on his face. I walked over to him and lifted up onto my toes, giving him a quick kiss.

"I'll see you when I wake up," I said.

Cade nodded, smoothing one hand lovingly over my hair.

I bit back a smile and slipped into my room, shutting the door behind me. To my surprise, I found my backpack, bow, and quiver of arrows neatly tucked into a corner. Before retiring to the bed, I took a few more moments to examine the room. It was shaped like a half dome, one wall traditionally straight, the other a sloping arc. Through one of the windows I could see the wrap-around ledge the Dagda had been talking about and beyond that, a gorgeous, unobstructed view of the other hills and rolling countryside.

Sighing, I plopped down on the mattress and started taking off my shoes. I was all ready to fall into bed when the soft murmur of voices caught my attention. I glanced over towards the flat wall. Ah, the infamous door that separated mine and Cade's rooms. On quiet feet, I padded over to the wall and pressed my ear to the crack where the door and wall met.

"Whom do you expect to make an appearance in Erintara?" the Dagda asked, his voice muffled and gruff.

Cade released a heavy sigh and I pressed myself even closer to the rough wood.

"Danua of course. Lugh, Nuadu and Epona. I spoke to Lugh and Epona in person, but I can't guarantee the rest. For many of the Tuatha De I simply sent out a royal message in Danua's name, requesting their presence. I can only hope they received the missive and will comply."

"And what of Donn?"

I froze where I stood, eager to hear what was said next and trying to remember who Donn was. I knew the other names; they were all key figures in the battle of Maige Tuired, the famous conflict that was the dominant subject of one of my Celtic mythology books.

"I fear he may be the one aiding the Morrigan."

The Dagda swore and once again silence greeted me.

"The goddess of war and strife and the god of death and the afterlife," he murmured after a while. "I was hoping it wasn't one of the Tuatha De, but I can't say I'm surprised. We have much to discuss and prepare for then. Now I regret the planned celebration later this evening. We should be discussing strategy, not drinking mead and laughing over the slaughter of a handful of the Morrigan's mindless minions. Donn may keep to himself most of the time, but his power is vast and he'll show no pity when it comes down to the final hour."

A heavy sigh worked its way through the thick wood of the door before the Dagda continued, "I'll leave you now. You and your Meghan need to get some rest."

Cade was silent for a while and I was so tempted to knock on the door and demand to know every detail of what had just passed between them. But something stopped me, a whispering voice against my conscious and the tiny, but sharp bite of my new magic. A warning. It was a warning from Cernunnos. I closed my eyes and let some of the tension ease out of my shoulders. The strange forest god may have insinuated I was on my own when it came to deciding the time to use his gift of magic, but this wasn't the first time he'd offered a hint. I wasn't about to ignore these small offerings.

"Very well," Cade's voice drifted through the door. "But don't regret the celebration, Dagda. A party would do us some good; help get our minds off of negative thoughts. Besides," he continued, his voice taking on a lighter air, "it is the eve of

Lughnasadh, and if Lugh were to learn we neglected to observe his holiday we might have his wrath to contend with as well."

I listened as the Dagda moved towards the door, his heavy footfalls causing the boards in the floor to creak. When the distinct click of a shutting door echoed in the circular hallway, I pushed away from the wall and crawled back into bed.

For fifteen minutes I waited for Cade to slip into my room and join me, but only bitter disappointment hit as exhaustion took over. Before I fell asleep, I registered the quiet sounds of him climbing into his own bed through the door that separated us. My wandering thoughts from earlier revisited me and again I wondered at his strange mood just after the battle. Was he angry with me? I bit my cheek and pushed against that idea. Now was the absolute worst time to create a rift in our relationship. With my recent epiphany about the fragility of life, I longed more than ever to have Cade close to me. If we were going to war against the Morrigan and another powerful god, then I wanted every moment to count.

Stop it Meghan, you're going to work yourself up into an emotional frenzy and then you won't be able to function at all. For once, my subconscious was giving me some good advice. I was tired of thinking; tired of analyzing and worrying. And I was tired of the comfortable, proper distance Cade and I had been so careful to keep between us. He had died for me and I would die for him if I had to, I was certain of it. Growling into my pillow, I fell asleep telling myself that before the night was out, I would make sure Cade and I were okay.

When I woke up again it was dark out. The fire in the hearth had died down to bright coals and I could hear the distant muffled hum of voices and laughter. I climbed out of bed only to find a beautiful dress, in the style of the Otherworld, spread out over a chair. Rubbing the sleep from my eyes, I padded over and reached out to touch the raspberry colored material. It was soft and cool; not too formal but not casual either. Sticking out of one of the folds was a note. Curious, I picked it up and started reading.

Meghan,

The Dagda has been saving this dress for you and would like you to wear it to tonight's celebration. Sleep for as long as you need to, we had a harrowing afternoon and you deserve the rest. I will meet you downstairs when you are ready.

Love,

Cade

Crinkling the note in my hands, I pressed it to my heart and glanced back at the dress, smirking. I wondered when the Dagda had commissioned the dress for me and had a suspicious feeling that the wardrobe in the corner held all manner of clothing that happened to be just my size.

Smiling, I stripped out of the clothes I'd slept in and slipped into the dress. To my great relief, I didn't require any extra help with buttons or ties. For a small moment I simply stared into the mirror across the room, strangely reminded of the last time I'd been in this situation, dressing up for one of the Dagda's famous parties. Shivering, I cast those thoughts aside. I hoped that this night didn't end with Cade and I racing across the countryside to face down an evil goddess. Fortunately, the faint sound of music decided to drift up the stairs at that moment and I quickly finished making myself presentable, taming my hair into something other than a tangled mass of dark curls. I quickly slipped into a beautiful pair of fuchsia shoes, then scooped up the string of pink topaz gemstones with matching earrings that had been left next to them. Suddenly I didn't feel so morose anymore.

Thirty minutes after waking up, I was weaving my way through party guests as I headed down the long hallway towards the dance hall. Men and women alike were moving freely through the Dagda's house, laughing and wishing each other a good Lughnasadh as they toasted the successful battle against the faelah with various tankards of mead. I ducked under most of them, smiling and returning their cheer as I searched for Cade.

The dance hall was even more crowded with people, and the murmur of lively voices and the joyous tempo of music mingled together in harmony. A sudden burst of laughter drew my attention away from my general surveying and I grinned when I spotted the Dagda, hands on his hips and head thrown back as someone spoke animatedly to him. He wore his finest, a beautiful green vest embroidered in gold, his beard braided in an intricate pattern that must have taken him (or more likely, some of the women of the house) the entire afternoon to complete.

The Dagda was standing closer to the far wall, but centered in the great dance hall. And next to him stood Cade. I paused where I was and just took a few minutes to drink him in. Dressed in pale cream pants and black knee-length boots that accentuated his athletic figure, he was very hard to miss amidst the Dagda's guests. His dark auburn hair was brushed back neatly and his face was clean shaven. A dark mulberry hued vest, made of the same kind of material as my dress, only made him look even more regal than he usually did. The effect hit my senses like a sledgehammer, and I had to grab hold of the wall to keep from falling over.

A raucous bout of laughter snapped me out of my daze and I shot my eyes towards the noise, sucking in a breath of annoyance as I did. Standing in the corner closest to the refreshment table was a familiar face. Dark hair and grey eyes brought back the memories from the night the Morrigan tricked us, but I couldn't remember the vile boy's name.

"Drustan!" a girl with dark hair shrieked. "You promised a dance with me."

Ah. That's right. *Drustan.* The little jerk who was too good to be within the same vicinity as me.

With a toss of her curls, the owner of the shrill voice marched over, shoving her way between the other young men and women gathered around the table, and grabbed Drustan's hand. It was in that same moment that he glanced up and caught me watching him. At first he started in surprise, then a sly smile curled at the corner of his lips.

He pulled the girl's ear up to his mouth and whispered something, then let go of her hand and headed in my direction. Oh, wonderful, he'd found his source of amusement for the evening.

I straightened and crossed my arms, a look of disgust taking up residence on my face. *Bring it on, pretty boy.*

The couple in front of me moved to the side and Drustan, in all his conceited glory, leaned an arm above my head, rocking forward so that he came uncomfortably close.

"Well, well, well. If it isn't the princess. Nice fighting this afternoon, but did you happen to see me out there? Took out ten faelah on my own."

He leered at me and I blinked up in surprise. Had he completely forgotten how he'd treated me the last time I was here? Or was this some sort of trap? Get the clueless little Meghan to gush and swoon at the attention so he can make a spectacle of her on the dance floor.

Oh, I don't think so . . .

"What do you want?" I snapped, crossing my arms and trying to lean away from him.

"I was hoping for a dance, then maybe afterwards we can find a nice little alcove and get comfortable. What do you say?"

Ewww! Not going to happen pal.

I gaped at him. "Have you lost your mind? You hate me, remember? Practically had a meltdown because you'd touched me."

Drustan shrugged. "That was several months ago. I've grown up a lot since then. And besides," he trailed his eyes over me, from head to toe, "my tastes have changed."

Suppressing a shudder, I opened my mouth to tell him off, but a hard voice broke through the music and did it for me.

"She's already spoken for."

Drustan's eyes grew huge and he jumped away from me, almost bumping into Cade. I froze when I saw the look on his face. That aggressive vibe was back, and Cade looked like he was ready to tear Drustan's throat out.

"Sorry Drustan, but my boyfriend's right." I smiled up at Cade, hoping to diffuse the situation. "He promised me the first dance."

I walked forward and linked my arm in Cade's. Holy crap he was tense!

Drustan swallowed and bobbed his head in a nod. "Uh, yeah, sorry. Didn't know."

As he scurried away, I placed a hand on Cade's chest and turned my face towards his.

"Thanks, but you don't need to look so fierce. I could have handl-"

Cade cut off my words as he pulled me into a ferocious kiss. My nerve endings fired and I lost complete control of my knees. Luckily, he had me wrapped up pretty tight in his arms, so I didn't collapse to the floor. The music, the happy chatter, the aromas of spiced apples and roasting pork fled from my mind and all I could sense was Cade. Man, if Drustan had any doubts as to who had a claim on my heart, he'd know for sure now.

Slowly, Cade drew back, his lips moving more gently against mine.

"Sorry," he mumbled huskily, "didn't mean to attack you like that."

I smiled up at him, my eyes half-closed. The tension in him earlier had drained and I just made myself comfortable in his arms.

"No need to apologize. And you got rid of Drustan, which just made my whole evening."

Cade smiled back, his eyes flashing from green to brown and back again.

The music, which had been rather upbeat and joyful, transformed into a more languid, smooth tempo.

"Would you care to dance my lady?" Cade asked, still pressed firmly against me.

He was already leading me in a slow rhythm when I answered, "Yes, I would like to dance. I'd like to dance with you all evening long."

It was well past midnight when I decided I'd had enough of the party. Cade had stepped away from me for a moment to talk with one of the Dagda's soldiers about the fight with the faelah, and I found myself yearning to head upstairs. I wasn't ready to go to bed, but the stuffiness of the dance hall was finally getting to me, and I wanted to move away from all the people. If I simply stepped out into the courtyard, I'd only run into more revelers, and maybe Drustan and his friends, so casting a look over my shoulder, I headed down the hallway and up the stairs that led to mine and Cade's rooms.

Instead of going into my room, however, I pushed open the heavy wooden doors at the top of the staircase and stepped out into the cold, crisp night. The wooden balcony was larger and wider than I'd imagined, and a section of it even extended further away from the hill. I spotted a bench and went to sit down, sighing as my aching feet thanked me. I sat still and listened to the sounds of the Dagda's guests standing and chatting around a bonfire below me, and the music floating through the open front door was a soft accompaniment to the still, moon-lit night. Now I was alone, and now my mind returned to the thoughts I'd managed to banish earlier.

Sighing, I leaned forward and sought out my well of glamour. There, that little blue flame dancing strongly next to my heart. I decided to practice with it, pushing it out until the magic suffused my every cell. I grinned as I held the power at my fingertips and the small rose next to it remained tightly shut. I'd come a long way since that first lesson with Enorah in the Weald.

A slight rustle behind me indicated that I was no longer alone. I stood up and turned before presenting a wide smile. Cade walked towards me, looking resplendent in his simple but elegant clothes. His face appeared shuttered, uncertain even, as he quietly moved towards me and I wondered if that odd aggressiveness was back. For the life of me, I couldn't figure out what had caused it. I wrapped my arms more tightly around myself and shivered.

"Are you cold?" he asked as he moved closer.

Yes and no, but not for the reasons you might think, I mused. I shook my head.

He stepped in behind me and wrapped me in his arms. Even though I wasn't all that tired, I wanted to fall asleep just standing there like that. The moon was bright above us, basking the rolling land in silver light. I took a deep breath, allowing the warmth of the mead from the party and Cade's closeness to fill my senses. I wanted to stay in this happy place forever and forget that an impending war was trying to force itself upon the Otherworld.

I took a deep breath and released it slowly. *No more dismal thoughts Meghan. Now's the time for living, remember?*

I turned in Cade's arms and rested my cheek against his broad chest, breathing in his scent and letting it flood over me.

Gently, Cade took a step back and lifted my face so that he could look me in the eye.

"What's wrong?" he asked, is own eyes dark with concern.

I shrugged, unwilling to burden Cade with all my worries.

"I can sense it Meghan, tell me."

Sighing, I decided to give in a little. "I hate that your world is facing down a war because of me. I feel this is my fault, no matter what you or Enorah or the Dagda says. If I hadn't stepped through that dolmarehn so many months ago, the Morrigan may never have decided to build up her army so that she could get at my glamour. If I had just accepted my life as it was, then your world might not be in danger now."

"Do you regret coming after me?"

There was no playfulness to his voice, no flirtatious glint to his eyes. He was dead serious.

"No," I breathed, "I don't regret it one bit. If I hadn't crossed over into Eilé, the course of my life may have taken a different turn and I might not be standing here with you now."

"Then why can't you see it, Meghan?" His voice became suddenly quiet and seductive. "This isn't my world; it is *our* world. And nothing, in all of Eilé, matters more to me than you."

He kissed me then, one that did not, in any way, hide what he felt. I returned the kiss with equal fervor, my heart racing and my mind losing control of rational thought as my magic flared to encompass us both.

Cade broke the kiss and pressed his forehead against mine. His breath was ragged and he was wound so tight I thought he might break.

"Meghan," he said roughly, "I've been so careful for so long, but I don't know how much longer my control will last. If we keep going like this, I might not be able to stop. I'm afraid-"

I pressed a finger against his lips and looked him in the eye. My heart was racing and I was terrified, for many reasons, but I whispered the truth that sang from my heart, "I don't want to stop Cade."

He searched my eyes then whispered softly, "Are you sure Meghan?"

I bit my lip and nodded, then admitted my other great fear. "We could both die when the Morrigan unleashes her fury. I don't want to miss anything. I don't want to have any regrets."

"I won't let the Morrigan hurt you Meghan," he whispered desperately against my mouth.

Then, without another word, Cade bent over and put an arm behind my knees. In one swift movement, he swept me up against his chest and carried me back to his room and for a while the both of us forgot about the Morrigan. We forgot about the possibility of an unstoppable army of faelah destroying everyone and everything we knew. That night, we forgot about all our worries and fears and simply lived.

Fourteen

Onward

I woke to the warmth of the morning sun on my face. Stretching, but not opening my eyes, I basked in the heat of the sun and the glow of my own happiness. I turned onto my side and cracked my eyes open. Cade lay next to me, his elbow propped to support his head as he watched me intently. My eyes met his and he grinned. I felt my cheeks flush as the memories of the night before bubbled to the surface.

Cade reached out a hand and brushed my cheek, his silent words blooming across my mind, *I love this.*

What?

Your blush.

Of course, that only made me blush harder. Guess my great epiphany about an early death had only scared my old self into hiding. Easily embarrassed Meghan was back in full force.

Cade dipped his head and kissed my arm where the faelah had scratched me. I had almost forgotten about it.

How are you this morning? I didn't hurt you last night, did I?

His words were tinged with the pale orange color of concern.

I smiled. I knew he wasn't talking about my arm. *No, you didn't hurt me and I couldn't be happier.*

Cade's answering smile melted my heart. He pulled me close and pressed his lips to my temple.

Onward

Do you know how long I've dreamed about this moment?

No, tell me.

Since the night you were attacked by the Cúmorrig, the first time we met, when you sat in the dirt, your nightgown bunched up around your waist, giving me a wonderful view of your long legs.

I gasped and punched him in mock outrage. It was a good thing he liked my tendency to blush because I could feel the heat spreading across my face again. Cade caught my hand and kissed my palm.

You were terrified Meghan, but even then I knew you had spirit; that you were made of something more. That, all the Celtic gods willing, I had finally, finally, found another Faelorehn who could understand me and maybe one day grow to love me.

I bit my cheek as hot tears spilled from my eyes.

I love you Meghan. I love you so very much, he sent to me, his thoughts smothered in bliss.

I sighed contentedly and snuggled up against his chest, reveling in how warm his bare skin felt against my own. Last night had been wonderful, scary and nerve-wracking and absolutely wonderful. When we had first entered Cade's room and he'd set me on his bed, I had sensed that uncharacteristic violence in him once again. As the night progressed, however, that darkness behind his eyes and beneath his skin slowly melted away, our glamour flaring up and mingling together as we let go of everything but each other. The sensation had taken my breath away and I wondered, what with the fact that my self-control had been all but absent last night, how I had managed to keep that other well of magic silent. A miracle. It must have been some sort of miracle.

Taking a deep breath, I decided now was as good a time as any to ask Cade about that strange darkness.

"Cade?" I murmured.

"Mhmm?"

"Yesterday, after the fight with the faelah," I paused, not sure how to go on.

A few moments ticked by and I took a deep breath. If I couldn't have an open conversation with him after what we'd done last night, then I was in trouble.

"You seemed different, like a piece of your battle fury decided to stick around. The way you kept looking at me all afternoon, and how you reacted to Drustan."

"That little asahl was trying to abscond with my girl."

He kissed my forehead and I bit back a grin. "What does *asahl* mean?"

Cade cleared his throat. "Something unpleasant I don't wish to teach you."

"Will you teach me the language of Eilé someday?"

"Yes," Cade murmured, "but not the crude words."

I giggled and then took a deep breath. Alright, where had this conversation started . . . Oh, yes, Cade's strange aggression.

"So, is that what happened then? Did part of your ríastrad linger behind after the battle?"

Cade drew in a deep breath and let it out slowly. I tensed up as I waited for his response, which was a bad idea. What with us being so close together, both physically and emotionally, Cade picked up on every minute detail.

"I'm sorry Meghan, please don't be afraid." He held me tighter, as if he feared I would bolt. "I don't really know what caused it, but I think your theory might be correct. At the end of the fight, while the battle fury was leaving me, I saw something that made it flare just a bit before I was myself again. I think the ríastrad was trying to stay with me as long as possible and when I saw you after the battle, and when Drustan was speaking to you, all I could think of was protecting you. My battle fury runs on pure instinct when it takes over, so although

I was mostly in control, I think that tiny lingering piece of it came out when I felt the need to keep you safe."

I tilted my head back so I could see his eyes. Worry was etched in their depths, but I couldn't see anything else other than the Cade I knew so well.

"What did you see?" I murmured. "At the end of the battle. What convinced that little part of your battle fury to linger?"

His eyes darted away from me and I noticed a struggle there. When his gaze caught mine once again, he took a small breath and whispered, "The Morrigan. In raven form."

I drew in a quick breath. So. He had seen her after all.

"I saw her too," I admitted, burrowing my head back into his shoulder. "I didn't say anything because I didn't want to worry you."

He nodded. "Me too."

Then he chuckled a little and dropped a kiss to the top of my head. "Look at the anxiety we cause in each other by keeping secrets."

A jolt of panic shot through me and I flinched.

Cade noticed right away. "Meghan? Are you alright?"

"Um, yes, just my nerves recalling the fight yesterday," I lied.

In the corner of my mind, I saw a sharp image of the spider, furiously working to gather up all the thoughts that suddenly sprang into my mind. Cernunnos's gift, the great secret I had to keep. Couldn't tell Cade, couldn't tell anyone . . .

The bitter bite of guilt soon followed my flush of alarm and I had to work really hard not to start shaking. *I'm sorry Cade*, I thought, careful not to send the words into the space that I used for shîl-sciar. *But I have to keep this secret from you . . .*

Eventually, I polished my intense worry down to nothing more than a smooth pebble of concern. I picked the pebble up for a moment, felt its weight in my imaginary palm, then tossed it away to consider at some future date. I was lying in bed with Cade, the two of us blissfully alone and wrapped up in each other's arms, and I wasn't about to let my stupid problems ruin the moment.

The gentle caress of Cade's hand down my spine quickly brought me back to the present. When he leaned into me and whispered playfully into my ear, "Are you up for a repeat of last night?", the only thing I was concerned about was answering him fast enough.

I mimicked his attentions and when he gasped against my mouth, I said with a grin, "What do you think?"

By the time Cade and I were ready to face the Dagda and the rest of his household, it was almost noon. I gathered up my dress from the night before and scurried over to the door that connected our two rooms, casting Cade a bashful glance over my shoulder. He was still reclined in bed, his hands folded behind his head. His auburn hair was unkempt and the sheets were bunched up around his waist, leaving his entire bare chest in plain sight. A few more tattoos, similar to the intricate knot work on his arms, decorated his torso. One stretched down his side from the bottom of his ribcage to his hip, the other was a circular design just below his collar bone on the opposite side. I had noticed them last night, but now that they were on full display in broad daylight, I could see them better. I must have been gawking because Cade cleared his throat. My eyes flicked up to his face and I was greeted with a lazy smile.

"Are you going to go get ready, or have you changed your mind? Because I wouldn't mind in the least if we spent the whole day up here."

"No," I answered quickly, my face warming, "the Dagda will worry if we never come downstairs."

Onward

I smiled and disappeared before I let the appeal of Cade's comment tempt me into running back to the bed and curling up next to him. I wouldn't mind staying upstairs either.

After seeking out the bathroom and teaching myself how to use the shower (luckily, it was very similar to the one at Luathara), I donned some fresh clothes and returned to Cade's suite. He must have been in the bathroom because he was nowhere in sight. Shrugging, I closed the door and glanced around the room, noting the sparse furniture and simple design.

A moment later Cade stepped around the corner, wearing nothing but a white towel around his waist, and I bit my cheek to keep from smiling like an imbecile. He strode past me, planting a kiss on my forehead, then reached out for the pair of pants draped over the back of a chair. I tried not to stare, but the image of male perfection standing in front of me was too tempting to resist. Before I could start drooling, however, I forced myself to turn around and study one of the oil paintings on the wall. A minute later I felt the heavy warmth of Cade's arms as they draped over my shoulders. Sighing, I fell back into his embrace. He pressed his face into my damp hair and took a deep breath before leaning forward and kissing me on the cheek.

"Good morning my love," he murmured, and I felt my nerves melt all over again.

I savored his touch, absorbing his heat and breathing in his own unique scent. I allowed my eyes to drift shut and the memories of last night flooded my mind. I sighed, no longer feeling shy or embarrassed.

"Shall we let my foster father know we are awake?" Cade asked, taking me by the hand and pulling me towards the door.

The Dagda's grand hall was empty and quiet except for a few servants bustling about their mid-day chores, and a small pack of wolfhounds snoozing by a crackling fire. Cade never dropped my hand, even when we made our way into the kitchen.

"There you are!" the Dagda roared, his face bright with amusement.

He wore the robe I'd seen him in so many times; an all-purpose garment meant for everyday lounging.

"I'm assuming you two must be hungry," a red-haired woman said.

"Yes Mairin. Thank you," Cade answered, leading me to an open seat.

The woman, Mairin, smiled warmly in my direction, curtsied, then left, claiming she had errands to run. When I turned around, there was a plate sitting in front of me, heaped with some sort of meat and vegetable pie, the flaky crust golden and already split open. As soon as the wonderful scent reached my nose, my stomach growled loudly.

The Dagda grinned and gestured towards my fork before picking up a steaming mug of tea. "Please. Eat! We've already had our morning and afternoon meals."

He nodded at Cade, his blue eyes almost sparkling they were changing color so fast. Cade grumbled something under his breath in that old language and got busy with his own meal.

A comfortable silence fell, but like all quiet moments in the Dagda's abode, it didn't last long.

"So," our host drawled after taking a long sip from his mug, "I take it you two had a splendid evening?"

My fork froze in midair and I cast Cade a startled look.

He arched a brow at me and then glanced at his foster father. "Of course, Dagda. Your parties, no matter how large or small, are always enjoyable."

"Oh, I was referring to the after party."

As calmly as possible, I set my fork down and glanced up at the Dagda. He looked as relaxed as a bear in his den after a huge meal, but his eyes were bright and his mouth was curved in a knowing smile. Ugh. He knew about Cade and me.

Onward

"Dagda, I should think that your hospitality has not waned over the years, or that you are so desperate for entertainment that you have taken up the practice of spying on your guests."

Cade's voice was formal, but beneath the cool tone was slight irritation.

"Relax my dear boy! I have never, nor will I ever, spy on my guests. Alannah went up earlier to check on your Meghan and when she didn't find her in her own room, she merely put two and two together. She came to me this morning, grinning from ear to ear, so I insisted on knowing the reason for her obvious joy."

He huffed out the last part of his sentence, as if Cade's tone had insulted him, and gave me an exasperated look. "Be warned Meghan, there are no secrets in this household. Just know that eventually everyone will know what you're up to."

I gave a half smile and got back to my meal. I wasn't comfortable with the idea that the Dagda's entire household knew Cade and I had spent the night together, but it's not like I was ashamed. Maybe I just needed to get used to the idea before everyone else did.

Cade's hand found mine under the table and he gave it a gentle squeeze.

I'm sorry, he said using shíl-sciar.

I'm not, I sent back. *I mean, I'm not thrilled your foster father knows, but I don't regret it.*

I turned to look at him and he smiled at me. My stomach did a flip and all the sensations from last night and this morning came flooding back to me.

Pressing my lips together to prevent looking like a lovesick fool, I got back to finishing my lunch. *Cade, you can't look at me like that. It's distracting.*

Then you had better get used to walking around with your eyes closed because I simply can't help myself.

That only made it harder to keep my composure. I tried to focus my thoughts on the Dagda's cheerful voice as he told us the most amusing events from the Lughnasadh party the night before. Cade's hand never left mine, but I made a point not to look directly into his eyes for the rest of the afternoon. I honestly didn't need the distraction.

Despite the relaxed atmosphere of the Dagda's house, the following week passed by swiftly, with Cade and I hardly spending a single moment out of one another's company. During the daylight hours, we would go for short rides on Speirling and Lasair, or Cade would help me practice my magic or teach me how to fight with my dagger. In the evenings we would join the Dagda and listen to him weave tales of the past. He was a wonderful storyteller and he loved our company (or so he claimed), so it was no trouble to spare a few hours indulging him with our presence. After the night of the Lughnasadh party, I moved most of my stuff into Cade's room. Having another body sleeping next to me was a new experience, but the sense of protection and warmth I got from sharing a bed with Cade was worth those first few awkward nights. By the time I got used to our new routine, however, it was once again time for us to go. The week was up and we would be traveling to meet with my mother and the other Tuatha De. The night before we left, I was even more grateful to have Cade so close to me.

The next morning the entire household was up early preparing for the journey to Erintara. Lasair and Meridian met me in the stables and I was glad to see that the red horse's injuries from the battle the week before were finally completely healed up.

As soon as I stepped into the hay-scented building, Meridian descended from the rafters to come to rest on my shoulder. I offered Lasair an apple while my spirit guide nestled up against my neck, then headed back out into the main yard.

The second we left the warm stable behind, Meridian pulled her wings in close.

Ice! she sent to me.

I nodded and wrapped my arms around my torso. It was freezing, but then again the bright colors of summer had begun fading a week or so ago. Autumn came cool and early in the Otherworld.

We followed the wide dirt path around a small hill and found several of the Dagda's guard, milling about in the open, preparing their own horses and packing their bags. Among them were Cade and his foster father, donning serious looks and giving out orders to the other men and women.

Cade looked up and saw me, his expression softening. He said something to the Dagda, then grabbed Speirling's reins and headed my way.

"Are you ready for this?" he asked quietly.

I knew he was talking about seeing my mother again and not the ride to Erintara. Pulling a slow, cold breath into my lungs, I glanced up at him and said, "I'm ready for anything with you by my side."

Cade's eyes glinted as his face split into a huge smile. He gave me a quick kiss then helped me climb atop Lasair. Once Cade was settled on his own horse, we turned to face the Dagda and his retinue.

"There is a dolmarehn a few miles from here that will take us to the woods behind Erintara," the Dagda said as he nudged his giant horse closer to us. "But we'll ride swiftly. I don't know if any of the faelah from the other day still linger."

Cade's foster father led us out of the hills and onto open ground. Once we were clear of his domain, the horses broke into a faster pace. I was no expert rider, but Lasair's smooth gait, along with the fact that he now had a saddle, made the ride easier than it could have been. Cade rode by my side on Speirling, and Meridian and Fergus trailed after us, keeping a lookout for faelah. At the pace we were going, we reached the dolmarehn in half an hour. The structure was huge, like the one behind Luathara, and in no time we were all through, emerging in the middle of a sparsely forested area.

The trees here were mostly beech and oak, their leaves wearing the first, burnished golds and rusts of autumn. Cade and I eventually caught up with the rest of the group, all who had stopped in response to the Dagda's raised arm. Cade urged Speirling forward and I followed him. The Dagda and his horse stood near the edge of the woods on a ledge that overlooked rolling farmland. He lifted an arm and pointed.

"Erintara," he said.

I raised my hand to shade my eyes and squinted. In the distance, the glassy surface of Lake Ohll stretched on forever. Rolling hills continued to the east of the lakeshore, and resting on top of the tallest hill was a great castle. Erintara. The home of Danua, high queen of Eilé. My mother.

I settled back down in the saddle and gave Cade a solemn look. The last time I had spoken to Danua things hadn't gone so well. She had told me to stay away from Cade and I had refused, informing her that she had no say in my life. Now I was returning, and Cade and I had grown closer than ever. I was afraid of how she would take that little morsel of news.

What's wrong? Cade asked me using shíl-sciar.

I sighed. *Just thinking about how Danua and I parted the last time we were here.*

He brought Speirling closer and reached out to take my hand. *It will all work out Meghan. Don't fret.*

That was easy for him to say. I'd been confident when we left the Dagda's home this morning, but now that we were within sight of the castle, those pesky nerves started their tap dance once again.

Gritting my teeth and telling myself I was silly to be nervous, I nodded and clicked Lasair on as the Dagda began leading us down the side of the hill. The countryside proved to be a welcome distraction, its beauty shining forth as it succumbed to fall's approach. Most of summer's green had given way to duller hues, but every so often we crossed paths with a pile of golden leaves or several red apples clinging to an orchard tree, waiting patiently for the harvest.

As we got closer to the city of Erintara, we began to see more people out working their land. Many stopped, leaning on a pitchfork or resting against their plow horse, gawking at the Dagda and his guard. Some even removed their hats and bowed, clearly aware of who it was passing by on their road.

Despite the cold morning, the city of Erintara was alive with people scurrying about, but once they caught a glimpse of the god riding the golden horse, they paused in their tracks and showed reverence. Some bowed like those in the countryside, others cheered. By the time we reached the gates of the castle, we had the entire city treating us like the spectacles of a town parade. Cade remained gallantly silent the entire way and I did my best to mimic him. I never liked being the center of attention and Cade had been alone for so long I imagined he shared my sentiment. But, despite what Cade had told me, I still dreaded the idea of facing my mother, and something told me he wasn't looking forward to it either.

I didn't see Danua right away. The Dagda, Cade and I were welcomed into the castle by the many servants who worked there while the men of the Dagda's guard were shown to their own rooms in the soldiers' quarters. My heart beat faster as we walked through the castle of Erintara, all the memories from the previous spring flooding through my mind: the cold, disapproving attitude of my mother, the general disdain of her courtiers, the disregard of Cade's presence . . . It all sent a chill through me, but I stood up straight and held myself with dignity. I had suffered far worse after leaving the castle last time. I could handle these memories.

A woman in a green gown greeted us at the top of the stairs. I suppressed a growl when I recognized her; the older lady in waiting who had been so rude to Cade the last time we were here. She clearly remembered me as well, if I was judging correctly by her unnatural stiffness and the sour look on her face.

"Three rooms, I presume?" she said with haughty formality.

I forced a small smile and said, before anyone else could answer, "Two, actually. Cade and I will be sharing."

Her eyes widened and she stopped some automatic response in the back of her throat. A strangled noise from behind me told me that the Dagda was doing his best to smother a laugh and the warm weight of Cade's hand caressing the nape of my neck gave me more confidence than I felt.

She turned abruptly and led us down the hallway, showing the Dagda to his room and then Cade and me to ours. She bowed quickly, informed us that the other Tuatha De had not yet arrived but were expected later that afternoon, then turned and scuttled down the hallway. I was convinced she was headed directly to my mother to inform her of the change of my relationship with Cade and the only thing keeping her from full out running was her own frigid sense of decorum.

The Dagda had excused himself and shut the door to his room, so all that was left was for Cade and me to settle into ours. Cade carried the bags with our clothes inside and set them in the corner. The moment I closed the door he pounced, wrapping me up in his arms and spinning us both around. I squawked and smacked at his chest, but I didn't put much effort behind it and by the time he pulled me down onto the bed with him, we were both laughing.

"What was that all about?" I asked, still smiling as I pulled a plush pillow under my head.

Cade shrugged and mimicked me. "No reason. I just felt like it."

I arched a brow at him, my mouth tugging up into a grin. Cade was always so careful and serious around me that it was nice to see him behaving like this. I even unabashedly gave myself credit for this change in his demeanor.

A piece of Cade's hair came loose and fell across his forehead. Reaching out a hand, I gently brushed it aside but let my fingers linger on his face. His eyes darkened, but they were anything but dull.

"I love seeing you so happy," I whispered.

And then my dreary thoughts returned, thoughts about dying under the wrath of the Morrigan. Thoughts about losing Cade again. My magic jumped in response, the flame flaring for a split second before settling down once again. I bit my lip and Cade reached up with his own hand to capture mine. He pulled me gently forward. I closed my eyes, anticipating his kiss, but someone knocked abruptly at the door.

Cade growled in frustration and released me, getting up off the bed to go answer the door. I sat up, crossing my legs and resting my elbows on my knees. One of my mother's many ladies in waiting stood on the other side of the door. She was younger than the woman who had showed us to our room, but still held the same frozen stiffness. She looked Cade up and down, then glanced past him at me.

"Your mother requests your presence," she said. "She is taking tea in ten minutes." She wrinkled her nose and added, "You might want to reconsider your wardrobe."

I glanced down at myself. I had put on a pair of dark jeans and a knit turtleneck that morning. Some of the clothes from the mortal world I had brought with me to the Dagda's. I shrugged then stood up and strode over to her.

Kathara

Crossing my arms, I came to a stop next to Cade. *Might as well get this over with*, I told myself.

"I'll wear this," I replied. "Please, take me to her now."

Fifteen
Tuatha De

$\mathcal{D}$anua waited for me in a spacious room that was located just off of her throne room. A floor to ceiling window let in a stream of weak light and a cheery fire crackled in the fireplace at the far end of the room. Bookshelves lined one wall while a collection of portraits decorated another. My mother sat in a stuffed chair beside a table holding a large teapot and several trays of small sandwiches and desserts. She sat regally, as always, with her hands folded primly in her lap. The dress she wore today was a creamy pink color inlayed with tiny rose vines that looked like they'd been embroidered by hand. Suddenly, I felt grubby in the comfortable jeans and turtleneck I'd insisted on wearing.

I sat down, squirming a little to get comfortable before realizing no matter how I sat, I'd never get truly cozy around Danua. Well, I might feel at ease if I had Cade sitting next to me to offer his silent support, but he had opted to wait in the hallway. Yet as much as I wanted him by my side, I couldn't begrudge him his decision. Danua had summoned me, not me *and* Cade, and I owed her, and myself, a chance to talk where it was just the two of us.

The moment I lifted my eyes to glance at Eilé's queen, she started speaking.

"It would seem you have gone against my wishes and developed a deeper attachment to Caedehn MacRoich."

She picked up her delicate teacup and took a sip as if we were discussing something as tedious as the layer of dust on the bookshelves.

I stiffened in my over-stuffed chair.

"I thought I told you to stay away from that boy."

So this was how it was going to start. Not so much as a "Hello darling daughter" or, "It is good to see you Meghan" or, "How have you been since I last saw you my child?" Fine. If she wanted to be unreasonable, then so be it. I wasn't going to apologize for my actions, especially if I didn't regret them.

"And I thought I made it clear that you had no say in the matter," I retorted.

I was nervous as hell, but high queen or not, my biological mother or not, she wouldn't be making the decision on who I wanted to date, especially since she'd been absent from my life until recently, and also because she went around insisting that her orders be followed instead of talking to me like a civilized person.

She sighed and leaned back in her chair, ignoring the tea cooling in front of her.

"Meghan, I have no wish to fight with you."

I opened my mouth to snap out a response, something along the lines of *then you shouldn't have started this conversation by trying to order me around*, but she held up a hand and continued. "We started off on the wrong foot the last time, and I'm afraid I'm still not reconciled with that. Unfortunately, right now isn't the best of times in Eilé and I'm afraid this upcoming confrontation with the Morrigan has kept my mind occupied. I haven't had the time to worry about the strained connection I have with my daughter, and the last thing I need right now is a distraction."

I gritted my teeth and took a long sip of my tea, disregarding the scorching sensation as the hot liquid went down my throat. As inconvenient as it was for me to show up now of all times, I resented being called a distraction.

"I called you down here to let you know that I do wish to try and salvage what's left of our shattered relationship, but that it will have to wait."

I tried not to feel hurt, really I did. Sure, I still disdained her for the way she treated me and the way she so callously cast me aside, but she was right. Now was not a good time to let our emotions get the better of us. If the Morrigan had any notion of the anger that brewed between my mother and me, she would pounce on it like a starving flea on a dog. Yes, waiting to sort out our differences, no matter how much it scraped at my raw emotions to put it off, was the best.

"Now," Danua said, clasping her hands together as if she were about to use her glamour to clean off the table, "the day grows late and some of the Tuatha De have yet to arrive. We will not meet until mid-morning to discuss this threat that looms all around us, so you are dismissed. Use the afternoon to rest and prepare yourself for tomorrow's schedule."

I stood to leave, a bit confused by her abrupt dismissal. Yet, perhaps her only reason for calling me down here was to chastise me about Cade and to inform me that she'd be willing to try out that whole bonded mother-daughter thing once the Morrigan situation had been taken care of. And she had handled the whole conversation as if it was simply a business meeting discussing the variety of wheat grown in her realm. I had to hand it to her, she had a talent for shrugging off emotion like an old coat.

"Dinner will be served to your rooms tonight," she said as she ushered me to the end of the room, "so don't bother coming down to the dining hall. We'll be having a more formal welcome when everyone has arrived."

Nodding, I stepped through the ornately carved door only to find the same lady in waiting ready to take me back upstairs. Cade wasn't in the hallway any longer, and neither was he in our room when I returned, so I killed time by browsing the bookshelves. Once I found something interesting to read, I settled into a great stuffed chair beside the fire place. The unremarkable day had faded into afternoon, and a gray wash of clouds on the horizon signaled an approaching storm.

Appropriate weather, I mused as I flipped through the pages of my book.

Cade arrived just before dusk settled in. I glanced up from my reading and lifted my eyebrows in surprise. His hair was damp and ruffled and his clothes looked muddy in some spots. I gasped and jumped out of the chair when I caught sight of a red smear near his temple.

"You're bleeding!" I exclaimed, lifting my hand to touch the small gash above his ear.

Cade quickly caught my hand, turned it over, and planted a kiss in my palm. His eyes sparkled and a grin tugged at the corner of his mouth. My stomach fluttered and I breathed a small sigh of relief.

"I was only sparring with Danua's guard," he said, sounding slightly sheepish. "How did the meeting with your mother go?"

My moment of joy faded and I took a breath. "Honestly, as well as I had imagined."

Cade grimaced. "I'm sorry Meghan."

Shrugging, I said, "All is not lost. She wants to mend the rift between us, but she wants to wait until after everything with the Morrigan blows over."

My heart twinged at that thought. I might not make it past the war . . . Shaking my head, I turned back to Cade and tried on another smile.

"It hurts that she doesn't want to work on our relationship now, but I can understand why."

Cade nodded and pulled me into a hug. He kissed me once on the forehead, his favorite display of affection, I'd come to learn, then disappeared into the bathroom to take a shower. I sat down on my chair once again and let my mind wander back to the meeting with my mother. She had been as cold as ever, but even as my own mind fought against her distance, I could sense something hovering just below the surface. A spark of yearning perhaps? A desire to reach out to her daughter?

A sharp knock at the door yanked me out of my reverie. I rose to open it just as Cade stepped out of the bathroom wearing his casual shirt and pants. A servant with a tray gave me a quick bow and I realized that dinner had arrived. Cade stepped up and took the tray, setting it on a small table in the corner. As we ate, he told me about his day and I told him about mine. Despite the uncomfortable and emotionally draining encounter with my mother, a cloud of comfort surrounded me. Who would have thought that such joy could be squeezed out of a simple conversation with the one you loved?

After taking my own shower, I pulled on some old pajamas from my bag and snuggled into bed next to Cade. He wrapped an arm around me and tucked his face up against my neck, his warm breath stirring my hair. A wash of happiness flooded over me, chasing my worries away, and I soon drifted off to sleep.

The steady rhythm of rain pelting the windows woke me the next morning. The fire had died down to tiny, glowing embers and the room had grown cold. It was still dark out, but not so much so that I couldn't see the objects in the room. Cade's soft breathing came from behind me and I rolled over so that I faced him. He was splayed out on his stomach, his arms reaching in front of him and his head turned in my direction. His hair, a tousled mess since he went to bed with it wet, falling against his cheek. Slowly, so I wouldn't wake him, I cuddled up against his side to keep warm. I hadn't realized I'd been shivering until my body came into contact with his. Heat flooded over me and I sighed, letting my eyes drift closed.

Cade mumbled something and took a deep breath. He shifted, rolling up onto his side and curling his arms around me, pulling me close. I welcomed the gesture without any complaints and fell asleep for who knows how much longer. The next time I woke, it was to the sensation of Cade stroking my hair out of my face. My eyes flickered and I found him staring at me.

"What's wrong?" I whispered.

He drew in a deep breath and let it out slowly. "Nothing," he answered in the same silent tone. *Just reminding myself how lucky I am,* he murmured into my mind. He leaned forward and kissed my forehead gently.

I could have easily fallen back to sleep, but I knew it was probably already getting close to mid-morning and Danua had expected us to meet in her throne room. I wondered if all of the Tuatha De Danann had made it last night. Cade and I had gone to bed relatively early and I couldn't recall hearing any sounds of a large party arriving in the courtyard far below our window.

Reluctantly, I got out of bed, Cade not far behind, and we donned our formal clothes. I had brought one of the dresses I'd found in the wardrobe at the Dagda's, this one a lovely dark plum color with some silver needlework. Once we were ready, we slipped from our room and headed down the hall, the soft patter of rain against the tall windows accompanying us along the way.

As we walked, I contemplated how the day might go. The last thing I wanted to do was sit in a council meeting with my mother and the other kings and queens of Eilé. Okay, I wasn't being completely honest with myself. I was dying to meet the other Tuatha De, excited but terrified at the same time. What would they be like? Would they shun me? Demand that I leave their secret meeting? I was also afraid to learn what the Morrigan was up to. Discussing it with the high queen and her brethren made the path towards an actual war valid, and I had been so enjoying this time out from real life with Cade.

Sighing, I tucked my arm into Cade's and moved in closer to him. He arched a brow at me, but I gave a nervous smile and said with shíl-sciar, *I'm a little nervous about meeting all the gods and goddesses of the Celts.*

He leaned down and pulled me closer with his free arm, almost making me trip over his feet.

You'll do fine, he responded. *They're not like the courtiers who think they are far above you.*

They're not?

Nope. They know *they're far above you, so they don't even bother with proving it.*

I blinked up at him, then caught the smile that was fighting against his tight lips. I smacked his arm and he let out a laugh. My apprehension didn't go away, but Cade's attempt at making me feel better helped.

Cade and I were the last to arrive at the meeting of the gods of Eilé. I had assumed we'd be gathering in my mother's throne room, but instead one of her guards led us through the massive hall into a side chamber. As soon as he threw the doors open and we stepped in, a blast of power, raw and unchained, hit me in a great wave. I stopped walking and wavered, both trying to catch my balance and keep control of my own power and the glamour right next to it.

"Steady, love," Cade whispered against my ear as he held me up.

I took several deep breaths and waited for my heart to slow its erratic beating. Fortunately, no one had noticed our arrival yet. The room was buzzing with conversation, both serious and casual. I stood up straighter, but kept my fingers wrapped around Cade's collar, and took a few moments to study the most powerful Faelorehn in the Otherworld.

There was of course my mother, Danua, reclining at the head of the grand table. Next to her sat the Dagda, his radiating charm spread out like an invisible mantle all around him. He had his arms crossed casually over his chest as he talked with my mother. His hair had been swept back and he'd trimmed his beard. When he glanced in our direction, he winked and smiled at me, never once losing track of his conversation with the high queen.

On the other side of Cade's foster father sat another familiar face. Epona, the fair-haired woman who ruled over the wild horses, spoke quietly with an intense, dark haired and dark eyed man. As I observed him, I noticed that one of his hands was hidden inside a finely-wrought glove of chainmail. My eyes and thoughts must have lingered on him too long, because I detected Cade's gentle words in my head.

That is Nuadu, the famous king from the battle of Maige Tuired. His hand was severely injured and it pains him if the bare skin comes into contact with anything other than the metal used to make that special gauntlet he wears.

I scrunched up my face and thought about the folktale that mentioned the famous battle. It had been a long time since I'd read it, but eventually the details came back to me. In the book, Nuadu had lost his hand and the surgeon of the Tuatha De had created a new one out of silver. I silently prodded Cade about it.

The story said he lost his hand, and therefore couldn't be king, because he was flawed. That's why the false hand was made for him. There was never any mention of a glove.

I felt Cade's smile as he pressed a kiss to my temple. *Legends often skew the facts a little.*

Well, I couldn't argue with that. Once my curiosity about Nuadu was satisfied, I let my eyes continue their journey around the table. A fire-haired giant sat next to Nuadu, Oghma according to Cade, and next to him another large man with brown hair and what looked like a few burn scars on his neck, face and arms.

Goibniu, Cade told me in his silent words when I asked, *our blacksmith. If anyone wishes to learn the art, they study under him or someone he's trained. He's the best there is.*

I took note of the handful of other attendees, most of whom were daughters or sons of those present, or Faelorehn of great power but not so strong as my mother and her brethren. Many of them looked my age, but then again, being from the Otherworld, they could be hundreds or even thousands of years old. I shivered a little. Yeah, I was still getting used to this immortality thing. My wandering gaze skidded to a stop when they fell upon a man with golden hair and beautiful blue eyes. For a few seconds my mind went blank as I admired him. This was no common Faelorehn.

Who is that? I asked Cade in awe.

He glanced up and searched for the god who had captured my attention. He laughed softly when he discovered who I was talking about. *That, my love, is Lugh. The Celts called him the Master of all the Arts, and he is one of our most talented and powerful rulers.*

As I ogled him, I had no doubt that he was everything Cade claimed him to be. He was stunningly beautiful, his hair such an unusual shade of blond and his skin almost glowing with life. He sat back and casually surveyed his fellow Tuatha De, joining cheerfully in a conversation every now and again. In fact, I was so distracted by his radiant presence that it took me a while to notice the quiet man sitting at his side. When my eyes finally left Lugh's striking face and caught sight of his companion, I nearly gasped out loud. How I hadn't noticed him before was a mystery, what with the antlers protruding from his head. Perhaps he had been making himself invisible before now, but at that very moment he was as real and present as the golden god sitting next to him.

Cade and I had been moving gradually deeper into the room, but after spotting Cernunnos I froze, my feet rooting in place. Cade stopped with me and gave me an inquiring look, but my thoughts and attention were somewhere else entirely. My gaze was fixed on the god of Eilé's wild places, and as the memories of our strange meeting in front of the Tree of Life poured forth, that little magical spider sleeping in a dark corner of my mind burst to life and started working frantically to gather up my thoughts.

I had not expected to see him here. Why I had thought he wouldn't heed my mother's call, I couldn't say. Maybe because he had seemed too unreachable, too wild, to be influenced by something as simple as Danua's summons. But here he was, leaning against the window pane, as close to the wild as he could get in this beautiful castle, his arms crossed as he listened to something Lugh was saying to him. Yet, he wasn't really listening, for he had seen and recognized me. His brown gaze was captivating, and his mouth gave a slight upward tilt, but that was all the acknowledgment I got. After having his thoughts in my head on more than one occasion, the gesture was almost ridiculous.

Cade, apparently, noticed the exchange as well. He moved in closer to me, stepping just so and breaking my eye contact with the antlered god of the woods.

"Why is Cernunnos looking at you like that?"

It was a murmur, but it sounded like a death threat. I gave Cade a troubled look. Had that sliver of his ríastrad returned? His green eyes had flickered to a dark brown and he looked almost violent.

I swallowed, only to find my mouth dry. "He-he spoke with me in the Weald, when you were gone those first several weeks after we arrived in Eilé."

There. That was all I was going to tell him. The gift Cernunnos had given me was still unknown to others; my little magical spider still keeping my secret wrapped up securely. My heart raced and I was afraid Cade would notice my pulse as he grasped my hand more tightly.

He stepped even closer and placed his hand on my face, his fingers splayed and trailing down my cheek. I sighed and closed my eyes.

"Did he threaten you Meghan? Did he try to seduce you?"

Wait, *what*? My shock must have been clear on my face because Cade continued with shíl-sciar, *He has a reputation, Meghan, of charming young women and taking advantage of them. Especially beautiful young women.*

I felt dizzy all of a sudden, both from the implication of what Cade had said and from his sincere compliment. *Had* Cernunnos been trying to seduce me? I frowned and tried to remember the details of that day in the meadow with the Tree of Life. As hard as I tried, I could not recall the horned god's conversation or actions being seductive in any way. Yes, he had talked me into accepting his gift of Tuatha De magic, but even then, when he touched me, it didn't seem inappropriate in the least.

No Cade, he was kind to me, I finally managed. *I was just surprised to see him here is all.* I grinned and looked Cade in the eye. *I didn't think my mother's influence was strong enough to entice the god of wild things to come to a fortress.*

The vice-like grip on my hand loosened and I could feel Cade physically relax.

"Good," he murmured, leaning down to press his lips to the top of my head. And then with a mischievous grin and a challenging glint to his eye, he said, "Because he can't have you."

I snorted at that, having half a mind to tell Cade no one could have me; I was not a possession, but then someone in the room cleared their throat. Oh. I guess we were causing a scene. I hooked my arm around Cade's and leaned into him a little, biting my lip to keep from blushing. Okay, I guess he could have me, just as long as I could have him back.

Danua eyed us with slight annoyance as we took our seats beside her. I was glad to see that she had reserved one for Cade as well.

The moment we were seated, my mother rose, the heavy skirts of her sapphire gown flowing around her like water. She lifted her hands and a cool flush of power poured over everyone. I actually shivered, but managed to stay calm.

The moment the friendly chatter ended, my mother took a breath and said, "As you all know, we are here today to discuss a problem that has been growing for quite some time. During the past several weeks, the young Caedehn MacRoich," she paused and acknowledged Cade with a formal nod, "traveled throughout Eilé seeking both counsel and aid from each of you. The fact that everyone is present today gives me great hope that we will come to some desirable conclusion with regards to our common plight. That plight being that the Morrigan has become more determined than ever to take my throne and unleash her evil power upon all of us.

"She plans on doing this by either enslaving or destroying my daughter and taking her magic," she paused and gestured towards me. Nearly every set of eyes turned to look in my direction and it took all my willpower not to shrink into the cushion of my chair.

"Why not take the magic from another Faelorehn?" a young man with dark hair called out. "She can't possibly have any more power than the rest of us."

Despite the slight sting of insult in that comment, I was thankful for the distraction. Everyone lost interest in me, and I joined them as we cast our eyes in the young man's direction. He was rather good-looking, I couldn't help but notice. Tall and broad, his dark brown eyes flashing to hazel.

My mother sighed and rolled her eyes to the ceiling.

"Bowen," the man next to Epona, Nuadu, growled in warning.

Danua held up a hand. "No, it is alright Nuadu. He has a point. The reason I believe the Morrigan is after my daughter is complicated."

I froze, utterly horrified. Where was Danua going with this . . . ?

"The Morrigan has never liked me, and when Meghan was born, I was forced to send her into the mortal world so that she would never know the evil of that goddess. Unfortunately, Meghan discovered our world and broke the geis of protection I'd placed over her. The Morrigan tried to take her magic then, since she was an easy target having not grown up in Eilé and ignorant in the ways of wielding her own glamour properly. But Meghan proved she was stronger than the Morrigan anticipated."

Wait, was it just me or was that a hint of pride in my mother's voice?

I blinked up at the high queen, and she gave me a small smile before throwing her mask of sovereignty back on. My heart nearly stopped. Was my mother, in her strange, silent way, trying to reach out to me? Despite the fact that she had wanted to put our healing process off until after this war?

Danua took a breath and continued, "Now I believe it's mostly about revenge for the Morrigan, and as we all know, when the war goddess is on a mission of vengeance, she is twice as dangerous."

Silence descended upon the room and I gritted my teeth. I appreciated my mother's sincerity, but now everyone knew my story and that the Morrigan was on a rampage because she couldn't handle being outdone by a pathetic Faelorehn who didn't know how to use her magic. Despite my general unease, however, I allowed Danua's small bit of praise and acknowledgment bring me some joy. Maybe she was warming up to me after all.

"Does that answer your question Bowen?"

The young man nodded once, shot me a quick, appraising look, then sat back down. For some reason, his quick yet efficient assessment of me made my skin tingle.

"Are there any further concerns?" Danua asked, casting her eyes over those sitting around the grand table.

When no one spoke up, she continued, "Then I'll give each of you a chance to speak. If you have any information or any ideas on how to take on the Morrigan, please feel free to share your thoughts now."

The Dagda rose out of his chair and cleared his throat. "My foster son and I spoke at length just recently." He gave Cade a nod of acknowledgement. "He informed me that the Morrigan has enlisted help from someone of great power."

A light murmur grew in the room and I clenched my hands into fists.

"How do you know this?" Danua asked, her voice sounding a bit strained.

I looked at Cade and his face was as serious as ever. Had he and the Dagda not told my mother about their theory?

"Because she has already launched two attacks on us, your Majesty," Cade said without getting up.

The high queen shot her eyes in his direction, her face paling ever so slightly. "When? How?"

"Just after Meghan arrived in Eilé," Cade continued. "A small army of faelah descended on Luathara the very evening Meghan and I returned from the mortal world, and we were overwhelmed by faelah once again on our journey to the Dagda's. The only way she could have gained enough power after losing it the day she tried to capture Meghan is if she had help. And not just any help, but the assistance of someone of great power."

A cool silence descended upon the room once again as everyone let Cade's words sink in.

"And I'm assuming by your tone that you know who this ally of the Morrigan is?" Danua said slowly.

Cade nodded. "Donn."

Surprised gasps, some louder than others, filled the room.

Before the chatter could get out of hand, Lugh stood from his chair, graceful as a lion, and the Tuatha De quieted down. He splayed his fingers out to support his arms as he leaned over the table and let his head hang.

"Caedehn is right. The moment he arrived at my doorstep a week ago, I sent out spies to see if what he claimed was true. The Morrigan has, indeed, enlisted the help of Donn."

"How on Eilé did she manage that?" the man with the scars, Goibniu, asked.

Cade shook his head. "We don't know."

"Donn has more power than any three of us combined!" Epona cried.

As the murmurs of disbelief made their way around the table, I glanced at Cade.

You didn't tell everyone your suspicion about Donn and the Morrigan when you left to summon them?

No, was his answer. *I told them I suspected the Morrigan had found an ally in her evil plot, but I never told them who I suspected.*

I thought about that, then took a moment to survey the faces around me. It was clear now that none of them were the culprits, but I could understand why Cade had been careful not to share his thoughts. Well, except with one of them . . .

Wait, Lugh . . . You told Lugh about Donn.

Cade's hand tightened on mine.

Why did you trust him and not the others?

The strange essence of a shíl-sciar sigh washed across my mind.

Because he is my grandfather.

This time, my hand tightened on his.

Your grandfather?! Lugh is your grandfather? And the Morrigan your mother and Cuchulainn your father . . .

I turned and gave him a fierce look. *Anything else I should know?* I tried to keep the bitter sarcasm from my words, but I suspected their color reflected my emotions too well.

Cade winced, then responded, *No Meghan, you now know all my secrets.*

And just like that, my irritation evaporated into thin air. He had to use that word, secret, didn't he? Who was I to be angry when I was the one keeping a huge secret? Nervous, I darted my eyes in Cernunnos's direction, only to find him regarding me with curiosity. I swallowed back my sudden fear and took a mental inventory of my spider. Yup, she was there, spinning away.

I let out a deep breath and sent to Cade, *I'm sorry I got upset. I guess you just never really got a chance to tell me about Lugh.*

I planned on introducing you two later tonight. I'm sorry you found out this way.

He pulled my head forward and kissed my hair and I no longer felt offended. Unfortunately, I was the only one. The room was still abuzz with the angry, distressed voices of the Tuatha De.

Lugh lifted a ring-encrusted hand and waited for the room to become quiet before continuing. "As you are all well aware, Donn and the Morrigan working together is a big problem. If we had every single able-bodied man and woman here with us to fight, we might be able to overtake the two of them. Unfortunately, I was only able to rally my guard and perhaps half of those living in my realm. What say the rest of you?"

A light murmur of ascent traveled through the room, most of those present agreeing with Lugh.

"We could always send word to our people," Nuadu said. "Perhaps we can stir them to action when they are aware of what has developed."

Danua nodded in his direction. "And you and your men and women are all welcome to remain in Erintara until we receive further word of the Morrigan's plans, if you wish."

Many heads nodded in thanks.

"Thank you, Danua," Lugh said. "But I feel we still have some time before the Morrigan acts."

"How much time?" Epona called out.

Lugh sighed, then glanced up at me. It was a quick, brush of his gaze, nothing more, as if he was trying to assess me without my knowledge. My stomach turned.

"I don't know for certain," he said. "But it's as if she is waiting for something."

More troubled murmuring broke out at the great table and I felt myself shrink inwardly. Right at that moment I imagined the Morrigan sitting in her own dark castle, pacing as she drew out another plan, one that had to take place before she launched herself into a war against her fellow gods and goddesses. A plan that involved capturing me and draining me of my magic so that she could be all but invincible. And how much more invincible she'd be when she got a hold of the magic Cernunnos had given me . . .

Unconsciously, I shot my eyes up and met the antlered god's gaze once more.

Yes Meghan, she waits for you . . .

I hissed and tore my eyes away, only to attract the attention of Cade and my mother.

"What's wrong Meghan?" Danua asked, her question plunging the room into silence.

Suddenly, every pair of eyes was on me. I took a deep, shuddering breath and released it slowly.

"Nothing," I mumbled, "sorry."

I felt my face flush.

My mother regarded me for a few moments more, then stood and said, "Is there anything more we need to discuss for today?"

When no one spoke up, she continued, "Very well. We will call this meeting to an end. As I said, you are all welcome to stay here for as long as you need. The Morrigan and Donn are preparing for a war, and so must we. I'll have my swiftest messengers travel to your lands with missives asking for help. Let's hope we get some volunteers.

"For now," Danua took a deep breath, "feel free to rest. In an hour's time I would like to welcome you properly with a formal dinner and after party. Regardless of the dismal circumstances for which we've been called together, I would be ashamed if I didn't offer you the proper food and entertainment you all deserve."

My mother gave a small grin, her eyes flashing between blue, green and grey, and then dismissed us.

Without a second glance, I bolted for the door, dragging Cade close behind me by the hand. His surprised grunt was drowned out by the light chatter of the Tuatha De as they followed us, but I ignored it. I couldn't wait to get back to our room. In one hour we would be thrown back together in the dining room, then the dance hall, and I knew every last one of them would want to meet me. The girl who had antagonized the Morrigan into starting a war.

Meghan? Are you alright? Cade sent as we headed up the stairs.

I just need to prepare myself is all, I returned, hoping he didn't pick up on the panic in my thoughts.

Finally we reached our room. When Cade excused himself to go meet with the Dagda, I shut the door securely behind him and then slid to my knees as the tremors took over.

Sixteen

Admission

I spent most of my free hour trying to wrangle my emotions into some semblance of normalcy. Fear, anxiety and anger reared their ugly heads, but I think the guilt clawed at me the most. A nice, long, hot shower helped get things under control, and when Cade quietly rejoined me, I was able to face him without bursting into tears.

Get a grip Meghan! No meltdowns in front of the Celtic gods! my oh-so considerate conscience told me.

Dressed once again in formal attire, Cade and I joined the Dagda and we headed towards my mother's grand dining hall. Fortunately, we were seated next to Danua again and I wasn't forced to make small talk with any of the Tuatha De.

A hand on my arm snapped me out of my self-loathing funk. I glanced up to find the Dagda's kind eyes regarding me.

"No one blames you for this Meghan. I know you don't want to believe me, and I know you weren't convinced when I told you before, but it's still the truth."

For some reason, his words comforted me. Maybe because when I set my fork aside and took the time to glance around the table, all I met were kind, curious eyes. Perhaps their curiosity had nothing to do with my connection to the Morrigan but with the fact that I was the daughter of their high queen. That thought alone helped warm me and dispel some of my fears.

Casting the Dagda a brilliant smile, I nodded my thanks then got back to my dinner.

Afterwards, we all converged on Danua's ballroom floor. There were only about fifty of us altogether, the soldiers having remained in their own lodgings. A small party of musicians were setting up their instruments in one corner, and soon the light, airy flow of music mingled with the many voices echoing throughout the spacious hall.

The young man from earlier, Bowen, wove his way through the crowd, heading in my direction. I felt myself tense and instantly Cade's hand was in mine.

Bowen stopped a few feet away and gave a polite bow. "I was wondering if Meghan would like to dance."

I froze. He'd called me by my name. Not 'Princess' or 'Lady'. And he had a very kind voice. I studied his brown eyes and couldn't find any of the vicious humor I'd seen in the young men who frequented the Dagda's party.

Go ahead Meghan. Bowen is honest and it will do you some good to get to know more of your peers, Cade spoke into my mind.

Are you sure? I returned.

Cade's answer was a light chuckle and a quick kiss on my neck before he nudged me forward.

Yes I'm sure. I have no fear of Bowen stealing you from me. He knows better.

Releasing a mental snort, I gave Bowen my full attention and said, my voice a little wobbly, "Sure, uh, Bowen. I'd love to dance."

Bowen took my hand in a firm but not overbearing grip. The first dance wasn't a slow one, but it wasn't too fast either.

"So, Meghan, daughter of Danua, why don't you tell me a little about yourself."

His words were friendly and he sounded genuinely interested, so I opened my mouth with the intention of only telling him little, insignificant things. But once I began, the floodgate came down and I simply gushed stories from my childhood and high school years, as well as those from my time spent in the Otherworld. After three songs, the band took a break and I found myself standing in front of Bowen, a bit dazed. Had I really just spent all that time babbling without once giving him a chance to share?

"I'm so sorry!" I said, pressing my hands to my cheeks. "I just spent a good fifteen minutes talking about myself!"

I was horrified, but Bowen only laughed. Man, he had a nice smile . . .

"Don't worry about it. I enjoyed your stories, but I'm afraid you'll have to ask me about mine some other time."

He nodded towards something over my shoulder and I turned to find Cade approaching. Grinning sheepishly, I thanked Bowen for the dance and rejoined Cade. He met me with open arms and as we moved to the rhythm of the music, he asked me if I had enjoyed Bowen's company.

He's very nice, and almost as cute as you. If you ever change your mind about me, I'm going directly to him.

Never! Cade returned, pulling me closer. I bit my lip against a smile. His shíl-sciar words had been pure conviction. *I would never give you up, my love.*

We danced for a little while more, and when the musicians stopped for a longer break, Cade took me around and introduced me to some of the Tuatha De. They were so overwhelming, what with their pure, raw magic practically pouring off of them and their ancient, all-knowing eyes. Epona and the Dagda I already knew of course, but when Cade pulled me over to Lugh, I broke out in a nervous sweat.

"Lugh," Cade said, "I would like you to meet Meghan Elam, daughter of Danua."

Admission

The magnificent god turned away from his companions to consider me, one perfect eyebrow arched over a sapphire eye. For several endless seconds, he studied me but then his face broke into a brilliant smile.

"Why young Meghan, I've heard a lot about you, both from my grandson and his foster father."

My knees almost buckled as relief coursed through me. "And I've read a lot about you," I blurted.

Lugh adopted a look of slight surprise and I felt my face flush scarlet. Brilliant Meghan, *brilliant* . . .

But then Lugh burst out laughing.

"Oh yes," he said once he'd regained some composure, "for some reason the Celts were extremely impressed with me."

His smile was enough to light the room.

Oh, I can see why . . . I thought as I self-consciously brushed back my hair. When I was certain my face had regained its normal color, I glanced back up, taking a few moments to study the Tuatha De king before me. Lugh. The Master of all the Arts. Cade's grandfather. Although it wasn't immediately apparent, I could see the similarities between them. They both had the same strong, straight nose and there was a familiarity in Lugh's smile I'd see so many times in Cade's.

Feeling a bit bold, I cleared my throat and said, "So, why do they call you the Master of all the Arts?"

The man who had been standing beside him, the one with the silver glove, Nuadu, rolled his eyes then tilted his glass of mead towards the blond Tuatha De. "Because he is well learned in everything there is to know."

I looked back at Lugh with a question on my face. Could someone really be the best at everything?

Lugh sighed and set down his own glass. He crossed his arms and focused all his attention on me. I did my best not to squirm.

"When we first crossed over into the mortal world, into the realm of the Celts, I was several thousand years old. Many of the skills that their people trained for, I had already mastered. Think about it for a moment, if you had an eternity of time on your hands, wouldn't you grow bored of the same old thing?"

He paused and waited for my reaction. I nodded. Anyone would get bored.

"So, since I was so well practiced in such a variety of skills, I have come to be known as the Master of all the Arts. In Celtic myth at least."

He grinned, picked up his glass once again, saluted me with it, then drained what was left.

We spent several more minutes talking to Lugh and Nuadu, but when the music started playing again, Cade led me off into another round of dancing. After several dances, I was ready for a break. As Cade and I headed away from the center of the dance floor, I spotted an open door leading onto a large balcony.

Breathing a sigh of relief, I turned to Cade. "I'm just going to go get some fresh air."

Cade nodded and lifted my hand to his lips, planting a kiss just below my wrist.

"I need to go speak with Nuadu and Goibniu. I'll come find you when I'm done."

I nodded then lifted my skirts and headed for the open door. Long, heavy drapes blocked most of the entrance, but I simply swept them aside and sighed at the cool caress of night air that met my heated skin. I hadn't realized how warm it was in the ballroom.

For fifteen minutes I simply stood there, leaning against the stone balustrade and studying the city far below. Erintara wasn't exceptionally large, but the buildings closest to the castle were crowded and several stories high. A few bonfires decorated the dark landscape like brilliant little stars, farmers burning off what remained of the harvest. I wrinkled my nose at the sharp smell of smoke and smiled. I loved that smell. Taking a deep breath, I imagined staying out here all night and forgetting about the room full of Tuatha De Danann and their plans for war. I could disregard what my mother had said to me and everything that had been discussed at dinner. I could simply be a young woman enjoying a break from dancing with a handsome young man. Unfortunately, my little fantasy didn't last for very long.

I felt more than heard someone approaching. I whipped around, expecting Cade, but felt a pang of unease and disappointment when I recognized the man who'd broken free from the crowded ballroom. So much for forgetting about the doom and gloom that loomed so close in my future . . .

Cernunnos smiled and sketched a neat bow. "I'm losing my touch, I can see. I'm usually able to sneak up on anybody, but I guess I can't fool you."

I stood up tall, the thick skirts of my formal dress pooling around the stone floor of the balcony. I tried to adopt an air of grace and importance that would do my mother proud, but I'm afraid I was shaking a little too much to pull off the whole haughty princess act.

"May I stand with you for a spell?" the antlered man asked.

I narrowed my eyes, but nodded. I didn't trust him. So far I'd managed to keep his magic nice and hidden, and under control, but I'd been doing a lot of thinking since leaving the Weald. It seemed strange how he had singled me out to give me that extra supply of magic. Kindness had been my first assumption, but why would a god want to be kind to me? Especially when he didn't know me? Then slowly, the truth began to reveal itself, the way solid earth became apparent once winter's snow gradually melted away. The Morrigan was after me, she planned on attacking *me*. I had more than thoroughly convinced myself of that fact, despite the constant denial of Cade and the Dagda. Cernunnos was aware of this little detail, and since I was still relatively ignorant of the ways of Eilé, why not give me a boost of magic and send me on my way? Give me the impression that I could handle the Morrigan on my own? What a perfect plan it was. Send Meghan out to face her enemy with her extra magic, to weaken the Morrigan so that she may be easier to deal with. Yes, these thoughts had been brewing over the past few weeks in the back of my mind, and here was the perfect opportunity to confront Cernunnos about it.

As soon as the antlered god was standing beside me and I was certain the noise of the crowded ballroom would cover our voices, I whispered harshly, "I know why you really gave me that extra magic. You needed a pawn to distract the Morrigan, and I was the perfect candidate."

He had the good grace to start, so I looked him square in the eyes. Yes, he was surprised, but not in a guilty sort of way. More in an I-can't-believe-she-figured-it-out sort of way.

I crossed my arms over my chest and released a bitter laugh. "I knew it. You're nothing but a coward. You strut around, flaunting your power and happily accept the status of godhood, but when one of your own decides she wants more power than the rest of you, not only do you turn a blind eye when she resorts to nefarious means to get it, but you seek out the naive people you believe to be your underlings to do the dirty work for you."

Cernunnos released a huff of breath. "I, and the rest of the Tuatha De for that matter, allowed the Morrigan no such thing. She has been performing her wicked deeds against our better knowledge."

I gasped in disbelief. "Unbelievable! How can you say that? How can you say that when Cade has been shunned from society for his entire life because of the acts of his mother?!"

My fingers curled until my hands made fists, and if it wasn't for his impressive height and the pointy antlers protruding from his head, I'd have slapped the man standing before me right in the face.

"Listen Meghan," he growled, his teeth gritted. "Yes, I did use you, but I didn't do it in order to avoid playing my part in all of this. For awhile the Morrigan did act in secret. We all knew what she was, yes, but by the time we realized her ultimate plan, her magic had grown too vast. So, we appeased her by fighting little battles to keep her power in check. She was happy with this arrangement because she could still play the war goddess but it never led to actual war. Now that she's had a taste of your power she wants more, and since you had the guts to stand up to her, she's even more determined."

"But why give me some of your power? Why not just join us and help us fight? What was the point?"

He released a heavy sigh and placed his hands on the balustrade, leaning his head over so that his chin nearly touched his chest. His antlers must have been heavy, because it seemed to take great effort to lift his eyes back up to mine. A sad, desperation lingered in their brown depths.

"I didn't give you some of my power, Meghan. I gave you *all* of it."

I felt like I'd been slapped in the face. Stunned, I gathered my voice and managed to ask, "What?"

Cernunnos sighed and drew himself to his full height. He was a robust character, what with his broad shoulders, lean build and the wild energy of the forest seeping out of him. A presence to be felt in every sense, just like all the other Tuatha De. But in this moment I noticed something was missing, something that had been present the first time I'd met him. He had hidden it well, but now that I gave him a good look, I realized he was telling the truth.

"You have in your possession all of my magic. Not the natural magic that all Faelorehn contain, but that special degree of glamour that only the Tuatha De possess."

So many thoughts burst forth in my mind, all of them concerning this great secret I held. The many legs of my hidden spider whipped madly about as she worked to capture them all. No wonder I'd had so much trouble getting his magic under control. My head was spinning, but again I managed to get out another word.

"Why?" I murmured.

"Because of a geis."

I blinked dumbly. Huh? Then I grew angry.

"Ugh, I'm so damn sick of that word! Is it a requirement or something? In order to be Faelorehn, you must have a geis placed on you? Everyone and their mother seems to have a geis around here."

Cernunnos stood straight and arched an eyebrow. "Trust me, it isn't something to take lightly."

I snorted. "Oh, believe me, I know."

"Mine has to do with something I learned one day while wandering the Weald. Every now and again I simply travel though my forest to make sure all its inhabitants are following the natural order of things. Sometimes, the Spirits of Nature speak to me. Other times, they offer me information."

He paused and looked at me to make sure I was listening. I flapped my hand. "Go on."

"About a month ago, the Spirits told me a great battle loomed on the horizon, a battle that could mean the end of the Morrigan's tyranny for several centuries. They also said they'd tell me how to defeat the goddess of war if I paid the right price."

My skin was prickling, and not because of the cold air of the open patio. This had something to do with the power I now held next to my own. Cernunnos's power. And that bud of magic knew as well. I'd been fighting it since he stepped out onto the patio; clamping it down with my own magic as it struggled to unfurl.

Cernunnos took a deep breath and continued. "They told me that if I gave my power over to another, a young woman who was new to our world but very important to its future, then I could learn of the secrets to winning this inevitable war. So, I accepted their offer."

"And?" I whispered, my voice coming out hoarse and demanding. "What did they tell you."

He smiled, his teeth reflecting what little light had seeped through the curtains.

"That, like your own secret, I cannot tell you lest I break my geis and forfeit all that I am."

I reached my hand backwards and was relieved when it came into contact with the back of a stone bench. I sat down, not worried about crumpling the rich, dark folds of my gown. For a few moments I simply took in air, breathing slowly through my nose. In and out. In and out.

Eventually I found my voice again. "What, what happens to your magic when this is all over?"

Cernunnos shifted his weight. "I get it back. As long as I keep my end of the bargain, my glamour will be returned to me. So, if you reveal your secret before it's time, or if you die before then or use it when it is needed, I'll get it back."

He smiled, a smug look on his face.

Anger shot through me then. So, in a nutshell, he gets his magic back no matter what happens to me. I rose to my feet, my hands clenched into fists.

"And when am I supposed to use this magic exactly?"

"Come now Meghan. I've given you a few clues here and there; nudging you along in the right direction so you don't flare out too early."

My jaw dropped. He didn't care. He had set me up for this and he didn't care. He had received all the information about how the outcome of the war against the Morrigan was going to go down and all he had to sacrifice was his glamour for a temporary amount of time. Which was no big deal because now he had me to go in and do the hard part for him. And no matter what happened, he'd get all his nice, lovely magic back. And what could I lose? My Faelorehn identity, my life, Cade . . .

"You *bastard*!" I hissed, ready to burst forward and punch him. I didn't care about his antlers anymore.

I drew my arm back to hit him, but he figured out what I was doing and grabbed my wrist before I could make contact. Unfortunately, at that very moment someone threw back the thick curtains separating us from the ballroom. I whipped my head in that direction and all the blood drained from my face. Cade stood there looking like a bull ready to charge. He darted his dark green eyes between me and the god standing only a few feet away from me, gripping my wrist as I fought against his hold. I could only imagine what he saw: Cernunnos looking as if he wished to drag me off someplace against my will. Oh, this couldn't end well . . .

Cade moved so quickly I hardly had time to see it happen. His fingers were wrapped around Cernunnos's throat and he actually lifted the god off the ground.

"If you hurt Meghan in any way, if you so much as make her frown because of something you say to her, you'll regret it."

Cade's teeth were clenched and his arm grew before my eyes, the muscles bulging, the bones lengthening and straining the sleeve of his shirt.

"Cade!" I cried.

He ignored me, his focus entirely on Cernunnos. "I may not be able to kill you, but I sure as hell can incapacitate you for a few days."

Admission

Cernunnos kept a tight grip on the fingers that were wrapped around his throat. Cade held him a few moments more, but then dropped him. The antlered man bent over, struggling to catch his breath. Before long the coughing turned to laughter.

He stood up, his eyes watering and his face slightly red. He smiled and his eyes were alit with mischief.

"Well done Caedehn! But have no fear, I mean your sweet Meghan no harm. A pity though. It would be fun to take you on in my stag form. But alas! Not tonight. Not with your foster father and grandfather just in the other room."

He stepped forward, but kept his distance from Cade. Before reentering the ballroom, he turned and gave me another bow, this one more sloppy than the one he'd greeted me with.

In my mind, his words whispered across my conscience. *Remember Meghan, you can't tell a single Faelorehn man or woman about that magic I gave you.*

My eyes narrowed. I knew this already, why was he repeating it? Did he think I was stupid enough to forget?

He must have sensed my irritation because his face softened ever so slightly before his words reached out to me again. *I am allowed to offer you one more sliver of information the Spirits of the Wild shared with me. You will have spent some time in the Morrigan's lair before you can act. That is all I am permitted to say.*

I drew in a sharp breath as my eyes grew wide. The Morrigan's lair? That could not be good. But at least he was giving me more to go on.

"Remember what we discussed, dear Meghan," Cernunnos said aloud, his dark eyes hard and locked with mine. "And keep an eye on that boy of yours. Quite the temper he has. It could get him into trouble."

I crossed my arms and glared at him but made no response. He chuckled and slipped past the curtains to join the other revelers.

Cade stepped forward, reaching out an arm. "Meghan," he said quietly.

I threw my arms down and shoved him hard in the chest. Cade grunted in surprise as he took a step back to catch himself.

"You idiot! What is wrong with you? Why on earth would you entice a Celtic god like that? Do you have a death wish?"

Cade merely rubbed his chest, frowning in slight confusion. I sighed and dropped my face into my hands.

"I was the one trying to hurt him," I grumbled.

Cade gently took one of my hands and pulled it away from my face. I looked up at him, my expression one of misery.

"Why?" he asked.

When I didn't answer immediately, his eyes grew hard again and he asked with a clipped tone, "And why was he out here confronting you to begin with?"

Oh yes, why indeed. What could I tell Cade without making him suspicious?

I shrugged, trying to shake off this new batch of unease. "We had a misunderstanding is all."

As I turned to head back into the ballroom, Cade's hand fell on my shoulder, stopping me.

"Meghan," he said, his voice gentle but insistent.

I cursed inwardly, my little spider working furiously to capture and bind all the thoughts about Cernunnos's magic that now poured into my mind. *Quickly Meghan, invent some excuse . . .*

"He wanted to introduce himself properly, so he said. Then he made some off-hand comment about Danua I didn't care for."

Cade's eyebrows rose. "Oh?"

Nodding, I swallowed and continued with my fabricated explanation. "Yes." I smiled and stepped closer to Cade. "He couldn't understand why the high queen of Eilé would allow her daughter to traipse around the countryside with a ruffian like you."

Cade returned my smile and pulled me close, molding me against his chest. I took a deep breath, inhaling his scent and letting his presence relax me. After what I'd learned tonight, I needed Cade's comfort like a fish needed water.

When the weight of Cade's heavy arms settled around me, I took a deep breath and closed my eyes, letting my mind drift off.

"I'm sorry Meghan," he murmured against my hair, "about the way I reacted. But when I saw Cernunnos's hand around your wrist . . ."

He trailed off and I felt his muscles tense and his body heat spike. With some effort, I imagined, he got his anger under control. The last thing either of us needed right now was for a piece of his ríastrad to rear its ugly head once more.

Cade sighed again. "I guess I just went blind with rage."

He gently removed me from himself and put his hands on my face. "I thought he was trying to hurt you."

I smiled and stood on my toes, settling my mouth against his. He accepted the kiss and transformed it into anything but the innocent caress I had initiated.

When he finally let me go, I put a hand on his chest, his heartbeat playing strongly against it. I bit my lip to hide a grin.

"I understand Cade. Just try not to anger the gods too much, okay? You need to be whole and healthy when the Morrigan decides to attack us."

And just like that, the little bit of peace Cade had created shattered. Why did I have to go and remember what lay ahead of us?

Cade drew me close again. "Don't think about that now Meghan."

Behind the curtains, where my mother and her court and all the other Tuatha De stood around talking and sharing news, the orchestra started in with a new song. The music was gentle, soothing, as if somehow the people playing the instruments knew I needed some comfort right about now.

"Dance with me princess?" Cade whispered against my temple.

I turned and nipped his ear. He grunted in slight surprise but I merely answered back, my own voice hushed, "Oh, of course my young man. But we must remain out here on the dark balcony so that my mother, the queen, doesn't catch me consorting with a rogue such as yourself."

He laughed and swept me around in a circle. I squealed and allowed my dismal mood to vanish as Cade drew me near again into a slower dance.

We spent a good half hour on that dark patio, dancing to the music drifting past the velvet curtains, before someone finally found us. My worries had been eating away at me for weeks, but at least for that one evening, for those few, precious minutes, I was able to forget my qualms and enjoy the cheerful music, the warmth of Cade's arms and the happiness of knowing I was loved.

Seventeen

News

Cade and I left Erintara a week after the meeting with the Tuatha De, returning to the Weald in order to wait for news from the Morrigan's realm. Although my mother had invited us to stay in the castle, I couldn't stand being there any longer than the seven days that had already passed. It wasn't that the Tuatha De were cruel or rude, or that my mother's cold indifference left me feeling drained (and it wasn't Cernunnos's presence either; he'd been kind enough to keep his distance since our strange confrontation), it was mostly a combination of other factors. The subtle build up of Faelorehn magic was grating away at me and making it harder to control my own glamour, and the constant undercurrent of aggression as everyone scurried about, preparing themselves for the coming war, didn't help either. I could sense the stress in Cade as well, his every muscle tense whenever I put a hand on his arm or leaned against him. It didn't take long before he insisted we return to the Weald.

"It's not so far away that we can't make it back here if anything should develop," he'd told Danua and the Dagda at afternoon tea the day before we left. "Besides, Enorah offered her help and now would be a good time to let her and her best fighters know we will gladly accept their assistance."

"Very well," my mother had replied, as cool and collected as ever. "We will send word when you are needed."

I hated the idea of hiding out, but staying in the castle with all that raw magic bouncing around was out of the question.

My mother rose early the next morning to see us off, the great hooded cloak she wore to ward off the cold hiding her face. To my great surprise, she reached out and took my hand in hers. "Be safe daughter, and know that we will do all we can to thwart the Morrigan."

I nodded once, fighting the tears that suddenly wanted to escape. Turning away, I called out for Meridian, my silent words brushing her mind. She'd been hiding out in the stable, and complained in her own avian way as she found a spot on my shoulder. The stable workers had saddled Lasair and Speirling, and as I spotted the two stallions, the odd sadness that had visited me vanished. The red horse pricked his ears forward at my arrival, tossing his head and whickering softly, his warm breath misting the air.

Cade helped me into the saddle, and once I had my loose riding cloak situated around me, I leaned forward and whispered, "Did you miss me boy?"

Lasair tossed his head again and dug at the cobblestones with his front hoof. I smiled. "Yeah, I missed you too."

Cade led Speirling around to me. "Ready?" he asked, his eyes glimmering with anticipation.

I smiled in return and nodded. I couldn't help but agree with him. The journey to the Weald would do our troubled minds some good. So long as we didn't meet any faelah along the way . . .

With one more wave to my mother and the Dagda, we were off, our horses' hooves clattering along the cobblestone streets of Erintara. The Otherworld had cooled down at autumn's arrival, but that lingering hint of summer still suffused the air. I laughed, despite the relative melancholy still clinging to me. Lasair's whicker matched my mood and he picked up his feet, dancing a little as we made our way down the road.

With my smile still bright, I turned around and glanced at Cade. He had the hood of his long riding cape pulled over his face, but the flash of his teeth told me he enjoyed my antics. My heart all but melted in reaction to his small but sincere gesture.

We climbed into the hills, and in no time we found the dolmarehn we had passed through the week before. Once on the other side, we encouraged the horses into a faster pace, Fergus increasing his own speed to keep up with us. We bypassed the Dagda's, the grouping of hills strangely still and quiet without the cheerful god's presence, and headed directly for the dolmarehn that would take us to Luathara. We had decided early on that we would spend the night at the castle and then head for the Weald first thing in the morning. How long we ended up staying in the magical forest, I couldn't say.

By the time we reached the wooded hill behind Cade's castle, it was nearly twilight. Cade pulled Speirling to a halt and I followed his lead. When Fergus left our side and disappeared down the hillside in complete silence, I knew Cade had sent him ahead to make sure all was well.

Fifteen minutes later the wolfhound reappeared and we urged the horses onward. Briant and his family greeted us in the courtyard.

"Lord Caedehn! Lady Meghan! We have worried about you since last time we parted. How is your sister my lord, and the Dagda?"

"You were supposed to remain in the village," Cade grumbled as he climbed down from Speirling.

Briant brought himself up to his full height. "We live at Luathara now, my lord. It is as much our home as it is yours.

Besides, someone had to make sure it didn't become overrun with the Morrigan's abominations."

Cade merely shook his head and sighed. Who could argue with that logic? As he filled his steward in on the past several weeks, I followed Briant's wife and daughter inside as the stable master led our horses away. Lasair called out to me, seeming agitated as the stranger took his reins. I whipped around and looked at him, his brown eyes flashing with unease.

Leaving my friends on the stairs of Luathara's main entrance, I walked over and pressed a hand to the red horse's forehead. He blinked once, twice, and then he seemed to settle.

"This is home, Lasair. Cade and I must travel to the Weald soon, but it is safe enough for you here. We'll return as soon as we can."

I hated the idea of leaving the horses behind, but they would not fit through the dolmarehn that would take us to Enorah and her wildren, and the people who had returned to keep Luathara's castle in running order would take good care of them. I only hoped the Morrigan was too busy preparing for war to bother with attacking Cade's castle again.

That evening, Cade and I shared a light dinner with Briant and his family. I chatted a little with Birgit, but my heart wasn't in the conversation and I was pretty certain she sensed it. I just had too many other worries on my mind.

Later that night, as I enjoyed the feeling of cozying up to Cade in his great bed, I contemplated what the future might reveal. We had a lot going for us, if I really thought about it. Sure, the Morrigan was the Celtic goddess of war and she had the god of the afterlife on her side, but we had everybody else. I had my own glamour and that extra helping from Cernunnos. And we had the Dagda's Cauldron. A piercing tingle of joy shot through me at that sudden thought. How on earth could I have forgotten about the Cauldron? Suddenly I felt much better about everything that had been keeping me awake at night.

Perhaps we weren't so lost as I had thought. Sighing in pleasure, I snuggled in closer to Cade as his arms wrapped around me.

The moment we arrived in the small village in the middle of the Weald, we were descended upon by dozens of children. The two guards who had spotted us a few miles out wandered off to fetch Enorah, and when she came stepping out of one of the many cabins, Cade let go of my hand and wrapped his sister up in a great hug. She grumbled and struggled to escape, but smiled the entire time. When he let go, it was my turn. Enorah grunted in surprise as I mimicked her brother's gesture.

"I've missed you!" I said, stepping away.

"And I you," she answered, looking at both me and Cade. "Why are you here? Has the war started?"

Cade shook his head. "No, but it shouldn't be long now. We've come to stay with you until Danua summons us. All that Tuatha De magic was wearing us down."

Enorah pursed her lips and nodded. "I can imagine. Well, let us make use of what time we have then. I'll have to get some of the other adults prepared for looking after the young ones while I'm gone. I have at least a dozen good candidates to take along with us when the time comes."

We followed Enorah as she led us to our very own cabin. Once we dropped off our stuff, we headed back out into the village square. We had gotten off to a late start that morning, so by the time we settled into the routine of the village, it was time for the evening meal.

"Tomorrow morning we practice, Meghan," Enorah proclaimed as we enjoyed the rustic cooking of the wildren of the Weald.

The fire felt warm and inviting, and the memories of my month spent here in mid-summer came flooding back. It was good to be within the embrace of the forest again, the safety of its ancient magic settling my nerves.

"Good," I said, taking one more bite of bread. "I haven't had a chance to use my longbow in days."

Enorah only grinned, her eyes glittering with anticipation. Before Cade and I headed for our cabin, we regaled the tale of the attack outside the Dagda's and what had been discussed in Erintara. Enorah listened with full attention, her usually jovial face slowly becoming weighed down with the bad news.

"We're going to have a real fight on our hands then," she finally said. "But that's the one thing about the Faelorehn. We do know how to put up a good fight."

As I drifted off to sleep that night, I tried to keep Enorah's positive attitude close to my heart.

We can defeat the Morrigan and Donn, I told myself. *We have all the Tuatha De and the Cauldron on our side. I just have to have faith.*

My thoughts sounded convincing, but for some reason they did little to ease my mind. Yes, it seemed we had a good chance against the Morrigan, but something I couldn't quite grasp remained hidden under the surface; something unknown and unseen. A haunted spirit that knew something I didn't, but couldn't tell me. I had a bad feeling that whatever it was, it wouldn't reveal itself until much later.

Suddenly, Cernunnos's words came rushing back to me: *Before you use my magic, you must first visit the lair of the Morrigan.*

I shivered and Cade, sensing my distress even in sleep, stirred next to me. Forcing myself to calm down for his sake, I tried to think happy thoughts and eventually I fell into a restless sleep.

Focused. I was utterly, and entirely focused. Breathe in, breathe out. Nice and steady. Eye on the target and . . . release!

I let the arrow fly and it hissed through the air, slicing the apparition in half.

"Good!" Enorah cried as she conjured up another false faelah.

We had been in the meadow a good two hours, Cade's sister creating targets for me with her magic while I practiced my archery skills. This exercise was a lot more difficult than aiming for the non-moving kind of targets, but then again, what good was it trying to kill stationary targets when the ones that mattered in the real world would be moving all over the place?

I shook my head and got back to my task at hand. Cade and I had been in the Weald for well over a month now, biding our time and passing each day in dreaded anticipation for news from Erintara. The temptation to cross into the mortal world and visit my family was great, but so was the fear of drawing attention to them in case the Morrigan was watching. Yes, she knew about my family in Arroyo Grande, but if I stayed away, maybe she wouldn't think I was attached to them any longer. Instead, Cade and I kept our minds occupied by spending most of our waking hours practicing any fighting skills we could think of. Usually Cade or Enorah or some of the older wildren would run me through one drill after another until the moves became second nature.

This morning, however, I had opted to practice archery with Enorah. Cade had left before dawn to check the perimeter and hunt for the evening meal with some of the adults and older children. I was happy to stay back with Enorah. My archery could always use some improvement, especially when it came to moving targets. Another shape came at me, and my focus sharpened. I blew out a great breath, took aim and shot, the arrow tearing through the center of the smoke monster. The magical form disappeared and another soon followed.

Ten more minutes passed before a frantic cry from Meridian forced me to lose my concentration. The arrow missed Enorah's smoke faelah and glanced off a rock.

What is it? I sent, trying to mask my annoyance. If she was just sharing her excitement about something she caught, then I'd be tempted to lock her in the cabin for the rest of the day . . .

Trouble. Village, was all she sent.

My heart nearly stopped. Every last nerve I possessed drew taught and my magic simmered in my chest.

"What's up?" Enorah asked, drawing her magic back into herself and following me as I headed back towards the settlement.

"Don't know. Meridian just told me there was trouble back at the village."

Enorah cursed and picked up her pace, jogging ahead of me. Dread curdled in my stomach as I trailed after her. Had the Morrigan finally made her move? Had she somehow found a way into the Weald? As I hurried down the trail, I pulled an arrow from my quiver and got it ready just in case.

A large crowd was gathered as we came upon the low cabins of the wildren's woodland town. Several of the children stood surrounding a stranger, murmuring and reaching curious fingers out towards his semi-formal clothes. Wait, no, not a stranger . . .

"Briant!" I shouted, dropping my bow and rushing over.

"You know him?" someone asked.

"Yes," I breathed, "he's Cade's steward. What are you doing here Briant? Did something happen at Luathara?"

The steward turned to look at me and the stress in his eyes made me cringe. Oh no . . . Had the Morrigan attacked them? What about his wife, his kids . . . ?

Before my mind could go into full blown panic mode, he held out a shaky hand. I blinked and looked down at a crumpled piece of paper clasped between his fingers.

I swallowed and took it, my eyes flying over the words.

Strayling,

I hope you are enjoying your time hiding away in the Weald with my dear boy, but I am tired of your cowardice. Since you refuse to face me like a true Faelorehn of noble blood, I took the initiative to entice you out into the open. I am just returned from visiting that hovel you once called home in the mortal world and I now have in my possession something I believe is rather precious to you. The next move is yours.

My hands were shaking by the time I reached the end of the note. It wasn't signed, but that made no difference. There was no question who the letter had come from.

"I'm sorry Lady Meghan," Briant said, his voice hoarse.

I didn't ask where he had found the letter, or whether it had been given to him. None of that mattered. I took a deep breath and I felt my magic swell with my emotions.

Cade! I called out using shíl-sciar. I tinged the words with my anxiety, letting him know it was an emergency.

Meghan, he sent back right away, *are you hurt?*

No, Briant is here. He's brought a letter from the Morrigan. She has taken something from my home in the mortal world . . . We have to go see my family.

I let my words trail off as I fought down a sob, but my anger helped burn it away. It would do me no good to lose it now.

I'll be right there, Cade replied.

I let the letter slip through my fingers, and before I knew what I was doing, I felt my knees hit the cold, wet, earth. Briant and Enorah dove for me, shouting my name, their voices strained. The overwhelming black cloud that threatened to take over lingered for a moment, but I clenched my teeth and forced it back to where it had come from. If I was to stand any sort of chance against the Morrigan, I needed to keep a level head.

The hunting party must have been close, because it seemed like only moments passed before Cade had me wrapped up in his arms. He cupped the back of my head with his hand and pressed me against his chest.

"What happened?" he demanded over my shoulder.

No one spoke, but I heard the distinct rustle of paper and knew that someone had passed him the note. After several seconds, he cursed harshly in the language of Eilé.

He sighed deeply and I felt some of the strength leave his body. "We were waiting for a sign," he murmured. "Looks like we got it."

Cade released me and tucked me into his side, then gave his sister a grave look.

"We're going to the mortal world right now, but I want you and those you have chosen to fight to head to Erintara. We'll meet you there as soon as we can."

Eighteen

Acknowledgment

An hour later Cade and I were racing towards the dolmarehn that would take us to the swamp. We urged Lasair and Speirling on until even Meridian and Fergus had trouble keeping up. When we reached the point where the horses could no longer pass, I threw myself off Lasair's back and nearly hit the ground running. Cade was right behind me, his mind and voice silent.

On the other side of the gateway, the swamp was characteristically silent and a light mist worked its way through the treetops. We ran up the equestrian trail, bypassing the backyard and squeezing through the fence with the 'dead end' sign. I hadn't been home in weeks, having been so caught up in my new life in Eilé, and being back so suddenly like this felt strange. It was as if I'd been gone for years. Without even pausing to knock on the front door, I turned the knob as if I was coming home from school.

Mom was sitting on the couch, Logan and Bradley and the twins trying to comfort her, while Dad paced in front of them. Their heads jerked up in surprise when they heard me come through the door. Mom reacted first.

"Meghan!" she screamed. And then she began to sob.

I hated to see my mom lose control like that, so I went to her and wrapped her up in my arms. My brothers piled in on top of us.

"What's wrong? What happened?"

I looked up and scanned the living room, trying to think of what the Morrigan could have taken. I wondered if she'd visited my room and rifled through my things. The only thing of worth to me in there would be some old pictures, and as much as I treasured them, they were here in the mortal world and hardly the type of thing that would draw me out into the open. I wasn't about to offer myself up to the Morrigan over some old photos.

I sighed and pulled away from Mom, sniffling a little and glancing around at my siblings. Logan and Bradley looked shell-shocked, Dad was still pacing and the twins were subdued. Wait . . . Someone was missing. My heart froze in place despite the sudden rushing sensation of fear and my magic surging forth.

"Where's Aiden?"

Oh, but I knew the answer to my questions. I already knew . . .

For an unbearable moment, the room went deadly silent. Then, in a small voice that was far from normal for him, Bradley whispered harshly, "We were playing down on the trail when this lady walked up to us. We thought we should just head back to the house, but she seemed so nice, so we waited a bit. Aiden was the first one to start pulling on us, as if she was a zombie or something. She tried to get us to come with her, but we told her no."

A strange, sick prickling sensation started creeping down my spine, joining in with the pounding of my heart and the flaring of my glamour. Next to it, the rose began to peel open. I bit my lip and forced the magic back where it belonged. I'd held onto Cernunnos's gift this long and I wasn't about to let it free, not when I knew I'd really be needing it soon.

Bradley took a quick, deep breath and continued, "She said she was from the Otherworld and that you needed our help, so we started to change our minds. But Aiden screamed, as if someone had burned him, and started pulling harder on us. I thought it was weird, but before I could tell him to knock it off, the strangest thing happened. The woman," he paled a little before finishing, "she started to do something like magic. Her eyes got red and the sky got darker. We all turned to run but then she grabbed Aiden."

Bradley sniffed as his eyes filled with tears. "We held on as long as we could and we screamed and screamed, but she was too strong."

"Dad heard us and came running out of the house," Logan cut in, "but the strange lady was already going back down into the swamp. Aiden wasn't making a sound or struggling any more but his eyes were huge."

Fear and anger churned in my stomach and I so desperately wanted to scream or hit something or both. The Morrigan. The Morrigan had come to our world and had taken my little brother.

Meghan.

I could hear Cade's words, feel his presence in my mind and I jumped a little. In the rush to get here, with the revelation of what had happened, I'd forgotten he'd been behind me the entire way. Now that my mind was open to his, I knew that he was just as angry as I was.

I turned to my mom, fighting back my rage and despair so that I could get as much information as possible.

Mom still looked rattled, but she was able to tell me the rest of what had happened.

"Meghan, your father followed her down there, down into that swamp. He said she disappeared into some sort of cave, but when he went in after her, it just dead-ended."

Kathara

I looked back at Cade, confusion written all over my face. Aiden was mortal. How could she take him into the Otherworld?

Cade must have been thinking the same thing because his face looked uncertain. He glanced over at Dad and asked, his tone quiet, "A cave at the end of a culvert littered with fallen trees? About a mile from here? She went in with Aiden and never came out?"

Dad could only nod and I felt that fear and anger that was swelling in my stomach take on one more emotion: disbelief. Only the sobbing of the person next to me drew me away from my stunned silence.

"The dolmarehn," Cade said, loud enough for everyone to hear him.

He didn't have to elaborate. Everyone in my family knew what a dolmarehn was and where it led. Ever since their daughter had told them she was from the Otherworld.

My mom became hysterical and I couldn't blame her. My head was spinning and it was becoming hard to breathe. I could feel my well of magic reacting to my emotions and I had to fight to keep it under control. What my family was telling me was impossible.

Mom grabbed my hands, her own shaking and cold. She looked up at me with frantic eyes and cried, "I thought you said we couldn't cross over into the Otherworld!"

"No," I answered, my throat growing dry, "no, you can't. It isn't possible for humans to enter Eilé."

"Then how?!" she cried.

I didn't know. I looked up at Cade. *Could it be possible? Could there be some humans who were able to cross into the Otherworld?*

He shook his head infinitesimally. *No. There are a few who have both mortal and Otherworldly blood in their veins, but they contain the essence of our world and can pass through the boundary. But no human being has ever entered Eilé.*

Acknowledgment

Maybe she's taken him somewhere here, in the mortal world. Maybe she used her magic to hide from Dad when she was in the cave.

I don't know. But her note said she had something precious to you, and Aiden definitely fits that description. And my instincts tell me that if she entered the cave, then she was returning to Eilé.

But how? I felt my eyes fill with tears once again.

Cade sighed, then sent, *I don't know Meghan, but I think we should get back and start planning. The Morrigan has finally made her declaration of war and if we wish to get Aiden back, we'll have to inform the queen and the Tuatha De of what has happened.*

I nodded, gritted my teeth, and looked my mom in the eye. She was a mess and my heart broke again at the sight of everyone looking so defeated.

I stood and glanced at all of them in turn. "We'll find him, Mom, Dad. We'll find him and bring him back."

Everyone remained quiet, but they nodded. I turned to leave but Mom reached out and grabbed my hand.

"Be careful Meggy," she whispered.

I squeezed her hand back and strode to the door where Cade waited for me. We returned to the dolmarehn in silence, both of us thinking furiously about what we had heard and what we were now going to do. According to my family, the Morrigan had carried Aiden into the Otherworld. I knew she intended to use him as a pawn to control me, but strangely, that wasn't what bothered me. What troubled me was that she had done it in the first place. Mortals could not enter the Otherworld, so how on earth had the Morrigan managed to get Aiden through the dolmarehn?

We returned to Luathara, feeling dejected and emotionally drained. The clouds that had been building that morning had finally arrived, and we decided that stopping for lunch was a good idea. Yes, it meant we'd most likely be traveling in the dark by the time we reached my mother's castle, but we couldn't afford to take the time to stay overnight. The Tuatha De needed to know about the Morrigan's recent move so they could start organizing their troops. We needed to arrive in Erintara as soon as possible.

The door to Cade's room creaked open and Briant's daughter walked in with a tray full of food. For some reason or another, my mind flashed back to the first time I had met her and my heart let out a pang of regret. If not for the Morrigan and her selfish, vindictive obsession with power, Birgit and I might be good friends by now, tending to the kitchen garden and laughing over frivolous things. Not that I was one who did much of that, but it would be far better than carrying around all the secrets and fears that had been weighing me down of late.

Birgit set the tray on a table and the tantalizing scent of roast beef greeted my nose. Too bad my stomach was too upset to enjoy it. I felt like tearing my hair out and screaming at the same time. I paced back and forth over the beautiful rugs, imagining I was wearing them out as I wracked my brain, trying to puzzle out how the Morrigan had done it. How had she brought my brother with her to the Otherworld? It was impossible for mortals to come to Eilé. Had she employed some unknown form of magic? And if so, what did that mean for us when we finally confronted her?

"Meghan, please sit down, you'll wear yourself out."

Cade walked over to me and tried to take me in his arms.

"No," I hissed, batting his hands away, "I can't stay still. I have to keep moving, keep thinking."

Nodding grimly, he returned to the windowsill where he'd been leaning and gazed through the rain-speckled panes. The fire crackled and popped in the fireplace and I detected the smallest flinch in Cade's shoulders. Sighing heavily, he braced his hands against the stone ledge and let his head hang as if trying to regain some misplaced strength.

Acknowledgment

I frowned, regretting the way I had pushed him away, but my emotions were too frantic to worry about Cade's feelings right now.

Think Meghan, think! I told myself. *How did she do it?*

Part of the problem was that I was angry, furious really, and I had to fight to keep my power from overwhelming me again. If that happened, I might finally lose control of Cernunnos's magic and end up breaking my geis. As if I needed any other disasters at the moment . . .

Calm down Meghan, calm down . . . But that bitch had taken Aiden. Aiden, of all my brothers! He was the most helpless, and the closest one to my heart. My small, autistic brother who had trouble letting the world know what he felt. He was so vulnerable and reminded me so much of myself when I was his age, what with his mumblings of sometimes seeing things that weren't there, and his dark hair and pale eyes and . . .

I stopped dead in my tracks and gasped so loudly Cade was beside me in an instant.

"Meghan! Alright, enough, you are going to lie down right now."

Cade grabbed my elbows and started leading me to the bed.

"No," I said, feeling my knees nearly buckle. My voice was a rasp and my skin felt clammy. "Cade!"

I looked him straight in the eye and I was sure my face was a haunting picture. The idea that had so suddenly bloomed in my mind was a shocking one. Yet, the strange tingling sensation that prickled along my spine told me my instincts were correct.

"Cade," I said softly as I allowed him to support me, "we need to go see my mother."

"Meghan, we were just in the mortal world," he said, his voice sounding tired. "And we need to get to Erintara."

- 271 -

"No." I shook my head, then added bitterly, "No, we need to go see Danua. Right now. I have some questions to ask her."

Our lunch turned cold in Cade's room as we flew to Erintara, driving our horses as fast as they would go. Kellston was quiet as we passed through, everyone locking themselves away from a sky that promised rain, and as we passed through the dolmarehn on the opposite end of town, I found it appropriate that the weather should match my own dismal thoughts.

When we reached the castle, we were ushered in by Danua's guards. Dusk had settled in and Erintara's hallways were gloomy despite the freshly lit candles and lamps. The only sounds that accompanied us as we made our way towards my mother's throne room were the cracking of our heels against the stone floors, a tempo that kept in time with my heart. Once we'd reached our destination, I burst through the great doors leading into Danua's throne room. As the huge planks of solid oak slammed against the stone walls, everyone turned to stare at me. Epona, Nuadu, Lugh, Goibniu. Even the Dagda looked annoyed. Lovely. I'd rudely interrupted a meeting with all the Tuatha De. So, they'd all decided to take advantage of my mother's hospitality and stuck around. Good. It would take us less time to get ready for an attack this way.

The gods of the Celts glared at me and Cade, taking in our mud-stained clothing and disheveled appearance.

"What in Eilé has possessed you two to burst in here like this?" Nuadu asked, his dark eyes flashing.

"I need to speak with my mother," I snarled. "Right now."

How strange it was that I could so easily throw my weight around like an all-powerful monarch. Even more shocking was the silent but obedient response I received from the men and women who had enough power to squash me like a gnat should they wish. Once everyone had shuffled from the room, I spun around and faced Danua, pain, worry and anger molding my face into a contorted mask.

Cade murmured somewhere behind me, "I'm going to go see if my sister has arrived yet," then made to exit.

I turned just enough to reach out and grasp his fingers in mine. We still wore our riding gloves, but I could feel his strength through the leather barrier.

"No," I whispered, "stay."

Memories from earlier that morning fought their way to the surface, pushing away my fear and anger for a split second. I had been far too agitated earlier to think straight and had pushed Cade away. But now I needed his strength if I were to face Danua, high queen of Eilé, my blood mother, and ask her the questions that fluttered around in my head like panicked birds thrashing against a confining cage.

He nodded and moved to the side of the room, his presence obvious, but giving my mother and me the space we needed. I turned towards Danua once again.

She stood waiting for me, standing tall and elegant and as cold and beautiful as a marble statue on her dais. Her hands were clasped just above her waist and her brilliant eyes shone with challenge, as if she knew the reason behind my abrupt appearance and was daring me to demand answers from her.

"You lied to me," I ground out, my hands curling into fists.

She didn't even bat an eyelash.

"You lied to me!" I repeated. "I am not your only child, am I? You have a son, younger than me, and you abandoned him to the world of mortals as well."

There. I'd said it. The realization that had been clawing at me since it dawned upon me earlier that morning at Luathara. I could feel the tears burning my eyes and the painful ache swelling in my throat. Aiden. My beautiful little brother, who I had always felt connected to but had never really understood why. Until now. Somehow, he was Danua's natural child, just as I was.

"What do you want me to say, Meghan?"

I sucked in a sharp breath. That was Danua, my mother, always calm and collected; heartless, callous, uncaring of the feelings of others. And to think, I'd been moved when she'd shown some compassion at our last parting.

"I want to know the truth! How is it that my foster parents think he is their son? Who is his father? Tell me!" I demanded.

Danua's mouth twitched and finally, *finally*, the mask she always wore began to crumble. She let out a soul-deep, ancient sigh and melted into her throne, pressing her forehead against a palm.

"I didn't lie to you about your father. I merely left Aiden out of it when I told you of your heritage."

She looked up and smiled at me, her eyes shining. My breath caught in my throat. Danua was showing emotion; she was finally letting me see that side of her the Dagda and Cade had always assured me was there.

"You have the same father Meghan, I have loved none but him these past twenty years and more."

My heart lurched. Aiden and I, we were siblings, full-blooded siblings. I wanted to cry out in joy, but then I remembered why I had come here in the first place. The Morrigan had taken him. She was able to bring him to Eilé because he wasn't human. Because he was Faelorehn like me.

The anger at my mother vanished and I looked back up towards the throne. We had to tell the rest of the Tuatha De that the Morrigan had sent her message loud and clear. We had to work out a plan on how to get Aiden back, but I had more questions for my mother.

Acknowledgment

"How could I not know he was Faelorehn? And why don't his eyes change like mine?"

My voice was a whisper, but it carried well in this cavernous room. I heard Cade shift his feet just to the left of me, but I fought the temptation to look in his direction.

His thoughts brushed my mind. *Beloved?* he sent.

He had never called me that before and the sincerity behind the endearment tugged at my heartstrings. I doused my own words with calm when I responded, *I am well Cade. I just need to get through this.*

Danua took a breath and answered quietly, "Because of the geis I put on him."

I felt my muscles tense and a cold dread filled the pit of my stomach. My mother must have sensed my reaction because she lifted a hand. "Only in the mortal world will he be restricted. In Eilé, he will be healthy and whole. He will be able to speak and act like a normal child."

"What did you do to him?" I asked, my voice a harsh whisper.

She looked up at me, her eyes haunted once again. "I suppressed his magic completely. This is why his eyes never changed like yours. Your brother had a very strong aura when he was born, and since it was such a big part of him, I had to hide it from the other mortals." She sighed heavily. "I had made that mistake with you. People notice you Meghan, because of your Otherworldliness. I would go back and do the same for you if I had known it would have helped you fit in more."

A hot tear made its way down my cheek. "Why would you do that to him? Do you have any idea what it was like for him the last nine years? Growing up as an autistic child in the mortal world?"

How could she do such a thing to her own son?

As if she could read my mind, Danua stood up in one swift movement, the room growing darker as her magic reacted to her sudden change in mood.

"I did it to protect him, just as I did it to protect you! Think Meghan, think! I made it so your magic would be with you, small and dormant, but with you. And look at the trouble it caused. Aiden had more power than you when he was born. Imagine what it might have done to him were it allowed to sleep unchecked! His magic might have come to life on its own, despite the drain the mortal world brings upon it."

I reeled back as if slapped. Aiden? More powerful than me? My skin prickled with pride and fear at the same time. What might he be capable of? What would happen if the wrong people found out about his potential? What if the Morrigan knew about his power . . . ?

I gasped and my knees buckled. Cade was at my side before I knew it, gathering me up in his arms, pressing my head gently against his shoulder as he murmured my name between words of comfort.

"I don't think she knows," Danua whispered. "The Morrigan. I received a letter this morning, and I'm assuming you received a similar message, or else you would not have burst in here like this."

She sounded closer, and when I had the strength to look past Cade's embrace, I saw that she had stepped down from the dais. I squeezed my eyes shut, trying to block out the pain. Oh Aiden . . . The Morrigan had been so desperate to have my power and now she had Aiden. He was only a little boy. How could he protect himself from her?

A gentle touch ran down my arm, and I could feel Cade carefully drawing me away from him. I turned towards the touch and found my mother's eyes, so like Aiden's, gazing at me. For the first time in my life, I forced myself to look deeper than the surface. I drew in a breath as I finally found what I had been looking for for so long. Beneath the hard shell of a queen who had ruled an immortal race for centuries there lived a woman who had been torn from the man she loved and had been forced to give up her children to keep them safe. I knew then that Danua wore her aloof, harsh demeanor as a suit of armor, to protect her heart from the terrible reality of the world.

A sob escaped my throat and I took my hands from Cade's shoulders and fell into my mother's embrace.

"I am so sorry my daughter," she whispered against my hair. "I am so sorry for everything. We will find him Meghan, my heart, we will find him and somehow we will be a family once again. I will bring you both here and we will be a family. Please, just let me in, give me a chance to prove to you how much I love you and Aiden."

I cried and I cried as she held me, all of her hard angles becoming soft and welcoming. I stood there and poured my heart out as she hushed me and rocked me and soothed away all my pain.

Nineteen

Atonement

I can't tell you how much time passed before I finally pulled myself together, but at some point my mind started registering lucid thought once again. I peeled myself away from my mother and sniffled. I could barely detect Cade, once again standing in the shadows of the room.

I was very grateful that Danua and I had somehow finally breached the chasm in our relationship, but the flimsy rope bridge that stretched between us was a far cry from the steel and concrete structure it needed to be.

"Tell me," I said as I exhaled a deep breath. "Tell me everything."

"Meghan," Danua said quietly.

"No!" I hissed, "I need to know, please!"

I clutched my arms to myself, shivering at the bite of cold air that filled the cavernous space. My mother sighed and gestured towards the chairs at the end of the room. I moved numbly along, trying to organize the questions in my head. Once we were both settled before the fire, I opened my mouth and said, "What happened to the baby Aiden replaced?"

I feared the answer to this question the most, so I figured it was best to get it out of the way. Mom had been pregnant, I had been old enough to remember that, so there had to have been a baby.

When Danua failed to answer me, I feared the worst. Before I could ask again, she finally answered in a small voice, "She was stillborn."

"Oh no," I said, "did you . . ?"

Danua gave me a harsh glance, her clear eyes slicing through the thick air. "No Meghan, I did nothing to make such a thing come about."

She sighed and began to rub her forehead with one hand. "I always knew what was happening with you, did you know that? I had someone watching you, making sure you were happy. When your foster mother got pregnant with her fifth child, I had every intention of sending my own unborn baby into your world."

She looked up and smiled at me, her own eyes filling with tears. "Your foster parents had already had twins, so it wouldn't be too unbelievable if they had twins again. My plan was to make it look like Aiden and their own child had come into the world together."

"How?" I asked, my throat feeling raw. "How could you pull something like that off? The doctors would know if Mom had been pregnant with twins."

"Meghan, there are so many ways to use glamour, some of which you haven't learned yet," she said almost to herself. "Glamour powerful enough to erase or even change memories."

She glanced up at me, her eyes sad but determined. "I would have had my most trusted advisors and assistants change the memories of all those involved in the birth of the infant and Aiden's joining it, but I learned early on in the pregnancy that the baby would not be born alive. I had a trusted friend use glamour to disguise herself as one of the nurses, then quickly change the memories of all those in the delivery room. Your foster mother never even knew her child had been stillborn."

Kaṭhara

It was all so horrifying. My mom, who had raised me as her own, who loved all of her sons beyond description, had lost a baby and didn't even know it. I wanted to jump up and slap Danua, to scream at her and tell her what a monster she was, but at the same time I wanted to thank her. What would life have been like for my parents if she hadn't given them Aiden? Would the Elams now have a cloud of sorrow and loss hanging over them? Would my brothers have turned out differently because my parents would always, in some way, be mourning the loss of their child? I shuddered at the thought, but there was still more I wanted to know.

"What happened to the baby?"

"She was buried properly in the cemetery of your town, with other infants who had been abandoned or parentless."

I shot up then, anger coursing through me once again. "She wasn't unwanted! How could you!?"

Danua stayed seated, her hands folded in her lap, her forlorn face gazing up at me. I wanted to shake her, and I was about to step forward to do so, but Cade materialized in front of me and wrapped me up in his arms. I couldn't hold the emotional wave back any longer. I broke down into tears, *again*, sobbing freely as he rocked me and spoke my name softly.

"You should have let her hit me Caedehn," Danua said from her seat. "I deserve it more than anyone."

"No, my queen," Cade murmured over his shoulder, "she would have regretted it."

I forced the anger and the tears to fade away as Cade comforted me. I was livid and hurt and confused. I wanted to claw Danua's eyes out, but another part of me wanted to hold her close. She had opened up to me only a few minutes ago, and despite all the times I'd told myself I didn't give a damn about what she thought, her willingness to let me in was like a balm to my soul. We all made mistakes and most of us spent the rest of our lives trying to make up for the worst of them.

Atonement

My mother, the high queen of Eilé, was no different than anyone else. She was trying to right a wrong she had made a long time ago and I could either continue to hold it against her or I could help her through it.

Sniffing back my tears, I pushed Cade gently away, smiling weakly up into his worried face.

It's okay Cade. I've got this.

Are you sure? he asked as he brushed a hand down my cheek.

He had finally removed his gloves and his fingers were warm and rough. I shivered slightly from his touch and reached up to take his hand.

I lifted his fingers to my mouth and brushed his knuckles with my lips. *It's just a lot to take in at once, but I can get through this.*

His fingers squeezed mine before releasing my hand.

"Meghan, I know you think that the Morrigan is after your magic, that this whole mess is your fault, but you're wrong. It isn't about you, it's about me."

I opened my mouth to argue, but she held up a hand, halting whatever speech I was about to make.

"No," she said harshly, her eyes growing hard again. "No, you wanted to know everything and so you shall. I lied to you Meghan, I know this, now give me a chance to make amends. Your father is Fomorian, I did not lie about that, but I wasn't honest about the details of our relationship."

She gazed up at me, her eyes growing soft once more. She quickly flicked her glance towards Cade before looking at me and continuing once again, "As you have now gathered, I did not stop seeing him after you were born. He crossed over into our world to visit me, and I crossed over into his. We tried so hard to stay apart Meghan, but we couldn't."

She glanced up from her lap and grinned crookedly as she looked at Cade again. "I can only imagine you understand what I'm talking about."

The soul-deep burn of my anger subsided a little. Was she no longer so averse to Cade? And then a strange, but very likely, thought invaded my mind. Danua had been so against Cade because she didn't want us to end up like her and my father, separated by the inconvenient conventions of society. I should have been furious at her, but if I listened to her words without letting my emotions tarnish them, then all I could see before me was a woman trying to protect her own heart and those her heart belonged to. Not a queen, not a powerful Faelorehn goddess, but a mother. My mother. And just like that, all my anger fled.

"The last time I saw your father was the day after Aiden was born. He was the one who took him to the mortal world and made sure he became part of your foster family."

Fresh tears filled my eyes, but my hatred and distrust was gone.

"I know you cannot forgive me Meghan, but please, for Aiden's sake and your own, please believe me."

I stepped away from Cade and he let me go. I knelt down in front of my mother, the all-powerful Danua, and took her hands in mine.

"I believe you mother, I believe you."

She cried out, standing up and pulling me into her arms as she did so. We both had tears in our eyes as we stood there, making that bridge stronger and allowing our hearts to heal, if only a little. I felt light on my feet as I finally allowed myself to forgive my mother, and although I welcomed the feeling like a gentle winter rain, the acrid sting of severe anger threatened to spike through me once more. One wound had been repaired, but another was still torn wide open. The Morrigan had my little brother; Danua's son, and from the sudden rush of magic swirling around us, I could tell the high queen of Eilé was thinking along the same lines as I was.

"Now," she eventually said, holding me at arm's length and screwing her beautiful face up into an expression of vengeance, "we get back your brother and knock so much power out of the Morrigan that she'll be nothing more than a legend for the next thousand years."

The moment my mother and I recomposed ourselves, Danua asked Cade to inform the Tuatha De to meet in her counsel room as soon as possible.

Cade gave her a short, formal bow then cast me a reassuring look before quietly stepping out of the room.

Once Cade was gone, silence descended upon us like a heavy frost. Yes, Danua and I had just taken that first step in healing our mother-daughter relationship, but it would take time for us to get used to each other. When a heavy log fell in the fireplace, crackling and sending up a flurry of sparks, the high queen cleared her throat and said, "Shall we?"

She held out a hand, indicating a door that I knew led to her council room. Nodding, I went ahead of her, opening the door and stepping into the familiar room from those several nights ago when I saw the Tuatha De gathered together for the first time. At the moment, the large room was silent, the huge, oval table sleeping like a beast in the darkness. In the next few minutes my mother used her glamour to light the candles and the fire, then summoned someone to bring us tea.

Danua sat in her chair, the one with the highest back, and gestured for me to sit next to her.

"And now we wait," she said simply as she took a sip of her steaming tea from a delicate cup.

I copied her, but before long the oppressive silence returned. I had absolutely no idea what to say to her. I wanted so badly to ask her about my father, but when I opened my mouth, the words just wouldn't come. *You've just been through an emotional blender Meghan, and now it's about to be set on high speed. No wonder you can't speak.* Thank you, conscience . . .

Instead of trying to come up with a meaningless conversation, I glanced out the window. An icy rain pelted the landscape, painting it in various shades of grey. I alternated between chewing on my fingernails and drinking my tea, trying so very hard not to think about what I knew was coming. This meeting that was about to commence would be it. We were going to war. And not only did I have to worry about protecting Cade and myself, but I had to worry about Aiden too.

Without knowing it, I took a deep breath and released a huge sigh.

"I know Meghan," my mother said softly, causing me to start.

I turned my eyes to her. Carefully, she set her teacup back on its saucer, the delicate chirp of porcelain meeting porcelain ridiculously loud.

"This is a terrible test on someone so young, but I want you to know, no matter what happens in the coming days, I am very proud of you."

Suddenly, I was blinking back tears again. I wanted to believe her, but her behavior from several months ago, when we had met for the first time, and even more recently, had me doubting.

Danua only smiled and shook her head, tears gleaming in her own eyes. "I was a fool, my dear daughter. Seeing you made me think of myself, so many years ago when I was young, and the anger I expressed was more towards myself than towards you. But you stood up to me; you refused to budge. You are far stronger than you think Meghan. Don't you ever forget that."

The tears streamed down my face, and as I lifted my sleeve to wipe them away, the door burst open and in poured Cade and the Dagda.

Atonement

For some reason, seeing Cade's foster father sent one final fissure through the dam and the flood burst free. I jumped up from my seat and threw my arms around him.

"Whoa! Meghan dear! What's amiss?"

I felt the heavy weight of his arms wrap around me, one of his hands patting me on the back.

"Your young man here woke me from a dead sleep. Has the Morrigan attacked?"

Without thinking, I peeled my head back and blurted, "She has Aiden! The Morrigan has Aiden!"

Confused cornflower blue eyes regarded me for a few moments.

"Aiden?" the Dagda said.

I bit my lip. Stupid emotions. I guess I should have thought this through before assuming that Danua wouldn't care if everyone knew about her other child.

"Aiden is my son, Dagda, born of the same father as Meghan. Like my daughter, we hid him in the mortal world, conveniently within Meghan's own family. The Morrigan somehow discovered this and passed through the dolmarehn, taking him from his foster parents. She holds him hostage here in Eilé."

I felt all the muscles in the Dagda's arms grow stiff, then he cursed.

Danua sighed deeply, her age showing on her face for a split second, then lifted her clear, ocean-colored eyes to Cade's foster father. "We no longer simply have a war to fight, but we have a rescue mission to attempt as well. I suspect the Morrigan wishes to keep Aiden as a way to bait Meghan and myself."

The Dagda carefully set me down, then crossed his arms. He furrowed his brow in that all familiar thinking stance I had often seen him in, then took a deep breath and released it.

"The others will have to be told. And we cannot make any plans until we know exactly what we're dealing with."

Danua nodded grimly.

"We'll have to create a distraction," Cade added, resting his hands on his hips and letting his head hang low.

After a while he glanced up at me, his emerald eyes gleaming. "If anyone knows how to antagonize the Morrigan, it's me. Besides, she isn't exactly pleased to know that my death didn't stick. She'll find it hard to concentrate on the big picture with me standing in her trail and reminding her of her weakness and failure."

"No," I blurted, stepping forward and grabbing onto Cade's arm. "No, you will not offer yourself up as bait."

"Meghan, we need a diversion," Cade said in a lower voice. "I'm the best candidate besides you, and there is no way-"

"Enough!" Danua said, throwing her arms in the air. "We will not discuss this any longer, not until the rest of the Tuatha De get here."

She picked up a large bell and rang it twice. "Now, let's have something to eat. Meghan and I had some tea, but we'll need several more pots soon."

In the next breath, a door at the side of the room swung open and two male servants came in carrying a tray. The tantalizing aroma of savory stew and fresh bread filled the room and soon our worries were set aside as the four of us paused to eat. I couldn't put Aiden from my mind, not entirely, but it was nice to have a distraction if only to let my emotions take a breather.

"Caedehn," Danua said looking up from her meal, "did you relay my message to all my guests?"

Cade nodded. "They told me they'll be down as soon as they can."

"What about Enorah?" I asked, suddenly remembering Cade had wanted to check for her.

"Not here yet. I'm guessing she had a slower time getting away from the Weald than us. I expect she'll arrive by tomorrow at the latest."

I nodded, but before I could get back to my meal, the door burst open again and in strode Epona and Nuadu, followed by Lugh, Goibniu, Oghma, Cernunnos and a few others. I gritted my teeth at seeing the god of the Wild, his magic flaring in my chest as it recognized his presence.

"What is the meaning of calling us all together on such short notice?" Lugh wanted to know. "Has the Morrigan struck?"

With all the grace she possessed as high queen, my mother calmly explained the situation, and as the details of her story unfurled, the tension in the room wound tighter and tighter.

When she finally finished with her tale, Nuadu spoke up, his voice silent but resonant, "Well then, there is no question as to what we must do. We must try and rescue the child."

I nearly melted in relief. I'd been so afraid they would meet our dilemma with anger and dissidence.

"It is clear she has tossed the first stone. Now we must prepare for war, as soon as possible," Epona said, pounding her fist against the table.

"Yes, it's inevitable, but let's go about this with as much reason as possible," Lugh added. "If we pool all of our resources and gather all the men and women willing to fight, we still stand a poor chance against the Morrigan and Donn and their army of faelah."

Cade's grandfather looked at me. "While you and Caedehn were away, we sent word to our people. We won't receive as much help as we'd previously hoped."

The room burst into worried argument, and I felt my magic stir in response to the frustration permeating the air. My own panic was threatening to overtake me. When Cade and I had left Erintara, I'd been convinced we stood a decent chance. Perhaps that was just another silly daydream on my part.

"Each of my men is worth fifteen faelah!" Bowen yelled angrily, his voice carrying over the commotion.

In the aftermath of everything that had happened since the night of the dance, I'd almost forgotten about the young man. He now sat next to his father, his dark eyes looking like they were on fire, his handsome face twisted with annoyance.

"And how can our combined power not be enough to defeat two Tuatha De?" Epona asked, her pale, flyaway hair taking on a life of its own.

"And what about my brother?" I added, but no one, except for Cade, heard me.

Lugh lifted an arm and tried to shout above everyone. "Wait, quiet, please! I'm not finished."

Reluctantly, everyone quieted down. I shot my mother a glance. She sat regally, looking cool and calm, but her fingers were hooked around the ends of the armrests on her chair, her nails practically digging into the wood. I knew exactly how she felt.

"The Morrigan alone we could handle. As everyone knows, she recently spent most of her power trying to destroy Caedehn and Meghan. She is weak, but she has two advantages over us. First, she has Donn's aid. The Lord of the Afterlife has been soaking in his glamour for centuries, allowing it to build up and become a nearly unstoppable force. He hardly ever uses it, and frankly, he really doesn't need to use it. If we assume he has given most, if not all, of his power to the Morrigan, then we have good reason to worry. Secondly," he took a deep breath, one I doubted gave him much relief, "she has the high queen's son. If we value his life at all, then we must act more carefully than before. Despite these obstacles, however, we do have a few things at our disposal."

And then the golden-haired god turned his gaze onto the Dagda.

"My Spear contains a bit of power, but not nearly enough to help us much. And I will need it during the battle. But Dagda, your Cauldron, it has been absorbing Eilé's magic for centuries, probably longer than Donn has been storing up his own power."

Cade tensed up next to me and a knowing stillness permeated the room. Wait, what was going on?

"Until recently. I used it a few months ago to restore Caedehn."

"But it still contains an incredible amount of fae magic, am I correct?"

The Dagda sat up a little straighter in his chair and said carefully, his tone harder than usual, "Yes. What exactly are you suggesting?"

Lugh sighed and took the time to look at everyone sitting at the table. When his pale eyes met the Dagda's blue ones once again, he drew a deep breath and said, "I am suggesting that we borrow the magic from the Cauldron to strengthen the natural magic of our soldiers."

An audible, unanimous gasp played across the room, but no one dared speak their opinions.

The Dagda's jaw worked and I could tell he was fighting against some emotion.

"If you take the magic out of the Cauldron," Nuadu, said carefully, his deep voice rumbling through the silence, "then it cannot be used to regenerate the dead."

Now I understood the reason for everyone's reaction. And now I knew why I could feel my own blood growing cold.

Nuadu continued to run his fingers up the stem of his goblet. He looked up from what he was doing, his dark brown eyes troubled. "You would be able to make our men and women harder to kill, but once they died, they would stay that way. You know the Cauldron would never regain enough power in time to save them."

"Exactly how long would it take, to absorb enough power from Eilé to work again?" my mother asked, her voice containing the slightest shake.

I trained my eyes on her. I was wondering the exact same thing.

The Dagda folded his hands and then pressed his mouth against them. I had never seen him look so troubled. Finally, he took another deep breath, cast a regretful glance in my direction, and said, "A few hundred years."

The room burst into conversation, partially angry, partially frantic. All I could do was sit there, numb. When my brain started working again, all I could think about was the epiphany I'd had the other night; the realization that we always had the Cauldron to fall back on. But if the Tuatha De agreed to drain the vessel's power, then the one thing I was counting on would no longer be available.

"Stop!" Lugh shouted, his frustration gradually transforming into anger. "We have no other choice!"

"Yes, we do!" Epona growled, standing up to face off her fellow Tuatha De. "We fight, as we are, with the power we have, and then use the Cauldron to regenerate those who fall!"

From the far end of the table Nuadu started chuckling, but it wasn't the laughter of someone amused. No, it was the laughter of someone who pitied others for their ignorant foolishness.

"Don't you get it?" he said, his voice almost a whisper. "This isn't a band of renegade Fomorians like the last time. This is the Morrigan and Donn. The Celtic goddess of war and strife and the god of the dead. If we don't borrow the magic from the Cauldron before this war starts," he continued, his voice growing in power, "then there won't be enough of us left standing to drag the dead into the Cauldron to bring them back.

Atonement

We ourselves, the Tuatha De, could be weakened so severely we might not be able to rise from the ground for several days. By then it will be too late!"

A hush fell over the room as everyone absorbed what Nuadu had said.

The Dagda cleared his throat. "He is right. We have a better chance draining the magic from the Cauldron and dispersing it amongst our people now, than if we wait and try to revive them later. It is the only chance we have of freeing your son."

He lifted his eyes and gazed directly at my mother, sitting at the head of the table. He was imploring her, his queen. He and Lugh and Nuadu had laid it all out before her. They had been honest and done their best to come up with the strategy that would be the most likely to succeed. They were telling us, telling Danua, that the only chance we had against the Morrigan and Donn was to pull the power from the Cauldron and to give it to those who would be fighting. It meant they would be more powerful. It also meant that they had no chance of survival if they were struck down. But they were leaving the decision up to her. Perhaps this conversation would have ended differently if the Morrigan hadn't taken Aiden, but I couldn't let that distract me now. We had absolutely no way of knowing Aiden's safety would have been part of this whole mess. Well, at least I had no way of knowing.

The Dagda released a great sigh. "We have to accept that there will be sacrifices. But I'm afraid it is the only way."

Suddenly, the part of me that wanted to believe them because they were far more experienced at warfare than I went into hiding, and my emotional side clawed its way free for a split second. *No!* I wanted to shout. *No, mother, don't agree to this!* Fortunately, my rebellious thoughts stayed in my head.

It took Danua a long time to respond to the Dagda, and I could only imagine what was going through her mind. We were not only fighting this war because the Morrigan insisted on it, but because she had something that was precious to the high queen and myself: Aiden. If the Morrigan didn't have my little brother, would this choice be easier for her? Whatever my mother decided, would she fear her personal attachment had driven her to that conclusion? I wanted to save Aiden more than anything, but the Cauldron had proven to me once just how important its magic was.

Finally, she squared her shoulders and glanced around the room. "Very well. We will go forward with the plan. We will utilize the magic stored in the Cauldron, and pray that it is enough to defeat the Morrigan."

"No!" I cried out, standing up out of my chair.

My protest went unnoticed, for I wasn't the only one to make an outburst. Everyone, save for my mother, the Dagda, Nuadu and Lugh had burst forth from their chairs, shouting or protesting in anger or disbelief.

Cade, who had remained sitting next to me, tried to draw me back into my seat, but I shrugged off his hands. We could not borrow the magic from the Cauldron. What if those who had less magic in them, everyone except for the Celtic gods, fell in battle? They would die; they would be lost forever. Enorah, Cade . . . *No.* I gritted my teeth and fought the panic rising in my chest. No, they couldn't take away the one thing that would keep Cade alive if he was lost in the fight. I couldn't watch him die. Again.

My magic flared in response to my emotional state, and that's when it hit me, above all the clamor and chaos, one resounding thought broke free. *Cernunnos's magic Meg, the secret you've been keeping all this time . . . perhaps now is the time to speak of it. You can use your extra magic and the Tuatha De won't need to drain the Cauldron of its life-giving force.* Cernunnos had said I couldn't tell any Faelorehn men or women, but the Tuatha De weren't technically Faelorehn, were they? And neither was Cade. He was the son of a goddess and the grandson of Lugh. Maybe that's why Cernunnos had been so adamant about reminding me who I couldn't tell. Perhaps he was trying to give me a hint. My eyes grew round and my hands, which had been clenched at my sides, stopped shaking. I licked my lips and opened my mouth to speak, but the words got caught in my throat. Something, instinct perhaps, stopped me short.

And then some unseen force made me whip my head around, my eyes hooking onto an earth-brown gaze. Cernunnos. Amid all the gesticulating arms and booming voices, Cernunnos sat in his chair, as still as a hunter in the forest, his arms crossed and his eyes trained on me. He didn't send any words into my mind, something I was expecting at this point. He only kept me still with that death glare of his, his mouth cut in a grim line, and gave a small shake of his head. I knew what that meant. *No, not now. Not yet. Remember, you must visit the Morrigan's lair first.* I didn't hear the words, but I knew he would have said them if he needed to.

I fell back into my seat, dropping my face into my hands in despair. No. This had to be the time! It had to be! They could use my extra magic instead of the Cauldron's.

No Meghan, that rich voice whispered across my mind, *my glamour isn't nearly vast enough to replace what the Cauldron can provide.*

I wanted to scream and leap across the table. I wanted to take those stupid antlers and twist them and break his neck. But I couldn't. He was immortal, in the most permanent sense. He could not be killed, no matter what. He was one of the elite few who would never die, even if taken down in battle or overcome by disease. My anger flared then, and so did my magic.

Calm down Meghan, do not let my power unfurl. Do not break your geis.

He sounded concerned this time, as if he really cared about my well-being. But I couldn't help that my magic was getting out of control. I was *so* angry. And it was so unfair.

Meghan! he shouted into my mind, and I jumped this time, lifting my tear-stained face to look at him. He was glancing off to the side, but his jaw was tight, his face strained.

Do not lose control. I understand your pain and anguish, but you will have your chance to prove your worth yet, I promise you that. Do not give up the fight now. You are stronger than that!

His silent words hit me like a slap, not because they were harsh, but because they mirrored the very words my own mother had spoken to me only a few hours ago. Suddenly, I felt my magic draw back as my nerves calmed. At first I thought it was Cernunnos helping me along, but then I realized it was me. He was right. Danua was right. I was stronger than this. After living for seventeen years in the mortal world, oblivious to the life that waited for me in Eilé, I had somehow overcome all my weaknesses and had proven myself capable of defeating every challenge thrown my way. Yes, this current obstacle was bigger and far more terrifying than all the others put together, but really it was my own terror that acted as a barrier. I could not let my emotions, my fear, rule me; I had to be practical; I had to figure out a way around this difficulty.

Cade distracted me from my internal pep-talk by pulling me close and stroking my hair.

"Hush, Meghan, hush," he crooned softly into my ear. "Don't be upset."

Easier said than done, I thought. Then I gave myself a mental shake as I absorbed Cade's comfort. *Time to be strong Meghan, remember?* I reminded myself.

I gave Cernunnos's words some more thought and as my tears dried up and the shaking stopped, I realized his reminder had reawakened my determination. Fate was trying to steamroll me again, but I wouldn't let it. I felt helpless and frustrated and angry, but I would take those emotions, give them their chance to run their course, and then I would stiffen my spine and face this thing head on. We were going to war, sooner probably than later, and we were going to drain the Cauldron of its power so that we had a better chance of winning. Several people would die, and we would not be able to bring them back. One of those people could be me, or Enorah, or Cade. I would just have to accept that. But I couldn't forget, I had that extra magic hidden away, and Cernunnos assured me I would get my chance to reveal it to help those I loved. All I had to do was stay strong, trust that he was telling me the truth, and trust myself that I would know when it was time to let my magic free to enact its wrath upon the Morrigan.

As Cade rocked me gently, and as my mother and her fellow Tuatha De, the gods and goddesses of the Celts, continued their out of control argument, I breathed in deeply and told myself that I would, somehow and someway, defeat the Morrigan and get my brother back.

Twenty

Conference

The Dagda left with his soldiers the next day in order to bring back the Cauldron. The rest of us remained cooped up in the castle for almost a week as we waited for his return. Outside, the sky remained slate gray and a mixture of ice and rain pelted the earth with vengeance. My mother tried to lighten the mood by providing entertainment, but the board games and music only just took the edge off of our anxiety.

At sundown on the fifth day, and an hour before the Dagda's return, we received a message from the Morrigan in the form of the puca who had tried to entice me out into the open at Luathara. Seeing the goat man once more made my skin crawl, but luckily I was in the room I shared with Cade when the creature arrived. Despite the dismal weather outside, Cade opened the window so we could sit on the ledge and hear what it had to say. Danua, unfortunately, had to stand in the massive doorway of her castle and listen to the monster's rattling voice up close and personal.

"Dawwwn tomorrooow. My Missstresss requests a meeeting to discuss the terrrms of waaar."

"How can we trust her word?" my mother shouted over the patter of rain.

Conference

"Youuu have nooo choiiice. Answeeer naaay to this requeeest and she shall attaaack toniiight. Answeeer yeaaa and you will haaave a channnce to speaaak with herrr."

There was a long pause before my mother said, "Very well. Tell your mistress we will meet her at dawn on the edge of her realm."

That night, the entire castle sought their beds early, but despite my weariness and Cade's warm presence, it took me several hours to finally fall asleep.

The sky had just begun to turn pale gray with dawn's approach as we left the grand courtyard of Erintara behind. Despite the early hour, many of the city's residents had risen to give us their blessings. Perhaps it was because the rain and sleet had stopped, even though the sky was still dark with more clouds building on the horizon. Or maybe they just knew we needed their moral support.

Lasair walked silently beneath me, his thoughts, like mine, kept to himself. All the other horses were also strangely quiet, as well as Meridian and Fergus. My spirit guide sat on my shoulder, but for once she didn't have her head tucked under her wing. She kept her sharp eyes trained forward, her mind as still as the frosty air. Fergus kept pace with Speirling, his feet drifting quietly across the ground. The only sound that met our ears that morning was the sharp clipping of hooves against cobblestone. And then there was Cade, raging like a soundless storm beside me, his intense silence scraping at my nerves like a cheese grater.

I know you think this is too dangerous for me, I sent using shíl-sciar, *but I am more a part of this fight than most.*

Cade growled, but I ignored him.

She can hardly do anything while I'm surrounded by Danua and her guard, I insisted.

Luathara

We had had this argument already, out loud, in our room upstairs earlier this morning. I insisted on going with the Tuatha De to meet with the Morrigan, and Cade had forbidden it. Blinking at him in surprise, I had burst out laughing, telling him he could go ahead and *try* to forbid me, but he'd fail. For once I played the whole daughter-of-a-queen card and reminded him that I was a princess and technically outranked him because my mother was the high queen. In the end it took the Dagda's intervention to first stop our fight and then get Cade to see reason. That had been a few hours ago and I still felt like we'd resolved nothing.

We traveled east for a few miles, passing through a wooded area, the trees bare of their leaves as they waited for winter. Not much conversation took place between the gods of the Celts and their soldiers, and I said nothing further to Cade. He knew how I felt, and even though he didn't like my coming along with them, he understood why I needed to be at this meeting with the Morrigan. Cade feared that this was just another trap to draw me out and capture me. I couldn't deny the thought hadn't crossed my mind, but the need to learn that Aiden was unharmed drove me despite my own nagging dread.

Gradually, the trees thinned and the land descended into a seemingly endless plain. In the distance I could just make out the white and violet tips of mountain peaks.

"The Morrigan's realm," the Dagda murmured, pulling his horse up next to Lasair. "Those mountains are miles upon miles away, but luckily we have the dolmarehn to bypass the distance."

He nodded towards the massive stone structure that stood like a beacon about a hundred yards away.

I set my jaw and nudged Lasair forward as the small army continued to crawl eastward. It took us a few minutes to reach the dolmarehn and I noted that it was even bigger than the one on the hill behind Luathara. Cade tried to dissuade me once again, to turn me back, but I stubbornly shook my head and said to him, *This is my battle as well. If I cannot fight to defend myself, then I hardly deserve to be Faelorehn.*

Cade moved Speirling so that we faced one another. He stretched out a gloved hand and gently caressed my face, his own expression grim and forlorn. *I just don't want to lose you Meghan.*

I reached up and touched the back of his hand with my own. *But you would leave me behind and go fight without me? So that I could wait in fear that you wouldn't return? No Cade, we fight together, you and I. And this is just a meeting. We won't be fighting today.* I hoped.

Cade sighed and dropped his hand, curling it around my own.

"Besides," I whispered hoarsely as we stepped beneath the cold arbor of the dolmarehn, "she has my little brother."

Cold. The first sensation I registered when we came out on the other side of the dolmarehn was cold. And not just in the temperature sense of the word, though it was freezing, but in the down-to-the-depths-of-your-soul cold. From the way the Tuatha De and their soldiers tensed on their horses, I could tell they felt it too. I glanced at Cade. He had hardly changed, though the bleak cut of his mouth seemed harsher.

Cade? I asked him, reaching out with my mind.

I am used to it Meghan, was his reply.

I settled back in the saddle, stretching out a hand to reassure Lasair. He'd grown restless below me, just like all the other horses.

As we traveled across the rock-strewn, desolate land, I thought about Cade's response. *I am used to it . . .*

It didn't take me long to realized that the reason he was used to this awful place was because he had been here so often; because his old geis had required it. I turned my head and blinked up at him. Oh, my poor Cade. Without saying or sending a word to him, I reached out and touched his forearm. He tensed a little, but his face softened when he saw that it was me. I merely smiled, trying to put as much joy on my face as I could.

We traveled in silence, my mother and her retinue, the Dagda, Nuadu, Lugh, Cernunnos and Epona in her horse form. The clouds overhead continued to threaten sleet, and as we approached a rise in the dead land, I squinted my eyes to make out the dark band of earth that rested on its crest. My stomach churned and my skin became even more chilled when I realized what it really was. Faelah. Thousands upon thousands of faelah. And then the Morrigan came into view, along with another tall figure standing next to her.

Danua ordered us to spread out in a line to match the Morrigan's formation and I stuck close to her and Cade as the other Tuatha De and their men and women dispersed.

My mother lifted her hand for us to stop when we were a hundred yards away, then she motioned for Cade and I to join her. As we closed the distance, gradually climbing the small incline, I gritted my teeth and forced my glamour to stay put. It sensed my unease and knew my enemy was near. Perhaps it had learned of her essence when it had driven her away last spring. In any case, I had to work hard to keep it, and the magic Cernunnos had given me, under control.

When we were a couple dozen yards away, Danua slowed her horse to a stop and we followed suit. Good. I didn't want to get any closer to the Morrigan and the domineering man standing next to her. I took a moment to study him. Other than being tall, his hair and beard were black, his eyes the same color. He emanated an evil coldness that had my every instinct screaming at me to flee.

Before I could consider him any further, the Morrigan opened her mouth and said, loud enough for everyone to hear,

"I called this parley in order to give you one more chance to hand over the girl and avoid war."

I blinked up at her, wondering why she was even bothering with the pretense of striking a bargain. The Morrigan I knew took what she wanted and never kept her word.

"I would never volunteer one of my children over to you. I've seen what you've done to your own," Danua retorted, jerking her head in Cade's direction, "and I know what you have planned for my daughter."

The Morrigan thrust her hands on her hips and glanced at Cade.

"Oh yes, my dear Caedehn. You broke your blood oath. It was never in our agreement that you use the Cauldron to undo what my Cúmorrig had already done. I have something extra-special in mind for you."

"And you broke your oath as well," Cade retorted. "Meghan was to be left alone."

"Well then, I guess we're back to square one." She sneered and turned her attention back to my mother. "Tell me Danua, is the daughter worth more than the son?"

Both my mother and I hissed at this, an instinctual response I was sure.

"They are both dear to me, Morrigan, but I will not trade one for the other, especially when I have no proof you have my Aiden."

The Morrigan lifted one of her hands and a ball of red magic swirled above it, small wisps of scarlet shredding away from the sphere in the slight breeze. The orb grew and its center became transparent. As we watched, a familiar face peered out at us. Dark hair, bright blue-green eyes . . .

"Aiden!" I screamed, almost kicking Lasair into action.

Cade grabbed the horse's reins before he could take a step.

"No Meghan," he growled, his voice hard and authoritative. "That's not Aiden, only a window to him."

I cast Cade an angry look, but he returned it with a sad one. Fighting my anguish and my glamour, I settled down, then took a deep breath and glanced at my mother. Danua's face had grown stony, her eyes flashing between their many hues; her own magic rising up to match the icy bite of our surroundings.

The Morrigan snapped her fingers below the sphere of magic and Aiden's image disappeared.

"So, as you can see, I have him locked away, nice and safe, where none of you will ever tread. You can only get him back by handing over your dear daughter. Of course, you can meet me here tomorrow on the battlefield, if you wish, but with that option comes no guarantee you'll see that half-breed son of yours again, win or lose. And there is always the chance you'll lose your daughter as well, should you choose to fight."

The faelah, which had been adding their own grunts and small squeals for the past several minutes, must have taken their master's words as encouragement, because they chose at that moment to make their voices louder. The baying and howling clawed at my soul, but I forced myself to keep my eyes on the Morrigan and her companion. The tall man, Donn I decided, for who else could it be, stood with his arms crossed over his chest, the black leather pants and sleeveless gambeson he wore matching his hair and eyes perfectly. He looked like death warmed over, or more accurately, death anticipating a great party. In this case, I could only imagine that the party he waited for was the war that would begin in a matter of hours.

"I will not sacrifice one child for another. We will meet you in battle tomorrow Morrigan, Donn," my mother nodded to both the Tuatha De standing before us, "and wipe your overbearing evil from this world for a good ten centuries."

Conference

The Morrigan threw her head back and laughed, her curling black hair swirling around her as her magic flared. When she looked back down at us, her eyes were like brilliant rubies.

"I was so hoping that would be your choice. Oh, how I love a good battle! Tomorrow morning then, my liege."

In the next breath the Morrigan vanished in a dark red swirl of smoke, a giant raven taking her place. The black bird let out a cackling caw and flapped her wings, heading north and east into the mountains. I watched her, my heart pounding, my resentment building, my magic urging me to follow. *No, not yet*, I told it as it burned to seek revenge and save my brother. *Tomorrow we fight.*

Another blast of magic drew my attention back towards the line of faelah, and instead of seeing Donn's silent, menacing figure, I spotted a huge black bull with burning eyes and an extra set of wicked horns. I gasped and tensed up, making Lasair dance below me.

"Don't worry Meghan," Cade said in a low voice, "he won't attack us today."

Cade's entire body was drawn taught, his muscles straining against his skin, his teeth clenched. It didn't take long for me to realize he was fighting his ríastrad. Yes, it would be bad for him to change at this moment; best to save his battle fury for tomorrow.

I reached up and ran my hand over his cheek, into his hair, murmuring his name until his wild eyes returned to their usual green. Once the initial aggression seemed to pass, he looked down at me. Cade grabbed my hand and pressed it against his face. I smiled as he took deep breaths and closed his eyes, the tension draining out of him.

"Thank you Meghan."

"I didn't know if I could soothe you or not, but I didn't think it would hurt to try."

His mouth quirked into a smile and he said into my mind, *Your presence always soothes me.*

I pursed my lips and arched one of my eyebrows, thinking about our fight earlier that morning. *Unless we're arguing,* I reminded him.

He smiled lightly and kissed my hand. *Even then, having you near is a blessing.*

The high queen and all the other kings and queens of Eilé stood their ground, watching as the faelah burrowed into the earth or turned and scattered, chasing after the raven and the bull. When we were certain none were left and none would attack after we turned our backs, my mother ordered us to return to Erintara.

"We eat well tonight from the Dagda's Cauldron and absorb the magic Eilé has poured into it, and tomorrow we return to fight the battle of our lives."

Everyone cheered and I couldn't help but notice the warrior coming alive in my mother. Her dark hair whipped around her like a banner, and despite the fact that she wore a beautiful dress best suited for court, I could imagine her in a suit of armor and bearing a sword. I smiled, a small speck of pride growing in my chest. So, I guess my relationship with my birth mother was healing after all.

The journey back to Erintara was a dismal one. Everyone seemed to be geared up for a fierce battle, everyone except me. At first I had been ready to take the Morrigan on, but as we continued westward across her desolate territory, the fight in me gradually burned off to be replaced by overwhelming helplessness. We had only been given a quick look at Aiden, but from those few moments I could read the terror in his eyes.

I held my breath and clenched my teeth as we passed through the dolmarehn because the anger threatened to take root again. As soon as we were back in the courtyard of Erintara's castle, I climbed down from Lasair. Cade was beside me in an instant, pulling me into his embrace. Like me, the tension coursing through him was almost loud enough to be heard. I immediately wrapped my arms around him, then buried my face into his chest and just breathed.

My mother's guard and those of the other Tuatha De gave us our space as they moved about, handing their horses off to eager stable boys and making their way back into the castle.

"I'm sorry Meghan," Cade rasped against my ear, "but I just need to be close to you for a moment."

Oh, you can take more than a moment Cade, I responded.

He sighed. *I'm so sorry about all of this. About Aiden, about my mother, about not being able to protect you well enough.*

I pulled away just enough so that I could look into his face. His eyes were stark, his expression drawn. How much of this mess did he consider his responsibility? How long had he been accepting the blame for all of this?

Cade, none of this is your fault, do you hear me? I sent, my words painted with the harsh color of conviction. *It wasn't your responsibility to protect Aiden, it was my family's and just because the Morrigan took him, it doesn't make it their fault either. You don't need to apologize for your mother. You are as much a victim of her evil as the rest of us. And I don't want to hear any more of this talk of not being able to protect me. I'm far more capable of protecting myself than I ever was and you have already done plenty.*

Can't help it, he sent, kissing my temple gently, *it's instinctual.*

I wiggled away from him just so I could get my next point across without getting distracted.

We fight tomorrow Cade. Together. I don't want you trying to send me off in order to protect me. Understood?

Yes, my Princess.

I punched him in the arm then grinned when he pulled me in for another close hug.

Before I could really get into the moment, however, the Dagda's booming voice cut into our privacy. "Enough lollygagging in the courtyard everyone! Let me fetch my Cauldron and begin the ceremony. We'll need all the power it can lend us, and it wouldn't hurt to have one last celebration before tomorrow's big fight, now would it?"

The men and women still lingering outside sent up an appreciative cheer. Soon, plans were made and messengers were sent to gather all those who would be taking part in the battle against the Morrigan and Donn tomorrow.

As the castle came to life with activity, Cade and I slipped upstairs to get ready. On our way, we learned that Enorah and her fellow fighters had arrived while we were gone. She had been put up in the spare room down the hall from ours, and when Cade and I were ready to head back downstairs, we first stopped to collect his sister.

When we knocked, Enorah opened the door with gusto. Her eyes gleamed and she gave us a wicked smile.

"I hear there is to be a party tonight," she said after giving Cade and I one of her death hugs. "Come on, let's get to it. I'm sure my men and women are already celebrating without us."

By the time we made our way back outside, a huge fire had been lit with the Dagda's Cauldron suspended above it. An aromatic steam rose from the great vessel and I caught a hint of beef and barley and onions. From the open castle doors, people poured out into the courtyard carrying baskets and trays full of fruit pies, fresh bread and everything else needed for the huge feast. My stomach growled in response and Cade gave me a rakish look.

It took quite a while for the stew to cook and as we awaited the meal that would feed not only our stomachs, but our magic as well, several people pulled out pipes and harps and fiddles. Cade drew me into a dance more than once and held me closer than what might have been deemed appropriate. For those several blissful minutes, I was able to forget about all that had been worrying me since coming to Eilé. Thoughts of the Morrigan and her hatred of me, of my mother's cold aloofness up until recently, of Aiden's capture, of the burden of the extra magic I carried and kept secret . . . All of it seemed to vanish as Cade led me in one dance after another. For a few hours I was simply the Meghan I was before, carefree and unburdened by troubles greater than not fitting in. That afternoon I caught a glimpse of what my life might be like if we won the battle tomorrow and everyone I loved came out of it alive. Cade and I would be together, happy, not worried about what his mother might do next.

We were in the middle of a slow dance when the Dagda called for everyone's attention. By now, the courtyard was crowded with men and women; all those from Erintara and those who had traveled with their Tuatha De king or queen to fight. Enorah stood off to the side with about twenty people dressed in the style of the Weald, all of them looking eager for tomorrow's battle. Cloth-draped tables, weighed down with a variety of food and dinnerware, stood waiting against the courtyard's tall stone walls.

As the cheerful murmur of voices died down, the Dagda lifted his arms and said in a loud voice, "I will now begin the ceremony to transfer the Cauldron's power into the food we shall eat. Remember, if you feel a little strange after eating, that is perfectly normal. It is only your body absorbing the extra glamour."

The crowd fell utterly silent, and we formed a large circle around the bonfire and the Cauldron suspended above it. Cade and I had managed to find a spot close to the Dagda, with my mother beside me and Enorah stepping forward to take a place next to her brother. The others were scattered about with their own people; Lugh and Nuadu were across from us, and next to them were Epona, Goibniu and Oghma. Much further out, Cernunnos watched like the silent tenant of the forest that he was. The antlered god caught my gaze and held it.

Soon, Meghan, his thoughts seemed to float on the air, *soon . . .*

I clenched my teeth and returned my gaze to the Cauldron. I was so tempted to curse Cernunnos for this so-called gift he'd given me. It had seemed to be more trouble than it was worth, but at least I'd get to finally set it free tomorrow during the fight. I only hoped it was enough to get Aiden back.

The Dagda lifted his arms, the strange silence of the courtyard and cold, damp breeze making room for his unmistakable presence. He closed his eyes and threw his head up to the grey clouds, muttering under his breath and slowly speaking the ancient words of Eilé.

For a while, nothing happened, but then I felt it. A tiny reverberation that started in my core, making my bones vibrate. It was a strange sensation and I wondered if anyone else could feel it. Suddenly, the courtyard flared with a brilliant, violet flash of magic. It lasted no longer than a lightning strike, but I blinked my eyes and took several shallow breaths, as if the air had been driven from my lungs. When I'd managed to blink all the stars out of my eyes, I looked up at the Cauldron. A deep purple glow emanated from the thick soup it held.

The Dagda drew a few ragged breaths and I glanced over to see that he was slightly bent at the middle with his hands on his knees. Sweat beaded on his forehead and he looked genuinely tired.

"Dagda?" I asked tentatively, releasing Cade's hand and reaching out to his foster father.

The Dagda lifted a hand. "I'm well. It just takes a lot of effort to pull so much magic out of the Cauldron."

He glanced up and smiled at us. I returned the gesture, though my own smile felt a bit weak.

Conference

Eventually, the Dagda straightened and gestured towards my mother. "Your Majesty," he said, his voice hoarse, "this is in your hands now."

Danua nodded once to him, cast me a look I imagined was meant to give me strength, then climbed the stone steps that hugged the Cauldron. A biting wind ruffled her skirts and tossed her hair into dark streamers, but she remained steadfast as she inspected the men and women crowding the castle's courtyard. Some were her own soldiers, others served under the Dagda, Nuadu, Lugh and Epona, away from their own realms to protect the wellbeing of all those living in Eilé. Some were formally trained for battle, others were merely farmers and business owners who knew their high queen needed all the help she could get. Or perhaps they were too familiar with what could happen should the Morrigan get her way and seize Danua's throne.

The people in the courtyard and the thousands more I could see crowding against the wide open castle gates grew still and silent as their high queen prepared to talk. Cade and I listened as my mother, with the diplomacy and elegance only a queen could possess, told her people about the common enemy they faced tomorrow. She explained that we fought not only to free ourselves of the Morrigan's terror, but for the life of her other child, Aiden, as well. At the end of her speech, Danua gave her people the opportunity to step down if they believed this fight was not theirs. Not a single person turned to leave, and I was touched by their loyalty. It seemed they had finally forgiven my mother for loving a Fomorian warrior.

As the sun dipped below the eastern horizon, many of the soldiers worked together to remove the Dagda's Cauldron from the fire. Several bundles of wood were thrown into the blaze and soon the flames were roaring higher and higher, lighting up the courtyard with their brilliance.

The party was just getting started, but I had no desire to stay. I wanted to be with Cade. I was resigned to accept whatever fate awaited me, but if either of us was destined to die tomorrow I wanted to spend as much time alone with him as possible.

Taking Cade's hand, I led him through the throngs of people, their boisterous voices working in unison as they regaled the war stories of old. We were jostled and saluted as I pulled Cade behind me, heading for the stairs that would take us up to our room. The castle itself was crowded with random people high on the Cauldron's power and the mead that had been passed around, but they paid no attention to us as we made our way upstairs.

Finally, I reached the door to our room. I threw it open, yanked Cade inside, and latched the door shut before reaching up and hooking my hand behind his neck. Cade let out a small noise of surprise when I jerked his mouth down to meet mine, but it didn't take him long to realize my plan. Soon he had his arms around me and he was leading the kiss and I was following.

"I don't want to feel anything else tonight Cade," I breathed as I pulled away from him to get some air. "I don't want to feel fear or sadness or regret. I only want to feel you."

"Well," he said, his own voice deep and raw with emotion. "I think I can arrange that."

He kissed me again, his lips trailing down my throat, then lifted me up and carried me to the bed. For the next few hours Cade kept true to his word, banishing all of my worries as our glamour and our love took us to a place no means of magic could ever reach.

Twenty-One
Omen

I jerked awake some time later only to notice that I was standing in the middle of a stone-littered field. My shoes were gone and I was wearing the clothes I'd had on the day before. Where was I and how had I arrived here? A cold wind drifted past me and I wrapped my arms tightly around myself, fighting the need to shiver. Maybe I had walked in my sleep again. If so, why hadn't Cade woken up?

Something, a small sound or my own intuition made me look up. I had been cold before, now I felt as if my body had frozen solid.

The Morrigan stood on that desolate plain with me, a dagger in her hand and a cruel smile on her lips. At first I was confused, but then I glanced beyond her and my eyes grew wide. I gasped as I brought both my hands up to cover my mouth. Cade . . .

He was naked and bound in chains, his skin pale and his eyes haunted, and surrounding him were two dozen Cúmorrig.

I cried out and moved to rush towards him, but the Morrigan held up a hand.

"Ah, ah little Meghan. Make any sudden moves and I'll instruct my pets to attack."

I balled my fists, the bile rising in my throat. "What do you want?" I managed to bite out.

She sighed, as if immensely bored. "You know what I want. The same thing I have wanted since the beginning, and rumor has it you've been keeping . . . secrets. Tsk, tsk."

My heart almost stopped as all the blood in my veins headed for my feet. Did she know about Cernunnos's gift? How could she know? Even now I could picture my little spider, working away to keep my secret hidden. I took a deep breath and pushed my panicked thoughts aside.

"You have another chance Meghan, another chance to keep your loved ones from harm. Before Danua and her army awaken, I must have you in my custody. Turn yourself over Meghan. Is it really worth all the pain and suffering the others will go through simply because you are too selfish to see the big picture?"

I clenched my fists, my arms shaking from fear and the cold. "You wish to use my power to harm others. How does sacrificing myself change the fact that many will still come to harm?"

The Morrigan regarded me with shrewd eyes. "As usual, you refuse to see things my way. Very well." She sighed, then continued as if I hadn't said a word, "When you wake, you will have exactly three hours to send word that you are on your way to the dolmarehn that separates my realm from Danua's."

"How am I to send word?" I asked, trying to catch her in a lie.

She only stared at me, her grin one of malevolence. "When you reach the edge of Erintara, you will know, believe me."

That made absolutely no sense. Angry at her arrogance, I shouted, "And if I refuse to give you what you want?"

She smiled again, and my spine turned to ice.

"Oh, silly, sentimental little Faelorah. I would tell you I'd release your pathetic little brother, but I fear that wouldn't be quite enough to ensure your cooperation, so, that is why I've set up this little insurance policy."

She gestured towards Cade. He wouldn't meet my eyes and I had the horrible feeling that his magic was nearly drained.

The Morrigan narrowed her scarlet gaze and continued, "The Dagda's Cauldron can't make your precious Caedehn whole again if you can't find all the pieces. This is what will happen if you fail to obey my summons."

She snapped her fingers and the closest Cúmorrig lunged, clamped its jaw onto Cade's shoulder, and tore away flesh and muscle.

I felt myself gag and the horrible vision vanished as I tore out of my deep sleep, screaming and choking on my sobs. As I came violently back to consciousness, a frosty whisper caressed my mind: *Three hours Meghan . . . You have three hours to decide . . .*

I swallowed back my horror, ready to release another scream when I felt strong arms wrap around me.

"Meghan! Meghan, what's wrong?"

Cade. Alive, safe with me. I immediately hugged him back.

He rocked me gently in his arms and I clung to him, the way a starved dog clings to a bone. He ran his hands down my bare back, over my face, through my hair, speaking soothing words in his ancient language. When my hysteria began to subside, he kissed me, carefully at first, but I reacted, purely on instinct. I laced my fingers through his hair and pulled his mouth back down to mine, kissing him so hard he gasped in surprise.

I broke away but didn't release him. Instead we simply lay there on the bed, gazing at one another in the dark. Cade ran a gentle hand through my hair once again.

Tell me about the dream, my love, he sent with shíl-sciar.

I sighed and closed my eyes, trying to force the images away. They had been so vivid; so real, and the last thing I wanted to do was relive them.

I'm alright now, honestly, I returned. *You know how dreams seem so realistic when you're lost in them. The edge has worn off.*

Huh, liar, my conscience accused. That had been the most realistic dream I'd ever had, as if the Morrigan had somehow plucked me out of bed in order to force me to take part in her macabre little show-and-tell.

Cade pulled me in closer so that our bodies molded together. Instantly, the coldness that had been gathering just underneath my skin vanished as his body heat and what I suspected was the gentle aura of his magic permeated my senses. I sighed and tried to relax; tried to convince myself it had only been a bad dream. Unfortunately, every instinct I possessed warned me that it had been a message from the Morrigan, one I could not ignore.

I forced the dream to resurface. As much as I wanted to forget it, I had to consider it. The horrible goddess already had my brother, and if any of that dream had been true, then I could now safely say she would take Cade away from me again as well. She coveted my magic, and in order to get it she needed to strike at everyone I loved.

I tried to curl up into a pathetic ball of despair, but Cade shifted next to me. I could tell by his breathing that he was asleep, but he still wouldn't release me. And that was how it would be. No matter what happened, Cade would not let me go. If I ignored the Morrigan's message, then tomorrow, when we pitted ourselves against her and Donn and all the horrors they had at their disposal, Cade would have me as a constant distraction. He would protect me instead of focusing on the fight, and his mother knew this. She knew he would be an easy target, and he'd be the first one she would go after.

I bit my lip in order to keep it from trembling. Carefully, I extracted myself from Cade's embrace so as not to wake him. Once I was free, I studied his face in the soft light of the dying fire in the hearth. When he was asleep, all the strain of this whole mess disappeared from his features. I felt tears prick at my eyes. It was all because of me and my family. He despised his mother more than anything, but because of me and Aiden and Danua, he would confront her once again.

Pain and anger shot through me then. Danua and I had been near enemies up until a few days ago and now I was on the verge of losing the family I had always wondered about. The family I belonged to. But the Morrigan had my little brother. Aiden, who had been so helpless in the mortal world, must be terrified and so confused. How powerless must he be here, in Eilé? He must think he's in a living nightmare, and he couldn't let anyone know, not with his autism . . . But, my mother had said something about that earlier. Aiden wasn't autistic after all. In the mortal world, his magic had been suppressed, so much so that he couldn't even communicate properly with us.

Frustrated, I shoved my face into my pillow and let loose a silent scream. All the events of the past several weeks went swirling through my mind, as if a tornado had picked them up. Returning to Eilé, the attack on Luathara, my four weeks in the Weald, learning about my magic with Enorah, Cernunnos's strange visit and the imparting of his magic, the Lughnasadh party at the Dagda's, the council with the Tuatha De, news of Aiden's kidnapping, the draining of the Cauldron's magic, the parley with the Morrigan and then her insufferable arrogance in my nightmare . . .

Around and around the thoughts went, scratching at the edges of my sanity until I wanted to tear out my hair. Gradually, the phrases of my memories became single words; *Magic, Cauldron, Cade, Aiden, Secret, Sacrifice, Cernunnos, War,* and the one that repeated itself the most: *Morrigan.*

Suddenly, my pain and anger honed themselves into a sharp point, one aimed directly at the goddess's heart. She had been controlling Cade's life, my life, for far too long. And then, in a powerful wave of realization strong enough to sweep the frantic tornado in my mind off course and force the air from my lungs, I understood what I needed to do. As the storm of confusion in my brain lost its bluster, a few words lingered before disappearing completely. It was something Cernunnos had said to me on that balcony the night he told me I had all of his magic, and then repeated at the council meeting with the Tuatha De: *You must first visit the lair of the Morrigan before you can use my magic. . .*

Hissing in a breath, I slowly sat up in bed, my eyes wide and my mind working once again. Only, this time I had full control of my thoughts. For several minutes I merely sat there, thinking hard, and finally, a plan began to form. It was as insane as it was brilliant; reckless, crazy, and dangerous as hell. But if I was right and it worked out, then I could save both Aiden and my new found family. Only problem was, there was a good chance I might not be around to enjoy those I hoped to save . . .

I looked over at Cade, his face relaxed in sleep. Tears spilled from my eyes when I thought about how my plan could go wrong. This could be the last time I ever saw him. *No Meghan, if you are to do this you must be strong, you must be willing to let him go.*

Silently, I crept out of bed, threw on a robe, and took up residence in the tall, stuffed chair closest to the fireplace. Three hours, the Morrigan was giving me three hours to hand myself over. Although I had already decided what to do, I needed some time to get the details straight in my mind. As the middle hours of the night slipped away, I fine-tuned my plan, going over every possible detail and outcome.

An hour and a half after waking from my terrible dream, I felt there was nothing else to consider; no stones left unturned.

I just needed to remain patient and follow the script I'd so painstakingly put together in my head. Digging deep into the recesses of my memory, I collected the ancient words Enorah had given me when I'd created my little spider. I was going to need another one, one that would hide every thought connected to my plan. When I had accomplished that, I gathered up my courage and recalled another spell Enorah had taught me, the one that encouraged deep sleep, and padded silently back over to the bed. I leaned forward and pressed my mouth against Cade's ear and focused a small cloud of my magic into a tiny pebble. I took a breath, drawing the speck of power up into my throat. As I exhaled, I spoke the ancient word that went along with the spell: *codladh* . . . sleep. I could feel the glamour traveling over my tongue, flowing into Cade's ear so that it could take hold and keep him unconscious longer than what was natural. I hated to do it, but it was the only way to guarantee my getting out of the room without waking him.

As the tension eased out of Cade's body and his breathing grew deeper, I leaned away from him. I sighed and ran my hand through his hair, down his perfect face, and over his shoulders. I studied his skin with my fingertips, memorizing every detail because I would need them to give me strength as I put my plan into motion. I counted his ribs, one at a time, and traced the dark ink of his tattoos. I felt fresh tears pool in my eyes when my fingertips lingered on the scars left by the Cúmorrig that had killed him. I pulled my hand back and leaned forward, kissing him once on the mouth, just as I had done before leaving him in the Dagda's care those many months ago.

"I love you," I murmured.

His eyelids flickered, and for a moment I thought the spell hadn't taken hold. I released a breath of relief when he settled back against the mattress. If Cade knew what I was about to do, he'd tie me to a chair and lock me in Danua's dungeon until the battle with the Morrigan was over.

With careful movements, I crawled out of bed. Cade's arms crept forward as I stepped away, his fingers seeking mine, but the spell held strong. I released the breath I'd been holding and quickly found my clothes and my warm cloak, pulling them on as swiftly and as silently as I could in the dark. Fumbling through my bags, I also pulled out Enorah's dagger and some of the hawthorn arrows from my quiver. Pausing and glancing back at Cade, I quickly snapped a few in half, shoving the broken shafts down my boots. They might come in handy later.

When I was ready, I turned and glanced back at Cade. His huge frame took up most of the bed now that I was gone, his face turned towards me. Unconsciously, I reached my hand up to my throat and brushed my fingers over the torque that had been there since spring, the mistletoe bead on its leather string just below it. The torque and the charm could not protect me against the Morrigan, but they would bring me comfort because they had been gifts from Cade.

Last chance to change your mind Meghan, my conscience told me.

Oh, how was I tempted to listen to it, but I knew that if I wanted to save Cade and my brother and everyone else I loved, I had to do this. With one last silent prayer sent to whoever might be listening, I squeezed out the door and crept through the dark castle.

Luck was with me in those early morning hours because no one was awake, not even the guards posted at the kitchen door where I slipped out, or in the stables where I managed to saddle up Lasair in record time. At dawn the fortress would be alive with activity, my mother and the other gods getting their troops and all those willing to fight ready to march against the Morrigan. I would not be with them when they did.

As I led the red stallion through the dark city, a sleepy Meridian clinging to my shoulder and my heart pounding in my throat, I thought about my plan. So many unknown factors relied on its success, and I only hoped that my instincts proved correct. One thing I was counting on was the Morrigan's greed and cunning. If the Morrigan wanted to take Aiden's power, it would be easier to do so if he didn't know how to use it. Since this was his first trip into Eilé, I was betting on this fact and the remote chance the Morrigan hadn't tried to get at it yet. After all, she needed Aiden whole and healthy in order to entice me and my mother into making a trade, and something told me that stripping him of his glamour would do far too much damage. Yet, if Aiden still retained all of his power and if I could somehow find a way to be alone with him, then perhaps I could teach him about his magic and then we could pool our resources and . . .

My thoughts were suddenly interrupted by the grating caw of a raven. Instantly, my senses came to life as Lasair whickered nervously and side-stepped on the road. Meridian clenched down with her claws.

Danger, she whispered into my mind.

Yes, I know, I returned, my head swiveling on my shoulders as I scanned our surroundings for a large, dark raven. I had been so caught up in my contemplation that I hadn't noticed we'd reached the edge of the city. Ahead of us stretched the hilly, wooded farmlands of Erintara, behind us, my mother's castle and Cade. Of course, the entire landscape was currently cloaked in darkness, but I could just make out the vague shapes of trees, hills and buildings.

The raven cawed again, snapping my attention forward. When I finally spotted it sitting in a nearby oak tree, I released a soft gasp. The bird was large, but not nearly as large as the Morrigan was in her raven form. And it was pure white. Nervous, I clicked Lasair closer, and the stallion obeyed me without any trouble.

Now that I was sitting just below the giant bird, I could see it better. The creature was blind in one eye, a great scar running down the side of its face, so it tilted its head to study me. That's when I noticed the feathers covering its ears. Despite the darkness, I could tell they were red, just like Meridian's. A spirit guide. And not just any spirit guide, the Morrigan's spirit guide.

Fighting back the urge to blast it with my magic, I took a deep breath and said with a shaky voice, "Tell your master I've decided to hand myself over to her. I'm heading to the dolmarehn that will take me to her realm right now."

The creature shook out its ghostly feathers and groaned out a long croak before flapping its wings and heading east, its pale form a stark contrast against the black sky. I heaved a deep breath and thought once more about what I was doing.

Once you step through that dolmarehn, there's no turning back, my conscience told me.

I clicked my tongue and tapped Lasair with my heels. "Come on," I murmured as a shiver shot through me, "I have a job to do."

Beyond the outer reaches of Erintara and my mother's kingdom, once the wooded and rock-strewn hills came to an end, there stretched a vast reach of nothingness. Well, it wasn't completely empty. There were stones and a random shrub every now and again, and small hillocks and lots of thick, tangled grass and low spots where water collected into shallow pools or deep ponds. But the land itself was desolate and wind-torn. Meridian, Lasair and I had passed through the dolmarehn an hour ago, the same one we'd crossed through just the day before with the Tuatha De Danann and my mother. I had no idea exactly how long it would take me to get to the Morrigan's castle, but I knew as long as I kept heading east, I would get there eventually. Until then, I had only my worrisome thoughts to keep me company.

Just before I'd urged Lasair through the stone gate, I'd heard Cade's voice in my head.

Meghan?

He'd been curious at first, his words fuzzy at the edges, as if he'd just woken up. I shook my head and tried to ignore him. I imagined him lying in bed, reaching out for me before he was fully awake, the way he always did. But I hadn't been there.

Meghan, are you with your mother? he'd continued.

I'd ignored him again, and planned to do so for as long as I could. I'd let him search for me, putting more space and time between us so that he wouldn't come after me right away. No matter what, I couldn't tell him where I was.

When he tried to reach me a third time, I wove a small shield of my magic and placed it around my mind, blocking out his words. It tore at my heart to do so, but I could not let his worry distract me.

That had been over half an hour ago, and I estimated another hour or so would get me to the base of those mountains. If the Morrigan's spirit guide had brought her my message, then perhaps she would be waiting for my arrival. And it would be too late for Cade to do anything to get himself into trouble.

Eventually, the relatively flat land started sloping upwards and the great, jagged mountains I had been staring at for the past few hours jutted up before us in stark contrast to the rest of the landscape. Small growths of stunted, half-dead trees dotted the earth and just beyond them, spread out like a thick, black mist against the top of the rise at the base of the mountains, was an army of faelah.

Meridian screeched and took off from my shoulder and Lasair trembled beneath me, eager to charge at the monsters who were responsible for his sister's death.

I was stunned. I knew the Morrigan had Donn's unfathomable wealth of glamour at her disposal, but the endless legion of monsters waiting up ahead still surprised me. There were at least a hundred times more faelah here today than there had been yesterday, if not more. So this was the army my mother and the Tuatha De would soon be facing. And the Morrigan was apparently breaking her word again. Despite the fact that I'd practically offered myself up on a platter, she was still going to attack my mother and her people. I had dreaded this. Yes, I had counted this in as a possible outcome while I formulated my plot, but I had hoped my sacrifice would be enough to appease the goddess of war. Silly me; of course it wouldn't be enough.

I gritted my teeth and fought against the well of pain growing in my throat. This complicated things quite a bit, but I still had other options. I had committed myself to this plan and I was going to see it through to the end, whatever that end might bring.

Lasair moved forward until we were only fifty yards away from the line of faelah. I could smell them, a horrible blend of death and rot and evil. They screamed in their ancient voices, snorting and cawing and growling and snarling, like a primordial roll of thunder, up and down the base of the mountain. The low fog from earlier had lifted, only to reveal a sky dominated by inky rainclouds. It wasn't raining yet, but it could start at any minute. A cold, damp breeze pulled at my hair and blew the hood off of my head.

Suddenly, the monsters stopped their chatter and parted just in front of me. Behind them and extending far into the mountains was a deep, narrow crevice, and from its mouth strode a pale woman in a black dress whose skirts unfurled around her like living darkness. I swallowed hard and fought against my building magic. The Morrigan.

She walked with the grace and ease of a practiced warrior, all confidence and malice. Just behind her and to her right strode the tall, dark-haired man from yesterday morning's encounter. He had his black leathers on again, and as they moved closer, I busied myself with counting the wicked weapons he carried. But it was his eyes that startled me the most. Black and sharp and crackling momentarily to silver when he looked at me. Power rolled off of him in waves and I suddenly felt trapped. I swallowed back the sudden horror that boiled up like acid in my stomach.

No Meghan, don't let them see your fear . . .

I could feel Lasair reacting beneath me, anger and aggression pouring off of him. I slid from the saddle and turned to look him in the eye.

"Lasair," I whispered as I leaned my forehead against his velvety nose, "I haven't known you long but you have proven to be a brave horse, full of honor and pride. What I have to do I have to do alone. I need you to return to my mother's castle and join the others. If we're all lucky, there will be no fight today."

The red stallion whickered his disagreement and dragged his hoof through the rocky soil. Somehow his thoughts reached me. He wanted to avenge his sister and protect me. He didn't want to run like a coward.

"No," I murmured, my voice growing rough, "you must do as I say."

I put as much force behind my words as I could. Slowly, Lasair's agitated state calmed. He backed away, threw his head in the air and reared up, screaming his irritation. But when he touched down he turned and fled. I breathed a sigh of relief, then turned my mind to my spirit guide.

Meridian, I said.

She dug her claws into my shoulder. *No*, she sent. *Stay. Love. Protect!*

Her own thoughts were full of despair and anguish and the lump in my throat grew larger. Tears formed in my eyes but

I dashed them away. I could not look weak in front of Donn and the Morrigan.

They will kill you Meridian. They will take you and strip you of your glamour. I love you too, but you must flee. Please! You must go and protect Cade. This is something I must do on my own.

With a heart-rending screech, Meridian threw herself into the air, crying out as she tore through the sky after Lasair. And then I was alone, accompanied only by the raspy grunts and restless shuffling of the faelah lined up behind me.

The Morrigan and her companion closed the distance between us and came to stand several feet in front of me.

"Well, well, well, if it isn't my son's little Faelorah come to pay me a visit. I'm pleased to see you got my message."

She crossed her arms and smiled. The images from the horrible dream slammed into my mind and I winced.

"What took you so long to come calling Meghan? You know my home is always open to you and I've extended an invitation more than once."

She sketched a fake curtsy, gesturing towards the canyon from which she had just emerged. A strange babbling of haunted voices came rolling down the ravine at that moment, a hint of warning and suffering in their tones. My trepidation increased. The Morrigan shook her head and clicked her tongue as her army of faelah hissed and grumbled at me. Donn merely stood there like a statue, glaring at me.

I took a deep breath and decided I had best get this over with. "I've come for my brother."

The goddess arched a perfect eyebrow. "Is that so? And do you really expect me to hand him over?"

"No," I said, standing up straighter. "I've come to trade. Take me and let him go."

The Morrigan had the good grace to look surprised. "Really? That is very noble of you my dear, and tempting, but you see, I don't want to trade anymore."

"Then what do you want?" I said, my teeth gritted.

She looked up at me, her violet eyes adopting a lazy expression. She smiled sweetly. It made me think of the scent of flowers in a morgue. It did nothing to mask her evil, or chase away my disgust.

"I want you both. Think of how strong I'll be with *two* Tuatha De-Fomorian bastards, both of you ripe with boundless, untrained magic."

"I'll fight you," I blurted, letting my control slip just a little.

The Morrigan laughed, but it was my turn to grin. "You weren't laughing when I nearly destroyed you after my magic broke free the last time. If I remember correctly, you fled in your raven form before I could hit you with its full force. And that was before I learned how to control it. You should see what I can do now . . ."

Her smirk vanished and the look she gave me next could strip paint from the side of a fighter jet. I tried not to feel smug at the slight look of fear in her eyes. *Don't push this too hard Meghan; you have to give her just enough so she doesn't suspect anything . . .*

"So, you can take me willingly, or we can fight. I may not win, but even if you manage to kill me, I'll be sure to take a good chunk of your entire army with me in the process. It will be easy for my mother and the other gods to defeat you then."

There. That should make an impression. I only hoped my nerves would stop threatening to give out on me.

The Morrigan seemed to consider it for a while, but as the clouds swept by above us and as the faelah that stretched for miles began fidgeting and grumbling again, she looked back up at me, a wicked glint to her now red eyes.

"Oh Meghan, poor, sweet little Meghan. Do you know what your problem is? You have too many people that you trust and care for."

She took a breath and glanced down at my neck, then flicked her gaze back up at me.

"That's a beautiful torque you're wearing my little witchling. You've grown awfully close to that abomination I so unfortunately call my son, and you're here now because of him. What did he promise you? Wealth? Fame? You may get both from him, but he'll always be his father's son. He'll feed you pretty words and shower you with gifts, but in the end he will always stray."

I flinched hard, and she must have noticed.

"Oh, I see. He's already begun the process of winning your favor, hasn't he? The torque, your spirit guide, that horse you chased off . . . Need I go on? It won't be long before you catch him with one of the serving girls of your mother's palace. Or perhaps with one of the maids at that run-down hovel he likes to call a castle."

I clenched my fists. Cade was not like that. He wouldn't do that to me, to anyone. *She is feeding you lies Meghan, she is speculating. Just because Cuchulainn got the better of her, doesn't mean that Cade will follow after him. Don't let her manipulate you!*

I forced myself to calm down, then gave her a long, cool look. "You lie. He wouldn't do that. I'm growing tired of your crap. Time to make a decision. Either you can let Aiden go and take me instead, or you can taste the fury of my magic and risk losing your entire army."

Her red eyes flared even brighter for a moment, then she sighed and said rather boorishly, "Very well. I had hoped last night's little preview would have been enough, but it appears I have no choice. It seems dear Caedehn means something to you after all, so I'll repeat my previous threat, if you don't mind. Perhaps it will sink in if you see the kind of power I now wield in person and not in your dreams."

Oh no. This couldn't be good . . .

"You know all about my sweet hounds, correct Meghan? You like to call them Cúmorrig, and you've seen the damage they can do, especially if I feed them a little magic."

I shivered as I recalled the nightmare from last night.

"Well, they are nothing compared to the Dótarbh."

I stared at her, not sure what to say.

She sighed pleasantly and turned to her silent companion. "Donn, do you mind?"

The dark god nodded once and, without speaking, strode forward to stand in front of the Morrigan. He took a deep breath and let his arms drift casually from his sides. He closed his eyes and titled his head towards the ground. The earth began shaking and all along the front line of the faelah, trailing off for miles on each side, small bumps in the ground began to form. The mounds grew in size until they were about as big as a horse, if not bigger. Then, with a final flourish of his arms, Donn released a silvery torrent of magic and the hills of earth burst open, revealing what grew within.

I almost screamed out loud. They were all identical, but my eyes were trained on the one closest to me. It was a bull. A giant bull with horrible, black horns and blood-red eyes, and there were so many of them. They opened their mouths and bellowed, revealing unnaturally sharp teeth and the same furnace-like throats the Cúmorrig had. And like the Morrigan's hounds, these bulls appeared to have been dead for quite some time. Their heads were nothing more than skulls covered in black hide, the rest of their bodies patched together carelessly. But I had no doubt they were strong, and there had to be well over a hundred of them.

"Magnificent, aren't they? You see Meghan, the Dótarbh are Donn's pets, and they will come in very handy when I march on your mother and my other fellow Tuatha De later this morning. But let me return to the point I'm trying to make. You have told me that unless I release your brother, you will use your power to destroy my army. Well, here's what will happen if you do. You are powerful Meghan, I won't deny that. But you aren't powerful enough to fight me and my faelah and stop Donn and his Dótarbh. Their master has given them an order, you see. If you continue to refuse my demands, then they are to seek out my dear, charming son and, how did I put it?"

She cupped her chin in one hand and tapped her cheek with a finger as she looked up into the leaden sky.

"Ah!" she cried, then lowered her gaze and glared at me with such malice I almost fell to the ground. "Rend him limb from limb."

"NO!" I shouted, unable to help myself.

"Yes, I will," she spat. "You know I will. And he won't stand a chance, you know he won't. Even in his ríastrad, he died fighting only ten of my Cúmorrig. He will certainly perish against a few hundred Dótarbh."

Tears stung my eyes, but I ignored them. "You said," my voice rasped, "you said that if you had me, you'd leave him alone, that you'd leave everyone alone! So here I am, take me and do what you will, but call back your army and let my brother go!"

The Morrigan's cruel laughter crackled through the magic-tensed air. "Foolish, foolish Meghan! When are you going to learn that I never stay true to my word? I have no honor and you cannot outsmart me!"

I shot the goddess a look of pure hatred. She knew my weaknesses far too well, but I knew hers also: she was far too arrogant for her own good, and that's what I was counting on. I couldn't have anticipated the Dótarbh, there was no way for me to know that they were to be a factor in this horrible game. But all hope was not lost, at least not yet. *Patience Meghan, patience. Your chance is coming soon . . .* Cernunnos's magic burned inside of me, but I tamped it down with my own as the spider worked to hide my thoughts. Yes, my chance was coming. I just needed to get into the Morrigan's lair, find my brother, and then let that godly magic loose to wreak my vengeance.

"Come, come little girl, your sniveling bores me. Come join your little brother and I'll leave Caedehn be. At least until he comes with your mother and her friends to confront my army. But by then you and that other whelp of Danua's, and your wonderful magic, will be locked away safe where I can use it to replenish my own glamour after the fight."

I hesitated for a split second. Every instinct in my body was screaming at me to turn and flee. Unfortunately, my heart was now running the show. If I wanted to save Cade, my mother and Aiden, I had to be willing to make this sacrifice.

"Surrender!" the Morrigan screeched, sounding like the raven she often embodied. "Your attempt at swaying me has failed and you cannot escape!"

Very well, I thought as I stepped forward.

Immediately, the faelah acted, several of them breaking free of their line and moving around to encircle me, locking the Morrigan and Donn in their ring as well. My heart leapt into my throat. Yes, I was doing this willingly and for the ones I loved, but that fact didn't banish my instinctual desire to run. As the god of the dead continued to study me, I tried very hard not to squirm or break down into a full out panic attack.

"Check her for weapons," Donn said, his voice trembling with the raw power of an earthquake.

I sucked in my breath as the Morrigan turned her gaze on me. Her eyes flashed red once, and then I watched the dark cloud of her magic creep across the ground. The tendrils of smoky glamour poked and prodded me like fingers. When they got to the top of my right boot, the Morrigan chuckled, "What have we here?"

The magic worked its way down into my shoe, extracting the broken arrows I'd shoved there before leaving this morning. The tendril of power wrapped itself around the makeshift weapon and returned it to the Morrigan like some sick, ethereal tentacle. I bit my cheek. I had expected them to find Enorah's dagger, but I'd hoped they would overlook the hawthorn.

The Morrigan eyed my rudimentary weapon and arched a brow at me. "What did you plan to do with these? Carve a whistle whilst in confinement?"

She let loose a soft snicker of amusement as her dark magic continued its job. When it moved up to my torso, I tensed. Under my shirt and wrapped securely to my back was the dagger. It was too obvious to miss, and if she had found the broken hawthorn shafts, then she would definitely find the knife. The black smoke caressed the blade and I closed my eyes slowly, waiting for the Morrigan's cry of discovery, but the magic moved on in its search for more weapons. Finally, the smoke pulled away and returned to its wielder.

"Nothing more," the Morrigan said to Donn in a bored tone.

I felt my eyes grow wide with surprise. Her magic had been all over that dagger. How had she missed it? Then I remembered how the blade had so thoroughly destroyed the faelah outside of the Dagda's abode. Perhaps Enorah's weapon was more magical than I'd previously thought.

I turned to the Morrigan, my face set rigidly in what I hoped was a mask of defiance, and felt an invisible rope of glamour bind my arms to my sides.

The Morrigan looked up at her partner. "I'll just be a half an hour or so. If you want to start without me, I can catch up."

The god of the dead looked up and narrowed his eyes. "I think I'll join you in case she tries anything."

The Morrigan snorted a laugh. "What could she possibly do now?"

Donn remained impassive.

"Fine," the Morrigan snarled, "but first instruct your pets to lead my army onward. We'll have plenty of time to catch up to them before we meet Danua and her allies."

Before the Morrigan tugged me forward, I thought I heard Donn turn and mutter something in the ancient language. The demon bulls, the Dótarbh, let out a resounding bellow that echoed up and down the line of faelah, then started forward, moving west. The Morrigan's monsters quickly followed suit, a black, oily wave of death rolling over the land and covering it with their filth. The earth trembled as the army moved out, and I couldn't tell if it was Eilé herself protesting their existence or the result of so many feet marching in unison.

The ice-laced rain began to fall as we took our first steps into the crevasse I knew would lead us to someplace unpleasant. My magic shivered beneath my skin, but I held it back. We weren't finished yet, oh no, not by a long shot. But when the time came, I would let all the magic I contained come boiling forth like a storm of vengeance.

Sending up a silent prayer to whoever was listening, I hoped I would see Aiden soon and that somehow, I was going to get us out before Donn and the Morrigan could destroy everything I loved.

Twenty-Two
Duty

The walls of the narrow canyon were practically vertical, the ground we walked on littered with stones of all sizes and the remains of unidentifiable, dead creatures. Three times I almost gagged as the stench cloyed at my nose. The few faelah that hadn't followed the Dótarbh scurried around us, fighting with one another as they picked at the rotting flesh and broken bones. Hurrah. Another scene that would be giving me nightmares for all eternity.

The Morrigan strode before me, her dress of dark evil swirling about her like a black cloud as Donn, still chillingly silent, took up the rear. Eventually the canyon came to an end. Ancient, Celtic ogham letters and knot work designs adorned a massive stone doorway pitted with large recesses. I nearly fainted when I spotted what resided inside the primitive shelves. Human skulls, or more likely, Faelorehn skulls. At least twenty of them formed a gruesome border around the entrance to the Morrigan's realm. Two great, dead trees, their limbs bleached white and free of leaves, protruded from the rock wall on either side of the door. A flock of ravens decorated their branches like nightmarish Christmas ornaments, the half-blind, white spirit guide who had brought my message to his master sitting higher than all the rest. The birds let out a chorus of caws when the Morrigan approached, and she smiled and scratched at their necks as they greeted her. Donn merely crossed his arms and gave a sneer.

Once the birds were appeased and they had returned to their guard posts, the goddess turned to the doorway and gently ran her fingers down its surface, muttering something under her breath as magic flared from her palm. I felt it as clearly as I felt all magic, a strange tugging at the back of my knees, as if someone had taken a rope and was trying to pull my legs forward into a bend. Could this be some sort of well-disguised dolmarehn?

The rock shifted and a stone slab in the shape of a massive door swung inward, the icy air hissing free like the first breath of the risen dead. Goose bumps broke out all over my skin despite my warm cloak. A black abyss yawned before us and as I peered reluctantly into the opening the Morrigan shoved me.

"Your cell awaits, princess. If you behave yourself I'll let you share with your brother."

I tensed, but forced myself to relax. Good. That's exactly what I was hoping for. Despite the fact that my every last instinct screamed at me to flee in the opposite direction, I made my shoulders slump and shuffled forward, attempting to adopt the guise of an acquiescent prisoner.

The Morrigan moved to follow me, but something stopped her. I peeked over my shoulder to see Donn's gloved hand grasping her arm. He pulled her closer and hissed something under his breath, his black, disheveled hair and beard hiding most of his expression. I strained to hear him, but he used the language of Eilé. If only I'd asked Cade to teach it to me earlier . . .

The Morrigan jerked her arm back and snapped at him, her eyes flaring red. "I hold everything she cares about in the palm of my hand. Believe me, once she's in that cage with her brother, there will be no escape for her."

Donn growled at her. Actually growled.

"You wish to put the two offspring of Danua and that Fomorian in one cell?"

The Morrigan snorted and grasped her skirts, turning to walk away and herd me further into the pit of darkness that gaped before us.

I braced myself for another shove when Donn barked out, "You fool of a woman! To come this far and risk combining their magic?"

I froze where I stood, my heart catching in my throat. No, no, *no!* Could Donn have any idea what I had planned? Was I that obvious, or had he figured it out? But if *he* hadn't, wouldn't the Morrigan know what I was up to? Was she, like me, playing dumb until all the dice fell into place? I knew they hadn't read the thoughts in my head. My second little spider was keeping the details of my plot nice and out of reach, but that didn't mean they couldn't read my actions, actions I'd thought I'd hidden from their immediate observation. Then I swallowed hard as another thought came to me. True, they couldn't see what I was thinking, but could they have detected the magic I used to hide the secrets I kept?

The Morrigan, who was trying, unsuccessfully, to force me into her underground lair, paused and let loose a deep sigh.

"Donn, I'll tell you one more time: leave the thinking to me. This Faelorah may have power, but it is in no way greater than yours or mine, and she has not had time to hone it either. As for her brother . . ."

She yanked on my arm so that our eyes met. *Look terrified Meghan. Appear meek and beaten, but make sure that burn of hatred shows as well.* Huh, like that was difficult to do at the moment.

"He is in absolutely no condition to be aware of his magic, let alone use it."

Another jolt of dread coursed through me then and I felt my eyes grow wider. What had she done to Aiden?

The Morrigan smiled and I could have sworn the temperature dropped a good ten degrees.

"That's right Meghan dear, you have lost and any tricks you planned on performing with your brother won't work. He's a bit incapacitated at the moment."

"Wh-what did you do to him?" I asked, my voice raspy.

"Nothing, though I did give him a draught to make him sleep. He'll make a wonderful sacrifice once this is all over. Unfortunately, I haven't had the time nor the means to do much more than drug him."

I choked back the bile that threatened to rise as the Morrigan shoved me further down the tunnel. A sleeping potion would wear off, sooner or later, and I was praying it would be sooner rather than later.

The trip down into the bowels of the Morrigan's domain was one of the most terrifying experiences of my life. The tunnel, though spacious and lit with torches hanging in cruel-looking sconces, gave me a sense of extreme claustrophobia. Every now and then the path would branch off, as if we were following the trail of a giant ant hole, and the distant noises of pain and suffering came floating up from their depths. Five minutes into our journey I could no longer feel my fingers or toes and by the time we reached our destiny my whole face felt numb.

Eventually we spilled out into a massive chamber. Well, I stumbled but the Morrigan, with her usual grace, took the small staircase like a fog spilling over a range of hills. Donn opted to stand at the top of the stairs with his arms crossed. It's a good thing I couldn't feel my hands because the small stones that lodged themselves under my skin were the size of lentils.

Shivering, I dragged myself to my feet, taking deep breaths of the icy, semi-fetid air and wondering why I felt so exhausted.

I glanced around and nearly gasped at what I saw. The chamber was, in reality, a huge cavern, complete with stalagmites and stalactites and a small stream meandering along the floor. That's not what surprised me the most, though. Several feet in front of me there was a natural formation of rock acting as a dais with a dark throne perched upon it. The tall chair resembled my mother's in Erintara, only this one was composed of black stone and the skeletal remains of several creatures I didn't know the names of. The perfect seat for a goddess of war and death.

The sconces, which housed the hundreds of blood-red candles and torches lighting the huge place matched the throne, but that was about as far as the macabre decor went. The cold floor was draped with thick, rich rugs in dark shades of red and gold. Delicate, tasseled curtains hanging from the walls suggested passageways into other rooms, and a great, roaring fire just behind the throne took away the bite of the freezing air.

The Morrigan turned to share a few clipped words with Donn. He nodded once, then turned on his heel, his boots grating into the hard ground of the cave and sending a raspy echo bouncing off the walls. I assumed he was satisfied with my impending imprisonment and was off to accompany his monsters to the battlefield.

"Is my domain not splendid?"

The sudden sound of the Morrigan's voice, cutting through the trickle of the stream and the soft breathing of the Cúmorrig sleeping by the fire startled me out of my stupor. I could only nod. As much as I hated the Morrigan and everything connected to her, this cave was beautiful, in an underground, Phantom of the Opera sort of way.

She sighed and brushed past me, her skirts trailing far behind her as she crossed the wide room and climbed up the stone steps and into her throne. She threw one leg over the arm rest and crooked one elbow up onto the opposite knee.

"It's a pity things had to end this way. If only you and Caedehn could have seen things my way, we might have been able to work something out."

She shifted in her seat and brought her leg down so that she could lean both elbows on her knees.

"Unlike your mother, I would have blessed your union with my son if you two had joined me in my plans. But now you and your brother will be mine, slaves bent to my will. Or I may just destroy you both and take what magic you have to offer. Of course, that all depends on how today's battle plays out."

She grinned, a wicked cut to her mouth, and her eyes glittered like rubies.

I kept my mouth clamped tight and stood as straight as I could.

"It doesn't matter," I said once I'd gathered my loose emotions. "Cade won't have to worry about protecting me on the battlefield now. I won't be a distraction to him and he'll have a better chance of defeating your faelah army. And besides," I said, taking a quick and pity-filled breath, "if you kill us after all this is over, at least I'll be with Aiden, to offer him what comfort I can."

I hoped with all my might it wouldn't come to that, but if it did, I would have to push aside all my regrets. *You knew this could be a possible outcome Meghan*, my conscience reminded me, *so you must live with that decision. Yes, there is still a chance that things will go your way, but this isn't over yet.*

The Morrigan narrowed her scarlet eyes at me and then started clicking her tongue as she slowly shook her head back and forth. "You see, still the weak little Faelorah you were when we first met. Letting useless emotions rule your decisions."

The goddess sighed again and pushed herself to her feet, the dark cloudy smoke of her magic swirling around her.

"Well then, as you know, I'm going to be quite busy for the next several hours, so I'll have to lock you up until I have time to deal with you. They say you shouldn't keep all your eggs in one basket, but in this case, I think it would be wise."

She leveled those eyes on me again then raised a hand and snapped her fingers, the sharp sound bouncing off the walls. The Cúmorrig jolted awake and quirked their half-rotted ears at her, only to pant when they recognized their master. I almost threw up at the sight of their decaying tongues.

The soft sound of a heavy blanket crumpling to the ground soon pulled my attention away from the hellhounds. Near the base of the dais, where a curtain had been hanging on the wall and covering what I had thought might be another passageway, was a small indentation carved out of the wall. Black iron bars ran from the tiny room's ceiling to its floor, a gate complete with a lock in its center. And there, curled up on a blanket in the furthest corner sat . . .

"Aiden!!"

My voice tore across the massive space, causing the Cúmorrig to jerk to attention once again.

I ran, just put my numb toes to the floor and ran, tripping over both the thick rugs and my own clumsy feet at least three times. I crashed into the bars, my frozen fingers wrapping around the icy metal, tears streaking down my face.

"Aiden! Oh, Aiden, can you hear me?"

"No, he can't. I drugged him, remember? He should be out another hour or so and I wove a spell of silence around him so he can't speak either. So sorry Meghan, but you'll not be able to ask him any annoying questions."

I gritted my teeth, anger and sorrow boiling up, enticing my own magic and the magic of Cernunnos to flare. Oh yes, now would be a wonderful time to use that magic . . .

You must visit the lair of the Morrigan before you can use my glamour.

Cernunnos's words revisited my mind, bypassing my emotions and settling themselves firmly between that wall of magic and the tiny grain of control I currently had over it. My nerves tingled and a rush of adrenalin poured through me. I let the magic build a little, and just before I was about to let my defenses fall and push all that power forth, I hesitated. Aiden was still in that cage and I was still an emotional wreck.

Wait . . . a tiny voice whispered into my mind. *Wait* . . .

Reluctantly, I released the breath I was holding and drew my magic back within me. There was one more thing I had to do before I let all hell break loose, and that was to get to Aiden and make sure he was alright.

Before any other thoughts could cross my mind, however, the bars I clung to gave way and I stumbled forward. I didn't have to look behind me to know that they'd rematerialized. The Morrigan's cold laughter filled the massive chamber and with a sharp snap of her fingers, the Cúmorrig stood and left their beds by the fireplace to lie in front of mine and Aiden's prison.

"Keep a close eye on those two and if, by some miracle of Eilé, they figure out how to open the door, kill them," the goddess snarled as she whipped her skirts around and headed for the exit.

"I hope you take this time, little Meghan, to think of all the horrible things I'll do to my son once I catch him. Because I don't plan on killing him on that battlefield, oh no, I've got something extra special planned just for you."

She turned and smiled at me and all I could see across that dark space was the white flash of her teeth and the low, smoldering glow of her crimson eyes. The scene from my dream the night before flashed into my mind, of Cade bound and surrounded by the Cúmorrig, of the Morrigan ordering them to attack. The sound of Cade's screams as they tore into his flesh.

A sob broke free of my throat and echoed throughout the cavern. I shot my hand to my mouth, trying to hide any other sounds, but it was too late. The Morrigan's laughter filled the room as she disappeared down the dark tunnel. The echo of a large stone slamming into place informed me that she was really gone and that Aiden and I were trapped in this hell hole with the hounds to keep us in check. I was distraught, Aiden was unconscious, and we hadn't a hope in the world. For a few brief moments I allowed myself to get lost in my despair, but then I gritted my teeth and shook myself.

Stop it Meghan, stop it! I told myself. *You spent four weeks of intense training with Enorah. Yes, it wasn't nearly enough time to become a glamour-wielding expert, but you can't forget what you learned. You must find a way to use it to your advantage.*

I closed my eyes and took several deep breaths through my nose. Eventually, my volatile mix of magic settled down and I could feel the distant warmth of the fire across the room. I glanced down at Aiden, wondering what the Morrigan had given him to sleep. I nearly gasped when he stirred, lifting his hand up to rub his eyes before curling tighter into a ball.

"Aiden?" I whispered, my voice mimicking the rasp of sandpaper. She had said the sleeping potion would last another hour. Could her calculations have been wrong? Could Aiden's own potent magic be protecting him?

My brother wiggled around again and moaned, but still didn't sit up.

"Aiden!" I hissed, sharper this time.

The ears of the closest Cúmorrig swiveled in our direction but I ignored it.

"Aiden, it's me, Meggy. Please wake up."

Slowly, Aiden opened one eye, the one that wasn't covered by his tiny hands. For a few seconds he simply gazed at me as if he wasn't sure he was awake yet. All the while I sat there, still as a statue, holding my breath. But then both of my brother's aqua eyes flew open and he leapt at me, crying out in a muffled voice. I hugged him back, my grip fierce, as tears streaming down my own face.

"Oh Aiden! I'm so sorry the Morrigan took you! I'm so sorry!"

He simply clung to me, shaking as his own tears flowed free. When I pulled him away to look at him, I found bright, blue-green eyes staring at me. He sniffled and frowned, pointing to his throat.

I furrowed my brow then felt a cold prickle trace down my spine. "What did she do to you Aiden?"

He lowered his eyes as his bottom lip trembled. A moment later a fat tear slid down his cheek.

With a thick voice, I whispered, "She made it so you can't talk, didn't she? With magic?"

Aiden glanced up at me, his eyes full of terror. But there was something else there as well. A slow-burning anger. Good. Both Aiden and I had to be strong if we wanted to get out of here.

I glanced past his shoulder, making sure the hounds were still asleep, then lowered my voice and looked him in the eye. "I have an idea Aiden. I know a trick that might make it possible for us to talk, but you can't be afraid, okay? Cade taught me. You remember Cade, right?"

Aiden's eyes grew big and he nodded his head, placing his hand on my heart. I smiled, my eyes shimmering with tears again. "Yes, I love him very much. And I love you very much, too. That's why I let the Morrigan capture me and bring me down here."

Aiden's lower lip started trembling again so I shook my head.

"No Aiden, shhhh. I have a plan to get us out of here, okay? But I need your help. First, I'm going to teach you something called shíl-sciar. I'm going to teach you how to talk inside my head and how to hear me inside of yours."

Aiden firmed his mouth and nodded.

"I'll send some thoughts your way, okay? If you can see them in your mind, I want you to try to send something back. It might take a while, but I think you can do it."

Crossing my fingers, I hoped that the Morrigan had only hindered his ability to speak and that entering the Otherworld really had awakened his magic.

Taking a deep breath, I closed my eyes and sent, *Aiden? Can you hear me? This is your big sister, Meghan.*

I opened my eyes and found Aiden concentrating. He looked confused, but I gave him a few more moments. Just when I was convinced my words hadn't reached him, his eyes and mouth shot open in surprise. Good. He'd heard my thoughts. I smiled, but before I could say anything else to him my mind was bombarded with words in vibrant, overpowering colors.

Meghan! She took me! Mom, Dad, Logan, Bradley, Jack and Joey! Are they okay?! She's so mean and her dogs smell bad and they growl at me and I didn't know where we were going and I thought it was a nightmare and it's so cold in here and she made it so I can't talk . . . but when we went through the first tunnel I could talk like you and Bradley and Logan and she understood me and I was so mad she made it so I couldn't talk because I could finally say what I was thinking . . .

I struggled to sit up, dizzy and overwhelmed by what was happening. Oh, Aiden understood how to use this magic, and he had figured it out really fast. Danua had said he had powerful glamour, but could the Morrigan know just how potent it was? My guess was that she didn't, or hadn't taken the time to check. My skin prickled and I had to swallow against my nerves. Perhaps this crazy, convoluted plan of mine would work after all. I had counted on the Morrigan bringing me here; I knew she couldn't resist my magic. I had also planned on being locked up with Aiden and to somehow find a way to combine our magic to break free. I hadn't counted on his magic being so strong, and as the realization flooded over me, I tried hard not to let my excitement show.

Settle down Meghan. You're still a long way away from being on the other side of that long tunnel, my conscience reminded me. Right. I just needed to take a few deep breaths and get my mind back on track. Unfortunately, I couldn't make it go completely go blank.

. . . And I wanted to see you because I knew you were here somewhere, but that mean lady just told me to be quiet and I wouldn't stop asking so she made it so I couldn't talk and then put me to sleep . . .

Ah yes, Aiden was still on his nervous rant. Not that I could blame him. I placed a hand on his shoulder and he immediately went quiet.

Okay Aiden, I sent into his mind, *we're going to get out of this, but I'll need your help. We need to use our magic, together, to break the Morrigan's spell on that door. Cade's sister taught me some tricks, but I'll need you to help me.*

I could feel my magic stirring, amping up as my body got ready for the fight ahead. Cernunnos's glamour burned right beside my own, but I still held it at bay. I wasn't out of the Morrigan's prison yet, and I was saving that for the last possible minute.

Aiden calmed and then nodded once, his face set in rigid determination. I took a deep breath and, not sparing another single moment to let my worry, anxiety and fear burrow into my heart, I began to teach him everything Enorah and Cade had taught me. First I showed him how to find his well of magic and how to draw it out and shut it down. Then I taught him how to become invisible and how to make a shield. I trained him how to transfer his magic to me and showed him what to expect when I wanted to give him some of mine. He learned fast, brilliantly, impossibly fast, and I thought for a fleeting second that perhaps the reason he was picking this up so quickly was because he'd been deprived the ability to learn for so long.

When we were done, I felt shaky and exhausted, but I drew Aiden close to me. We must have been at it for hours, and I feared that we were running out of time. That Cade and Enorah and my mother and all the other gods and goddesses were running out of time. Guilt hit me and stung fiercely. Saving Aiden was only the first part of my plan. We needed to get moving.

I took a shaky breath and pulled myself to my feet, dragging Aiden up with me. He felt lighter than I remembered and I gritted my teeth in outrage. The Morrigan would pay for her cruel treatment of him.

"We need to get this gate open," I whispered so as not to wake the snoozing Cúmorrig.

Aiden pulled his hand free of mine and placed the palm to the locking mechanism. I furrowed my brow and bent over to examine it.

The Morrigan said some strange words to open it, Aiden sent with shíl-sciar.

I felt my shoulders slump. Great. Probably words Aiden hadn't understood.

Suddenly my mind was flooded with a string of phrases that looked suspiciously like the language I'd heard so often here in Eilé. I blinked in total shock.

What was that? I asked my little brother.

The words the Morrigan used to open the door.

He repeated them again, and several more times until I got the hang of them.

"Um, so how exactly did she do it? Did she just say the words?"

Aiden shook his head. *She placed her hand on the lock and then said the words as her hand glowed.*

No. It couldn't be that easy. She simply said some fancy words and released a stream of magic? Then again, how was she to know Aiden had a memory like a trap. I didn't even know that much. Shrugging, I turned towards the gate. It was worth a shot.

"Okay," I whispered as I reached around my back to pull out Enorah's knife. I still didn't know how the Morrigan's magic had missed it, but I wasn't about to complain. "The Morrigan said that her hounds would kill us if we broke the charm on the gate, so here's what we're going to do. You're going to stay in here, behind me, and I'll stand just inside the doorway so they can only come at me one at a time."

I replaced Aiden's hand with my own, gathered my magic at my fingertips, cleared my throat and repeated the phrase.

When my knees came into contact with the stone floor just on the other side of the bars I knew it had worked. Unfortunately, I didn't have much time to celebrate. The ruckus of our escape had woken the hellhounds.

"Behind me Aiden!" I hissed as I shoved him back and moved to stand in the door-sized gap in our prison.

He let out a whimper and dug his fingers into my coat.

I readied the long dagger and adopted a fighting pose.

The first Cúmorrig leapt and I shoved my hand forward, stabbing its rotten heart with the blade. The hound yelped and fell to the ground, smoke pouring from the hole in its chest. I didn't pause to watch its demise. I fell back just behind the doorway and waited for them to come at me again. I managed to kill seven more before one got in a bite. I gasped as the hound's teeth sank into my thigh.

Meggy! Aiden screamed into my mind, trying to rush forward.

No! I returned, the pain making me grit my teeth as I shoved him further into the alcove. *Stay back! Only five more.*

I managed to cut the remaining hellhounds, but not before getting a few more bites, one on my arm, the other on the same leg as the first one. Once the horrible dogs were on the ground, writhing in pain as the magic of Enorah's blade slowly incinerated them, I limped around the cavern floor, plunging the dagger into the beasts' hearts and watching in macabre satisfaction as they turned to dust.

A light tug at my back made me turn around. Aiden gazed up at me with wide eyes, his skin looking slightly grey. Despite the pain in my arm and leg, I reached down and lifted him up, smoothing out his dark hair as I murmured in his ear.

"We're getting out of here now Aiden," I said, leaning my head against his, "but this isn't over yet. Outside we're going to find a war, and the Morrigan will not be happy that we got out. I need you to be strong and to do everything I tell you, okay?"

He nodded. *Will Cade be there?* he asked me as his arms encircled my neck.

I swallowed back a lump in my throat and kissed my brother's forehead.

Yes, I responded, *he'll be there.*

Aiden sighed. *Good. Cade will help us, won't he Meggy?*

Yes, but this time I hope to help him.

Although it was a struggle, what with my bum leg and Aiden's weight, I climbed the stairs, leaving the beautifully morbid cavern behind and making my way back down the tunnel. I had no idea what awaited me on the edge of the Morrigan's territory, but as I limped along, something began burning deep in my chest, and I had a feeling it was more than just my magic and Cernunnos's combined. It was the burn of vengeance, the demanding need to protect all those I loved.

Duty

No longer was I the naive Faelorehn girl who quaked in the presence of the almighty goddess of war and strife. Oh no, I was a warrior, my instincts honed to a fine point, a point I planned on driving straight into the heartless soul of my enemy. I almost laughed and I could feel the adrenaline pumping through my body. I had so much to lose, but I was through with being afraid. Win or lose, live or die, the Morrigan would grow to rue the day she ever thought to cross me.

-Twenty-Three-
Conflict

The moment I drew my first breath of air on the other side of the stone doorway, a single, frantic word bombarded my mind.

MEGHAN!

The brilliant letters actually seared my eyes and forced a hiss from my mouth. I fell to the ground, my knees digging into the sharp rock shards that littered the dead canyon leading from the Morrigan's underground fortress.

Meggy! another internal voice cried out.

Oh, right. Aiden's. He reached for my elbow, trying to help me up.

I'm okay, I sent to him, pressing my hand against my pounding head.

Meghan! For Eilé's sake, where are you?!

I gritted my teeth and took another sharp breath. Looks like I'd let my shield of magic fail. Not that I was surprised, what with all that had just happened in the Morrigan's cavern. Drawing on some of my glamour, I quickly protected my mind again before I was tempted to answer Cade.

Conflict

Aiden and I moved as swiftly as we could to get out of that canyon. I had a sense from my short connection with Cade that the battle had either begun or was mere minutes away from commencing, and we were several miles from the dolmarehn. I could only hope that the Morrigan's army moved at a very slow pace. Regardless of the fact that there was no way we were going to make it to the edge of her territory in a hurry, I held out hope for a miracle. After all, I had come this far and I was still alive. Perhaps Fate had one more use for me.

Once clear of the imposing granite walls of the ravine, Aiden and I paused a few moments to catch our breath.

Where are we going now Meggy? he asked me, his words, though not spoken, quiet nonetheless.

There was no point in lying to my brother. He had been exposed to enough horror already; it wouldn't hurt to tell him the truth.

We're going to fight.

The Morrigan?

Yes.

Good. She is evil.

That she is Aiden. But we're going to try and be careful.

Is that where Cade is?

My heart took another plunge and I fought against the panic and sorrow that tried to take over me.

Yes Aiden. He is fighting with all the kings and queens of Eilé, of the Otherworld, and with our mo-

I was about to say, 'and with our mother', but I wasn't sure how much Aiden had been told about our birth mother. Best not to shock him as well as scare him.

I took a deep breath. *And the high queen of the Otherworld is with him as well.*

Aiden squeezed my hand. *The Morrigan has lots of monsters, and that scary dark man as well.*

Scary, dark man . . ? Oh, Donn. I found it odd that the god of the underworld was so silent and complacent with regards to the Morrigan. Then again, his part in all this was to lord over the lost souls of the underworld whereas the Morrigan's job was to stir the pot that sent them there. She would be the more violent one, naturally. Didn't mean Donn didn't scare the crap out of me, though.

Come on. We need to keep moving if we want to help Cade and all of our friends.

Your friends, not mine, Aiden corrected. His words were the color of doubt and sadness.

They'll be your friends too, I promise.

Just as I took the first step on what would definitely be a long, grueling journey, a sharp whinny cut through the air and brought me to a jolting stop. A fiery red horse came bursting around the corner, trampling what plants had managed to live in this desolate place. The stallion danced around wildly as several small, ugly faelah snapped at his heels.

"Lasair!" I cried, dropping Aiden's hand and moving to run towards him.

The horse let out another irritated scream and pinned his ears to his head, baring his teeth and snorting. I stopped my forward progress and instead flattened myself against the closest stone, Aiden at my back. Guess the stallion wanted to dispatch the faelah first. Who was I to argue?

With efficient grace, Lasair crushed the rotten creatures under his heavy feet and came trotting up to me, throwing his head back and digging at the earth with his hoof.

I stepped away from Aiden and the rock, crossing my arms and wincing against the lingering pain in my injured arm and leg.

"I told you to leave this place!" I demanded, though I couldn't hide the raw joy I felt at seeing him.

He tossed his head again and then nickered, as if reminding me I was wasting time.

"You're right," I breathed.

Grabbing his mane, I pulled myself into the saddle and then reached out a hand to Aiden. My brother gave me a wary look and swallowed hard, his aqua eyes filled with fear.

"Aiden, this is Lasair. He's my horse here in Eilé and he is very smart."

When my brother remained where he was, I tried again. "He won't hurt you, he only kills faelah."

Lasair rumbled and lowered his nose to try and sniff at my brother.

Please Aiden, I whispered into his mind, *Cade needs our help.*

Taking a deep breath, Aiden stepped forward and reached out a tentative hand. I didn't give him a chance to change his mind. With a sharp tug, he was atop Lasair and sitting in front of me.

"Let's go!" I shouted, giving the red stallion full permission to head westward towards the epic battle that awaited us. As we left the canyon and rocky hillside behind, another screech filled the air and the sting of tears broke free of my eyes as Meridian landed on my shoulder.

"Does no one listen to me?" I sobbed as she nibbled at my ear.

Protect, she insisted. *Never leave.*

I hugged Aiden close as Meridian took off again, screaming her own battle cry as she led the way. I wanted my friends to be safe and I was unhappy that they hadn't listened to me, but I was also happier than ever to see them.

Luckily, the time it took us to breach the distance between the Morrigan's hold and the dolmarehn was so brief with Lasair running at full speed, I didn't have too much time to think about all that could go wrong now that everything was coming to a head. After what seemed like an eternity of monotonous landscape, the flat terrain began to lift into a patch of small hills. I knew the dolmarehn that would take us to the edge of the Morrigan's realm couldn't be more than a mile away now.

"Almost there," I breathed, pulling Aiden close.

As we crested one final hilltop, Lasair slowed to a stop and whinnied in distress. Far below us all hell was breaking loose. Literally. We couldn't have been more than fifty feet up, but on the flat plain spread out before the looming dolmarehn in the distance, a sea of carnage awaited our arrival.

For several heart-wrenching minutes I simply sat in Lasair's saddle, my mind numb as my eyes scanned the battlefield, seeking out those I held closest to my heart. Donn's Dótarbh dominated the scene, their black shapes barreling through faelah and Faelorehn alike, trying to cause the most damage. Quickly, I located most of the Tuatha De: Lugh using his Spear from horseback, impaling faelah like marshmallows, their rotted corpses going up in flames and burning away as soon as their flesh touched the wood of his magical weapon. Epona, in her horse form, stood out like a beacon, her pale coat and mane stained with the dark blood of faelah. The equine goddess and her fellow horses used their teeth and powerful legs to bring down the enemy. Lasair let out an eager whicker as he watched his friends run down and destroy any faelah standing in their path.

"Alright Lasair," I growled softly, sliding off his back before helping Aiden down.

I quickly removed the stallion's saddle, then his bridle. Before he took off, he turned to give me one last appraising look.

"Be careful," I murmured as moisture pooled in my eyes.

He tossed his head, then let out his own battle cry before charging down the hill. I wiped away the tears and made sure one of my hands held Aiden's tightly before I returned my attention back towards the fight.

The sights, sounds and smells of conflict bombarded my senses. The screams and roars of animals and Faelorehn alike scraped at my ears and forced goose bumps to break out on my skin. Death, its aggressive smell akin to a malicious parasite, made me sick to my stomach, and the grand image of suffering all around me, like a serial killer's slide show gone berserk, was almost enough to make me turn tail and run. But I couldn't. My loved ones were down there and if that wasn't enough to motivate me, I had that bone to pick with the Morrigan and the conviction that the Tuatha De needed me if they wanted to win this fight.

Gritting my teeth, I continued my search. I wasn't doing anything until I found Cade, so I kept scanning the ongoing carnage, holding my breath and hoping to see some sign of the one I loved the most. I spotted the Dagda and my mother next, both of them on horseback and holding their own. The Dagda used a great battle axe to take out his enemy, while my mother threw arcs of magic that blasted the faelah into clouds of black dust.

A sharp scream followed by the tell-tale *thlunk* of several arrows striking flesh jerked my attention to the small patch of trees off to the left. I squinted, then grinned when I spotted Enorah and her archers in the branches of the trees, picking off faelah with arrows. Good. She was still in the fight and still alive. But where was Cade . . . ?

My eyes darted around frantically, but it wasn't long until they came to a screeching halt. Just at the base of our small hill, something large and dark rose above all the dead monsters surrounding it. The Morrigan. She sat astride a great horse. No, not a horse, but a faelah that looked like a horse. She wielded a curved, black sword and the sleeves of her dress were torn away. Wild, unfettered bloodlust gleamed in her scarlet eyes and the skirts of her dress billowed around her like a black cloud of death.

Ice pooled in my stomach and I forced my hands to stop shaking. I could not lose it now.

Something big slammed into the goddess's demon horse and she was thrown from its back, only to land soundly, her sword ready to do more damage. I watched in horror, unable to look away, as she mowed down men and women with that weapon of hers. When someone wearing the uniform of the Dagda's guard caught the sword on the handle of his axe and tore it from her hands, she simply threw the smoky edge of her skirts over him, the black substance sucking the life right out of him and making him age before my eyes. When the Morrigan pulled her skirts back, nothing but dust and a bleached skeleton remained.

"Meghan!"

The familiar, guttural roar dragged my attention away from the slaughter. My eyes flashed to the left and my bones almost melted. *Cade.*

He was coming out of his ríastrad, his arms shrinking to their normal size, his huge frame returning to its usual proportions. He looked utterly spent and he stumbled as he tried to make his way towards me. Too much blood. There was too much blood covering his body and I could only pray it wasn't all his.

The Morrigan stopped dead in her tracks. She had been busy burning her way through a group of soldiers wearing Lugh's colors. I looked up and gritted my teeth. They were in the way of a direct path to Cade. The scorn and malice that gleamed red in her eyes only confirmed my suspicions. She wasn't even bothering to check and see if she had killed any of her adversaries; she was far too intent on getting to her son.

Conflict

Over my dead body, I thought with fury. I took in a deep breath and let my magic grow and surge. Aiden clung to me, but I felt him tense up, as if he were about to bolt.

Once her path was clear, the Morrigan gave her son one hard look, then followed his gaze up to where it rested on me and Aiden. As the shock rippled over her face, pure hatred and anger took its place. Her ruby eyes darted between Cade and I, and before Cade could close the gap between us, the goddess spoke a string of ancient words and sent the edges of her living skirts unfurling towards her son. The black cloud pooled at his feet and began climbing up his legs. He stopped mid-stride and lifted his hands to his throat, gasping for breath as the Morrigan continued her chant, her words becoming lost in the cries and screams of the battle still going on all around them.

"No!" I screeched. My magic reacted with me, bursting forth and saturating my every cell.

Not yet, I told it, *let me get her a little closer first . . .*

"Morrigan!" I shouted even louder.

This time she heard me. Jerking as if she'd been slapped, Cade's mother dropped her magical hold on her son and whipped her head around. As soon as the Morrigan's attention was on me, Cade fell to his knees, coughing to catch his breath, the aftermath of his battle fury having sapped all his energy. A few faelah noticed he was down, but out of nowhere something white blurred by and attacked. Fergus. A small flush of relief joined the rush of my magic as the wolfhound made mincemeat out of the Morrigan's abominations. Good. He would keep Cade safe for now. As the magic in my veins pulsed and cried out for action, I turned quickly to Aiden who had remained plastered to my side.

No more self-control, no more holding back. This was it. The final hour. My final dance with the woman who had been making my life miserable for the past two years. This ended, right now.

Taking a breath, I crouched down so that Aiden and I were eye to eye. Speaking into his mind, I tried my best to make my shíl-sciar words seem calm, controlled.

Aiden, this is it. I'm going to use my power to try and end this. I'd send you away if I could, but I don't know where you could go that would be safe at this point.

Aiden's eyes grew large and worried and he shook his head.

No, listen, okay?

I had to take a few deep breaths to gather my bearings. I needed my brother to hide Cernunnos's magic; to create a shield of his own glamour to stretch around me as I allowed it to bloom to its full extent. This way the Morrigan would only be focused on his magic and not mine, and if I could gather Cernunnos's power and throw it at her in one large blast, I might just be able to obliterate her. But if I told Aiden about my extra glamour, then I would break my geis. How ironic it would be, to make it this far and lose everything. I gritted my teeth. The magic had to be hidden from the Morrigan. She had to believe I only had my little bit to use against her. The element of surprise would not be there if I revealed my extra glamour too soon.

Think Meghan, think . . . What did Cernunnos say to you? About your geis, about his magic, about not telling a single person . . . And then it dawned upon me, like brilliant, pure golden light bursting through an ocean of storm clouds after a week of rain. His words came rushing back to me: *You cannot tell a single Faelorehn man or woman Meghan . . .* That's right, I couldn't, and Cernunnos had told me this twice. Why? Because he'd wanted me to remember his exact words. I couldn't tell any Faelorehn men or women about my gift, but he hadn't said I couldn't tell any Faelorehn *children* . . .

I quickly turned my attention back on Aiden, the ridiculous urge to smile like an idiot flitting across my mind.

Conflict

Unfortunately, my intense fear and anxiety pulled the plug on that plan. Taking a deep breath, I prepared the words in my mind. *Well, here goes*, I told myself.

I have my magic Aiden, I sent to him, *but I also have someone else's magic as well. I'm going to let it free, and I'm not sure what will happen, but I want you to stay by my side.*

I paused for a moment to take a shaky breath, realizing that I had to use everything I had to make sure the Morrigan didn't rise again this day. It meant risking more than I was willing to sacrifice. It meant taking the chance that my own flame of magic might burn out, but as I cast one more glance over my shoulder to survey the fight below me, I also realized that this might be the only way to save Danua, the Dagda, Aiden . . . Cade.

A light touch pulled my thoughts back up to the hilltop. Aiden had placed a hand on my shoulder.

Don't worry Meggy, he whispered into my mind. *I'll protect you.*

I pulled my brother close, fighting the warning in my head that kept telling me not to do this, not to risk my own life. But I had no other choice. I would not lose Cade again, nor would I lose Aiden or anyone else if I could help it. I drew in a deep breath, my body shuddering as I did so. I had to make a sacrifice, and the only sacrifice I could live with would be one of my own offering.

I glanced over my shoulder and checked on the Morrigan's slow climb up the low hill. Her immense power was gathering and crackling around her like a scarlet web of electricity; her skirts of smoke and death billowing out over the ground, smothering anything that dared approach.

Meggy? Aiden asked, his own silent words tainted with terror.

I closed my eyes and let the tears fall silently as the clash and shouting of battle continued to rage on just below us.

It'll be okay Aiden, but you have to do exactly what I say, okay?

He nodded and hugged me closer. A twinge of bitterness coursed through me, matching the tingle of the magic I was building up in my blood. I had to push it away. It would do me no good to reflect on what I was being forced to give up. No. I would not dwell on regrets.

I knelt down on the damp grass and looked Aiden in the eye. *I'm going to use my magic to stop all this*, I repeated as the first icy raindrop fell from the black clouds above, *but I need your help.*

Aiden nodded, his dark hair ruffling in the wind.

Remember what I taught you about your magic? How you can never let the candle go out?

He nodded again.

And remember how I showed you how to build a shield with that magic?

Yes.

Good. I blinked hard and took a deep breath.

How is all this possible Meggy? Why do we have this magic? Does anyone else have it?

I knew he meant the rest of our family in the mortal world. Biting my lip, I shook my head. I reached up and placed my hand on his cheek. *Just us buddy, and when this is all over, I'll explain it to you. But first I have a job to do and so do you. I need you to build a shield and I want you to place it around both of us. But Aiden, you must never, ever, let your candle go out. That is the most important thing. Do you promise me to never let the candle flame go out?*

I knew my fingers dug into his arms, but I could not loosen my hold.

Yes Meggy, I promise I won't let my candle go out.

I pressed my head against his small chest and murmured, "Thank you Aiden."

Then I pulled back and reached my hands up, lifting the mistletoe charm from around my neck. I never took it off anymore, but today I had good reason to.

Conflict

This was the first thing Cade ever gave me from the Otherworld. It is a charm to protect you against evil. I want you to have it.

Aiden shook his head fiercely. *You need it to keep safe.*

No. I have my torque, see? I brushed my fingers against the smooth metal.

Reluctantly, Aiden took the necklace and looped it over his head.

I stood and carefully removed Enorah's dagger from its hiding place. I remembered what Cade had said to me long ago, about how magic was more potent when the barrier between blood and skin was breached. Despite the wounds I'd received from the Cúmorrig in the Morrigan's cave, I didn't think they were enough.

"Look Aiden, look at how dark the sky is over there. I think I saw some lightning."

Once he turned away, I dug the sharp edge of the dagger into my arm. I gasped, but bit my lip so I wouldn't cry out. I made several more cuts, two at the base of my neck, two on my palms and one on each of my forearms. I could feel the blood trickling over my skin and I could smell the metallic tang of it. But I could also see the pale blue aura of my glamour gathering around me like a small storm. And for the first time since acquiring it, I allowed the magic Cernunnos had given me to join my own. It flowed free, an exhilarating, cooling rush of darker blue as the rose burst into bloom. The strength behind the antlered god's glamour made me gasp, but I refused to give it full control, at least not yet. Behind Aiden's shield, away from the Morrigan's immediate sight, I let my magic and the foreign magic build and grow until it nearly consumed me. I had one shot to end the Morrigan's assault for good, and I couldn't blow it.

I took Aiden's hand, my own bloody from the cuts I'd made.

His blue-green eyes held concern, but I smiled at him as the tears gathered in his eyes once more.

Now Aiden, keep the shield nice and strong. But remember, never let your candle flame go out.

What about your candle Meggy?

I gritted my teeth and fought the tremor that tried to take over me.

Don't you worry about my candle Aiden. You just take care of yours.

"Hold onto me Aiden," I breathed down to him in my best big sister voice, ending our silent conversation, "hold onto me no matter what and when I say let go, I want you to let go of me but keep the shield of magic over yourself, okay?"

His bottom lip quivered, but he sniffled and nodded, then buried his face into my side. Taking a deep breath, I sent a prayer out to the spirits of Eilé and then I turned and faced the Morrigan once more.

My power crackled down my arms, making the small hair stand on end, and a supernatural wind stirred around me, but the goddess of death was undeterred. Pure fury engulfed her, her black skirts like a great cloud of death and strife spreading out behind her, the dark tendrils of smoke seeking out new souls to ensnare as she finally breached the crest of the small hill.

"How did you two fae straylings escape my fortress!?" she hissed.

Oh yay, we were going to have a little chat before we attempted to obliterate one another on this hilltop. Fine. I had lots to say to her.

"You put Danua's two children together then left us to be guarded by your worthless hounds," I retorted, my voice shaking a little. "What did you expect?"

"The bars on that gate were charmed!" she ground out. "You should never have been able to break free!"

"That was your mistake," I responded, calling my combined magic to gather into one, solid sphere of power.

Just a little longer, I whispered to myself. *You just need to keep control a little longer . . .*

A screech and a white flash flew into my line of vision, breaking my concentration for a split second. Meridian . . .

Too late, I realized what she was doing, but I screamed nonetheless. "No!!"

A red flash of power zapped through the air and slammed into my spirit guide, sending her cart-wheeling into a thicket of oaks growing up the side of the hill, white feathers flying everywhere.

Crying out in pure anguish and hatred, I turned my eyes on the Morrigan and almost charged at her.

No Meghan, you've come too far and suffered too much to let it all fall apart now, my conscience reminded me.

Gritting my teeth and fighting back a new wave of tears, I glared at my enemy. The Morrigan merely returned my look of disdain. I didn't have time to wonder about Meridian's fate, because in the next breath the goddess continued on, as if taking out my spirit guide were as noteworthy as smashing a mosquito.

"So then Meghan, after escaping my lair and killing my hounds, do you still think you are strong enough to fight me?" she hissed in a quiet voice that suggested she had a very thin hold on her own temper. "Even with the paltry power you're siphoning out of your brother, you stand no chance against me. Do you think I've simply been killing these Faelorehn scum and leaving them to rot?"

She cast her hand around, gesturing towards the plain below. "Do you have any idea the amount of power I've accumulated since this battle started? I've given you every opportunity to join me and I am weary of this game. You die today, Faelorah, you and your worthless brother and that pathetic son of mine. You all die and I get all that power I've always wanted without the headache."

The Morrigan wiped the blood and sweat from her forehead, seeming to take pleasure in the act.

"Your words don't frighten me, Morrigan," I retorted. "I have survived your murder attempts twice already, and you know what? I learned something from those experiences as well. I'm not the ignorant little *Faelorah* you once thought I was. But Donn was right; you let your superiority get in the way of caution."

I lowered my voice, though it was still hard to speak over the building wind of the storm and the continued percussion of the battle below. "Just think about it. You laughed at him for believing it unwise to leave Aiden and me alone. Looks like he had a point, huh? Makes one wonder what else you've been wrong about."

The Morrigan's eyes shifted, and for once I saw something other than anger, hatred and conceit in their crimson depths. I saw doubt. And I saw fear.

"You may be the most powerful goddess in Eilé, but everyone has a weakness, and I know yours," I said, my voice harsh and angry.   "Your arrogance has caused you to underestimate me, to become lazy on the details. All I had to do was behave the way you expected me to behave and bide my time. Well Morrigan, your time is up!"

I drew the immense ball of power closer, sending it spinning into a spiral just in front of me. I could feel Aiden's shield of glamour wavering. He had done so well, considering how little he knew about magic, and I understood that it was now or never. One shot, I had one shot to either end the Morrigan's reign or annihilate all that I loved.

"You cannot kill me!" the Morrigan screeched as she covered the last several yards that separated us, lifting her arm as that dark power crackled along her skin.

"No," I said harshly, my voice not sounding like my own. I could tell that my eyes glowed brilliant blue, like the magic I was building. "No, I cannot kill you, but I can destroy you."

The Morrigan's eyes grew wide and she pulled in a deep breath, calling upon every last reserve of her own immense glamour as it condensed into a brilliant crimson blaze in her hand. But before she released it, I screeched at Aiden to pull the shield away and simply let the power I controlled pour forth, the great, spinning sphere surging forward as it continued to pull more magic from my self-inflicted wounds and every pore in my body. It stung, the way a healing dose of medicine stings away infection, and the air was swooped from my lungs. I felt suddenly like an empty shell and I collapsed to the ground just as my magic crashed into hers. An explosion that rent the dark sky and sent shock waves rippling across the land rumbled like the roar of the earth itself. Above all the chaos and cacophony and pain from the magical explosion, a primitive scream, filled with hatred, anger and anguish, rang out.

It felt like my eardrums would burst and I recalled a few things before the darkness came. One, I didn't feel any pain anymore, which in its own way was a blessing. Two, I could sense more than hear Aiden's sob of realization when I crumpled beneath him. Good, that meant he had listened to me and hadn't let his flame of magic go out. And the last thing I experienced before I lost all sensation was Cade's anguished voice and his words splaying across my mind in brilliant red, *Meghan! NO!*

I floated in darkness for a long while, waiting to be taken to the afterlife of the Faelorehn. Did we have an afterlife? Or did we just drift around in nothingness? It didn't seem fair, that we would have a conscious and have nowhere for that conscious to go once our bodies died. But maybe it was different for us because we were immortal; we weren't supposed to die.

I inhaled a deep breath and let it out slowly, wondering why I was breathing if I was dead. Maybe it was something that followed the spirit; something done more out of habit than necessity.

Time passed, how much though I could not say. Eventually the darkness that surrounded me faded away and I was shrouded in mist. Not a single sound disturbed the quiet, and as the mist swirled and unfurled before me, I saw something familiar. A huge tree, its many branches and upturned roots tangled together to create a sphere. The Tree of Life. So, I really was dead, my spirit returning the great Tree. It made sense and I had, after all, used up every last speck of my magic. I only hoped that I had taken the Morrigan with me, or at least hit her so hard she wouldn't be solid again for centuries.

The Tree seemed to beckon me, but before I could so much as set foot on the first stepping stone, I glanced down and saw my reflection in the water. The mist had parted, blown away on a gentle, indiscernible breeze, and the grey and white monotone of the glade became suffused with a golden light.

What I saw in that pool was shocking. The girl, no, the young woman, who stared back at me was absolutely beautiful. True, she had the same color eyes as me, only they were a clearer, brighter hazel than my own, and my hair . . . that tangled, curly mess that had more than once tempted me into shaving it all off, fell in perfect, dark curls down my back. A beautiful white, long-sleeved gown replaced the torn and bloody clothes I had worn when confronting the Morrigan, but my feet were bare. I looked like some little girl's guardian angel but without the wings.

"Yes Meghan, that is you."

The voice startled me, and I jerked my head up. A tall man, a pair of many-pronged antlers protruding from his head, stepped out of the pale mist that remained and came my way. Cernunnos.

"It is you, but it is how Caedehn sees you."

"I don't understand," I answered.

And I didn't. I was dead, lost in the spirit world, I assumed. Cade was safe, I hoped, and alive in Eilé. Along with Aiden. So why was Cernunnos here talking to me? Had he died in the battle too? Maybe because he didn't have his magic to protect him?

Cernunnos only grinned and gave a slight shake of his head.

"Not many of us ever know how lovely we look in the eyes of the one who loves us. This is my gift to you; to know how Cade sees you. This image represents more than just physical beauty, but your spirit also. As you can see, I chose well."

I blinked at him, confused.

"I thought my gift from you was your magic, the magic of a god."

"Yes, but that gift you paid for. You kept your word Meghan; you didn't tell a soul about it, except for Aiden, and you used it when it had the best chance of helping others. When it could show you just how strong and great you could be."

I tried not to feel bitter. "And yet, I am here."

Cernunnos's brown eyes sparkled and became almost green. "Yes, you are here."

I gritted my teeth and tried not to regret my choice. I had known this could happen, so I had to live with it, so to speak. But now that this was all over, and now that I had the woodland god here with no one to interrupt, I took a deep breath and asked the same question I'd asked him the day he bestowed his magic upon me, "Why me? Why did you give this gift to me? Of all the Faelorehn you, or the Spirits of Eilé, could have chosen, why did you choose me?"

Yes, he had already given me an answer, but there had to be more to it. And now that we were both in the spirit world, I thought maybe he'd be more honest with his response.

"Because you were the most innocent. Of course, your brother would have been an even better choice, but he is far too young to understand. You, Meghan, you who knows next to nothing of our world, who is not yet blinded by the power you possess, no one but you could have done this."

"But to keep it secret from everyone, to let them live in fear for that long? To have sacrificed so much when they could have known my gift of power would make things right in the end?"

"Ah, but what is a sacrifice worth if it is not given from our hearts? It is worth nothing, Meghan, if there is nothing to lose. That is what makes it a sacrifice; that is what allows it to hold its own power."

I glanced at him once again, then at the Tree looming only yards away.

"I think I have to go now," I murmured.

As I took a step towards the Tree, Cernunnos reached out and grabbed my hand gently.

"Oh no Meghan, not today," he said, his own words quiet.

"But," I turned towards the Tree again. "I think-"

"No," he said more firmly this time as he pulled me away from the stepping stones and deeper into the mist. "The Tree can wait."

Slowly, the warm, fuzzy orange glow of the enchanted meadow faded away and an image of Cade's worried face appeared before me. I smiled, my eyes prickling as they filled with tears. Oh, how I had missed him, floating around in this strange state of death. But then my grin vanished and I felt a stab of pain. This was wrong. I had died so he wouldn't have to. Had my sacrifice come too late? I bit my lip and choked on a sob. Not fair. Not only had Cade died too, but shouldn't the afterlife be free of such painful emotions?

Then his hand found my cheek and he stroked my face gently. His eyes shone and he released a great breath.

"Oh my love, oh Meghan."

He sighed again and drew me close, pressing his forehead against mine.

"I thought I had lost you."

I was confused. What?

But you have lost me Cade. I'm sorry. I lied to you about my extra magic, all this time. But don't you see? I did it to protect you, and Aiden and everyone else. Please forgive me. I thought it would be enough. I thought I could save you.

I didn't realize I had been using shíl-sciar until Cade's lips met mine as he answered me. *No Meghan, no. You did not die, but you almost did. Gods, you were so close I nearly went crazy. My ríastrad is nothing compared to the state I was in when I found you.*

His arms wrapped around me as he trailed kisses across my face. It felt as if he would never let me go and I sighed, enjoying this comforting fantasy while it lasted. There was no way what he told me was true. I couldn't have survived that fight. My candle flame had burned out.

Eventually, Cade stopped kissing me and took a deep breath as he pulled me even closer, tucking my head in against his chest and under his chin, his strong hands splaying across my back. I melted into him, barely registering that it was our bare skin that touched. I sighed again and grinned, wishing with all my heart that what Cade had told me in this afterlife dream was true.

A moment later everything went dark again and I knew that the next time I woke, this bliss would be nothing more than a memory.

Twenty-Four

Consequence

I woke again to the sensation of someone stroking my face. Blinking the blurriness from my eyes, I noticed that Cade was with me.

"Where am I?" I murmured.

"In our room at Erintara," Cade responded quietly.

"Am I dead?"

Cade grinned, his eyes filling with tears. "No my love, no. You are very much alive."

But what about the Tree of Life? My conversation with Cernunnos? Then I remembered the dream I'd had of Cade just afterwards. Perhaps it hadn't been a dream after all.

I took a shuddering breath. "Are you sure?"

Cade tilted my chin up and kissed me gently, his lips lingering on mine.

Very much so.

My voice was rough when I spoke again. "How?"

And then he told me everything that had happened.

"I was halfway up the hill when your glamour hit the Morrigan, and the shockwave knocked me off my feet for a good thirty seconds. By the time I made it to your side, Aiden was there, crying silently over you with his hands pressed to your skin."

Cade shuddered but then forced himself to continue. "Immediately I sought out your magic and couldn't find any. I panicked, thinking the worst, but then I felt a steady stream of another's glamour keeping the tiny spark of your candlewick going."

"It was probably Cernunnos's magic, not mine," I murmured without thinking.

"No. It wasn't his," he replied, no question in his voice.

I stiffened. How did he know?

"Once we got you safely inside Erintara and I knew you were going to stay with us, Cernunnos pulled me aside and explained everything."

Cade pressed his lips to my temple and I could feel his mouth curve up in a grin. "I gave him a black eye and a few broken ribs before the Dagda pulled me off of him."

"What?!" I cried, struggling to sit up.

Oh no, that wasn't going to happen. It felt like someone had thrown me into an industrial strength drier full of broken glass and gravel and then hit the heavy duty button. I hurt all over.

"He deserved it for what he put you through, and he even said so after his nose stopped bleeding."

Ugh. I was so tired of people getting hurt. "Will he be okay?"

"Now that he has his glamour back he will be," Cade answered.

I sighed and snuggled back against him. "Cade?" I murmured.

"Hmmm?"

"Not that I'm complaining, but why are we naked?"

He chuckled and said, "Helps with the magical transfusion. I've been sharing my glamour with you to help you get stronger. That's what kept the spark of your magic from going out you know, the magic that was being poured into you."

Ah yes, the conversation we'd been having before I got sidetracked with my concern for the antlered god. "So who was it then? Who kept me alive?"

Cade turned my face so that I looked directly into his dark green eyes. "Aiden," he said quietly, "Aiden was the one who kept your magic from dying."

Tears welled and fell before I could even register them.

"Is he okay?" My voice was hoarse and my throat hurt, but I didn't care.

"He's with Danua right now. He's a bit weak, but she managed to break whatever spell of silence the Morrigan placed on him and when you're both well enough to travel, we'll pay a visit to your family in the mortal world."

I nodded. Now that I knew everyone I cared about was safe, sleep pulled at me. Before I drifted off, however, one more thing came to mind.

"The Morrigan?" I mumbled.

"Gone, my love." Cade kissed me again. "And when Eilé raises her again in a thousand years or more, we will make sure she never gains back the power she once had."

I later learned that I'd been unconscious for three days, during which time the Tuatha De gathered their people to head back to their own realms. They possessed the task of spreading the news that the Morrigan had been vanquished and that those faelah who survived the battle, the ones not controlled completely by her power, had scattered to hide until she returned again. Or to cause their own mischief. As for Donn, well, Cade told me he had disappeared after my blast of power hit the Morrigan. No one thought that the god of the dead would be making an appearance any time soon.

Consequence

On the fourth day after the great battle, I woke up to find a familiar set of dark eyes regarding me from the bed post.

"Meridian!" I cried, a sob catching in my throat.

Cade stepped out of the bathroom with a towel around his waist when he heard my cry.

I shot my glance to him, the joy at seeing Meridian distracting me from his splendid state of undress.

"I thought the Morrigan killed her," I said.

Cade shook his head, a small smile on his face. "We found her in a grove of trees under the care of a small colony of twigrins."

I continued to stare at him, confused.

Cade crossed the room and took a seat on the bed next to me.

"That's right, I never told you about that characteristic of your favorite Otherworldly creature. Twigrins like to fix things, well, repair things that are damaged. They use their special magic to mend broken branches or crushed flowers, or sometimes heal the twisted ankle of a fawn."

I was smiling broadly now. "Or cure a white merlin who has been hit with a blast of bad magic?"

"Precisely," Cade said, giving me a quick kiss on the top of my head.

I reached up and gave Meridian a scratch. She cooed and closed her eyes.

Safe, she sent on a mental sigh. *No more hurt.*

"What about Lasair?" I asked, my joy drying up only to be replaced with fear.

"He returned home with Epona," Cade said. "The faelah hurt him pretty badly, so he needs time to heal among his fellow horses."

I nodded, pained to hear he'd been hurt, but grateful he was alive. Then I asked the next question, somewhat afraid of the answer. "Will I ever see him again?"

Cade put his hand behind my neck and pulled me into a deep kiss. My nerves tingled and my fingers drifted towards his towel, but he escaped my grasp with a quick twitch of his hips, lifting up off of the bed and pulling away from me so that he could dress for the day.

"He told Speirling that once he has returned to full health, he'll be back to serve as your devoted companion."

Despite my disappointment at Cade's escape, the bright smile he sent me, along with the news of Lasair's impending return, kept my thoughts positive.

I started to get out of bed, insisting on a shower. Cade helped me, of course, because I could barely walk. I guess using up almost all of your power in one fell swoop took a while to recover from. Who was I to complain, though? It was better than being dead.

Once I felt clean and was dressed, I asked about Aiden and my mother again.

"Danua sent a message up earlier while you were still asleep. They are waiting for us in the parlor beside her throne room with tea."

I moved to stand up and as my legs crumpled beneath me, Cade stepped in and took charge, lifting me up into his arms.

"As much as I admire the chivalry thing," I grumbled, "I don't need you carrying me from room to room."

"Yes you do," Cade answered cheerfully, maneuvering us through the door.

As we passed down the hallway, people paused and stood aside, bowing and greeting me as if I had grown up here in this very castle. I guess risking my life and taking out their enemy improved my status in their eyes, and against my better judgment, their kind acknowledgment warmed me.

Danua and Aiden were waiting for us when we arrived, my mother in her usual, court dress and Aiden in a pair of fancy clothes that looked personally tailored to fit him. When he saw Cade carrying me in, he jumped up from his chair and came running over.

"Meggy!" he cried out.

Cade set me down just in time for Aiden to slam into me, wrapping his arms around me in a tight grip. Cade held onto my shoulders so I wouldn't fall over, and I reached down and ran my hand over my brother's dark hair. I couldn't help it. I started crying again. Aiden. My autistic brother, talking to me as if he'd done so his entire life.

"The lady says she's our real mother Meggy, is that true?"

Aiden looked up at me with those big eyes of his and I bit my lip, nodding. "Yes Aiden, she's our real mother."

He furrowed his brow and I waited for him to deny it, to break down and insist she was wrong. Instead he gave a little sigh and just leaned into me. "Then that means we're true brother and sister."

I sniffled and pressed my hand against his back.

"Meggy," he said again, looking back up at me. "If she's our real mother, why did she send us away to Mom and Dad?"

Danua had stood up and was moving our way, but upon hearing Aiden's words she froze and gave me a sad look.

I cleared my throat. "Because Aiden," I said, returning my eyes to his face, "she loves us very much and thought that we would be safer if we grew up with Mom and Dad."

Aiden seemed to turn that over in his head for a few moments, but then nodded again and closed his eyes as he rested his cheek against my hip.

I looked back up in time to see Danua approaching me with her arms open. I had to swallow back my surprise when she wrapped all of us, Cade included, into a great hug. Her shoulders shook and when she stepped back, tears streamed down her face.

"I never thought in a thousand years that I'd see the two of you again," she said softly, looking first at me, then Aiden. "And now I have both of you here."

After that, we all sat down to tea. Aiden asked one question after another as we enjoyed our meal, and he got an answer for each of them. I couldn't believe how comfortable he was here, sitting in Danua's castle and talking to us as if he had never had a timid streak at all. But maybe that had never been the case to begin with. Perhaps he had just been awkward about his inability to communicate with others. Whatever it was, I was beyond happy to see him so vibrant.

Cade trailed his hand across my thigh, seeking my fingers. When both our hands were clasped, I looked up at him. He grinned and whispered into my mind, *Danua has sent a message to your parents, telling them that you both are well. She has also requested that Aiden start spending his summers here in Erintara.*

I blinked in surprise at him. I hadn't thought about where Aiden would live. I'd kind of been too busy trying to rescue him and get rid of the Morrigan. What Cade suggested sounded like a good plan, but I only had one question.

Does Aiden know about this?

Cade nodded. *He was present when we discussed it.*

And?

He said as long as he got to spend time with his big sister, then it was fine by him.

Smiling like an idiot, I leaned back in my chair so that I pressed up against Cade. It would take me a bit longer to heal, but as soon as I could walk and function like a normal person once again, we would take a little trip to the mortal world and tell my parents everything that had happened.

That evening, my mother hosted a small dinner in my honor. Her entire court attended (along with their new, positive attitudes with regards to me) and when I entered the dining room and found the Dagda and Enorah waiting for me, both dressed in Erintara's finest, I almost fell on my face as I bolted away from Cade's side. I'd forgotten my legs still weren't working properly.

Aiden came in after me, flying away from Danua and latching onto my arm. I introduced him to Enorah and the Dagda, and although he hid behind the folds of my skirts at first, by the time the main course arrived, he was as chatty as he'd been with our mother earlier that morning. I still couldn't believe how much my brother had changed, but it was quickly growing on me.

The next morning, Cade, Aiden and I left for Luathara. I was well enough to travel, and it was long past the time we return Aiden to my parents in the mortal world. Danua came to see us off, her regal, controlled mask back on as she said farewell to a son and daughter she had almost lost.

"I'll come back again," I promised, squeezing her hand, "and hopefully our foster parents will agree to summer visits for Aiden."

Danua smiled, a tiny quirk of her lips, and nodded her head once. I turned to join Cade and my brother, but before I could take one step, Danua pulled me back and gave me a fierce hug.

"I am so sorry for all the pain I caused you before, and I'm proud to call you my daughter."

Sniffling, I hugged her back just as fiercely. "And I am glad to call you mother."

The Dagda and Enorah joined us on our trip back since their destinations were along the way, and by late afternoon we were gazing upon Cade's castle from the wooded hills above Luathara. Speirling, happy to finally be home, let out a cheerful whinny while the borrowed horse Aiden and I rode gave the black stallion a questioning look.

Briant and his family were there to greet us when the horses clattered into the courtyard. In no time we were ushered into the castle and taken directly to the dining hall where the staff who had remained for the evening insisted on hearing every little detail about the great battle against the Morrigan.

It was nearly midnight when we finally clambered up the stairs, Aiden out cold and draped over Cade's shoulder.

"Tomorrow morning we'll cross into the mortal world," Cade murmured closing the door to one of the spare rooms after tucking Aiden into bed.

Nodding my head and yawning, I happily used Cade as a crutch as we headed towards his bedroom. I don't actually remember making it to the bed, but I do know that my dreams were filled with light and joyful things.

I rose early the next morning, rubbing my eyes as I stumbled into the bathroom to take a shower. Cade was still asleep, so I did my best not to wake him as I fumbled around for a fresh towel and soap. Once I was clean and dressed, I returned to the bedroom to find the bed empty and Cade missing. Assuming he had gone downstairs to get the horses ready for our trip to the dolmarehn, I stepped up to the window, gazing out over the beautiful fields of Luathara. Far below, I could see people getting ready for work and I almost laughed when I recognized two familiar white shapes chasing each other around the courtyard.

A few moments later the door clicked open and shut. Cade stepped up quietly behind me and wrapped his arms around my torso a few seconds later. I leaned my head against his shoulder and drew air deep into my lungs, breathing in his scent. Closing my eyes and smiling, I said, "I could get used to this."

"As much as I'd love to stay here all morning," Cade murmured, "we have a quest to undertake, and I have something to show you first."

I turned and arched a brow, but Cade had already pulled away, taking me by the hand and leading me towards the bedroom door. I followed, my curiosity getting the better of me, and soon we were out in the courtyard and heading towards the garden gate. The sun was just peeking above the horizon and those helping with the castle's ongoing renovation were just arriving. We maneuvered around the neatly trimmed herbs and made our way through another archway that opened up into a smaller, secluded garden. A tiny section in the wall had been removed so that water from the stream could trickle into a pool, and a continuous stone bench wrapped around the four walls. Above, the branches of oak and ivy, bare of leaves this late in the season, intertwined to form a natural lattice. Once we were both tucked safely inside, Cade stopped and turned towards me, his face bright with a wide smile.

"Um, why'd you bring me out here?" I tried to make my voice sound curious and not accusatory. I think I might have failed.

"Look," he said, his voice barely above a whisper as he inclined his head upward.

I glanced up again, but this time I saw something that hadn't been there before, or maybe I just hadn't seen them. Looking down at me with big, kind eyes, their limbs interweaving and blending in with the branches above, were at least a dozen twigrins. I gasped in delight, pulling my hands free of Cade's so I could cover my mouth.

"I had Enorah bring some from the Weald to live here in our garden. For your birthday," he said smugly.

"My-" I began, but then stopped short. "Wait, what's the date?"

Cade's smile only widened. I groaned and buried my face in my hands again. Had I really lost track of that much time?

"What kind of a girl forgets her own birthday?!" I complained.

Laughing, Cade pulled me close, but sobered up the second our eyes met. He brushed back a loose strand of my hair and said in a quiet voice, "The kind that is too busy saving our world."

I sighed and succumbed to his embrace. For once, everything in my life seemed to be perfect. I had finally found my place in this world, and it was a very pleasant place indeed. I no longer had to worry about the Morrigan, for a long while at least, and my mother had finally opened up to me. I had so many new, wonderful friends and I had a brother who, assuming my mortal parents agreed, would be visiting me every summer. And I had Cade. Never in my wildest dreams would I have thought my life would end up here, standing in an enchanted garden with the young man I loved beyond all reason and who loved me back just as fiercely.

As the bright rays of the early morning sun streamed in through the branches above, I felt my magic rise to meet up with Cade's, enveloping us in a mantle of contentment no amount of words could describe.

Epilogue
~Imbolg~

The sun dipped low on the horizon, painting the fields of pure white with its golden light. I wrapped my cloak more tightly around myself and watched as my breath made small clouds in the frozen air. The waterfall at the edge of the patio was nothing more than a trickle this time of year, but I welcomed its simple melody as I let my mind wander. Nearly three months had passed since the Tuatha De had won their battle against the Morrigan; three months since I'd torn myself free from her wrath. Luathara's castle was nearly complete, but with the approach of winter the masons and construction workers had to postpone until spring's first thaw. I didn't mind. The interior of the castle was finished, so we were able to stay warm and protected from winter's wrath.

Today, though, had been pleasant. No snow had fallen and the sun had shown all day. I only hoped this trend continued through tomorrow for our Imbolg celebration, a holiday to mark the end of winter. I grinned as I rubbed my hands together. For some reason, thinking of Imbolg and the arrival of spring brought to mind the Solstice party my mother had hosted a month and a half ago. All the Tuatha De had attended and I had been so pleased to see them once again, even

Cernunnos. I only hoped that our own small bonfire and festival would prove as joyful.

Sighing, I cast my eyes back over the fields and rolling hills of Erintara, wondering when Cade would be back from his outing. Once a month he insisted on taking a few days to ride Speirling throughout his property to make sure any stray faelah hadn't moved in. Sometimes I went with him, especially now that Lasair had returned from his stay with Epona's herd. The memory of his arrival flashed across my mind, and I allowed myself another small smile. He had just shown up one day, a red flame standing on the hilltop, and I had run to him while Meridian swooped down and chattered happily.

At the moment, however, he was most likely snoozing in the stables while I rested from my long day of preparation. Yes, the reason for my staying behind this time. I had to make sure everything was perfect for all of our guests tomorrow. Cade and I had invited the entire town of Kellston, as well as the Dagda and Enorah and several of the other Tuatha De. My mother received an invitation as well, but we weren't surprised when she politely declined. She was the high queen, after all, and could not leave Erintara at the moment.

Thinking of Danua made me think of Aiden, of course. I had wanted to invite my little brother to the Imbolg celebration, but Cade had made a good point. Aiden needed as much time to get over the shock of his kidnapping and the following trauma he'd been through. Even though he seemed like a changed boy, exuberant and cheerful just after our ordeal, the evil that had surrounded him for those few days had to be dealt with, and the best way to help him heal was to let him soak in the normalcy he'd been so used to in the mortal world.

Four more months Meghan, I told myself as I rubbed my hands together and blew into them, *four more months and he'll be here for the summer.*

I grinned, remembering how grateful I was to my mortal parents for understanding Aiden's need to get to know his mother and the world he'd come from. Although, telling them about how Danua had deceived them was hard. They had taken their time to grieve the loss of the child they never knew while at the same time rejoicing in the fact that they'd had me and Aiden for so long. I don't know how they could show such strength after all they'd been through, and I only hoped that someday I might show that same courage.

A distant whinny followed by sharp barking snapped my attention away from my reminiscing. Far below, a black smudge interrupted the perfect, snowy landscape and my face broke into a wide smile. Cade was back with Speirling and Fergus. Several minutes later they entered the courtyard, and Cade sent me a few words using shîl-sciar.

Where are you?

Look up, I said.

He glanced up to find me gazing down at him from our patio. I waved and sent, *Come join me, the sunset is beautiful.*

Ten minutes later, the great wooden door leading into the third floor hallway creaked open and Cade stepped out onto the frost-encrusted terrace. I turned to study him, drawing in a deep breath of admiration. He looked resplendent in his dark green riding cloak, his hair tousled from the wind and his cheeks slightly flushed from the cold. With boots crunching against the thin layer of snow, Cade closed the distance between us and took me in his arms. I sighed and simply leaned into his solid warmth, closing my eyes and pressing my cheek against his shoulder. The day had been long and busy and I was ready for a break.

"I missed you. You were gone longer than usual," I breathed quietly as Cade rocked me gently in our very own slow dance.

"Yes, I had a few extra stops to make this time around," Cade murmured, his lips pressed against my ear and dispersing my wayward thoughts. "You see, I've been doing some thinking . . ."

I grinned and looked up at him, his arms still encircling me. "Have you now?"

He nodded, and then dipped his head as he fished something out of his pocket.

"I have," he continued, lifting his hand, his closed fist hiding something.

I blinked in confusion. With his other hand, Cade pulled my left arm from his waist and proceeded to wrap what looked like a gold string around my wrist. What on earth . . . ?

"I was hoping that you might want to make our current arrangement a little more, well, permanent."

I lifted my arm and stared at the armlet, stunned. It was absolutely beautiful, a long, thin thread of gold bedecked with tiny chips of pale green, blue and topaz jewels, woven into an intricate knot work pattern to form a bracelet. It looked strangely familiar, as if I had seen it before.

And then it hit me like a ton of bricks. I *had* seen this before, on the people of Eilé. On men and women alike. It was symbolic, a token of love. A representation of a bond made when two people wished to live and love one another forever. Cade had just wrapped an engagement ring, uh, *bracelet*, around my wrist. And when I glanced at his own arm, I could see he too was wearing a similar one, the gold thread of his a bit more masculine and the jewels a shade darker than my own.

I felt my mouth fall open in shock and tried desperately to say something, anything. Before the words would form, however, Cade took my face in his hands and tilted my eyes up to meet his.

"Marry me, Meghan," he whispered, his voice soft and sincere. "Bind your spirit to mine. Give your heart over to my keeping, just as I have already given mine over to yours."

I said something, but I have no idea what it was and I think it might not have even been an actual word. Oh, *very* romantic Meghan . . .

Cade grinned, his eyes gleaming a beautiful jade green. "Is that a yes?"

Finally, some real words got out. Yay! "But, Danua?"

Ugh, why had I said my mother's name?

Cade's grin widened. "She was the one who suggested we go through with the bonding ceremony."

He reached down and gently kissed my cheek, just below my eye.

"A princess of Eilé cannot remain unmarried for very long once she reaches a certain age. It would be shameful and the last thing I would want to do is bring shame upon yours and your mother's names."

I took several shallow breaths and stuttered, "M-Mom will want to know about this . . ."

"She's the one who helped me pick out the right bracelets."

He kissed my other cheek, his lips lingering on my skin.

"Wait!" I breathed, my heart hammering against my ribs as I grabbed at his hands and pulled them away from my face. I could not think straight with him kissing me.

"What about Dad?"

Cade sighed gently and stepped in closer. He pulled his hands from mine and ran them along the sides of my face, threading his fingers into my hair.

"He said the same thing he did when he took me aside at your house those many months ago," he murmured.

"Oh," I managed, "and what was that exactly?" Why wouldn't my heart stop beating so wildly and why were my palms so clammy?

Cade looked me in the eye and answered, "That if I ever hurt you he would find me and kill me, even if he had to cross into the Otherworld to do it."

I bit my lip and stopped fighting the tears that were forming in my eyes. "And what did you tell him?"

Cade's lips quirked up and his eyes took on a mischievous glint. He leaned forward and pressed his mouth against my ear.

"I told him," he whispered, his warm breath sending goose bumps down my spine, "that I had already died for you once and that I would not hesitate to do so again."

At some point I had curled my fingers around his shirt collar, but now my grasp was so tight my knuckles actually hurt. It was getting harder to breathe and I felt flushed.

"So Meghan Elam, daughter of Danua, high queen of Eilé," Cade said, kissing my neck, "will you marry me? Will you be my better half and live with me here at Luathara and help me destroy what faelah the Morrigan has left behind? Will you take care of me and let me take care of you?"

Finally, the answer I had been trying to give him all this time pushed its way past all the other silly, insignificant thoughts that had flooded my brain and burst forth.

"Yes Caedehn MacRoich of Eilé, of course I will marry you. Of course I will stay by your side and help you rid this world and the mortal world of evil. And yes, I will take care of you."

I laughed then, my smile hurting my face as he scooped me up into a great hug, twirling us both around on the stone terrace of Luathara as he kissed me again and again.

We remained outside until well after dark, dancing to our own music and to the natural rhythm and song that could only be found in Eilé. Three years ago I was nothing more than an awkward teen, ready to move on with my life even though I hadn't the slightest idea where I wanted to go. And then Cade had stepped into my self-conscious, pitiful little world and turned everything on end. I had survived the wrath of a goddess, had made peace with a mother who had abandoned me, had discovered a brother who could share my life in the Otherworld, and had fallen in love with a young man who I knew, without a doubt, would always be by my side to help me through anything. I knew this because, let's face it, he'd already proven his devotion to me.

As Cade and I slow danced under the moon and stars of Eilé, I finally let my joy spread through me. I was so very happy, truly and blissfully happy, and I had an eternity to spend adding to that happiness. For once in my life, I couldn't wait for the future to start.

Acknowledgments

I want to take this opportunity to thank all of those who have been with me on this long journey, including my family and friends and everyone who inspires me and encourages me every day to continue with my grand writing endeavors. I especially want to express my appreciation towards my readers, who have, over this past year, sent me wonderful messages and comments about the Otherworld Trilogy. I am exceedingly grateful for your dedication to Meghan and her friends, and I'm so very happy that my books have brought some joy into your lives. Finally, I especially want to thank Jodi Moore, Kaitlyn Ikenouve and Keisha Martin for their help in adding the finishing touches to *Luathara*. Once again, thank you all for being there right beside me on this wonderful adventure.

About The Author

Jenna Elizabeth Johnson grew up and still resides on the Central Coast of California, the very location that has become the set of her Otherworld Trilogy, and the inspiration for her other series, The Legend of Oescienne.

Miss Johnson has a degree in Art Practice with an emphasis in Celtic Studies from the University of California at Berkeley. She now draws much of her insight from the myths and legends of ancient Ireland to help set the theme for her books.

Besides writing and drawing, Miss Johnson enjoys reading, gardening, camping and hiking. In her free time (the time not dedicated to writing), she also practices the art of long sword combat and traditional archery.

For contact information, visit the author's website at:
www.jennaelizabethjohnson.com

Books by This Author:

The Legend of Oescienne Series
The Finding (Book One)
The Beginning (Book Two)
The Awakening (Book Three)
Tales of Oescienne - A Short Story Collection

Otherworld Trilogy
Faelorehn (Book One)
Dolmarehn (Book Two)
Luathara (Book Three)
Ehríad - A Novella of the Otherworld

A Sneak Peek at *Ehríad - A Novella of the Otherworld . . .*

A Single Thread of Magic

The sharp snap of a twig and a low, almost imperceptible growl informed me that the creature I hunted was now only a few yards away. I assumed his snarl of frustration was aimed towards the branch he'd broken, giving away his presence, and not by any means meant to intimidate me. No matter. I had planned it this way. I had known he'd been following me for a good fifteen minutes now. It helped when you had another pair of eyes, and a good nose, to lend a hand.

How close? I sent to my spirit guide.

Ten feet, to the right, Fergus answered.

His mind was sharp; focused on the hunt. Even better.

I let my body ease out of the tense stance it had taken at hearing the sound of the snapped twig. *One more minute Fergus.* I'd let the creature stalk me for sixty seconds more.

The thing about faelah is despite their vicious, blood-thirsty tendencies, they aren't very smart. I was only a few feet from the dolmarehn now, boxed in on most sides by the steep walls of the culvert, and the faelah was somewhere above me, close to the edge but remaining out of sight.

What exactly are we dealing with? I asked my spirit guide.

About my size, dark, no hair. Small eyes, big teeth, sharp, thin claws and a tail like a rat.

I nodded to myself. This particular monster resembled most other faelah: the grotesque, zombie-like imitations of animals created from the long-dead body parts of many others. If the people of the mortal world could see it, they would be cursed with a lifetime of nightmares to disrupt their sleep.

Fortunately for them, the faelah's glamour kept it invisible from sight. No, only my people, the Faelorehn, could see the faelah. At least until they were destroyed and a small window between the time their glamour faded from their bodies and their flesh turned to ash did the mere mortals get a chance to catch a glimpse. This was one of the main reasons I lured as many as I could back into the Otherworld, or at least deep enough into the woods to kill them where they wouldn't be seen by anyone.

The crunch of dead leaves met my ears again, along with Fergus's words: *Get ready.*

I slipped my hand into my boot, pulling out a long knife, pressing the dull side against my forearm so that I could stab if necessary.

In the next breath, the faelah leapt from the edge of the ravine and used the trunks of dead trees crisscrossing my path like ladder rungs to make its way down. The faelah came to rest only fifteen feet in front of me, a monster looking very much like a partially decomposed mountain lion. It growled at me, showing several long teeth, and twitched its reedy tail. Just as I had suspected, this one wasn't going to let me lead it back into the Otherworld. Looks like it would have to be a kill. Not that I regretted it much. Most of the faelah had been alive at one time, but not anymore, not really. I bared my teeth in a grimace, hoping to intimidate the beast.

A flash of white caught the corner of my eye and a giant wolfhound joined us, using the same method the faelah had to reach the gully floor. He landed behind the creature, bearing his teeth and laying his rusty ears flat against his skull.

Kill? he sent to me.

Yes, this one will have to be a kill.

The beast howled and snapped its jaws before hunkering down on its hindquarters.

A Single Thread of Magic

With preternatural speed the faelah leapt, mouth gaping open, massive paws tipped with needle-thin claws outstretched. I froze for a fraction of a second, then with one swift movement, jerked my hand diagonally across my body, swiping the sharp edge of my blade against leathery skin.

The yowl in the monster's throat died and I quickly sidestepped, letting the body hurtle past me. It landed in a tangled heap in the dirt, the head nearly severed from the rest of the body. Its limbs twitched a few times as black, putrid blood spilled from the open wound. I wrinkled my nose at the smell, but didn't gag. I was used to the stench.

As I cleaned my blade I felt the faelah's glamour swell like a bubble, growing larger and larger until it burst. There was nothing to see really, but my own well of magic felt it all the same. If there had been mortals around, they would now be gaping, dumbfounded at the atrocity lying at their feet. I didn't even stay to make sure it turned to dust.

"Come on Fergus, time to go," I said to the wolfhound.

Wounds? he sent to me.

No, not even a scratch. I was, after all, very good at my job.

We hiked out of the woods and through the small swamp that rested behind a sparse neighborhood. I often patrolled this area because my home resided just on the other side of the dolmarehn hidden at the end of the ravine. I longed to head home, back to Eilé, but I needed to return my car to the small garage I used as storage when spending any extended amount of time in the mortal world.

I crossed over the lowest part of the swamp and headed up the trail that veered off from the one the local horse owners often used. Five minutes later I found my car, a classic black Trans Am complete with a silver Phoenix emblem emblazoned on the hood. I grinned. I wasn't a big fan of the machinery and technology of the mortal world, but I had a soft spot for this car. As I approached, I ran my hand along the hood, petting it as if it were a dog.

Fergus snorted next to me and I gave him a look over my shoulder. He returned it with a canine grin, his tongue falling out of his mouth in a pant.

"We all have our indulgences, Fergus," I murmured, smiling as I dug the keys out of my trench coat pocket.

Teaching myself how to drive had been quite an adventure, and I had to be careful because being from the Otherworld the only driver's license I owned was a fake one. This was the main reason I never took the Trans Am out to test its racing capabilities; couldn't risk getting pulled over and questioned.

I unlocked the door and swung it open, but before I so much as set a single foot into the car, something familiar brushed against my senses. My well of glamour flared and I drew in a sharp breath, clutching a hand to the middle of my chest.

What in Eilé . . . ?

I shot a look at Fergus, but he only back-stepped a few paces and whined.

My breath was coming in short bursts and it took a while for the sensation to burn off. It wasn't unpleasant really, just unexpected. I glanced up and gazed down into the small valley dominated by the acres of eucalyptus trees and swampland. That burst of sensation hadn't come from any faelah I'd ever encountered, and I've encountered more than most. Yet, it had felt so familiar.

I shook my head to get rid of the feeling, gritting my teeth as I sunk into the driver's seat of my car. I gripped the steering wheel until my knuckles showed white; until the feeling faded away and my heartbeat returned to normal. Fergus whined again and I leaned over to open the passenger side door for him.

I turned the key in the ignition and the car rumbled to life. As I pulled onto the highway, my mind was completely occupied with the small burst of power that had slammed into my own glamour like a raging bull. What was it, and would I be able to find its source? Taking a deep breath, I made a mental note to seek it out the next time I was in the swamp.

A Single Thread of Magic

The wheels of the Trans Am crunched over gravel and the rumble of the engine set the dogs in the junkyard beside my place into a fit of barking. I hit the button to open the garage door and glided in onto smooth concrete. I had purchased this small place several years ago, when it became apparent that the faelah wouldn't stop visiting this particular area on the Central Coast. It wasn't much: a garage large enough to fit my car with a studio above it. I didn't stay here more than a few days at a time, but it served well as my headquarters when I needed to track down renegade Otherworldly monsters.

Before closing the garage door, I stepped out onto the asphalt and scooped up the newspapers from the past several days. I had been gone a week in the Otherworld and now I needed to check the headlines for any 'strange sightings' while I was away. Humans couldn't see faelah because of their glamour, but sometimes the little beasts stayed longer in the mortal world than they should and that glamour started to fade away. Any time I picked up the paper and read reports of odd things happening, I knew there were some Otherworldly creatures that had to be dealt with. I didn't particularly enjoy my job, but because of the geis, or curse, set upon me several years ago in Eilé, I was now Ehríad, a faelah bounty hunter with no true connections to anyone. My occupation was simple, really: I would enter the mortal world and round up anything Otherworldly. Then I would either send it back to where it came from or destroy it if it proved difficult, like the creature today.

Fergus barked at me as I re-entered the garage, carrying several rolls of newspaper with me. I opened the door and let him out just before hitting the button to close the garage door. My place wasn't in the best part of town, but it suited my purposes. The neighbors on one side ran a welding shop and those on the other, a wrecking yard. Let's just say it was seldom quiet. Luckily, this wasn't my permanent home.

Whistling to Fergus, I jogged up the stairs and the single room studio greeted me in its usual fashion. A couch hiding a fold out bed, a small kitchen, a bathroom with a shower, and a single, broad window that looked out over the street and the storage center beyond it.

I walked over to an old beat up desk and threw the newspapers on top, then stepped towards the tiny kitchen. Hunting down deadly faelah had a way of working up one's appetite. I checked Fergus's bowl and quickly poured in some dog food as I pulled out a frozen dinner from the freezer. Fergus sniffed at the food and huffed.

I glanced at the frozen dinner and nearly mimicked him.

"I know, but we won't be going back to Eilé until tomorrow, so you had best eat it."

A half an hour later we were both enjoying the mortal world's food to the best of our abilities. I poured myself a glass of water and sat down at the desk, flipping open a laptop, my latest investment. Yes, I wasn't a fan of technology, but having a computer in the mortal world was more useful than having an umbrella in the rain. I opened a file from my desktop and a detailed map of the area took up the screen. I scanned it, taking note of all the dolmarehn I knew of. Only the one in the swamp was big enough for someone my size to fit through. The rest were small. And that is where the problem lay. The faelah normally didn't sneak through the big dolmarehn because I kept a pretty close eye on it, but when the entire Central Coast area was riddled with smaller portals to the Otherworld, then someone had to visit this world every now and again to keep the vermin under control. For some reason, faelah enjoyed hunting in this world more than their own, and more often than not, they grew accustomed to the taste of small rodents and house pets.

Sighing, I flipped through the newspapers, searching the pages for anything out of the ordinary. Local pets gone missing, coyotes suspected . . . Okay, that might be a lead. I scanned the paragraphs. Nope. No remains ever found. Coyotes often ate most of what they caught. Keep reading. Burglaries, aggravated assault, a string of car thefts . . .

My eyes skidded to a halt when I turned the page. The headline read: *Chupacabra Sighting in Santa Maria*. Bingo. I read the first few lines of the article and felt my mouth tugging into a small smile. Horrendous looking creature, puncture wounds in the necks of the cattle, attacked at night . . . Yes, all the signs pointed towards something Otherworldly. I took note of the location, Costa Robles Ranch, and searched the internet for directions. I shut down the computer and went to take a shower. When I came out ten minutes later, I found Fergus lying on the couch. He perked his rusty ears forward and cocked his head to the side.

"Off the couch Fergus. We need to get some rest if we're to go out hunting tonight."

Fergus jumped off the couch so I could pull out the bed. Five minutes later I had my arm flung over my eyes as I tried to block out the crashing of metal in the junkyard and the familiar crack-pop of welding next door. Despite the noise and the light streaming through the cracks in the blinds, I managed to doze off into a half sleep.

Sneaking onto the ranch was not an issue. Located just north of the Santa Maria River and just off the main highway, the Costa Robles Ranch covered several acres of rolling land scattered with oak trees and the occasional dry gully cutting between the hills. I wasn't too worried about being spotted since it was, after all, the middle of the night. The moon provided just enough light to see by, and what I couldn't detect myself Fergus helped with his canine senses.

I pulled my car off the highway and onto a side road, killing the engine and turning off the lights. Fergus and I climbed through a heavy ranch-style gate and began our trek across the fields. I moved as silently as the broken earth would allow, trying not to startle the cattle I could sense dozing in the distance, their black shapes barely standing out against the pale moonlight. Fergus loped ahead of me, disappearing over the hilltop crowned with a copse of oak trees.

Death, he sent.

A chill ran down my spine. *How fresh?*

Very.

I gritted my teeth and crouched even lower, but kept my forward movement smooth. The odor of cow dung and dried grass was soon obliterated by the sharp metallic scent of hot blood. I maneuvered through the low oaks, drawing my broadsword from its sheath on my back. In the daylight, I'd be comfortable with my single edged blade, but in the darkness I needed something larger; something a little more lethal. When eliminating faelah, hawthorn worked the best, but any weapon forged in the Otherworld would also do the job. A white shape appearing against the darkness and a low growl informed me that I'd found Fergus. I wrinkled my nose as the smell of blood grew stronger.

In front of us lay a calf, the dark stains on its pale hide all that remained of its blood. Wonderful. A bloodsucking faelah. Those were the worst kind of Otherworldly aberrations because they let their desire for blood rule them. No fear, no caution. If you were warm and full of blood, then you might as well be a walking all-you-can-eat buffet.

The sharp cry of cattle and a low hiss drew my attention from the dead calf.

Fergus growled more loudly, his hackles rising along the ridge of his spine.

Twenty feet. Faelah draining one of the herd.

Go around wide, I sent back to my spirit guide, *there may be more than one.*

I lifted my sword into a front guard, not wanting to be unprepared in case the monster lost interest in the cattle.

The herd slept in a small clearing, the moon shedding just enough light for me to see that something wasn't right about the cow closest to me. An odd shape protruded from behind its neck. The shape moved, like a snake striking, and the cow bellowed out a sound of pain before falling onto its knees. No more time to hesitate. I swept my sword wide, bringing the blade down, biting into the back of the faelah. The creature squealed in pain, but it had been too distracted by its warm meal to realize I was there.

The creature slumped off the dying cow and I kicked it with my foot so that it landed in a patch of moonlight. About the size of a fox, it had a round head with large, bat-like ears and a nose like a pug. Short forearms ended with three fingers tipped with long, sharp claws. The hind legs were a different story.

They'd be several feet long if fully extended. This thing was meant for jumping. A hide resembling that of a dried up frog and a short, hairless tail completed the grotesque ensemble.

Letting out a breath I hadn't realized I was holding, I used the tip of my sword to peel back the thing's lips. I blanched. Four long, wicked canines crowded out the other teeth in the front of its jaw.

Fergus whimpered behind me. *There are more!*

Before I had a chance to turn back around, something hit me with enough force to knock the air from my lungs. Unfortunately, whatever it was also clung to me like a leech. I tried to gain my balance and shake it off, but the cloak I had decided to wear for this hunt only tangled with the monster and gave it something to hang on to.

Finally, I got my feet under me, but in the next second a sharp pain ripped through the muscles of my shoulder. I shouted in anger and agony, trying my best to shake the faelah off. Fergus was barking like mad, snapping and growling at what I could only assume were more monsters. My attacker was too close and I couldn't get my sword around to cause any damage.

I panted and reached down for my dagger. The faelah dug its teeth and claws in deeper, and it took all my strength to keep from blacking out. The glamour that rested beside my heart flared, bearing its own teeth as it demanded to be set free. No . . . no I couldn't let it out. This was another part of me, one I kept hidden unless all other options failed. If I let it break free, I would lose all control and might not have the strength to return to my car once this was over . . .

Grinding my teeth together, I fought the pain in my shoulder and the angry demand of my power. I worked my dagger free and brought it up, slipping it under the ribs of the faelah and driving it directly into its heart. The creature released its hold and gave a guttural gasp before falling to the ground.

Fetid blood stained my shirt and cloak, but I bit back the pain and turned to see how Fergus fared. The shadows of the night hindered my view, but I was able to count three more faelah still moving. Fergus had killed two, and I one, not including the first one.

Kill? Fergus asked, his teeth bared as he panted.

Yes, I sent, my sight almost going red with fury. *All of them.*

The final three faelah were easy to dispatch, now that I didn't have one clinging to me and turning my arm into mincemeat. I waited until all the bodies turned to ash, then sent Fergus to scout for any more we might have missed. By the time we returned to the car, the eastern horizon was awash in the pale turquoise of dawn.

Three times I almost fell asleep on the way home, Fergus barking every now and then to keep me awake. The fight had taken far more than I expected and despite the need to see to my wounds and the desire for another shower, I parked in my garage and started out across the highway. Thank goodness the swamp was only a thirty minute walk away. Fergus trotted ahead of me, checking for cars and other obstacles. My glamour was dangerously low and I was beginning to suspect that the chupacabra-like faelah might have been venomous.

The air was cold and damp and grew even more so as I descended into the swamp. When I took the first step into the culvert that housed the dolmarehn, I stumbled. I gritted my teeth and clutched at my shoulder, fighting the waves of pain that threatened to overtake me. Beads of sweat formed on my forehead and my knees felt like rubber. This wasn't good.

"Just a few more steps Fergus." My voice didn't sound like it belonged to me. It was dry and raspy and it hurt my throat to speak.

Fergus yipped.

They didn't bite you too, did they? I sent.

No. Tried, though.

I nodded. Even that hurt.

The dead trunks of eucalyptus trees crisscrossed the gorge ahead of me and I let out a shuddering breath. Not much further. Crossing between them took more effort than it should have, and just when I thought my legs wouldn't carry me another step, I spotted the cave entrance. I collapsed to my knees just inside and exhaustion overtook me.

Fergus whined again and I felt something tugging on the hood of my cloak.

Twenty feet, he sent. *Rest when in Eilé.*

I didn't want to move twenty feet; such a distance seemed too far, but Fergus wouldn't stop tugging on my cloak. And this was my good cloak. Didn't want him to tear it. Groaning, I dragged myself up onto my hands and knees and crawled deeper into the cave. I didn't dare stop until I felt the familiar tug of the Otherworld's magic. After that, I gave in to the fatigue and lost consciousness before reaching the other side.

☙ ☙ ☙

I woke up to the sensation of Fergus licking my face. Grumbling, I shoved him away with my left arm, sighing in relief when I registered no pain. I blinked several times, removing the sleep from my eyes, and caught a glimpse of oak trees layered in moss, a gray sky and several stone monoliths gazing down on me.

I sat up, scratching Fergus on the head to let him know I appreciated his loyalty and slowly removed my cloak and shirt. The misty air of Eilé was cold against my bare skin, but I had to make sure my wounds had healed. I ran a hand over my shoulder, feeling the small knots of new scarring, but no festering wounds. My arm proved to be in the same condition. I shrugged my shirt back on, frowning at the tears and bloodstains. Oh well. Perks of the job. One couldn't complain when they had the magic of the Otherworld to revive them.

I stood and stretched the stiffness away, yawning and running my fingers through my hair. It was slightly tangled and disheveled, but that didn't surprise me.

"How long was I out?" I asked my spirit guide.

He panted and flicked his ears forward. *Three days.*

I winced. Those bloodsucking faelah must have been more venomous than I had thought.

"I guess we'd better head back. There's no telling how many faelah have crept over into the mortal world while I've been napping."

Fergus yipped, as if to tell me I thought too highly of my own importance. I shot him a wry grin and turned towards the cave that was framed with the stones of the dolmarehn.

The next several weeks passed this way, with Fergus and I darting back and forth between the mortal world and the Otherworld. Every now and then, after tracking a faelah and either killing it or herding it back into Eilé, I would detect a tiny hint of the strange magic that had overwhelmed me the day I destroyed the bloodsucking faelah. And every time, the magic would fade away into nothing and I'd be left grasping at straws.

One autumn morning as Fergus and I were hiking up the equestrian trail behind the swamp, an invisible stream of power slammed into me. I stopped dead and shook my head, leaning over and resting my hands on my knees. What in the world . . . ? My own glamour flared in response. I rubbed at the spot on my chest and took a few deep breaths. It was the same strange yet familiar magic I'd felt those several weeks ago, but fresher. Where was it coming from? I had to find out.

Being what I was, being Ehríad, meant that it was my responsibility to keep tabs on anything Otherworldly that existed on this side of the dolmarehn, faelah or not. An idea came to me and I closed my eyes. Perhaps if I simply felt for the magic . . . In my mind's eye I saw a faint, crooked string of pale turquoise blue twining off into the distance above the horse path leading to one of the neighborhoods.

Fergus whined softly next to me.

"Hold on Fergus, I've found a trail of weak glamour," I murmured, my eyes still closed.

I breathed in deeply through my nose, drawing on a small amount of my own power, pushing and pulling it into a shell that would erase me from view. Opening my eyes, I left the path running to the road and followed the thread of magic instead. Fifteen minutes later I stumbled upon a house perched at the edge of a small hill overlooking the swamp. The yard backed up into the woods and small spots of vibrant blue glamour pooled around it.

"It's as if something from the Otherworld has sprung a leak," I mused.

At that very moment, a door slammed shut and someone walked from the house. I stayed put, relying on my magic to keep me hidden. I couldn't see the girl very well; she wore a light jacket with the hood pulled over her head, but she carried a backpack and looked too old for middle school.

I should have turned around then and gone back to my apartment. I could have written down the address and looked the girl up later on the internet from the safety of my garage, but I felt compelled to follow her, if just for a few minutes.

Fergus, hide yourself with glamour. We're following the girl.

The white wolfhound obeyed without a sound and we continued silently up the path, staying several feet behind her. I may have been invisible, but I could still scrape my boots against the asphalt and give away my presence, so I used the distance to help hide any sounds I made. As I walked, I shut my eyes for a split second and noted the ribbon of blue unfurling behind her. So, the glamour was coming from her, but how? Perhaps she'd had an encounter with some faelah or carried an object from the Otherworld.

I gritted my teeth. I didn't like the idea of following her around. It was intrusive and it went against my personal honor to be intrusive, but I also had to know where the glamour was coming from. It was never a good idea for Otherworldly and mortal things to mix.

Once at the end of the street, the girl stopped and chatted with another girl her age. I heard them say something about a high school, one I knew was only a few miles away. Before turning to leave them in peace, I picked up on the shorter, blond girl calling the other girl Meghan. So, I had a first name now. Breathing a sigh of relief, I turned around and headed back down the street. When I reached the end of the road, and before disappearing down into the swamp, I glanced back up at the house the girl had come out of. Above the front door was a carved wooden sign that read *The Elams.*

Ehriad

So, miss Meghan Elam, I won't have to work too hard to discern your identity after all.

Shaking my head, I tried to dispel the knot of guilt that was growing in my stomach. I didn't make it a habit to stalk young women, but when someone was so obviously shrouded in Otherworldly magic, I couldn't just ignore it.

Pushing the uneasy feelings aside, I continued on, seeking the path I knew would lead to the high school. The faelah had mostly stayed put in Eilé this week, and whether I wanted to or not, I needed to learn more about this girl with a string of blue, Otherworldly magic trailing after her.

I reached the outskirts of the high school within fifteen minutes of leaving behind the swamp. As I caught my breath, I studied the students pulling into the parking lot and reluctantly spilling out of their cars. I shied away from the barrage of smells and sounds that attacked my senses. Several dozen perfumes and colognes clouded the air, along with the high-pitched laughter and false promises being thrown from one person to the other. Combine that all together with the general angst and unavoidable desperation that permeated the atmosphere and it was enough to give one a headache. I was very glad I never had to attend high school in the Otherworld. I would not have survived it.

Fergus and I had been in this area only a week or so ago, checking into a possible faelah problem. I'd been wearing my old trench coat and had used my glamour to adopt the guise of an elderly homeless man. Most people left me alone when I took up that particular costume, so I wore the same cloak of glamour now: one of a decrepit, retired veteran down on his luck, lingering in the woods for no apparent reason.

A few more minutes ticked by before I caught a glimpse of that brilliant blue magic again. It trickled out of a gold minivan. I felt my muscles tense as the van pulled up and parked. The door rolled open and the girl, Meghan, stepped out with her friend. I took a small moment to wonder why I hadn't detected her strange magic here last week, but then brushed that thought aside once she started moving across the parking lot.

A Single Thread of Magic

I focused my attention on the group of teenagers, especially the girl I had discovered earlier that morning. They were a good distance away, so I sacrificed a fraction of my glamour, pulling it away from my disguise and using it to enhance my vision just enough to get a clear picture of my quarry. The girl turned and looked in my direction. My relaxed pose stiffened. Pretty little thing, but not in a typically human way. In fact, I wouldn't be surprised if her peers thought her to be strange-looking. Humans were often a bad judge of real beauty, in my experience.

I continued to study her, grateful my hood covered most of my face. She was tall with dark, curling brown hair and high cheek bones, but it was her striking eyes that gave me pause. Hazel, flashing to gray, then green and blue, and back to hazel. My heart sped up and I felt my own well of power begin to burn, like a coal coaxed to life by a bellows. Not just a human tainted by glamour. Oh no, this girl was Faelorehn. Suddenly I felt winded, as if someone had punched me in the stomach.

There were plenty of Faelorehn and half-Faelorehn people living in the mortal world. Some chose to live here, some merely liked to visit. But there was something different about her; something I couldn't quite place. Most Faelorehn wore their glamour like a mantle, hiding their true identity in the mortal world. But this girl . . . Hers was locked away and almost impossible to see, like something lurking beneath a sheet of dark water. Yet the magic that trickled off of her was as visible as the stars in a moonless night sky.

The girl and her companions glanced away and I took the opportunity to slip behind the trees. I would look into who this girl was, this Faelorehn with hidden glamour. And while I was at it, I'd try to forget those eyes and her alluring face, too.

🐉 🐉 🐉

I visited the high school the next day to catch another glimpse of Meghan, just to make sure she was real, but the following day I had to return to Eilé. The Otherworld greeted me with the cool caress of fog and ancient magic. I sighed, shivering a little as the sensation poured over me. The mortal world's magic was much more subtle than this; much more concealed and gentle.

The glamour of Eilé took hold of your senses and demanded that you pay attention, and if you chose to ignore it then more likely than not, that same magic would find a way to make you pay attention, and usually not in a pleasant way. Fortunately for me, I had lived a very long time in my homeland and I knew how to show respect to its raw, natural power.

Fergus and I traveled from the dolmarehn through the wooded hills, past the collection of ponds dotting the rolling fields, and on to Luathara, the castle that was left in my care. It more closely resembled a ruined pile of old stones than anything else, but there were a few rooms that were habitable with working fireplaces. The largest room on the third floor was where I often slept. It had a comfortable bed and a full-functioning bathroom (not a rarity in Eilé, but definitely an uncommon luxury at Luathara). I had dreams of one day returning the castle to its former glory; of settling down, to some extent, if I ever found a way to break free of the Morrigan's geis. As I thought about making a life at the castle, for some odd reason Meghan Elam's image flashed through my mind.

I stopped, just as my foot was about to hit the first step leading up to my rooms. Oh no. I shook my head. *None of that now Cade,* I told myself. Currently, I couldn't risk the luxury of thinking about young women in that way, and I most definitely couldn't think of the young Faelorehn girl I'd discovered hiding in the mortal world, either. First of all, she was too young for me and secondly, I knew nothing about her.

You know some things, my annoying conscience crooned. *She is very pretty, and she has strong magic, like yours . . .*

I growled and continued my progress upstairs. I would not think about Meghan Elam, and not only because it was a bad idea for my own sake, but for her sake as well.

"Stay here Fergus," I threw over my shoulder at the white wolfhound who followed me like a shadow. "I'm going to see the Morrigan."

My spirit guide whined softly and paused, watching me as I strode past my rooms and through the great gaping hole in the castle wall. I crossed the patio on the other side, my coat growing damp from the spray of the waterfall to my left. I took the stairs at the end of the terrace and descended into the caves that housed the dolmarehn to every imaginable destination in Eilé. I could take one to the edge of the Weald to visit Enorah, my sister, or I could take one that would bring me to the other side of my foster father's abode. But no, today I had to travel to the Morrigan's realm. My geis required that I check in with her once a month. And that was another reason why I had to stop thinking about Meghan, because if the Morrigan found out about her, her life might as well be over.

Eilé was a very large place, and many Faelorehn would tell you that it had no boundaries. They would also tell you that Erintara, the city of our high queen, was located in the exact center of our world. All the old kings and queens, the gods and goddesses of the ancient Celts, had their own realms, or large expanses of land they considered their own. The Morrigan's dominion was located on the easternmost stretch of land that nestled up against the endless mountains just on the other side.

I stepped through the dolmarehn and all of my muscles immediately seized up. The air was so frigid here it felt like a layer of ice coated my lungs every time I drew breath. I had walked out of another cave and into a small, rocky canyon devoid of anything living. The stones and skeletal trees that surrounded me reminded me of the bones of the dead. I gritted my teeth and made my way towards the mouth of the culvert where there stood a crude stone circle. Beyond that circle was a diseased forest full of dying trees, and even further past that were miles upon miles of desolate land littered with stones and shallow bogs. The Morrigan's kingdom was a place of death and despair.

I had been hanging my head as I walked, the sadness of this place acting like a weight to pull me down, but as I came upon the clearing and the stone circle, I glanced up and winced. She was waiting for me, the Morrigan, standing utterly still and wearing a dark blood-red cloak with the hood drawn over her head. An entourage of ravens sat scattered in the bare branches of a dead tree just behind her, watching me with baleful eyes. A pair of

Cúmorrig, the Morrigan's personal hellhounds, stood by her side, their rotting flesh and putrescence making me gag.

As I closed the distance between us, she lowered her hood and crossed her arms casually. Though she stood more than a foot shorter than me, the very sight of her made my blood turn cold. Beautiful, like all the Faelorehn, with pale skin, black wavy hair and eyes that flashed red to reveal her powerful fae magic, the Morrigan was the most terrifying and dangerous person you could meet in Eilé. Her only desire was to cause war and strife and gain immeasurable power. Therefore, she had no concern for the feelings or well-being of others.

"Have my pets been misbehaving?" she asked in her seductive voice.

"Yes," I said shortly.

She sighed and rolled her eyes to a gray sky that threatened snow.

"How many did you have to destroy this time?"

I did a mental count in my head. "In the last month I've killed around thirty faelah."

She sneered, but didn't look too terribly disturbed by this information. "Such stupid little creatures. I wish I knew a way to make them more intelligent. It tires me to have to replace them all the time."

My jaw clenched at her callous tone of voice. It may tire her to construct her obscene creatures, but it cost others far more than that. In order to bring her dead creations back to life, she needed the living essence of innocent victims, sometimes animal, sometimes Faelorehn.

Before I could help myself, I bit out, "Then stop making them."

She arched a perfect brow at me, her face blank with surprise, then her lips curled into a smile and she laughed.

"Oh Caedehn! You are so silly sometimes. After all these long years it still bothers you, what I do, doesn't it?"

I clenched my hands into fists. "It would bother anyone."

She snorted and dropped her arms to pace in front of me. "Please, don't be so pathetic. Those I use in my sacrifices are weaklings. They do not deserve to live if they cannot resist my power."

I turned on her. "You are a goddess! How can they stand a chance? Your power out-rivals even that of your Tuatha De brethren!"

She whipped around, her eyes flashing red, the dark clouds above grumbling their discontent.

"Do you wish to challenge me Caedehn?"

Despite my anger and the slight twinge of fear that burned inside me, I gave a small smile. I stepped back and took on a relaxed stance, crossing my arms loosely over my chest. "You cannot kill me. My geis forbids it."

The Morrigan released a deep breath and pulled her magic back into herself.

"Yes, that little catch has proven inconvenient on many occasions, but alas! Despite your many annoying characteristics, you have proven handy over the years. One of these days you'll outgrow your stubbornness."

"Unlikely," I grunted.

"So," she breathed, dismissing her more somber mood, "besides killing my poor faelah, is there anything else you need to tell me?"

I found a young woman the other day who possesses strong Faelorehn magic.

"No," I said flatly, my muscles tensing once again.

She studied my face for a moment or two, her eyes narrowed and her lips pursed as if she suspected something. My heartbeat increased and I willed it to slow down. For a split second she opened her mouth and I was certain she was going to accuse me of lying, but then a flash of crimson lit her eyes and instead she grinned. The expression was very unnerving.

"Very well, you're dismissed." She flapped her arm at me as she turned to leave, the ravens hopping from branch to branch in order to follow her every move while the Cúmorrig trailed after her.

"I shall see you in a month's time, then. Try not to kill so many of my pets if you can help it. You know how much it inconveniences me to perform a creation ritual. And you know how much you enjoy attending them."

I turned and headed back down the dead canyon, punching the trunk of a bleached tree along the way. I would love to kill all of the Morrigan's faelah, but that was the thing: the more I killed, the more she would create. And that meant standing watch as she tortured the living to reanimate the dead. I didn't need any extra horrors to add to my list of troubles.

I spent a glorious week at my castle, just enjoying the free time and the constant caress of Eilé's magic. My last few encounters with the faelah had drained my reserves, and it was nice to feel the pleasant tingle of glamour running through my veins once again.

I would have stayed longer, but my malevolent employer had decided to cook up a whole new batch of particularly annoying faelah that could somehow reproduce on their own. Thankfully, she hadn't insisted upon my presence for the process of their creation, and I had a feeling that they weren't true faelah after all. Eilé had many creatures of magic, some benign and some not. These particular beings, duínba, or toad people, had a tendency to gravitate towards evil magic. My guess was that the Morrigan had captured an entire colony of them and was manipulating them to bend to her will. It would explain why they were able to procreate. And if I didn't know any better, I'd say she was purposely sending them through the dolmarehn near my home just to bother me. She must have suspected I was hiding something after all.

The duínba were coming through the passageway in such large numbers that I had taken to camping out in the swamp. Even then, hordes of them managed to get past me. By the third night of my stakeout, Fergus and I had killed almost a hundred of them and I hoped we'd finally made a large enough dent in their population to slow them down. For the present, all I could do was grit my teeth and bear it until they stopped pouring through the dolmarehn altogether. I was desperate to get back to my research on Meghan Elam, but it would simply have to wait. If I even took an hour to leave the swamp, the little demons would completely take over. I needed to remain vigilant at least one more night to make sure we'd diminished them for good.

🐉 🐉 🐉

Cúmorrig!

The sudden, frantic thought flaring to life in my mind ripped me from my sleep. My heart pounded against my ribs and I had to take several deep breaths to slow its pace. Was it a nightmare that woke me?

Again, that bright, piercing thought came. *Cúmorrig! Girl in danger!*

I bolted from my sleeping blanket, grateful I had gone to bed fully clothed. It took a while for my sight to adjust to the dark, but I think I managed to move through the forest mostly on instinct. I cut through the trees, running full-out towards my spirit guide, his internal voice leading me on. Something had happened. Something involving the Faelorehn girl and the hounds of the Morrigan. Just a few days ago Fergus and I had been exterminating duínba, and now there were Cúmorrig around? My blood turned to ice when realization hit me. The Morrigan knew about Meghan. Somehow she had found out about the girl and she must know that I knew of her as well. My stomach lurched as I sprinted onward. Had the Morrigan suspected my lie after all?

Yes, my conscience whispered. Oh no, nothing good would ever come out of this . . .

I gritted my teeth and hissed as a long, thin blackberry vine sliced across my neck. I ignored the burn and kept moving. If the Morrigan's hellhounds were involved, then the girl was in real trouble. Could the goddess know what Meghan was, or was she just interested because I had been interested? Or was I simply overreacting? The Cúmorrig could have wandered into the mortal world on their own; it had happened before.

Growling, I picked up my pace, hurdling over a fallen eucalyptus tree and landing in the middle of a small meadow where, it seemed, all hell had broken loose. Off to the side the girl was trying to crawl away from an onslaught of two or three of the hellhounds while Fergus fought off one of his own. I didn't spend much more time studying the scene. With the moonlight to help aid my sight, I reached for the closest Cúmorrig, the one trying to get to the girl's neck.

I quickly took care of the other hounds, breaking their necks and crushing their skulls to ensure they didn't resume their attack, all the while keeping the angry beast that was my fae magic in check. I threw their carcasses deep into the brush where they could disintegrate out of sight. I would be punished for it later; the Morrigan did not appreciate a waste of her favored minions, but at the moment I didn't care.

Silence, like a dark shroud, descended upon the small glade, punctuated only by Fergus's gentle panting.

All clear? I sent him before turning to glance at the girl who was doing her best not to be noticed.

Yes, he returned, *no more faelah.*

Good. Setting my mouth into a firm line, I slowly turned and began studying the young woman sitting on the ground in mute shock. Her face was pale, her eyes wide and her hair a mess. She wore a nightgown of sorts, something that looked more like a long t-shirt. She sat stiffly, obviously terrified, but trying very hard not to let her panic take over. I smiled, impressed with her resolve. Most humans would have lost it by now, after having been attacked by faelah. But she was Faelorehn, made of stronger stuff than your average mortal. However, if I was judging correctly, I'd say she'd never seen anything Otherworldly in her life. But perhaps I was wrong . . .

Taking a small breath, I lowered my eyes, years upon years of training forcing me to study her entire person to make sure she had no obvious injuries. My gaze dropped further and I caught my breath. The nightgown had gathered at her waist, baring her naked legs, pale as her face in the moonlight. For a moment I was blissfully distracted, that is, until my conscience kicked in.

Don't stare Cade. Remember, you want to help the girl, not convince her you are some twisted degenerate . . .

Unfortunately, I think it was too late for that. I could only hope that the hood of my trench coat hid my face from her view. I turned my eyes away, just in case she could see me, though I wouldn't mind studying those shapely legs a bit longer.

A Single Thread of Magic

Focus Cade, the poor girl's been traumatized. She needs help, not ogling.

While my conscience was busy scolding me into behaving like a gentleman, Meghan decided it was safe enough to talk.

"Who are you?"

Her voice trembled. Time to play it smooth. *You've been dying to learn more about this strange girl for weeks now. Here's your opportunity. Don't mess it up. Slow, careful movements and gentle words . . .*

I dropped into a crouch, trying to make myself smaller so I wouldn't appear so intimidating. Apparently that was the wrong thing to do. She made a small noise and tried to scoot back further, her exposed legs still causing a distraction. I took a breath, ready to say something with every intention to reassure her, but she beat me to it.

"Hobo Bob?"

I could tell right away that she hadn't meant to say those particular words, for she seemed to shrink in on herself and even in the dim moonlight I could see her blush.

"Sorry," she mumbled, scraping at her hair nervously, "I mean-"

I released a small laugh, hoping it would lighten the mood, then spoke before she had a chance to continue, "Is that the title you have awarded me?"

"Huh?"

I chuckled again and stood back up. Crouching was uncomfortable and the fear pouring off of her eased a little when I backed away.

"I often heard the spoken insults of the young people attending your school, but I never paid them much attention."

And it was true. The times I spent loitering around the high school, trying to sniff out faelah and then that thread of glamour she trailed around, I'd allowed my own magic to enhance my hearing and managed to catch several conversations traded between the students. Most of them were tedious, bland or the typical cruel gossip I often found in such places. But on several occasions I'd caught them eyeing me warily and using the moniker 'Hobo Bob' while pointing indiscreetly. I didn't mind. It kept their curiosity at bay. No one ever bothered to pay much attention to a vagrant.

I sighed and lowered my hood. I was through with being Hobo Bob. If I was going to learn more about this girl and in turn help her, then she needed to know I wasn't going to harm her. Though this was not how I planned on introducing myself.

I glanced at her out of the corner of my eye and caught her studying my face. She didn't seem afraid, but almost fascinated. A smug smile pulled at the corners of my mouth and I allowed myself to believe she liked what she saw. Since she was scrutinizing me, I let my gaze drop once again to her legs. Nice legs, long and lean like most of the Faelorehn. I wondered then who she belonged to. She obviously had no idea where she had come from, so I suspected she'd been under the impression she was human for a very long time.

Meghan emitted a small gasp and quickly scrambled to pull her nightgown down. I guess I had been staring a bit too long. I felt my face turn hot and almost laughed out loud. When was the last time I'd flushed like this? Probably not since I was no higher than Fergus's shoulder. Now, why should I care if Meghan caught me admiring her? Oh, this girl was definitely going to cause some turbulence in my already tumultuous life.

"Forgive me," I finally murmured, shrugging off my trench coat and placing it over her shoulders. I hoped it didn't smell too terrible after spending half a week in the woods with me.

"What were those things? Those . . . dogs?" she asked after a long moment.

"Hounds of the Morrigan. Cúmorrig."

"What?"

I huffed a tiny breath. Well, I *had* decided to help her discover who she was, hadn't I?

"Most folklorists would call them hellhounds," I offered. *Yes Cade, break it to her slowly. She's been through a terrible shock.*

We were both silent for a long time and I had a feeling she was either trying to take this all in or simply figuring out how to get away from this nightmare. I couldn't say I blamed her.

"Thanks for helping me, but, um, who are you?"

Not quite what I expected her to say next, but at least she was still talking. I wanted more than anything to spend the rest of the night speaking with her, but what she needed most right now was a good night's rest without any nightmares to trouble her sleep. There was only one way to make that happen and it involved doing something I really didn't want to do.

Every Faelorehn being had the power to erase another's memory, but none of us was ever supposed to use that power. Some, like the Morrigan, exploited it whenever it suited them, but others were careful to use it only when necessary, and sometimes it *was* necessary. Like right now. I wanted to help Meghan and in order to do that I had to erase as much of tonight's ordeal from her mind as possible. It would be like erasing the chalk from a board; all one did was smear the white powder around until the words were no longer visible. That's what I'd do with Meghan's memories. I'd smudge them to the point where she couldn't read them anymore.

"You were right in guessing my identity earlier," I said as a way to distract her a little. A distraction always helped with the erasing process.

She leaned her head back to watch me, her expression one of pensiveness. Okay, good . . .

"Our first meeting wasn't supposed to go this way."

Alright, I wasn't really sure how our first meeting would have gone had I had any control over it, but it definitely would not have included the Morrigan's hounds.

Suddenly, she tried to stand up so I reached out a hand and said her name, then blanched. *Not smart, Cade.*

She shied away and murmured something that might have been an expression of gratitude as she tried to hand me my coat. Wonderful. She looked ready to bolt.

"You can't go on your own," I blurted, desperate to salvage what I could from this terrible night.

"Please," she rasped, "I just want to go home."

I stiffened and drew away from her. "You're afraid of me."

Well, of course she is you dolt! Sometimes I really hated my conscience.

It was too late to try to calm her, so I decided to go ahead with my plan. If I was lucky, she'd forget this entire night.

"I screwed this all up, I know, but it's best if you forget any of this ever happened."

She became fully alert, her eyes darting back and forth like a cornered deer.

I moved slowly forward. "Tomorrow, this will all seem like a dream. I'll send Fergus in a week. Follow him and I'll introduce myself properly."

"What are you doing?" she squeaked.

Before she could dart into the forest, I let my glamour flow from my fingertips, enclosing her in an invisible web of magic.

She gasped and started to collapse, but I caught her gently in my arms.

"Who are you?" she murmured blearily.

This time, I answered her.

"You can call me Cade," I said softly, "but you won't remember any of this, so it doesn't matter."

She went completely limp and I scooped her up into my arms, holding her close to my chest. I savored her comfortable weight and breathed in her unique smell for a few moments. The scent of lavender and spring surrounded her and all of my aches and pains from the last several weeks of faelah hunting seemed to disappear.

You could have handled that much better, Fergus said into my mind.

I grumbled and glanced down to find him panting up at me.

Oh, if that isn't the understatement of the evening, I don't know what is, I sent back.

You like her, he returned.

I ignored him and turned to walk up the equestrian path. As we made our way through the dark towards Meghan Elam's house, I could have sworn I heard the echo of canine laughter in my head.

The door to Meghan's room was unlocked and wide open. Fergus had admitted to leading her down into the swamp and I had chastised him for it.

You wished to learn more about her and since the duínba were gone I thought it an opportune time.

First of all, we weren't absolutely sure the duínba were all gone, and secondly, don't you think it's a lot more dangerous leading her into a swamp infested with Cúmorrig?

He sniffed and said, *I was unaware of the hellhounds.*

I shook my head. I would never understand canine logic.

Checking to make sure there were no other humans about, I stepped through the door and crossed the room. It was dark, but I could pick out a few details. The room was a bit cluttered and it resembled the typical teenage girl's domain: a lava lamp in one corner, posters adorning the walls, a desk, a small couch, a TV, a computer . . .

I side-stepped a few piles of clothing and came to the bed, laying Meghan's unconscious form gently on the mattress and pulling the sheets up around her. Before I left, I simply watched her for a moment, reaching out a hand and caressing her face. Her skin was smooth and cool and an image of her reaching up and pressing her hand to mine shot through my mind. I pulled my hand back and sucked in a breath. It was dangerous to have such thoughts, especially if the Morrigan knew as much, if not more, than I did. I would have to play this all out very carefully, and if I was smart, I'd assume the goddess knew everything.

Taking a deep breath, I moved away from Meghan and left her to her rest, hoping that I was able to successfully erase those horrible memories form her mind. I slid the glass door into place, trying to be as silent as possible. I lingered for a few more minutes on that small, concrete slab just outside her room, my eyes cast down as I considered the young woman sleeping mere feet away from me.

Fergus's tiny yip snapped me out of my reverie. Against my will, my mouth tugged into a smile as I glanced down at my spirit guide. His tongue lolled and he gave me that canine grin of his. He didn't have to tell me what he thought this time, for it was apparent in those intelligent brown eyes of his. I released a slow, deep breath as I turned to make my retreat back into the swamp.

"I believe you're right Fergus," I murmured softly as we left the house behind. "I have a feeling this Meghan Elam is going to have a far greater influence on my life than I had previously thought."